T0343651

THE
GREATEST
GAME
OF ALL

ANDREAS ROMAN

CATALYST PRESS, El Paso, Texas, USA

Copyright © Andreas Roman, 2025
All rights reserved.

No part of this book may be used or reproduced
in any manner whatsoever without written consent
from the publisher, except for brief quotations for reviews.

For further information, write info@catalystpress.org

In North America, this book is distributed by
Consortium Book Sales & Distribution, a division of Ingram.
Phone: 612/746-2600
cbsdinfo@ingramcontent.com
www.cbsd.com

In South Africa, Namibia, and Botswana,
this book is distributed by Protea Distribution.
For information, email orders@proteadistribution.co.za.

FIRST EDITION
10 9 8 7 6 5 4 3 2 1

ISBN: 9781963511000

Library of Congress Control Number: 2024942202

This is a work of fiction. Unless otherwise indicated, all the names,
characters, businesses, places, events and incidents in this book
are either the product of the author's imagination or used
in a fictitious manner. Any resemblance to actual persons,
living or dead, or actual events is purely coincidental.

To mum and dad,
*   you were always there*

THE
GREATEST
GAME
OF ALL

ANDREAS ROMAN

ONE

A BUSY
LITTLE GHOST

Chapter 1

THE BEGINNING

It makes sense to start at the beginning. So I won't, because I don't make much sense these days.

Of course, you could argue that anyone self-aware enough to point this out makes more sense than most.

But as you'll eventually see, you'd be wrong.

Anyway.

In the beginning, before Lisa but after Calvin, there was a soft rain outside my window, one of those early spring falls that made you forget about the winter and hope for the summer. It dropped like a slow beat against the ledge and had a hypnotizing quality, like a mother's lullaby for the restless child.

I was in bed, looking at gray skies. They weren't cloudy, just covered by a filthy veil. They stirred and moved as unseen leviathans slowly drifted through their space.

On a typical day, I was like the Swedish weather. It didn't matter what the forecast said. You just never knew. Getting out of bed could be as easy as smooth sailing over the waters of a calm mind, or as death-defying as navigating through a maelstrom of incoherent impressions.

There was the usual nosebleed involved, stains on the pillow and dried patches on my lips. I probably looked like a hungover vampire. I say probably, because looking at myself in the mirror was a Herculean effort beyond ambitions of any kind. All the same, I eventually rose and shambled to my favorite window, the deep one facing the park, where the trees had been naked just a few days ago but now displayed cautious sprinkles of green.

The rain stopped and the sun broke out. This was Stockholm at its finest, between the seasons when people emerged from months of hibernation to enjoy just a sliver of light. Put out a chair and a table by a busy street, and people would flock around it for coffee, snow be damned.

For a moment, these sights worked like a soothing balm. I could breathe, make an effort to stay in the now, forget about it all. Enjoy the beauty outside and be content with that.

But there was someone outside my door.

Knocking, like a ghoul rattling his bones at the gates.

He had a groove, this fiend.

He was banging away with a pattern of four by four like a disco beat on the dance floor.

Bang, clap, repeat.

I flinched as these beats threw me around, until I had no choice but to do what any man wrapped in filthy robes would do and retreat to the couch. The sun poured through the high windows and touched the oaken floors. It didn't reach the shadows around me.

That was the thing with these century old city apartments—they had the space and height to offer plenty of echo for a ghostly drum. And even though I wasn't sure if the beat outside was real or just a headache that came with my morning routine, I didn't open the door to find out. The possible outcomes were too many and when the knockings didn't stop, I left the couch to hide in the closet. It was one of those walk-in versions, big enough to count as a room (or a home, if you didn't care much about space), and I found some comfort in the faint smell from an old perfume. It came from my favorite shirt, mixed with just a tint of salt.

I hadn't worn nor washed that shirt since our last Midsummer Night party. It felt like many years ago. When our country was at its darkest, summer was a memory you weren't sure ever happened, a season too good to be true.

I stayed in the closet for hours. I pretended it was a burrow in an oak, perhaps one that had grown for a thousand years on a green-grassed hill. I could nest there, live comfortably in the shade of earth and wood, and never leave. I don't think anyone would miss me. I was okay with that.

But then I got up. A man had to eat, after all. Or this man, at least.

As I passed the hall on my way to the kitchen, there was an envelope on the carpet by the door. Someone must've finally decided to hell with it and slipped it through my mailbox.

I looked at it for a while, chin resting in my palm. To pick it up, or not.

I approached it and picked it up. It had a few words neatly typed on its cover.

Enough with the drama, Elliot. We just want to throw our money at you. Review this and get back to us with your damn signature already.

Ta,

Sean

Chapter 2

THE ATARI 2600

I'm sure that when you were young or at least younger than you are now, there was something you wanted more than anything, more than life itself.

For me, when I was a kid, this something was an Atari 2600.

Man, did I want one. The worlds it offered, the places I could go to, if I could just get me an Atari console.

I had no idea what a video game was or what a console did, or that a company like Atari existed. But once I found out...a place where people made games for a living? For real? Screw all the astronaut dreams or firefighter ambitions. Making games would have to be just about the coolest thing you could do on this planet, on any planet.

When I was old enough to join Dad on his working trips to Gothenburg, he dropped me off on an early Spring morning in a big toy store and said: "Don't leave, Elliot. Stay here until I come and get you. Ask the staff for water if you get thirsty."

And that's where I saw the Atari 2600 for the first time.

It pulled me in with its crude pixels and harsh voice, offering a suggestive beauty that contained more depth and truth and clarity than I had ever experienced before. I was twelve at the time, so while I was no journeyman yet, I'd had my fair share of lies.

I camped at the toy store for hours, looking at the screen as it browsed through the games on display. I was dehydrated when my father came to pick me up. The owner said in a passing comment that if we wanted the Atari, we'd get it cheap. It was outdated, they couldn't return it, and while he liked its vintage looks with wooden panels and all, it was time to make room for the new and shiny. Nintendo and such.

But cheap is still a fortune for those who can't afford it, and Dad only said to me that he was sorry that he'd been gone for so long. We took the one-hour bus ride home and he talked about how proud he was of me, that I was old enough for responsibilities now, that things would get better from here on.

You and me against the world, Elliot.

That's what he said, my father.

I didn't really pay any attention. I was on an asteroid somewhere or running with E.T. through the forest or fighting space invaders and hunting for treasure.

That a bunch of pixels which hardly resembled anything but a deformed mess could feel more real and honest than anything in the actual world just made so much sense to me. So much sense.

Chapter 3

THE SARA JOHNSON RUMOR

And there was a rumor going on.

Apparently, Sara Johnson had an Atari.

In our small town, rumors about such a hot item spread fast.

Life wasn't easy for a kid who spent most of his days alone under the blue skies, but I figured it could hardly get any worse, so I asked her about it on a schoolyard break between math and geography.

"And besides," I said to Sara, she and her friends rolling their eyes while chewing gum, "did you finish *Pitfall* in just one evening? I thought that game was huge. I mean, there's all the levels and the monsters and the crocodiles and...well, is it true? Did you?"

I'd stared myself blind at the toy store, at *Pitfall* in particular. I felt I knew the coves and crevices of that game better than the lint in my pockets.

But Sara looked at me as if I'd insulted her. She had long, dark hair, tied into a perfect braid. Her eyes were green and she even wore lipstick. Yeah, she was on that level.

"You're so weird," she said.

Her friends observed her, suddenly gleeful, wondering if the time had come to dethrone Queen Johnson. The other kids approached from whatever they'd been doing, creating a crowd.

"I heard you had an Atari." I tried to sound casual about it, but I was more nervous than eager. "Can we play? I mean, not play play, not with Lego or toys or stuff, I mean, but I can come over and...yeah..."

Sara laughed. It was as much a diversion as a taunt. A really sharp one. It had to be. If the school's most popular girl was into video games, that was ammunition to bring her down for a year, maybe two. Sara, who kissed boys. Sara, who wore a bra.

"*Pervert*," she said to me.

"No," I said. "*Pitfall.*"

Sara's friends giggled and whispered about my patched Manchester jeans and stained t-shirt. Some of the others mumbled and pointed, calling me Smelliot or versions of the kind. Others turned away, almost on the beat as they always did, or pretended it wasn't that bad and that's why they didn't have to notice. There was nothing here to see. Just the usual old banter between schoolyard pals. Elliot would be fine. He'd brush it off, get up, and get on with it.

And in a way, this was true, because this routine didn't bother me anymore. Even the more creative thugs had forgotten why they came after me. They went through the motions and I accepted the assaults in a numb kind of state, as if we'd agreed that things needed to be this way. That's what the years did to you, I guess.

They all looked at Sara, though. They'd formed a circle around us now. She looked at me. There was something in her eyes. Not contempt, but fear. Maybe curiosity. It felt odd, as if only for a moment, something tipped and I was the one in control.

I'd seen that look before. I'd known her a long time, after all.

"I guess I heard wrong," I said.

I turned around and moved through the circle. Someone pushed me, someone else tripped me, and I did stumble but I didn't fall. There was an insult or two and a rising wave of laughter. Someone said something about my mother, like they always did when they ran out of material, but Sara cut them off and told them to leave me alone. This caused a stir and for a second, I wondered if she'd change her mind and call me back, take my hand and lead me away from the crowd.

But when I slowed down in my steps, she said that I was a nobody after all, I wasn't worth the attention, just look at my clothes and when did I last shower anyway, and the others raised the chant as she whipped up the mood.

I looked over my shoulder as I broke out and left the yard. Sara pointed at me and laughed as their sermon shifted into climax. She was as faceless as the rest of them, as insignificant and mean as only a kid can be to another kid. But even so, I could still see the fear in her eyes as I left the schoolyard behind me and took my bike to the shores instead.

Chapter 4

SOME KIND OF ABYSS

During the time in my apartment, come heavenly tears or sunshine divine, one step forward took me two steps back. This wasn't a philosophical statement. There were times when I literally couldn't walk forward without moving backwards. When I tried to brush my teeth, I combed my hair. The fridge became the freezer and I put the remote to my ear when I wanted to watch a movie. These short circuits had gradually faded as I recovered over the seasons, but they still made the world seem so dangerous, I had to scramble to my favorite chair (which was also my only chair) to rest until my brain cooled down. I'd bury myself under blankets until I could make coffee without burning down the house.

In my defense, though, anyone would've been confused by the raging snow outside, when you'd witnessed the trees reveal their early green just the day before. I thought we were done with this fire and ice thing. Weren't the days supposed to be brighter now?

"You still there, Elliot?"

Ah, yes.

I was on the phone. With Doctor Larson. I'd been distracted by the white kaleidoscope patterns.

"Yes. Sorry. You were saying?"

"I was saying, you're the only one not seeing this for what it is."

"Well, what's to see? Is there an audience?"

"Don't be smart with me."

"But what is it, then?"

"You soared too close to the sun, Elliot. And like Icarus, you got burned."

"So I'm a tragedy. A Greek one."

"Your wings certainly were on borrowed time. There's beauty in that, though. If you can accept that, then you can embrace it. Make something of it."

Doctor Larson always took the opportunity to embed his professional evaluations in amateur poetry, with no regards to the quality of his output. I wanted to snap something witty back at him, but trying to come up with a reply that could be perceived as clever just exhausted me.

"It's all there," Larson said. "You're still there, buried within... ah, within..."

Waaait for it.

"Within that inner self, the essence that we call your soul."

"Oh, I'm done," I said. "I've retired. I really don't mind. I won't go back to work. I could use the break."

"I agree with the last part. Your brain unplugged for a good reason. Now, you have to understand that it's okay to be bored. But don't make this into something it's not. You'll recover."

"Is that what you think I am? Bored?"

"It's perfectly all right to create something that amounts to nothing. The act alone makes it worthwhile."

I paused at those words.

I sensed the smell of salt again, from my shirt. And I was on a pier where the sun washed over the waves and warmed my skin, and I was with someone, and it was the kind of memory you shouldn't return to but were grateful that you could.

The act alone makes it worthwhile, said the doctor.

"You're justifying waste."

Larson sighed. "Don't play the victim, Elliot. A man with your wealth only has options. Any conception you had of duty was self-imposed. You'll find another reason to ram your head into a wall, until you decide not to."

"I don't need your pity."

"Then stop asking for it. Go see a psychologist. One that specializes in neuro. I've given you a list. Linda's the best. You wanna get an appointment with her. I've told her you'd call. But of course you haven't. I know you haven't. You don't call people."

"You're a psychiatrist. What else do I need?"

"I'll prescribe stuff. Which is fine sometimes, but not this time."

"Maybe I don't need anyone," I said and stood up. I walked towards the window.

"Well, all right. But you're at the edge of some kind of abyss, and you need to understand that. You need to be okay with that. Otherwise, you'll never get well."

"We can't all be level, can we? Why do you even have to label me?"

"Hah, well. You're asking the wrong person."

I looked down through the window on the people taking one step forward but slipping two steps back. The snow was toying with them. I had to give it to them—at least they put up a fight.

"For what it's worth," Larson said, "I'm sorry."

"You shouldn't be."

"All the same, Elliot, all the same…"

"Yeah."

We were quiet for a few moments.

"I appreciate you saying so," I said. I heard him shuffling papers now. He always did that when he tried to shift into casual.

"You been to see her?" he said, as if this was just a byline before we hung up.

"Who?"

"Oh, come on." All of a sudden, he was done shuffling.

"What's that got to do with anything?"

"I'm just asking."

"I haven't."

"If you did," he said, "what would you do this time?"

"You're not supposed to ask me that."

"You should not go there again. Not until you know what you want out of it. For your sake. But for hers, as well. That's at least one habit broken, that might be for the better."

I was losing my patience with Larson now.

"You're a good person, Elliot. Don't let anyone else tell you otherwise."

"I gotta go now. Got stuff to do here. Important things."

"You take care no—"

I hung up and squeezed the phone. The smell of salt was gone. I didn't feel the sun against my skin anymore. The water had frozen around the piers and I was cold. If there had ever been anyone there with me, that presence was as vague and unreal as the summers I dreamed about.

Chapter 5

BLOOD ON THE CARPET

Apparently, you could get treatment over the phone, or arrangements could be made for the psychologist to come to you. You could cry in a safe place designed by you or an interior designer of your choice, next to your favorite plant, and the psychologist or therapist or whatever they called themselves would politely take notes while wondering where the bathroom was.

But even if I could get Larson's favorite shrink to come here through all the snow, I wouldn't want her anywhere near my plants. Especially not my Eucalyptus tree, which was *my* favorite plant, groomed and nurtured from a small seed I'd smuggled out when Calvin and I had visited a studio in Melbourne once. Sean had sent us there, to review what remained of their development and see if there were any titles worth buying. It was one of the last things we did for him.

Calvin and I had debated creative hiding places for this seed, to avoid customs, and we eventually decided it was best I put it where captured soldiers (apparently) hid their clocks during times of war. On the plane home, I read an article about manure and its qualities for the urban gardener, and I thought about the bud of life that was resting inside me. Perhaps the soil in my netherworld would be particularly fertile and the seed would grow roots before I came home.

"You might branch out," Calvin suggested. "If you did, I'd plant you in my garden. You'd be as old and wise as one of those trees in the Zelda games. I'd come talk to you about things and ask for advice when the world was in turmoil."

"Kind of like now," I said. "Only I'd be a tree instead."

Calvin drew a picture of this, on one of the napkins you get with your gin and tonic. He made a big trunk with my face in the middle and the branches vaguely resembling my messy curls. We laughed so hard, the stewardess said we had to calm down or she'd have to stop serving us.

I wouldn't mind, though. It would be a good life.

I'd rather be a tree in a garden than a man who could only assume he looked like a hungover vampire. Especially if Calvin had planted me there and came to visit every now and then.

The sudden turn from spring back to winter suited me just fine. I wasn't really communicating with the world, unless it was Doctor Larson calling. And most of the time, I didn't answer when he called either.

But the world tried to communicate with me. It called, texted, and e-mailed. Skye, in particular, bugged me with messages, even though she knew I almost never used my phone even when I was at full capacity. I wanted to see what happened if my phone kept piling up unread messages, if it eventually texted itself into a corner and died like the miserable instrument it'd become, designed to collect and transmit the affection of people you didn't know.

Not that Skye was sending me any kind of affection. I didn't need to read her messages to know that they contained nothing but drill sergeant insults to pull myself together and do the right thing. Whatever that was. She didn't say, I didn't know. It might've had something to do with Sean's envelope, the one suggesting that I should get off stage and take the money. But since I hadn't opened the damn thing, how could I know? I guess Skye kept trying because out of all of us, she was the one with the most time on her hands. Though the days when we all had nothing but time, yet felt that what we had wasn't nearly enough, were long gone.

Except for the fiend outside my door.

Like a perfectly calibrated clockwork, it arrived at 9:30 every morning. And it kept knocking. It seemed to have all the time in the world.

"I got your message," I shouted. "Leave me alone."

There was no answer. Eventually, the sounds faded.

Maybe it was Sean outside my door, maybe it was someone else. But while I was loathe to meet him now or ever again, there was still some comfort in knowing that it could potentially be him out there, provoking me to act through one of his mind games. Because if I opened and faced an empty stairwell but still heard those sounds, how would I know what else was real?

But then I remembered.

Sean had been in that room.

You know the one.

The one with all the blood on the carpet. The kind of carpet that didn't wash easily, the kind of blood that wouldn't stop pouring.

That had been very real.

This memory overwhelmed me, and I had to drink to manage. I didn't much like what the vodka did to me, but I didn't much like it the other way around either.

Then, as the storm howled through the nights, I slept for days.

I dreamed that a stream of light slipped through the front door. It raced across the floor with a giggle and a glee.

A shape walked towards me.

This was actually happening. Someone was in my home. The ghoul had grown weary and knocked down the door, and I was too sedated to do anything about it. But maybe it was for the best. Maybe it was time to go.

The shape drew closer.

Chapter 6

ADRIFT in FJELLHAMN

I grew up Fjellhamn, a small coastal community on an island in the western part of Sweden, where the difference between those who had and those who had not was embarrassingly obvious. Not a place where the video game community thrived, exactly. Not a strong foundation to nurture your recently ignited passion for otherworldly digital experiences. The fact that I'd believed that Sara Johnson had an Atari, or that it even was the hot item to get, just shows how desperate I was.

Wealthy or not, the people who lived here had no idea what the word video meant and only a vague conception of what a game was. The rich didn't care, the poor couldn't care less. The guys were into soccer, the girls were into guys. They were clusters of kids who did and liked the same things, separated into groups based on their parents' income and the brands they favored. Worn houses, ravaged and beaten by the wind and the rain, cluttered Fjellhamn's cobbled-stoned streets like old people who had nowhere to go. They had been built in an earlier era, during the days when people could make a living out of working with the sea.

Their neighbors were the expanding number of modern villas, towering with architectural glee on plots sold by fishermen who no longer could afford to stay in a house that was colder inside than outside. These homes in white stone eradicated the red houses with tiny windows, turned the soil upside down (usually with explosives), and finished the deed with a box designed by someone from a big city. Now you could say you had a house by the sea.

The rest of us couldn't or wouldn't move, and we remained in homes where plumbing worked only occasionally, heating was a fire in a stove, and visiting the bathroom involved a trip from one house to another. Which was fine in the summer, but in the winter...well, let's just say that your prejudice of a Swedish December isn't far from the truth, disregarding the polar bears. Who came up with that, anyway?

I had been drifting through Fjellhamn for years, becoming adept at staying out of school. For a long time, my dad was engaged with my teachers in talks on how to get me back on track and at least work up my attendance again, but what are you going to do with a kid who just doesn't care? They kept talking and I spent my time at the piers and watched the fishermen work their nets, asking them what their favorite games were. They said they didn't have much time for such things, but they shared their lunch with me, coal-grilled fish wrapped in foil. I went to the library where the librarian gave me cookies from his eleven o'clock tray. I asked him if he had any books on how to make games. He smiled and shook his head, but we could always play some cards if I wanted to. I had a glass of milk in the café owned by that guy who hardly knew a word of Swedish, but I didn't really ask him anything. He looked at me from behind the counter with a sad expression, and it felt like he wanted to say something, like he had a lot on his mind. But nothing ever came out, so I had my milk and left.

I went on bus rides. At first, when I was around seven, just a stop or two, within Fjellhamn. Then, as I grew older, I took longer trips. To the first station outside the community. After that, over the bridge, to the neighboring island. And from there, all the way to Skaresund and back. That could take hours, if you didn't time the rides right. I snatched some pocket change from Dad's jar, bought a chocolate bar and a Coke, and waited until the skies turned purple before I took the return ride home. I wondered what would happen if I missed the last bus. I'd have no idea how to get home. Or maybe I could take the ride to Gothenburg and find the store that kept the Atari, hide behind a mountain of plush toys until they closed, then crawl out and play *Adventure* until opening hours.

I wondered how long it would take before Dad would realize I was gone. Would he raise some kind of hell to find me, or just hammer away on his typewriter, figuring that I'll make it home eventually? I had so far, after all.

He was always working, but not always in an office. He brought his job home often enough, and sometimes I woke up to the drums of his words when he was jabbing away on his typewriter in our kitchen. On those days, when I came out from my room, he sometimes stopped writing, turned to me, and asked if I wanted to go for a walk.

It didn't seem to matter if it was a school day or a Sunday. If the house was quiet, if that sense of solitude lingered in every room like it could on an early Spring morning or the first winter dawn, we got dressed and took a walk down to the bakery by the old cinema. We talked about the quality of a dragon's egg in an omelet or what it'd take to get strawberries to grow in the winter as well, and we bought cinnamon buns. Dad carried them in a brown paper bag as we walked back to our house, saying that he wasn't sure, but it's possible that these pieces of pastry right here might be the best buns we'd ever have. He was funny that way, always saying extraordinary things about things quite ordinary.

When we came home, he'd put the buns on a plate and let them fill the room with their scent of butter and cinnamon. He made coffee and poured me a glass of milk. We ate slowly and in silence.

If it was winter, I'd watch the sun's orange glow in the ice taps from our window ledges, thinking they were swords made of frost but capable of wielding fire. If it was summer, we'd open the windows and listen to the sea gulls and the distant sound of the engine from small skiffs traveling across the ocean.

When we were done, Dad got up, ruffled my hair, and said: "Now go and fight the dragons, Elliot." Then, he sat down by his typewriter, smiled at me, and got back to work.

He'd told me once, about a year or so after things had taken a turn to the left, that I should always carry pen and paper with me. He'd make sure I'd never run out. It's like he knew that this would be perhaps the only gesture of any lasting value he could offer, because he took my hands and he told me I was great. That as long as I learned to separate my imagination from the lies, it would take me to amazing places.

Anything that could take me to any place that wasn't here made sense to me. So from that point on, I always had pen and paper with me. I wrote things down. Watched the people and imagined them in other contexts. The posh sailors fighting giant squids, the old women uniting against an army from the archipelago kingdom, the school transformed into training grounds for kung fu monks. There were stories everywhere, if you knew where to look. Or more specifically, if you had a desire to find them.

Which made the disaster that was Fjellhamn's local toy store even more depressing, especially now that I'd tasted the sweet fruit of what the one in Gothenburg had to offer.

You'd think that this was a place where imagination wouldn't have to work so hard. But it was nothing but an insult to kids of all ages. The most exciting thing it carried was last year's collection of Playmobil or the Star Wars figurines that no one wanted. This seemed to be its specialty, to carry the toys that everybody in other places had already deemed outdated.

And yet, or maybe just because, not too long after my visit to the city with my father, which had only made me yearn for more, I saw something flashing in the window.

Was that...

Why yes, it was.

An Atari 2600.

Man, our toy store was awesome.

Chapter 7

CALVIN

Now I went to the store every day. At first, I orbited around the Atari console for hours, like a man lost in the dunes, led on by a mirage. Once the shimmer had faded into something more real, I started taking notes.

I watched the demos on repeat, wrote down anything that came to me, made sketches and drawings, sparked ideas for improvement, and jotted down concepts for games of my own. The guy working there didn't like it, but that's okay, because I didn't like him. Also, he was ginger, no doubt one of the reasons for his foul mood. Sometimes, a customer showed up and asked to try a game or two, potentially looking to buy the Atari. These were the highlights for me, when I could follow a more consistent flow from someone who actually grabbed a controller and did something. I tried to understand the coherence that held a game together, how to get a point across when I didn't control what the next action would be, how to tell a story when the audience was so much in control. It was as mind blowing as it was sweet.

Eventually, I knew so much about defender spacecrafts or crystal castles that I could pilot a ship of my own or build a palace in my spare time. I'd definitely do a better job of pitching and selling the damn games, since it didn't take me long to learn more about the depths and nuances of the Atari than the freckled jellyfish behind the counter ever did. All that by just looking, paying attention, taking notes.

But sometimes, there was another kid there.

He was short and thin with a dirty face and wispy, blonde bangs that fell over his blue eyes. I didn't recognize him, which was odd, considering that Fjellhamn was the kind of town where no one was a stranger unless you actually were a stranger. So I guess it wasn't so odd, after all.

He, too, carried a sketch pad with him. He never seemed to notice me and after he'd studied the screen, he walked across the street to the small diner. Then he sat in one of the booths for the rest of the day, working with his tools. A towering woman circled around him from time to time, gesticulating wildly as if in constant battle with a hurricane. They seemed to laugh a lot together.

He kept coming back. I was wary at first. I wasn't expecting him to be any different than the other kids around here. At best, not interested. At worst, another thug.

But he had a calm appearance. His way of watching his surroundings with a constant curiosity made me think that perhaps he really was from another place. Besides, he did circle the Atari with pen and paper, just like me, so like it or not, we were in the same orbit. After a while, we sort of got to know each other, in the way that you can without saying anything but visiting the same place at the same time so frequently that something had to grow from there.

So one day, I said, "Hey."

He didn't answer, but looked at me with caution.

"I'm Elliot," I said.

"O-okay."

We were quiet for some time. But eventually, he added, "I'm C-ca-calvin."

"Cool."

He shrugged, agreeing to the obvious.

"Have you tried it?" I said and pointed to the Atari.

"N-nah. I asked once, but y-you know..."

Calvin nodded towards the guy behind the counter. And I don't know why I did what I did next, or I do know now but I didn't know then, it just felt right to turn to the man and say, "Hello."

But apparently, he didn't feel it like I did. He didn't answer. Not that I'd expected this to go down easy.

"Can we try the Atari?" I said.

"No."

"Why not?"

"You're never gonna buy it," he said and turned a page in the paper he was pretending to read. "You keep coming here. And you'll never stop if I let you try it, and then you're gonna keep playing that fucking thing and just waste *my time.*"

Calvin looked at me. *Told you so,* he said with his eyes.

"You got plans or something?" I said.

He looked at me now. "What did you say?"

"How do we know we'll like it if we can't try it?"

He held up his magazine. "Read a fucking review."

"You read a review."

Calvin failed to mute a giggle.

"Oh, you're really pushing it," the man said.

"All right. Show us then."

"Show you what?"

"How to make a game."

A vacant expression fell over him then, as if he just realized that even if he dyed his hair, he'd still be ginger at heart and everybody would know and whisper behind his back.

"How to...I don't...fucking kids...the fuck do you mean?"

"If I wanna," and I looked at Calvin's sketch book (quite impressive stuff in there!), "come up with a cool idea and Calvin could do all the art for it...you okay with that, Calvin?"

He nodded. *Hell yes.*

"So if we wanna make our own *Adventure* or *Space Invaders* or whatever, how do we do it? Can you show us? Does it take like a day or maybe two days? *Pitfall* takes longer, don't you think, Calvin? Lots of monsters and stuff in there, after all, and crocodiles and treasure."

Calvin put his hand in his chin, thinking hard. Yes, he concluded with a nod. Pitfall *would take longer.* There was a complexity to the level design as well as the pacing, which *Asteroids* or *Missile Command,* due to their emergent nature, didn't require.

Ginger leaned forward, his cheeks as red as his hair now.

"You can't make games with this box, little man. You can only play games on it."

Now, the vacancy fell on me. I looked at Calvin, who seemed to share my surprise over this turn of events.

"But why would we want an Atari," I said, "if we could only play someone else's games?"

"The fuck do you mean?"

"Well...what if our games are better?"

"That'd be your problem."

"Well, we're making it your problem, sir!"

"It's not our fault you're ginger!" screamed Calvin.

Chapter 8

SARA SMILED

He threw us out, shouting that we should get a fucking computer if we were so smart, and while we always told people afterwards, when we recounted this day, that we'd somersaulted through the air and landed on our feet first, we most certainly didn't. But we got up and brushed the dust away, and Calvin picked up his sketches while I collected my notebooks.

"Hey," Calvin said. "L-let's get pancakes."

"I don't have any money," I said.

"D-don't worry about it. C'mon."

"Nah. I should go home."

Calvin looked surprised. "Oh. Okay."

We shuffled our feet, shoved our hands in our pockets.

"Pancakes, huh?" I said.

"Yep."

"Okay, then."

We walked across the street, Calvin leading the way to the diner where I'd seen him sit and do his work. It was almost empty when we entered. The towering woman, who was actually quite short now that I saw her up close, approached us. She wore an apron and a hat and her stride indicated purpose, like she was ready to face that damn hurricane again and again until she'd worn it down to a breeze. She had black hair and a charismatic nose and she hugged Calvin and kissed him on the cheek.

"Where the hell were you drifting this time, honey? I was worried about you. Damn," she called out and looked around as if we had an audience, "I always worry about you."

"Mom," Calvin said. "This is Elliot. He's my...f-f-friend."

At this, I felt a tickle and a tingle.

A friend, huh?

Just like that.

A friend.

She slowly turned to look at me. I felt like a rare bird, found and filed by a zoologist who was the first to ever spot me in the wild and claim me to her legacy.

She smiled.

"Well, now," she said.

And if ever there was a smile that could cut through the dark, this was the one. It missed a tooth, it was a bit crooked, but that only contributed to its edge. Besides, it complemented the nose quite nicely. I looked at Calvin and he looked at me. He was grinning.

"Would you look at that, Calvin darling? Oh baby, I told you you'd make friends. See," she said to me, "we're new here, and it's always hard, you know? Course you don't, you've lived here all your life, haven't you? I'm Cornelia, and that'd make you..."

"E-Elliot," Calvin said. "I t-told you. We're making a game together. He's got all these cool ideas and I'm gonna do all the drawing."

Cornelia turned serious. "I see. You're gonna be needin' some pancakes then. With whipped cream on top and on the sides. And by some, I mean a lot."

She hugged Calvin again and looked at him, her pirate smile growing wider as if she never tired of watching her treasure.

"Now listen, Calvin, my boy."

Calvin listened.

"Before I go into that kitchen, you gotta know that I love you more than any piece of pie or any cup of freshly brewed coffee. And you know I love my coffee, Calvin, honey."

"I know, Mom." He turned to me. "S-she's impossible before she gets her first cup."

"That's the kind of love I offer, baby."

It was exhausting to see all this family affection on display. I focused on a stain on the floor until Calvin's mom left and went into the kitchen. I was confused and angry at feeling so good and so bad at the same time. Fuck, being a kid was hard. And Dad who kept telling me on his worst days that being a grown up wasn't any easier. I shrugged off any thoughts about my parents. I didn't want them here in this moment, so I put them away and sat down in a booth with Calvin.

"Okay," I said. "I've got some stuff already. You wanna hear about it?"

"S-sure. H-hit me."

He opened his pad and the lines poured out over the edges. As he shuffled through his pages, there was this half-finished clearing with a small pond, where I could smell the morning dew; a beach with no end, by a sea with no horizon, and I heard the slow waves reach higher with the tide; there was a man standing on a grassy hill, his beard unkempt and his long hair a mess, his eyes old and sad.

It was so beautiful, it hurt I couldn't go there.

Cornelia served us pancakes and coffee.

It was the best pile of pancakes I'd ever had. And I didn't even like whipped cream.

"Hey," I said as I tasted coffee for the first time in my life (yeuch!). "Our game's gonna be great."

"The g-greatest game of all!" Calvin shouted, almost knocking his cup from the table.

"Yes," I said. "The greatest game of all."

"W-who's that?"

"Who's who?"

"That."

Calvin nodded to someone standing on the other side of the street, looking in our direction.

I was surprised to see her there, and yet I wasn't.

She was carrying a wrapped bag of sorts. It contained a box about the size of a cartridge. One that might slide into, say, an Atari 2600. No idea which title. Maybe that *Pervert* game she'd been on about, maybe something else.

But it didn't matter.

No, what really mattered was that Sara Johnson saw me. And she smiled.

A faint smile, cautious, with no promise attached.

But a smile, all the same.

"You know her?" Calvin said.

"I used to," I said.

I didn't smile back, and turned away.

Chapter 9

IT'S NOT WEDNESDAY

Except for the bathroom and the small bedroom with the walk-in closet, there was nowhere to run or hide in my place, or in this case nowhere to make coffee except right in the middle, which is what Jason had done while I was sleeping.

If I should mention just one thing about Jason, it would be that he took his mustache seriously. He always made sure its perfectly groomed edges were in symmetry with his dark curly hair. Sometimes, it felt like it had a life of its own and that he actually had to groom it, because it whispered to him in the morning that it'd tell the world about his filthy little secrets if he didn't nurture it and love it.

I'm not going to mention just one thing about Jason, though. But if I did, that'd be the one.

He sat by my kitchen table now and enjoyed his coffee, wearing a uniform that implied craftsmanship of some sort. There was neither rain nor snow outside, but a dim light from a sun rising through the morning mist.

"Mornin'," he said.

I said nothing.

"I was just checking to see if you wanted the place cleaned."

"But it's not Wednesday."

As if I had any idea.

Jason looked at me with a thoughtful expression.

"That must've been the last of it," he said and turned to the window. "Here, I made you coffee."

I got up and shambled to the table. He had prepared a perfect cup of black. His cleaning gear was by the door, fresh from the supplier in mint condition, the bucket shining like a plastic mirror, the cloths perfectly folded into a pile next to the bag of chemicals.

"How long you worn those robes?" he said.

"Since I fell asleep."

"That's a good title right there. You working on a new game?"

I looked out. The thaw was almost gone.

Jason sighed. He put a pen on the table.

"The lawyer gave me this," he said. "And a bunch of papers to go with it."

I looked at the pen. It seemed to be of good quality. I'd consider using this pen, if I had something to write about.

"I love my kids, Elliot. And I don't understand my wife. But he says it's for the best."

"Your wife's a he?"

"Nah. The lawyer." He spun the pen slowly. "You ever been married?"

I looked at him. Despite my condition, I was amused and confused. We'd shared coffee for years. He'd been around since I bought the place. Yet he always asked.

"Kids, then?" he said.

"Yes, Jason. I have kids. Five or six of them. They're around here somewhere."

He smiled as I made a gesture to underline the potential this place held for children unleashed. Property worth a fortune would be destroyed in less than a minute. A first gen NES 8-bit console, in gold and signed by Miyamoto. One of the PlayStation One prototypes with a copy of *Wipeout* burned into its ROM. The white, transparent Xbox with a note from Seamus Blackley attached to it, wishing me good luck. One of the first hundred prints of Super Metroid. The handgun used for the motion capture sessions in *Resident Evil.* A *Terminator* skull. Gordon Freeman's crowbar (which we stole from Valve during a pool party at their offices), and a picture of me and J.K. Rowling, from a dinner we'd had when I was involved in the adaption of *Harry Potter and the Random Item Of Legendary Awesome* (her suggestion for the title—I was strictly told by the Executive Producer at Electronic Arts to only laugh at her jokes, not make any of my own. They always were an anxious bunch, despite their mafia nicknames).

"It's a strange thing," Jason said as he refilled his cup. Now, the sunlight poured through the (unclean!) windows, the wooden floor glowing like a (filthy!) pond in a hidden grove.

"You marry someone you love. And she's the most important person. Even when you get kids, she's a close second. And yet, she's like the human dumpster of all your psychological garbage."

"And the other way around as well," I said. Coffee and clichés were all I had to offer today. But Jason seemed fine with that and to be fair, that's about the only thing he did when he was here, drink coffee and talk. Occasionally, he cleaned the place, but I couldn't count on it nor remember when that last happened. He was scheduled to work here every Wednesday between 9:00 a.m. and 11:30 a.m., but according to him, that was just a formality.

"There has to be something on the paper before you sign," he'd said once. "So there's a roughly mutual understanding of our expectations for one another."

"I don't know," I'd said. "On this paper, it says Wednesday 9:00 a.m. and 11:00 a.m. That's not rough at all, really."

"In case we agree to disagree at some point, there's a paper, and we can point to that paper and say, 'Look, this is what we said.'"

"But that paper says when you're going to be here and what you're supposed to do. And you're not doing that."

He nodded. "I can see some truth in that." He raised an eyebrow. "Do we have a disagreement, though?"

I'd shrugged my shoulders. "Not really, no."

But this was Jason's forte, that he seemed to know when the time was right to swoop in on his broom and provide enough diversion for me to gather strength for whatever was coming next. It's a good thing he used the broom for something.

We were silent for a while. Then he looked at his watch. "I've got another customer, Elliot. Thanks for the coffee."

"Sure."

As he collected his (unspoiled!) gear and headed for the door, he turned to me and said: "How come, though?"

"What?"

"You never got married?"

He'd never asked me that before.

"Is that something you're supposed to do?" I said.

"There's not a lot of things you're supposed to do."

That made sense, coming from him.

"I was just wondering," he said. "I do recommend it, though."

"But you're getting divorced."

"Yeah. That, I don't recommend. Brutal."

As if on cue, this morning's knock-knock rap-tap-tapped on the door. The Fiend was back.

I looked at Jason, suddenly terrified. I wanted to know if he, too, heard the knocks or if this was the moment where I'd realize I'd imagined the whole thing. I was hoping I'd gone insane. That'd be easier.

But Jason returned the look, eyebrows raised and all. He reached for the handle.

"Don't," I said.

"No?"

"No."

"Oh, come on. Where's your sense of adventure?"

"Never had one."

"But you gotta open the door at some point."

"I'm not sure I do."

"Fuck it. I'm coming in, Elliot."

This last reply came from the other side of the door, from the depths of the stairwell and beyond. And as whoever had just said this rattled with a set of keys in the lock, in a casual and not very ghoulish way at all, Jason looked at me. I was going paler by the second, my heart racing in all kinds of directions. I knew that voice from the other side of the door and not in a million years had I expected this one to come talk to me ever again.

"You've given your keys to someone else?" he said.

"Apparently."

He seemed truly offended.

"To a *woman?*"

Chapter 10

THE EYE OF THE BEHOLDER

Her hair was shorter than I remembered and despite her fair color, I saw tints of gray. She didn't have a pony tail anymore, she'd always had one even when she'd cut it really short, but not now. She wore a beige coat and a shoulder bag, black stockings with boots. I think she would wear that that even if the storm still raged outside. She'd always been the first to defy the winter and welcome the spring, though she was never one to fully embrace the summer.

Jason lit a cigarette.

"Hey, Lisa," he said.

She didn't answer. She entered slowly, sighing as she did.

I felt a sting, a current traveling from my toes to my head and back again. I should've known my ghoul was of an entirely different shape, so unlikely to appear I wouldn't even go there with my mind's eye. Anyone else, I could've handled. But this...her...well... wasn't this supposed to be the other way around?

Lisa looked in my direction. Not exactly at me, just at a point very close to me.

A faint smell of something from a long time ago filled the place.

That could've been Jason's cigarette though, which he had in the corner of his mouth now, trying to look like James Dean.

Lisa pierced him with her gaze.

"Hello, Jason."

Then, she swept the place with her eyes.

"You're doing a bad job," she said. "As always."

"That's in the eye of the beholder," Jason said and exhaled.

"You're using him."

"That's okay. He's not paying me."

"He smells."

"It's not my job to wash him."

"Hey," I said. "You smell." After a pause, I added: "Both of you."

"What are you doing here?" Jason said to Lisa.

"I could ask you the same thing."

"I was about to leave. But now, I'm thinking I'll stay."

Lisa shrugged.

"It's okay," I said to Jason. "You can go."

He nodded. Lisa appeared lost in thought as he collected his gear, cigarette still in his mouth, but before he left, he put his hand on my shoulder and said: "I'll come back as soon as I can. Wednesdays be damned."

"Yes. Damn them all. Thanks, Jason."

"Sure."

Then he left.

Lisa sat down, still not looking at me.

I wanted to say it was good to see her, but her being here made me feel bad, so I didn't. Yet, she seemed okay and that made me feel good, so I wanted to say that. Of course, I wanted to say how sorry I was as well, but as the conversation played out in my head, she took those words, spun them around and hurled them back at me, and that made me feel bad again. So I guess all I wanted was not to lie, really.

"I'll have some coffee," she said. "Can you get me some coffee?"

Her voice trembled. It was an odd thing to ask for, so casual and every day. Like you'd ask for a glass of water before you headed into the storm.

But for what it was worth, Jason's brew was still warm so I poured her a cup as she stood up and walked into the kitchen, bringing the bag, adjusting the strap on her shoulder. It looked uncomfortable, not like any kind of bag she'd usually wear. She wasn't a purse kind of person either, but had always kept her phone and keys in her pockets and that was about it. Like me, she traveled lightly through life when it came to stuff.

"Skye wants to know if you've signed Sean's papers yet," she said.

I took a few seconds to consider this.

I would ask her, How long has it been, Lisa? And she would smile, exhausted but relieved that we could have this conversation, and we'd talk about the things that really mattered and she'd laugh, not a roaring *Saturday Night Live* laugh but a sad, searching one that told us despite all, the sun would rise tomorrow. And this wouldn't be so bad after all.

"If Skye wants to know," I said, "she can ask me herself."

"You're not answering your calls. Or mail. Or text messages."

"You're here, aren't you? And you're persistent. Coming here every morning, knocking on my door."

Lisa frowned.

"No," she said. "Just today. You didn't open. I still had your keys."

"Whatever Sean wants, I'm not interested," I said.

"Come on, Elliot." She pushed the coffee away when I gave her the cup. "We're lucky anyone wants to buy what's left. Even if it's Sean."

"Have you signed it?" I said.

"What do you think?"

"Do you need the money?"

She seemed genuinely shocked that I would say that. I'll admit, it was crude.

"How have you been, Lisa?"

"How do you think I've been? Why do you think you got the

right to ask me that?"

"You're here, after all."

"I'm already regretting it."

We had a few moments of silence.

"Sean's buying the rights to humiliate us," I said.

"Please, Elliot. You always were a self-made man."

"Okay, forget about us, then. What about Calvin?"

Lisa slammed her hand on the kitchen table so hard, it must've hurt. It sounded like thunder on a clear day. I felt a strong pain over my chest as she suddenly went from dead calm to furious. She remained cool in her voice, though.

"Sean doesn't care about us, Elliot. He's buying a bunch of games, a list of properties long dead. That's it."

"It's not just a bunch of—"

"You just had to keep going, didn't you?"

Suddenly, she was shouting.

"While the others left and did new things in new countries with new people, you didn't know when to quit, did you?"

"There was always—"

"Shut up. Shut the fuck up."

"Why do you care anyway? It's not like you ever were a part of it."

"Where's your fucking dignity? You always had that, at least. And integrity. Where's it gone to now?"

"I'm working on it," I said.

She took a deep breath.

"Skye told me," she said. "How you bled out on the carpet. In that room, with all those execs watching. And Sean, even joking about it."

She drew closer. I pulled back.

"But it did put you out of your misery, Elliot."

When I didn't answer, she flared up again.

"No publisher wants to talk to you. No studio wants to work with you. Sean's your only option. Take it."

She put her hand on her bag, protecting it from me now.

"You don't need to come here and tell me this," I said. "I wasn't planning on ever trying to find you. What's your real reason?"

She hesitated and looked over her shoulder at the door. Then she sighed and opened the bag.

She pulled out a folder, worn and stuffed like an old teddy bear that had rested on the attic for years. While the folder contained only papers, some of them yellow and torn at the edges, others surprisingly fresh (at least it was a surprise to me), she struggled as if it contained only lead. She almost dropped it and I almost reached out to help her, but she pulled away and slammed the folder on the table.

I had not seen this for quite some time.

Years, in fact.

I started pacing. Slowly, working on that dignity I was lacking.

Lisa gave me a minute.

"You know where he kept this?" she said.

The question annoyed me. In some damn box somewhere in some random basement in whatever house he used to live in.

"On his desk," she said. "Not in the basement or buried in a box in the garage." She tapped her fingers on the folder. "On his desk. Always open. When he couldn't walk anymore, he kept it in his bed."

"Why do you come here...how do you even know..." I stopped and looked at her. Her eyes glowed in the morning light. It was a cold, blue fire.

She stood up, straightening her coat. "He told me to give it to you. That's why I'm here. I couldn't care less about you. But he did. He still cared."

I looked at Calvin's folder from the corner of my eye. It hurt. I felt like the boy who couldn't sleep, listening to the silent cries that slipped through the cracks, cries like precursors to a larger haunt.

"And with that, I'm done," Lisa said. "We're done."

She walked towards the door.

"You could've just sent me this," I said. "Why didn't you?"

She stopped.

"Aren't you sorry, Elliot?"

"There it is. This is the conversation you really want to have."

"Well, aren't you?"

"I could ask you the same."

She looked at me now. "Are you serious?"

I didn't answer, because now I felt more cornered than ever. It brought out parts in me that did me no good. If ever I had a chance to say the right things to Lisa, this would be my shot. I'd imagined this meeting many times. But it didn't go anywhere near as I'd hoped, or thought.

"I just don't get it," she said. "After all these years...I just don't get it. I think he did, maybe. He told me not to call you. To not reach out. So I guess he knew you best, after all."

"I didn't want it to go this way," I said quietly.

She turned away when I tried to catch her eyes.

"I'm sorry," she said. "I don't know what hurts the most. That you're this person, I mean, you are who you are...I guess that's what it all comes down to...or the fact that I can't even look at you anymore." She pulled her arm over her eyes but suddenly I only felt anger. She only seemed to want me harm, even if I'd do my best.

"It's such a strange thing," I said, "that you'd want to see someone you can't wait to never see again. To come here and tell me what a miserable human being I am and hand over a bunch of papers. Implying what I did or didn't do."

"Oh, that's sweet," she said between the sobs. "You thinking I'm using this as an excuse?"

"You're here. You don't have to be."

"Not all of us wants to be that kind of asshole."

And I just had to ask, didn't I?

"And what kind would that be? Just tell me, Lisa. Just get it over with, so we never have to see each other again."

Now, she looked at me, her eyes burning through the walls.

"Oh, you know the kind," she said.

Then, she put my keys—the ones I'd given her so many years ago—on the table and left.

Chapter 11

THE GRAETEST

He was always at peace when he was working. Watching him as his hands traveled over the paper was a serene experience. He was like a conjurer, lost in his art to summon the essence from another world.

While paper was his preference, as we grew older, it didn't really matter. Whatever piece of gear he learned, he mastered and seemed equally comfortable with. He moved without friction between texturing and modeling in software (in *Maya*, if you must know, though he was okay with using *3ds Max* if he had to) to sketching something on a pad with just a black ink pen. He didn't much care for tablets, considering them a gadget for hipsters who imagined creativity had to be practiced in parks or not at all.

Sometimes, during a crunch for whatever game we were working on, when we were the only ones still there in whatever studio we were located in, I felt surrounded by that wide darkness that came to fetch certain people after midnight. I could almost see the shadows reaching for me, wanting something to bring back to their lair. But a light still burned by Calvin's desk. We'd sit there together and work on our game, and the monsters couldn't touch me. Even if Calvin wasn't involved in whatever I was doing for the moment, he'd stay. Help out, make some coffee or sleep on the couch until I woke him up and said that it was time to go.

It's a good thing we met when we did, because as brilliant as I was at design and writing, as criminally inept I was at drawing and sketching, I'd always wanted to learn. It seemed like such a relaxing skill to have, to sit down and see where your fingers took you. But I could not draw. Dad had paid for a class once, whose very title was "Everyone can draw."

But after a few sessions, the teacher put his hand on my shoulder and said, "You know, Elliot. Maybe everyone can't draw, after all."

Looking at my work, resembling more the output of a man insane than an artist rising, I had to agree.

But with Calvin around, this wasn't an issue. He'd already produced art that impressed me more than the mightiest of illustrators. Which was fortunate, since we had a lot of ground to cover. We had a game to make, after all. It also seemed that fate had not only brought us together, but also given us oceans of time, perhaps the only real luxury we had as kids and the one commodity we always seemed to lack as adults.

If my attendance in school was random at best, Calvin had made absence into an art. He just didn't show up. I could always find him with his sketch pad and a cup of coffee at the diner and on some days, I went straight there and didn't even bother with class. He smiled and waved at me from the window before he was eclipsed by Cornelia who laughed so loud, any seismographs on the western coast had to be recalibrated.

Not long after we'd met and Calvin told his mum about our game, she gave him a folder. It was old and worn, made in leather with strings to tie the binders. Cornelia told Calvin it used to belong to his grandfather. But that old fart, as she called him, never used it for anything other than cut-outs from magazines that no one should read, especially not old farts, so it was time the family's real talent put it to use.

"Save all your brilliance right here," she said to her son. "But remember that you're glowing so bright, it won't hold all that's good about you. And you wanna put Elliot's stuff in there, too, Calvin, honey, because without your friend, your glow's gonna pale. So make it your place, the one you'll go to that's only yours. This'll be your sanctuary, love."

For Calvin, a boy who owned hardly any clothes and such a limited supply of paper that he sometimes used the leftovers from toilet rolls to get his work done, this folder was like one of those rare power-ups from a tough-to-beat action game. It shined from all the stuff Cornelia poured into it, because the risks she'd take for her little boy were like the love she held for him—it blurred her judgment but knew no ends. Me, I had my walks with Dad to the bakery by the old cinema and the never-ending supply of notebooks. He certainly knew his ends.

You really think the folder was inherited from Calvin's grandfather, though? I didn't think so. Calvin had no grandfather. Cornelia had stolen it from a luxury store in Gothenburg. But Calvin would defend this folder as if his life depended on it. Which eventually turned out to be the case.

So when he composed the title for our game, and slapped it on the folder, it felt right. I looked at the letters and knew that no one else could've come up with exactly that. Because if I couldn't draw, then Calvin couldn't write.

It said:

the Graetest Game of All

Calvin showed it to Cornelia. She smiled and said: "I love it, honey. Oh, it's beautiful. Don't you think it's beautiful, Elliot?"

"It's the best title ever," I said, and Calvin beamed.

Chapter 12

THE REAL HAUNT

After Lisa left, I sat down and leaned against the wall. I was expecting an anxiety attack and maybe a good old-fashioned vomit or two. And guilt, from hell. But that didn't happen. I was dead tired, but that was it.

I closed my eyes.

That faint smell from a long time ago, it still lingered.

I felt a warm summer rain on my skin. I saw party lights and long tables on a lawn. In Midsummer's June, the nights up north became just a sedated shimmer that rolled down from the mountains as the skies turned into matte blue. Each summer felt brighter than the one before, until we'd reach the point where the sun would never set.

After the party, we'd all gone down to the sea in the hour before dawn, carrying our sleeping children in our arms. The water had glowed like turquoise fire as we swept through the waves.

When was this, again? Last year? Ten years ago? I think it was five years ago.

But they'd all been there. Lisa and Skye, still sharing an apartment. Simon, with his second wife. Benjamin brought his newborn twins. And Helene's sons were old enough to stay up late.

Even Pete showed up, like the long-lost son, but without his wife. We never met her actually, though we always assumed she existed, since he eventually got first one and then another and finally a third kid with her. Filip was dating some guy from Japan who liked the schnapps but hated the herring. Sean had stayed for lunch, but then he'd left after no one talked to him or wanted to sit next to him. He shook my hand, thanked me for the invite and said he had a plane to catch. No one walked him to his car or took the time to say goodbye.

But Calvin had been quiet that evening.

Lately, he'd pulled back and been more withdrawn. Skye and I had been busy with one of our most critical crunches yet and I'd meant to ask Calvin how things were, once things had settled down. Clearly, there was something going on. But I'd assumed he'd be around for that talk, once our next game had shipped. Why wouldn't he be?

I sometimes wonder what could've happened if I'd done this the other way around. If I'd approached him earlier, if I'd taken the time to hear him out and talked to Lisa before she left again. Just to settle things, to clear things up.

But I'd learned that picturing what could've been or trying to imagine what might be tomorrow was what took you from the present, the only reality you could actually change. I don't know. I always considered that was nonsense, created for people who couldn't face their past or accept their future.

But in the present now, outside my window, the sun took a stroll across the skies. I guess that was worth a moment.

It headed west, towards the darkening rim.

I felt an ache, a desire to get back to a place where there was someone around who asked me, "How are you?" Someone who was serious about listening. I was that boy again, the kid who couldn't sleep because the sounds that slipped through the cracks from the other side scared him, made him fear that no one would be there to fight for him if the ghoul came around.

It wasn't until the shadows had grown so long, they were reaching for my feet like ghosts wanting to give me a tickle, that I realized I'd been sitting here through the day. The front door was still open and it seemed that Lisa had left only a few minutes ago. But unless I'd been part of a time lapse, the twilight was real.

With no lights on, my home was submerged in a deep blue shade, the corners so thick they could be black holes to another dimension.

Perhaps this was the real haunt.

Not Sean's attempts to get me to sign, or Lisa's fury unleashed, or Skye trying to reach out. But this. Whatever it was.

I hurried to close and lock the door, but it was too late. Something was in my apartment and it wouldn't go away.

I slowly turned around to face the folder.

Chapter 13

ONE LAST THING TO SAY

It seemed harmless. An item on the kitchen table, charmingly worn by weather and time. But as I got up and approached it, I felt a strange comfort that led me away from that lonely fright, as if I still remained on the pieces of a wreck after the storm had settled. Behind me, the thunder would rage, tearing up the sea.

I made myself some coffee. Slowly. Grinding the beans. Measuring the pot. Pouring the water. One step at a time.

Then, armed with a warm cup, I approached the folder.

It was stuffed with so much material, the straps couldn't hold it. A mix of sketches and words, maps and characters, scenes and buildings, on yellowed paper from a time I still wasn't sure ever existed. While most of the words and scripts in there were mine, I believe I was guilty of a sketch or two as well. Hell, at some point I even made a draft of a production plan, drawn by hand and neatly folded on an A3 sheet which my father took from one of the agencies he worked for. But even though the title on Calvin's folder said it all, I considered calling Sean and accepting his offer. In fact, I'd more or less decided I'd do just that, and this last look was just an attempt to amend a failed farewell.

Yes. I should've called Sean and told him I'll sign.

You bring the lawyers, Sean. I'll get a good, proper shave and a haircut, we'll have a nice meal, shake hands, and then I'll move to France and grow old, maybe prepare a room with a spare bed for Skye if she ever comes to visit. Which she won't.

I'd just forget about Lisa. She'd stepped out of my apartment and away from my life, as it were.

So I called Sean.

Or I almost did.

I browsed my phone and found him in my contacts, and held my finger on the screen.

I put the phone away.

I opened Calvin's folder.

Or no, I didn't.

But I certainly thought about it.

Back to the phone again.

Then I went to the bathroom.

And there it was, the good vomit and a banging headache that sent the world spinning and my chest aching, leaving me to wonder if I'd die today, like these attacks always did.

I washed up and returned to the kitchen.

My place was dark now. I tripped on something but made it to the kitchen table. Sat down and put my hand on Calvin's folder.

I turned on the kitchen light and opened the binders.

I felt I owed us one last stroll down memory lane. So there was that. Maybe I was curious to see if I could bring back something good from that time, something with healing qualities. Or if it would bring back the hurt, if being alone was the entire point, and perhaps I deserved this and needed the hurt to move on. Most importantly, I was aware of how tiring it was to feel sorry for myself, especially since no one else seemed to have any sympathy to spare.

But there was also the fact that some of the material in Calvin's folder was clean, almost fresh from the printer.

Concepts I'd never seen before, words that weren't mine, images I'd never known.

These new prints were not from some time that maybe never existed, from when we were young or at least younger. They were real, fresh from the water and as mysterious as Santiago's marlin.

I had no idea what these new concepts contained.

I had no idea why they were there.

And I'd known this material since we were kids.

I leaned closer. On top of all those papers was a small, black notebook. Well-used, it seemed. It had a small, yellow post-it taped to its cover that said, "*Spellbinder Software.*"

I smiled.

The book rested on the picture of that man on the grassy hill, his beard still neglected, his long hair ever the mess, his eyes the same old, sad. I touched my face and the picture came alive, the grass waving to the clouds as they traveled over the sky, the man looking not at some point on the horizon but at me instead. The air was crisp and cold, the wind a silent hum.

I picked up the notebook. It let out a small gasp. Someone had worked the pages good.

I opened it and saw a stick drawing of two boys sitting on a pier.

I'd seen this stick drawing once before. But only once.

It wasn't nearly as old as much of the material in the folder, but not as fresh as the pages that seemed brand new.

The boys in the picture were laughing at something. It was made up of just a few lines of ink, but perfectly balanced, so exquisitely composed, it was painful to see such beauty on display and know it wouldn't be appreciated by all that needed to see it. He'd written, in small letters under the drawing, "*Remember?*"

I touched the drawing, hoping it would pull me in and take me to that place of ocean sunsets and long, warm nights drenched in the light from flickering screens. To a time when a friend was only a bicycle ride away, when he had your back because you had his. That'd be golden for anyone in this world, but for a kid who grew up wandering the hills of Fjellhamn on his own, it was something only a picture could describe.

Behind that picture, there were pages with words and sentences that struggled with coherence, letters bouncing around but written with a beautiful hand, each line so meticulously crafted that the purpose of the design almost triumphed the meaning of the words.

Apparently, Calvin had one last thing to say to me.

And like everything else in life, he'd worked long and hard to get it right before he left.

Chapter 14

HALL OF FAME

Dad would've been thrilled if I'd brought home a friend. None of us could remember when that last happened and he'd stopped asking why, since my answer might hurt him more than me. I was the kid, but he was the one who struggled to accept our situation.

Even so, when Calvin suggested we work on our game at my place, I felt all dry in my mouth. I'd seen this coming and I feared it more than I thought I would.

I know he'd be cool with my father. In fact, if Dad had one of his good days, they'd get along just fine. Maybe, if he wasn't too busy with work, he'd even ask if Calvin wanted to join us for a stroll down to the bakery.

But Mum, though.

There's no way I'd let her meet Calvin.

So I didn't tell Dad about Calvin and I didn't tell him about our game. I knew he'd love to hear about it, that it'd make his day for a year, and he'd do his best to make Calvin feel welcome in our house. But it didn't matter. I couldn't risk it. So I said nothing and our home remained as empty as ever.

We weren't fools, Dad and I. We knew that just because we didn't speak of it didn't mean it would go away. It wasn't a secret, what had happened to our family. Everyone in Fjellhamn knew. And if you'd moved here recently, it wouldn't take long before someone told you.

But in our family, there was a simple truth to the fact that what wasn't mentioned didn't hurt as much as when it was. There were no therapists around, nor any safe places with eucalyptus plants nurtured in the netherworlds. These were the eighties. You had to be insane before you went to see someone that helped you be sane. Honestly, we did try, the three of us, all the way to Gothenburg for a series of sessions with a bearded man who wore thick-rimmed glasses and a denim jacket. I was about six years old then and didn't remember much from those meetings. Dad said the guy had tried his best. But your one chance to deal with reality was to first accept it and then take it from there. You could only hope for, but never count on, a change with another person but yourself.

A harsh enough concept for an adult to deal with, but try explaining that to a child, or even make the decision that you had to. Well, whatever I was going through, scaring away my new friend wasn't gonna be part of it.

One day, when we met by the red storehouses at the piers, Calvin was quiet and eyed me from the side. He had his hands in his pockets. After some time, he said, "Mum said we could work on the game at our place, as much as we like. And if you wanna sleep over, that's fine, too."

I nodded. "Sounds good."

"Oh, and a-another thing."

"Yeah?"

"You're my b-b-est fr-friend, Elliot."

"I am?"

"You are."

"You're my best friend, too."

He smiled. He pulled out his hand from his pocket. He showed me a few coins and a wrinkled bill.

"W-wanna get some ice cream? I'm buying. You can have any ice cream you want."

"Sure."

We were wrapped up in a comfortable silence as we walked down the road to the ice cream cart by the water. The sales man waited with kind patience as Calvin got his stuttering in order and picked out a soft one with strawberry sauce around it. I bought a vanilla and blueberry mix with chocolate topping and caramel sprinkles around. We walked out to the end of the farthest bridge and sat on the ledge and dangled our legs over the water as we had our ice creams. We remained quiet, watching the boats and the fish in the clear, blue water.

I've had many ice creams after this one. I'd had a few before as well. But the man must've put something special in the mix on this day, because over the years, I'm sure this was the greatest slice of ice cream I've ever had.

Chapter 15

DINNER AT THE CALVINS

Calvin and Cornelia rented their home from Mr. Svensson. That man lived in a big house. But when his wife died and his kids moved out, he was alone in his castle and built a cottage on his oceanic lawn, renting it to people who couldn't afford a decent place but badly needed one. He ran a few restaurants on the islands around Fjellhamn. Most of the time, he got out of bed, put on his khakis and a white shirt, had his breakfast, got into his car, and solved restaurant-related problems. His expression was a bit distant, as if he wasn't quite there.

But when his kids came to visit with their kids, Mr. Svensson smiled and wore patched jeans and sweaters. He opened the windows and music from his old record player filled the gardens, while his son's toddlers pulled his beard and his daughter's twins told him that his waffles were the best.

The house Mr. Svensson rented to Calvin and Cornelia couldn't even be described as small. It was a room with a cooking area, a table for two, and a couch you made into a bed in the evenings. But it faced southwest. And it had big windows and a small porch that offered a view to Mr. Svensson's garden. It was clean, bright, and warm.

One day, when Cornelia worked the morning shift, Calvin and I cluttered the few square meters they had with pictures and papers, sketches and ideas, notes and drawings. We wrapped the cottage in concepts, from top to bottom, left to right, up and down. We only stopped when Calvin approached one of the walls with a black ink marker, ready to make a few notes next to one of the sketches. I put my hand on his arm and said that if he drew a line there, his mum would draw all kinds of other lines after that.

When Cornelia came home and saw the house all dressed up with monsters and people, oceans and skies, she said nothing. We watched her as she made herself a cup of coffee, humming like a philosopher while measuring up the water. Then, she went outside, sat down in her chair on the porch and had a sip.

"You know, boys," she said quietly.

We said nothing. How could we? We didn't know.

"These might be the best goddam paintings on a wall that a home could ever hope to have."

She closed her eyes and had another sip.

"Your mum's pretty cool," I said quietly to Calvin.

"Y-yeah," he said, looking at her and smiling.

We didn't need all that much space anyway. The library had tables and the librarian fed us with cookies as we dived deep into the conceptual challenges of pre-production. We went down to the piers and shared our ideas with the fishermen. They wondered if our game had boats in it and if you could go fishing. We decided that it wouldn't be the greatest game of all if you couldn't, and they said it sounded like a game they'd want to play. Just remember to watch the clouds, they'd say, to know the right time for fishing. There was nothing as deceiving as clear, blue skies with just the occasional streak of a white cloud.

We brought our stuff to the diner and knocked out sketches and designs as Cornelia made us pancakes, and we even spent some time in the café with the dark man that had crossed the sea.

He gave us free soda and then watched us from behind the counter, smiling as our enthusiasm leveled up with the blood sugar. Once, he sat down with us and said, "If there is laughing, there also must be grief."

We looked at each other, wondering what the hell he was talking about. When he smiled, it made me wonder—why was he always alone? I could imagine a woman next to him, as dark if not darker, chatting to the customers while making some kind of stew that you'd not find anywhere else if your life depended on it. They'd kiss as they passed each other while serving the guests, and there were kids running around and between their legs, filling up the place with giggles and mayhem. Or he could've been a guy who'd been to war and who'd patched up so many, the wounds eventually wore him down. Maybe both. He felt like someone who knew how to patch up people, somehow.

"I think," he said, "if your story is only about things you win, then it will not be true."

"We're not making a story," Calvin said. "We're making a g-game."

He smiled. "I do not understand the difference. But you will show me when you're done."

I dived into our folder and pulled out the sketch Calvin had made, of the sad man on the hill. I showed it to him. He took it, touched the lines, still smiling.

"It is beautiful," he said.

Then he got up and made another pot of coffee, the first one cold and untouched.

Whenever we got stuck on an idea, we took our bikes to the cliffs and dived into the ocean from the highest peaks, the ones the grown-ups had told us not to dive from. Someone had been ambitious enough to put a sign there, with a stickman that dived into the water and hit his head in an awkward position. Calvin brought out a pen and added some fish, a few seagulls, and a pretty sun in the background. Then, we went over the edge with Indian cries, spinning through the air like a perfect smash in a tennis finale.

Afterwards, we rested on the rocks to dry in the sun, talking about all the cool underwater levels we'd have in our game and that you'd have to have scuba gear before you could get there—or even better, a magic potion that grew gills on your throat! Though you would have to find the anti-potion before you could return to land again, or you'd choke from fresh air.

Calvin was usually at home when Cornelia wasn't working and before long, they made a habit of inviting me for dinner. I didn't even bother calling Dad and asking if it was okay. I knew it was, I knew he'd be relieved, though he'd pretend to make an effort and say that if I came home now, he'd have dinner ready. Maybe even Mum would join.

We sat by their kitchen table, sharing whatever meal Cornelia had cooked up with beans and chicken, vegetables and bread, and worked the books. Yep, that's right. Dinner at the Calvins was of the educational kind. He studied math, science, and geography under Cornelia's tutoring, and he did okay until it came to the written word. He could barely put the letters together, much less braid them into a proper sentence. It was just the way it was, but it frustrated him. Cornelia put her hands on his cheeks, looked him in the eyes, and said:

"You're the smartest person I know, Calvin. Do you know why I know that?"

He shook his head.

"Because you're making the greatest game of all. Now, you tell me—can a stupid person make that game?"

"I g-guess not."

She turned to me. "You two boys, you're wired just the right way. You just gotta remember that school's not for everybody."

"Then why does everybody go there?" I mumbled.

Cornelia leaned back and crossed her arms over her chest.

"That's a damn fine question right there, Elliot, honey." She looked out the window and fell into one of her moods again. She lit a cigarette. Then, she took us in with her dark eyes and fired up that predator smile.

"That's exactly the kind of thought only a smart person would think. The kind of thinking that don't necessarily happen in school."

Seeing as I'd stopped going and Calvin never even started, it was hard to argue the point.

Chapter 16

BETTER THAN E.T.

Also, not going to school meant less of the bullies and their bully-ing about. Like flies in the summer, they were part of the ecosys-tem. You had to accept them and deal with it, like the therapist had told me and my parents while we'd been in session.

There might've been a time when I feared them, but if so, I don't remember when that was. Maybe before all that stuff hap-pened, when I still had something to lose. But with no stakes, there was no fear, and with no fear, I went to my own place when they came after me and I emerged when they were done. They weren't particularly fierce or inventive, anyway. Most of the time, they weren't even around. But sometimes, they found us and circled us with their bikes, throwing about taunts of the kind that we had computers for brains and eyes like screens or that we were gay.

However, Calvin was fresh meat from the factory. Once they'd figured him out, they came after us with a new intensity.

"C-c-calvin!" they howled, like hyenas over Fjellhamn. "C-c-c-c-c-calvin! We're c-c-coming for youuu!"

They attacked him from all angles. They hit him for the way he talked, the way he looked, the way he lived, the fact that he didn't go to school. He was too stupid, too ugly, too strange, and too dumb. I wanted to hit them back. But he put his hand on my arm and pushed me gently back. Well, all right. If we weren't gonna fight, at least we could do a dignified flight. There's no way I was gonna let them keep striking at Calvin like this. I took him by the hand, he held his folder tight to his body, and we ran through the alleys and in between the houses, around the cliffs, and across the yards. If my years of exploring had led me to places I could now show to a friend, they had also branded a map of the town's quickest escape routes into my subconscious. I'd be an awesome bank robber, if Fjellhamn ever had any banks. We lost the bullies at the first turn but kept going. This was a place for lightning runs and daring leaps, a scene for death-defying stunts over bridges and water, if you knew all its edges and gaps.

Gasping for air, we stopped long after we were safe and sloped to the ground.

"We gotta have running levels in our game," I panted.

"Really fast ones," Calvin said.

I wiped the sweat from my forehead.

"I d-don't care, Elliot. Just so you know. I'm used to it."

I looked at him.

"I don't think that's okay," I said.

"I didn't say that."

This time, we'd found shelter in a small alcove under the cliffs, close to the rock beaches. A slow rain poured down as gray clouds swept in from the sea.

"Mum and I, we move a lot," Calvin said. He buried his feet among the pebbles.

"Why?"

He shrugged. "After some time, she says it's n-not working anymore. There's always some boss who's dumb or a teacher who doesn't get it or a neighbor's upset about something. So we move. We get into some kind of fight. And we move."

"What kind of fight?"

"A fight."

"Okay."

"Don't tell my mum," he said quickly.

"About what?"

"About this."

"Is this a fight?"

Calvin frowned. "I don't know. I mean, we've had worse." He laughed. "A lot worse."

We looked out over the water. A small skiff struggled against the wind, taunted by the sea gulls.

"I don't wanna move, Elliot."

"Sure. I mean, we gotta finish our game, right?"

"Right."

I paused.

"Ginger's right, though," I said.

Calvin nodded.

"W-we need a computer."

"But computers are expensive."

"Yes."

"Do you know how to use one?"

"How hard can it be?"

Calvin put his hands in his pockets, briefly closing his eyes.

"D-do you think our game's gonna be better than *E.T.*?"

We laughed so long and hard at this, even the seagulls chimed in.

Once we calmed down, me wiping my tears, Calvin sighing in affection, I stated the obvious, just to make sure the importance of the matter didn't get lost in the joke.

"It's like you said, Calvin. It would be the greatest game of all."

Calvin nodded. "Why else would we make it?"

"Why else indeed."

"Why do you think the *E.T.* guy made his game?"

"Maybe he thought he was making the greatest game of all."

"Maybe he thinks we're the ones who didn't get it."

"Maybe."

"Let's ask him, if we meet him."

"Let's."

We did meet Howard Scott Warshaw, many years later on the E3 fair at Los Angeles Staples Center. He was a nice guy and we had a lot of fun together. But that's a different story. Maybe I'll tell you someday, maybe I won't. Suffice it to say, he did think that *E.T.* was great at the time he made it, isolated and alone in his own house for several weeks, and he certainly didn't plan to make it one of the worst games ever.

"Look, guys," he said to us after his fifth beer.

(I'm telling you now anyway, aren't I?)

"Is there anyone who seriously believes there are people out there who set out to do miserable things? On purpose, I mean? Do they go like, 'Oh, I'm gonna cause some serious damage now, because I can? I don't think so."

We were all pretty drunk and at this point, if you were with friends, everything made sense.

"Isn't there always some cause or faith in what you do? Even when you hurt people?"

We all agreed on this and had another beer.

But I don't know, Howard. You tell me.

Do you think Atari seriously believed *E.T.* would be a good game despite only five weeks of development?

Or did Atari figure that it wouldn't matter, because *E.T.* is an amazing franchise and we've got Steven Spielberg on board so it'll sell like cupcakes anyway? Just give us something to put in the box.

You tell me.

The rain stopped. We climbed out and walked back into town.

So yes, the bullies were to us like the flies I mentioned. You just had to be aware and work out a strategy. Avoid them if you could, endure them when you must. The rules of engagement were clear.

Until Lars came around.

He was of an entirely different breed.

While his stay in Fjellhamn was brief, he changed our entire game.

That was a fight, for sure.

But I'll tell you about him when we get to the part about the heat. And we're not quite there yet.

Chapter 17

THE TOASTER

As we tuned in to the challenge of making the greatest game of all, we struggled to find one that would match ours in quality. We needed references beyond the Atari 2600, since the world of video gaming as we knew it was found lacking.

Sure, there were a few installations out there that did all right, but we had debated their pros and cons over blueberries and strawberries from Mr. Svensson's garden and we pretty much agreed on everything, including *Pac-Man's* weak character design—who wants to play a slice of pizza, anyway?—and *Space Invaders'* lack of coherence in its plot. So not a single one of these aliens, this super intelligent race, would stop to consider if their invasion plan to go left-and-a-right-and a left-and-a-right-and-down-and-a left-right-left-and-a-down aaagain, would benefit from some improvement? However, as Calvin pointed out, the game always ended with the invaders winning, so I guess they knew something we didn't.

Our game would be better than *Pac-Man, Space Invaders, Adventure, Galaga,* and *Donkey Kong.* I mean, who could argue the monkey's unfair lot in *Donkey Kong,* anyway? Just the fact that he'd been confused for a donkey would be enough reason for his barrel-related aggravation against Italian plumbers.

We had moments when we were overwhelmed by the depths of how easy this came to us and how difficult it must be for other people to make games, seeing as their output never amounted to anything else than mediocre. Even our favorite—still *Pitfall*—would be about average, compared to ours. We decided that this three-out-of-five standard was a result of the developers being grown-ups, chained by adult stuff such as work and going out for groceries and taking care of kids that just seemed to randomly multiply.

But now, it was our turn.

It's been said, but let's say it again—everybody now, including you people at the back with the cheap seats:

We would make the greatest game of all.

We even had a folder to put all our ideas in.

And fortune favored us, because as unlikely as it seemed, there was a place in Fjellhamn that had a computer in stock. This place was Mr. Parkvik's Hardware Store. While Mr. Parkvik mainly attracted customers that needed parts or tools or chains or screws for their boats, he had the soul of a pioneer. He'd been looking for an opportunity to challenge his customers. Getting a computer was that opportunity.

You had to give it to the man for trying. Fjellhamn wasn't exactly a bleeding edge community when it came to technology. Why he ever decided to set up shop here, I'll never know.

When the computer arrived by FedEx, Mr. Parkvik signed and accepted the parcel in an almost ceremonial manner, smiling like a gracious king to any pedestrian that happened to stroll by. He put the computer on display in his window, where it would wait for the citizens of tomorrow to lead the way to organized grocery lists and other such emotionally involving interactive experiences.

But when the people of Fjellhamn realized you couldn't bake

cupcakes with it and it didn't wash your car, it was dismissed as a kitchen appliance, possibly a toaster with a communist agenda wired into its circuits. Eventually, Mr. Parkvik's smile faded. Sometimes, when he thought he was alone, he looked at the people moving about in the world outside his window. He held a cup of coffee, his lips trembling as he whispered silent curses over the computer like Moses once cursed the people of Egypt.

But when you switched it on.

Man, oh man. What a toaster.

There was this blue screen and that blinking cursor waiting for you to work your magic, like the wand of a modern conjurer.

"Whoa."

Calvin said it like it was.

And he said it when that televised canvas of boundless creativity spread out before us, like fields of virgin rye under a sky with white clouds.

For once, I was the one lost for words. Our eyes glowed like the only remaining stars in an eternal darkness.

Chapter 18

PANDORA'S BOX

We knew that Mr. Parkvik had no idea he possessed the modern-day equivalent of Pandora's Box. Once the computer was gone, it would never come back. Someone would become equally hypnotized by that blue within blue mirage and buy it, and we were pretty sure the next store to carry one wasn't a bicycle ride away. Time, as they say, was of the essence.

We sat by the cliffs, thinking hard about how to get a computer when we didn't have any money. I squinted as the sun came out.

"We must think outside the box," I said.

Calvin nodded. "What box?"

"I don't know. It's something my dad says."

"Does he have a box?"

"He has a typewriter."

"Who's thinking inside the box?" Calvin said.

"I dunno. No one, I guess. You're not supposed to."

Calvin covered his eyes with his hand. "If no one's thinking inside the box, isn't it smarter to not think outside the box? If that's what everybody's doing?"

"You mean that inside is the new outside?"

"I don't know."

"I wonder how people with a lot of money ever earned it."

"They stole it."

An awkward silence followed.

"We can't do that," I said.

"I know."

"Unless we rob a bank," I said and fired guns into the air. "I know all the escape routes through town."

"But there's no bank in Fjellhamn."

"Hmm, yes."

"We can make our own." Calvin had already drawn a bill on his pad. He showed me. It looked credible.

"What if we just told Mr. Parkvik we had money, and then we didn't?"

"I don't k-know. I don't think he'd go for it."

"All right. We'll marry a millionaire, then."

"Do you know one?" Calvin said.

I poked my feet at some rocks. "Sara Johnson seems to do well. Or her dad, at least."

"She's older than you. She'd never marry you."

"Guess not."

"You think she has a computer?"

"Nah."

"We could always get a job."

I was about to say, "Who's gonna hire us? We're twelve." But then, lightning struck. Out by the sea, as bad weather was approaching. But also right here, right now, from the skies and straight into the rocks where Calvin and I were brainstorming.

"Come on," I said and jumped up, pulling Calvin with me, his feet bouncing off the ground. He turned around to grab the folder and we dashed into town.

When Calvin and I entered Mr. Parkvik's store again, he was murmuring a curse over those more fortunate. According to him, this was everyone, including the no-legged mute down at the old theater who lost his eyes last year in a train wreck accident.

"Hello, Mr. Parkvik?" I said. Calvin stood one step behind me, observing the man with anticipation. He didn't know what the plan was, but he was looking forward to whatever was coming.

"Boys," Mr. Parkvik said.

"We're gonna work for you this summer."

Calvin split up in a grin, bobbing his head like a drunk to the music.

Mr. Parkvik replied: "May you burn in hell for all eternity, where demons will cut off your penis with scissors so blunt it will take them hours to finish the job until it grows back on again and the torture is repeated every dawn until the end of time."

I looked at Calvin. He looked at me. Mr. Parkvik's infernal visions weren't without merit. We were impressed. He sighed.

"Excuse me. I was daydreaming. You boys were saying?"

"We're gonna work for you this summer."

He blinked.

Calvin stepped up.

"H-h-he said, we're gonna work—"

"How's your mum doing, son?" Mr. Parkvik looked straight at me. "Your father's holding it together?"

This annoyed me. "Fine, fine. She's just fine. They're fine."

Mr. Parkvik was quiet for a while. I hated it when people looked at me like that.

"I can't hire you. You could use the money, I'm sure. Your father's a good man. But I can't afford any help this summer."

"Why not?"

He spoke to himself, in almost a whisper: "My store is cursed. Yes. And I deserve it. Bring on the locusts and the eternal night, the red running rivers, and the angels of death. I am ready."

This man would do better on stage than in a shop.

"We're gonna work for you this summer and we don't want any money."

He looked at us again, curious now. He put his cup aside.

Calvin and I pointed in unison to the weakly illuminated parts of the store, where the computer currently rested, switched off like an old lady not even courted by the bards anymore.

"We want that."

Mr. Parkvik looked at me. Then, at the computer. Then, at me again.

"I was gonna put it on display at the Fjellhamn Festival," he said.

"And now, you don't have to."

"Mm-hmm. You'll work here all summer, then? All I have to do is give you that horrible toaster from Commodore?"

Calvin and I nodded. Hell, yes.

For the first time in many weeks, Mr. Parkvik's smile was for real.

Chapter 19

FEVER

On the night when I opened Calvin's folder and read his notebook, I had a fever.

My temperature rose to over 39 degrees (about 102 in Fahrenheit, for those unfortunate of you who still stick to that system). I hadn't had a proper one for years and I'd forgotten what it felt like. How much I loved it.

It burned in me like fuel in the desert as I dashed around, whirling papers around me with slices of adhesives to slam these pictures to the wall or on the floor. I had a ladder and I brought it out from the walk in-closet where I'd kept it since I bought it, to build not just to the left and right but to reach for the sky as well, making full use of the fact that I had a home where the space between floor and ceiling was over five meters. I consumed post it-notes like there would be none left for the bearded agencies of our age, and I used up more pens than I could remember (but probably not more than two or three—I mean, we're just talking about one night here, after all).

I was sweating and took off my robe. I paused to drink water, but couldn't finish it quickly enough and spilled most of it on the floor. During the quiet hours, when Stockholm was half asleep, I opened the windows to let the cool air in. A soft rain fell against my skin, an early scout from the still distant summer, and that was the only break I took, to cool off before I hit the last shift, the in-between hours when the clubs had closed and the convenience stores were resting, when the only one on the bus was a nurse on her way home from work. I'd lived in Los Angeles, London, Montreal, and Tokyo, but I liked that Stockholm, for all its angst on its metropolitan inferiority, had moments when it was quiet, where the city itself reminded us that we're just not there yet and you should consider that a good thing. I had done some of my best work here, during these hours of the wolf when sometimes all I heard was a baby crying or a night stroller talking on the phone.

As the dark skies hinted at a light blue, I looked at my work. My home felt like an old library, where first editions and hand-written tomes towered like giants between the aisles.

I called Skye.

She answered immediately.

"Oh, that's just great," she said. "This is so fucking you. For months, you're not returning my calls or answering my texts, and I know you're not even reading your fucking e-mail. And now, his Majesty the Creator, decides that it's time to talk, at..." I could hear her groping around for something, a crash in the background. "Fuck!" And then: "...at four in the morning, that's when he decides to call me, because now it suits him, the Mayor of Arrogance, to let the world know he's alive. Hang on, don't go anywhere."

She moved away from the phone. She said a few words to someone, along the lines of, "Why are you still here?" and "Get the fuck out," and then she was back.

"I had to call Doctor Larson, Elliot, just to make sure you weren't dead. Suffer through his damn poetry. I should charge you for that. Who the fuck gave him a copy of the *Divine Comedy*, anyway?"

She was shouting these last words, the membrane in my phone vibrating from the strain.

"I think I did," I said.

"I fucking knew it."

"Look, Skye, I've got something for you."

Another crash, probably she rolling out of bed, feet first.

"Put on some coffee. I'll be there in fifteen minutes. You're not at the studio, are you?"

"We don't have a studio."

"Don't you think I know that? I'll be there in five."

Chapter 20

ON POT

During the time when Calvin and I were still working for Sean and his Biosoft publishing house, he kept asking us if he could see what we'd made with this great game of ours.

"Maybe there's a gem there," he said, "if you got the right producer to look at it."

"Skye has seen it," I said. "She loves it because it's nonsense. And she's right. It doesn't even make sense to us."

"Well," Sean said and smiled. "I'd love to take a look at it. There are other producers than Skye."

"We're not showing it to anyone," Calvin said. "That's sort of the point."

"You might have to show it to me," he said. "You work for me, after all."

"It's not a project," I cut in quickly. "It's our spare time thing. Our refuge, you know."

Sean lit a cigarette. He looked at me. "You're too young to have spare time," he said. Calvin laughed nervously.

He leaned forward, cigarette between his fingers. "You can build it on your terms," he said. "You have that leverage now. There's a story here. Your childhood concept, a game in development over generations, finally ready for the audience it deserves. Wouldn't that be something?"

But we shook our heads in unison.

"Don't worry," I said. "You're not missing out on the next *System Shock*. At best, this is like a failed indie title from Nintendo."

Sean kept smiling. "I've worked with Nintendo. I like it when they fail."

I know he didn't believe us. I think he was waiting for the right time to get his hands on our folder, open it, and see what powers it could offer. If Sean was good at anything, it was to find potential where no one else was looking.

That's how he'd found Calvin and me, after all.

Skye arrived within minutes and she wore that odd lipstick she always managed to apply on the run, her short dark curls messier than ever but her green eyes studying with such intensity, such fascination, the mayhem I'd built that I felt nothing but a deep affection for her.

She was a short woman, broad over the shoulders like a wrestler but with a slender impression all the same. She wore that blue jacket I'd given her after we'd visited a studio in Copenhagen that made a game in clay and failed spectacularly. Original stuff usually did. But the studio had showed some promise, so Skye and I had gone there to do a due diligence on Sean's request. Calvin had respectfully declined to join. He knew some of the guys working there and he was pretty sure that this would amount to nothing but substance abuse.

And yeah, once we got there, it was like he said. The team was on pot. All the time.

Skye, who was a When In Rome kind of person, laughed and took a smoke with one of the senior developers, sucking it in and listening to old chip tunes by Rob Hubbard before we sat down with their CEO Bjork Larsen to tell them this wasn't going to happen. He was surprisingly cool about it, maybe because he was smoking something, too.

"Most of the time," he said, "the developers come back from their trips, so it rarely hurts production anyway."

Skye giggled. I said nothing.

Bjork turned to his executive producer. "I don't recall our parties ever causing any substantial delays. Do you, Karen?"

"Well," Karen said, "if you compare this to whatever bullshit a publisher throws at you every day, there's hardly a dent in our production."

Skye and I looked at each other. Karen had a point.

But it had to be said. And like always, Skye was the one who said it.

"But you made a game in clay. And you thought that might work."

"And with your money," Bjork Larsen said, "we'll make another one! Sequels for the win! So let's talk about the merger. Coffee, anyone? No? Sandwiches? Wine? Smoke? We've got some freshly rolled shit from our urban poppy plantation, straight from the studio's rooftops."

Chapter 21

WE NEED COMPUTERS

Anyway.

This night, when Skye came to my place, she wore that jacket. It brought back memories, as you can tell. She had a white t-shirt underneath and a pair of military khakis. She'd run from her apartment in sandals, those leathery ones that looked like something you'd wear if you were in a Greek think tank and had a lot of wine before lunch. Given that Skye's feet were molded from the same stuff that made cheese mature into something only Stephen King could've imagined, you'd think that she'd stay away from sandals or at least take better care of her feet. If I tell you that Skye was aware and didn't care, you'll know all you need to know about her.

There was no hug as she arrived, no "Oh Elliot, how are you, it's so good to finally see you up and about," no muted version of I Get It, But Let's Just Get To It. Nah. Instead, Skye stepped in without knocking (I was tired of all the knockings, so I didn't mind), went straight to the kitchen, and poured herself a cup.

"Right," she said. "Let's see what you got."

But as she passed me on her way to the stuff I'd taken from Calvin's folder and put up on the walls, she roughed up my hair and laughed. "You look good in a beard, Elliot."

"I have a beard?"

She took a sip and studied the work in progress on the wall. "Hoo-kay. So there it is."

"Take your time."

She took another sip. Me and my beard sank down in our chair and looked at her.

She walked slowly, touching the drawings, a mix of sketches thirty years old and artwork finished just a few months ago, pictures made by hand coupled with laser-printed material, stuff created by a kid and finished by a man.

She grabbed the ladder and climbed a few steps, looking at the stuff I'd put closer to the sky. She stopped at scattered mockups of a lush oaken forest. When the pieces blended together, the woods seemed to stretch into forever, the entire world an explosion of red and yellow leaves.

"This was always one of my favorites," she said.

She climbed down and sat on the floor, legs crossed. She seemed so small against the wall. To view the game in its entirety, she had to lean back and tilt her head.

"I didn't think I'd ever see this again," she said.

I got up from my chair and sat down next to her.

"You didn't know?" I said.

"No. I mean, I knew he kept the folder. But I didn't know he still worked on...well, on this. But once he got kids, he was a bit of a recluse, I guess. Not always easy to reach. I don't think any of the others managed to stay in touch with him, after he left."

If that was aimed at me, I deflected it. I wasn't ready to have that kind of talk.

She frowned.

"Some of these sketches," she said, "they can't be more than a few months old."

"I know."

"Why would he spend time on this? Especially in the end? It was always just a charming mess. Wasn't that the point?"

"Yes."

Skye looked at me.

"It all went so fast," she said. "Once he got sick. I barely understood it, before he..."

"Don't," I said. "Please. Not you."

She nodded. "Okay," she said gently. "For now. Okay. But for what it's worth, he missed you. That's why he did this, I'm sure."

I didn't answer.

We sat on the floor as the sun rose, looking at the pearls and gems from Calvin's folder.

I slipped his notebook into her hands. She looked at it, wiping something from her eye.

"What's this now?"

"Calvin made a few notes."

"Calvin don't do notes. You do. He don't."

"Things change."

I got up. My shoulders felt heavy. Skye opened the notebook and touched the pages. She quickly closed it again and was about to say something, but I interrupted her:

"No, Skye. You're gonna have to read it for yourself."

"Oh, come on."

"It's Calvin, Skye. He's written about a hundred words in his life. Half of them are in there. They're spelled right, too. I guess Lisa must've helped."

She laughed.

"But it's his words," I said. "I figured you'd enjoy hearing his voice again."

"That, I would." She got up and shambled to the sofa.

"You're not gonna read it?" I said.

"Why did you call me?"

"What do you mean?"

"What do you think I mean?"

"You ever came here knocking?"

She dropped with her back to the cushions, giving me an angry look. "What? No. I mean, I respect your decision to stay away. It's a fucked-up call, but it's yours to make."

"Just asking."

"I've tried to reach you. Last time I saw you, we were in an ambulance. You were bleeding. I wasn't. And then you locked yourself up. Like you tend to do."

"You know why."

"No, I don't know why. I can think of a few reasons, but I don't want to guess. I want you to tell me."

"It's not that easy."

"Like fuck it is. You just open that goddam mouth of yours and let the words pour. That's your forte. How can that be a problem? Oh, who am I kidding?" She took in the wall with her arms. "I don't need nostalgia. We're in our forties. I drink, smoke, and I don't sleep. I'll be dead before I'm fifty. Why should I care?"

She pulled out a cigarette and lit it.

"Given that you fucked up everything," she said, "and behaved like a dick about it, no one would want anything to do with you. You'd be lucky they even answered your call. Who's gonna publish you anyway? No one and his cousin. Oh, you're thinking Pete might? Forget it."

"He wouldn't be running Activision if it wasn't for us."

"He's not running Activision. And even if he did, he'd never take your game. Look, you're a pariah, at best. A good looking one, but a pariah nonetheless. Fuck, you'll die right with me. We'd make quite the couple."

She took another smoke.

"I wasn't that bad," I said.

She exhaled. "Who am I to judge?" She looked at me. "You've given this some thought, I'm sure."

"I'm thinking we could just sign Sean's papers."

"We'd be rich."

"I would move to France. I'd keep a room with a spare bed for you."

"I wouldn't come to visit."

"You could bring the kids."

Skye smiled. "They'd love France. And my kids would love your kids."

"They'd be best friends."

She yawned. "Well, everybody enjoys a good redemption." She looked at the cigarette with a puzzled expression, and then put it out in a small glass on a table next to the sofa.

"Just read Calvin's notes," I said. "For closure."

"That's a reason. And a cliffhanger. You're good at those. Let's sleep. Then we'll see."

But instead of laying down, she got up and walked towards me. She leaned forward and kissed me on the cheek.

She smelt good, she always did, a mix of salt and sweet as if she came directly from the beach. Maybe all those years by the sea became part of her skin, eventually. I looked away, on a spot on the floor or a stain on the kitchen table.

"They don't know you, Elliot. They've got no right to judge you."

"If you say so."

She lingered for a brief while, then sighed and walked up to the sofa. She cuddled up among cushions and blankets, looking at me from over the shoulder, already half asleep.

"Ginger was right. We need computers. Lots and lots of computers."

I looked at her with confusion as she fell asleep. She always did that, shifted between so many states that I couldn't keep up, but that's also why she'd resolved so many impossible situations during the years when one of our games was heading for disaster. In development, you were in crisis unless you had someone like Skye at the helm.

I reached down and picked up the notebook and brought it to the kitchen table. I sat down and read the words again, the ones that came after the picture with the two boys down at the pier.

Just a few lines, enough to fill the page. Calvin, who never wrote. Who couldn't spell. How he must've worked to get those words right.

The dim light fell with straight lines through the window. In this space, when dawn was as bright as the day that would follow but still folded in a gray veil, I wondered if the world itself felt it was too early to rise. There should be no light before 0600, it said. But the beams reached the deepest corners of my apartment. There were no real shadows, only silhouettes that slowly moved across the floor with the sun's pace. This was the time when my place was at its brightest.

I read Calvin's words again.

He was there with me, on the chair next to mine.

He spoke slowly to me, stuttering and smiling, pushing away his bangs.

I bit my fingers and wiped my eyes.

"I'm so sorry, Calvin," I said to the silhouettes. "I'm so, so, sorry."

Chapter 22

FLABBERGAST

Calvin and I anticipated how easy it'd be, once we had the computer, to build our game and how much we'd enjoy playing it ourselves, once it was done. Not yet knowing exactly how long it would take to write a game, we had to run with assumptions until we did. We decided to play it safe, work with margins, and leave room for the unexpected (probably a common mistake among the less gifted developers, to assume that things always went as intended).

Thus, we figured it would take the greater part of a week to make our game but we scheduled for two. We'd copy it to tape, which would take maybe an evening to set up and another evening to create duplicates, and then we'd sell our piece to the masses. Calvin already had ideas for boxing and wrapping, such as a package built like an iron gate where there was a key included and you had to unlock the box and then open the gate to pick up the cassette, or maybe one of those flowery arrangements which we'd make into a clearing with a pond, and you'd have to retrieve the cassette from the chest that was at the bottom. Mr. Parkvik didn't have a disc drive option for the computer in his store, so we had to go for the cassette version, anyway. Which was fine, since that made the game accessible to everyone. In fact, we were flabbergasted (such a fantastic word!—if I ever had a pet ghost, I'd name him Flabbergast) over the fact that anyone would make the decision to launch a game only on disc. Why would you want to exclude part of your audience? We could find no reason. Again, we prescribed this to the lesser gifted and their flawed judgment.

But when Calvin and I arrived to work for Mr. Parkvik a few weeks later, he looked at us with a sad expression.

"I'm sorry, boys, but I don't have any work for you."

"But the sailing season has started," I said. "You need help. Lots of it."

Calvin was quiet. He thumbed the folder. It was getting fat and juicy, stuffed with papers and notes, drawings and sketches.

"I...well, yes. I do, but..."

"You've sold the c-c-computer," Calvin said.

This hadn't even occurred to me but when I looked at Calvin, who stared at the floor, it was as if he'd expected this and was already dealing with the aftermath.

Mr. Parkvik was uncomfortable now. "I'm running a business, boys. It's a pricey item. If someone wants to buy it...what am I gonna do?"

"You could tell them it's not for sale," I shouted. "'You promised us. We were gonna work in your stupid store all summer, and all you had to do was keep your promise. How can that be so difficult?"

"Look, you can have anything from the store, anything you want."

"Why is this so hard?" I shouted.

Mr. Parkvik squeezed his hands together. "What's hard, Elliot?"

"For all of you. To keep a promise. To say something and then just do what you said you'd do."

Mr. Parkvik looked at me with pity, and that made me more furious. I know what he wanted to say next, if there's anything else he could do for me and my family, he'd do it, and he's really sorry, he can offer discounts and maybe come over sometime and help out with the house, but the tears burned in my eyes and while I was the kid, Mr. Parkvik remained the lost one. Why did it always seem like the youngest guy in the room was the only one who had his shit together? Or more precisely, why didn't anyone care if he had his shit together, busy as they were with their own emotional crap? Essentially, it had become a survival mechanism. If I didn't keep it together, no one else would do it for me.

"There's absolutely nothing you can say," I said. "Just shut up."

"I'm so sorry, Elliot."

"About what? Your store? You should be. It's a tragedy."

I turned around to tell Calvin that we should go and hope that Mr. Parkvik really would die from all the horrors his imagination had conjured up, but he was already gone. The door was half open.

"I hate you," I snarled to Mr. Parkvik and left.

Calvin really was gone. My heart beat so fast my chest hurt and I had these visions that he'd never been there. I'd summoned him like a make-believe friend, and our entire idea of making an amazing game was just a result of me not being able to stay in reality anymore. I did not have my shit together. In fact, my shit was all over the place. I wanted to get back to that other place quickly, because the rising tide that approached with thunder and lightning would drown me for sure. But I'd rather sleep on the street than go home, sit down with Dad, and have another conversation about dinner and school.

"W-we need pancakes, Elliot."

I turned around.

There he was.

Very real and very much smiling.

He looked so much like his mother when he did.

Okay, good. I still had a best friend. My shit was back together. I calmed down. As long as he was real, I could handle home. I was not alone.

Calvin kept on grinning.

Out from the shadows stepped a girl on a bike. She looked around, cautious and wary. Calvin looked at her, nodding and smiling to some unheard funky beat.

"Hey," Sara Johnson said. "So...what's up?"

Okay, so now I was confused again. Maybe I was in a strange place after all.

"Anyway," she said. "That game you're making? I want in." When she saw my expression, she quickly added: "I've got a computer."

Calvin laughed.

"Because we're gonna need computers," she said.

I nodded slowly. That much was true. I could latch on to that. Sara Johnson, who wore a bra and kissed boys. Who joined the bullies in the chorus. Who apparently had not played *Pitfall* on an Atari she didn't own, but still bought cartridges from our toy store. Sara, who smiled.

And yet, there was that look in her eyes, fear and curiosity and like last time, she seemed to have the upper hand but without the control that came with it.

She looked away.

"Why are you here?" I said.

She scraped her foot on the asphalt, biting her lip. Then she sighed, gave me a brief glance, and pushed away on her bike.

"W-wait!" Calvin cried. "Elliot, what are you doing?"

"We're not working with her," I said.

"What the fuck?"

Sara and I looked at Calvin. I'd never heard him curse. Seeing as words didn't come easy for him in any shape or form, I always assumed he'd be careful with the ones that got out. He was red in the face now and while his bangs covered part of his eyes, there was no mistaking his anger.

"She has a computer," he said. "She wants in."

"It's okay," Sara said. "Elliot's right."

"About what?" Calvin looked at me but pointed at Sara. "Just because she's an asshole doesn't mean we have to be. Give her a chance."

I folded my arms and looked at the ground. "She's had plenty, over the years." I raised my head and glared at her. "Why would I give her another one?"

Calvin was about to answer, probably ask what the hell I was talking about, but Sara cut in: "'Because you're better than me."

She had her eyes locked on me now. They were green but dark, like stones in the Mediterranean.

"What're your friends gonna say?" I said. "When they see you with us?"

She didn't answer.

"You'll just make sure that doesn't happen. But you still want our help."

"Look," she said. "I wanna show you something. Come with me. Just give me an hour."

Man, she was bossy. She always had been, ever since we were little.

"No," I said.

Calvin moaned and he was about to unleash another curse on the moment, but I also said: "But we'll come with you anyway."

Sara dared to smile, just slightly. Calvin grinned again. He didn't get it, but how could he? I hadn't told him about Sara yet. Maybe that was a good thing. When Calvin didn't understand, he pushed ahead and dragged me out of my comfort zone and made me do things I didn't want to do but probably should.

"All right," I said and got up on my bike. "Let's see what you got."

Chapter 23

SKYE, HONEY

She took us to the part of Fjellhamn where there were only lawns and white houses, oak alleys and streams, and we followed her on our bikes along a windy path that led to a small house with a picket fence. It could've been something from the Brothers Grimm, a place shadowed by a larger estate that had no doors but gates, not a backyard but a patio, not a bathtub but a pool (or so I assumed, at least—actually, I assumed they had both, but you get the idea). This is what money looked like in a picturesque west coast community.

The burning twilight filtered through the trees over the house, but that light paled compared to the hypnotizing glow that came from within, as frightening as it was comforting. I'll admit, I couldn't help being scared and excited, or maybe something new that I just didn't have the words for yet. I kind of knew and I kind of didn't know what was in there. Calvin, who'd looked like a smiling fool as we rode our bikes to Sara's house, had changed his expression to that of legendary awe, his face frozen in a sense of wonder.

The door was open. Someone was tinkering inside. There was the sound from a drill. Sara waved at us to continue.

"Hey, Sara," a man called from inside. "Is that you?"

"Yeah, Dad. I'm here with the boys."

"You can see boys when you're thirty. And even then, it's still up for negotiation." He came out, eyes on fire, monkey wrench in hand. Might as well have been a shotgun.

He had his shirt pulled out with the arms folded to his elbows, his neat pants tugged up like a rough pair of shorts. He had no shoes, no socks, and his hair was perfectly groomed into a lawyer's cut, with just a small string that dangled across his forehead. His clothes looked expensive but his appearance was casual, like a carpenter who came to work dressed for a wedding or the other way around but didn't care either way.

Sara groaned.

"Sorry," her dad said and looked at us with a smile. "Ah, Elliot. Haven't seen you in a while."

"Yeah. Hello." I shuffled my feet.

He hesitated. "How's home?"

"Okay."

"Sven's busy with work?"

"Yeah. With work."

He turned to Calvin. "And you are?"

Calvin swallowed. He tried, but the words didn't come.

"You're welcome, all the same. You're a fresh change from Sara's other friends. None mentioned, none forgotten, though I wish they were."

As he went inside with his tools again, Calvin whispered, "A-are we going to die now?"

I shook my head. "I don't know, Calvin. I don't know."

"He's all right," Sara said. "He's just trying to be cool. You know what he's like, Elliot."

"Right," Dan said as he came out again. "I'm almost done. Why don't you check it out, and I'll be back with snacks. Good to see you, boys. You're always welcome here. I'll be your worst nightmare if you touch my daughter."

"T-touch her how?" Calvin said.

Dan laughed. "And now, I'm not so worried anymore."

He walked past us and gave Sara a hug. "Build something great, Skye, honey."

She rolled her eyes but smiled. Then, as he left for the big house, she faced us. "Well," she said. "Come on."

And in she went, embraced by that shine from that little house. I mouthed wordlessly to Calvin: *Skye?* He shrugged his shoulders but stated the obvious with a smile—Sara was a cool name, but Skye was in a league of its own.

And with that, we had no choice but to follow, if you can believe such a thing.

Chapter 24

MY ONLY REAL FRIEND

In a way, this brought me back to that time in the toy store in Gothenburg, where I'd first seen the Atari 2600. It was one of those moments when a part of you that'd been resting in a dreamless sleep was now stirring. This day would never come again, you could never repeat it and only remember it, only hope that it was as important as it felt, that it would lead you to the next such moment that defined you even more.

We stepped into Sara's house and there it was, the computer on a wooden table.

It was hooked up to a big TV, the screen radiating those shades of blue that looked like oceans within oceans, the cursor flashing with a perfect beat, waiting patiently for our creations. Notebooks, pencils, and sketch pads were neatly organized into shelves around the workspace. In the other corner, there was another, smaller TV connected to an Atari with a sofa and a table that held two controllers, ready for play. It looked worn and properly used, its wooden cheeks treated with love by years of light and dust. The evening light dropping through the windows, the dimmed brightness from the interior lamps and the alien glow from the two screens, created a sensation that we were moving, as if the room had a pulse, breathing slowly like a sentient being traveling through space.

Pitfall was up and running on the Atari. I looked at Sara, who was browsing a stack of magazines in a box next to the computer table. She caught my eye from the corner of hers.

"I did finish it in one evening," she said. Then she dived deeper into the stack.

"You've had it for a while," I said.

"I got it for my..." Her voice cracked for just a second. "When I was eleven."

I looked around, and things made a little more sense now. Sara pulled up a magazine and threw it on the table. It had a lot of zeds on it.

"Read this. They're running a special on video game studios. The *Space Action* guy is there, there's a cover on Stavros Fasoulas, they've got photos from the Epyx and System 3 offices and I think Greve Graphics is in there, too."

Calvin looked at me. I shrugged my shoulders. But Sara smiled.

"It's okay. You're console guys. I get it. Sorry, I don't have a Nintendo. Yet." She smiled. "You're gonna love this."

She pulled out a drawer from the table and brought out a box of cassettes. I hadn't noticed before, but I did now, that there was the classic tape recorder there on the table that went with the computer and a small screwdriver next to the keyboard.

"We'll start with *Attack of the Mutant Camels*," she said. "It created a lot of buzz when it launched. Apparently, the guy who made it has llamas in his backyard."

"That's cool," I said. "But we have to go now."

"We do?" Calvin said.

"Yes. Good luck with your game, Sara."

I turned around and walked away.

"Hey," Calvin called. "What're you doing? Wait for me."

He ran up to me and we went towards our bikes. I didn't check to see if Sara followed us or what she did, but I felt bad about doing this to Calvin. Here it was, the opportunity we'd been imagining, and now I wondered if we'd always known this wasn't gonna happen, that our idea of making a game was just an ongoing play that held us together.

Calvin got up on his bike and said: "You hungry? I'm sure Mum's got pancakes at work."

I hesitated.

I'm not sure I deserved a friend like Calvin. Maybe that's why I'd been alone for so long.

But I owed Sara nothing and she owed me the world.

Well, okay. Maybe not the world. But she did owe me. A lot.

She came running down the path towards us, calling for us to wait. Her dad was standing in the doorway, looking at us with his arms folded, leaning against the wall. She stopped, panting, and brushed her hair to the side.

"My mother used to call me Skye," she said under her breath. "She said my eyes reminded her of the endless horizon. Such a rare sight."

Calvin looked at her, a bit puzzled. I'd turned away and locked my eyes to the road between the maple trees that led back to Fjellhamn.

"C-cool," he said. "I like it."

Sara smiled. "Yeah. Thanks. You know…I've never told anyone this. Well, no one around here, that is. I mean, my friends know my dad calls me Skye, but I'm telling them it's just a thing, you know. Just something he does."

"Why?" I said.

She sat down on the small bench by the picket fence, her hands on her knees. "I don't wanna give them too much. Of course, they know my mum is dead and all, but you know…if they knew…if they took that, and made it into Skye Schmade, or that I'm a video game freak, or whatever…you know."

I looked at her now.

"You're Sara Johnson. They got nothing on you."

She laughed. "I don't know much about your world these days, Elliot. You gotta believe me when I say I'm sorry. I mean it. I miss you. But you don't know anything about mine either. I'm watching my back. They're looking for a reason. Whoever comes next, if it's Ida or Sally or Mabel, they'll have to watch their back, too. That's how it goes."

She stood up. "You're the only real friend I ever had, Elliot."

"That was years ago," I said. "You've had plenty since."

"I'm sorry I fucked it up."

"You didn't," I said. "Things just happened. You're the popular girl now."

"Why did you bully him?" Calvin said. Sara looked surprised, as if she'd forgotten he was there. While the question surely was loaded, he was calm and curious.

"I...I don't know," she said.

"You c-called him names, didn't you? Taunts and stuff."

She didn't answer.

"Y-y-you could've just shut up. If you didn't wanna stand up for him. At least just shut up."

I hadn't told Calvin about Sara's part in any of this. But maybe it wasn't so hard to guess.

"Hey," I said. "It's okay. I don't care. We're done here."

He turned to me. "N-no. It's not okay. You said so to me. And y-y-ou're right. I didn't know. Maybe giving second chances is a stupid idea."

"Yeah," Sara said. "Maybe."

She turned around and walked back to the house. Calvin squeezed his handlebars and looked at the ground.

"Hey, Sara," I said.

She stopped and looked at me over her shoulder.

"I'm sorry about your mum," I said.

She smiled faintly. "She bought me the Atari. They were gonna give it to me on my eleventh birthday. It was her idea."

We watched her as she walked up the stairs. Dan gave her a

hug and waved to us as Sara leaned her head on his shoulders with his arm around her. I waved back.

Calvin shook his head to get the bangs out of the way and kicked his bike into gear.

"Come on, Elliot," he said. "I've got some cool new sketches to show you. Mum's working the evening shift. We can stay up for as long as we want. You can sleep over at our house, if you don't wanna go home."

"I don't."

"I know. C'mon."

We left the gardens with their bridges over brooks behind us, and reached the cliffs where the skies opened up and the sea stretched out. We let go of our handlebars and rolled down the road with our arms in the air. The wind blew in our face and we screamed as our bikes went faster. If we'd met a car, we probably would've died. But right now, the world was a constant stream of possibilities, because we were going for pancakes and we were going to look at the latest sketches for the greatest game of all, and nothing was gonna stop us now or ever again.

Chapter 25

CALVIN'S WORDS

Skye snored like a drunk through the morning, while I hardly got any sleep at all. I wasn't tired. Exhausted, maybe, but in the same way you are when you've unleashed streams of endorphins after a good run. I'd gone far and found this raw energy that flowed from a rare source, and it kept me going because I had to show her something before I could sleep, before we could continue. She had to know.

I could've woken her up, but it felt wrong. As if I'd distort her impression of what would come next, a kind of brain damage to the situation.

Skye woke up around noon, stretched out her arms, and blinked at me.

"I haven't slept this well since I was baby," she said.

I was by the kitchen table, watching her.

"What's wrong?" she said.

"Nothing. Come over here."

"Look, if this is gonna be one of those seduction—"

"Don't make a joke out of this."

She sat up. "Okay. I'm sorry." She ran her hands through her hair. "Coffee first?"

"No."

Skye woke up and walked towards me, still a bit drowsy but pulling it together as she sat down next to me. I gave her Calvin's notebook. She took it but looked at me instead.

"Am I losing you again?" she said.

"You know you said no one ever wants to work with me?"

"A bit harsh, I know, but there's truth in it."

"Oh, I know. Believe me, I know."

"Always a start."

"What if I told you they'll come, if I call for them?"

"All of them?"

"All of them. Well, not Pete. But sure, the rest of them, yes."

"You better have your arguments together."

I put my hands on her cheeks and gently directed her head down, so that she'd look at the page I'd given her.

"Read this, Sara."

Skye took a deep breath.

"He figured it out," I said.

She sighed. "Yeah. I was afraid he would." She looked at me. "Will you stay here with me when I read this?"

"No."

I got up and headed for the bathroom.

"Seriously?" she called. "You gonna ruin the moment by taking a dump?"

"I'm gonna to take a shower," I said. "And then, I'm going out. Sun's up. I want a croissant."

"You'll shave and cut your hair first."

I touched my hair and my beard. "I don't know. I kind of like it."

"It wasn't a question."

I smiled when I went into the bathroom. When I looked over my shoulder, Skye had started reading. As I closed the door, she wiped her arm over her eyes to get rid of some dirt or dust or whatever it was that had found its way there now.

Hello Elliot.

As I'm writing this, I'm about to die.

It's all gone very fast. I've looked for extra life or healing potions, but the store's all out. The coins I have won't buy me extra credits. If there's a boss fight waiting around the corner, I'll lose for sure. As that guy in Gauntlet said: Your life force is running out. Time's up.

I know I won't see you again. I would've liked to, but it won't happen. This is my one regret in life. That, and never working with Nintendo. Anyway, I've asked Lisa to give you our folder when I'm gone.

I don't mind dying. I've had a good run. But I feel bad for Lisa. She'll manage, I know, but still. And it hurts when I think about Isabelle and Alexander. I was looking forward to seeing them grow up, graduate, have some kids and come see me on my birthdays.

My children, these little disruptors of career and concentration, are the best things I've ever made.

A while ago, I had this idea. Maybe the greatest ever. I wanted to tell you about it. But I wanted it to be so strong that you'd have no reason to turn me away. I had this hope that my idea would help you remember all the good things about us. That we'd be friends again.

Obviously, that didn't happen. I got sick instead. And now, here we are. I'm all out of lives, and you're not. I don't like to leave things unfinished. I just didn't realize the value of closure, until my own became clear.

We always said the Greatest Game of All couldn't be made. It was too big, too scattered, too deep, too difficult. But as Skye used to say, that's why it was so beautiful. We could go to that place and don't mind the world outside. Try to build it, and it would become one of those tragedies that died by its own hype. All the good things about it would be destroyed.

Unless.

Yeah. That's right.

I've figured out a way to do it.

That's what you'll find in the folder, among all our old stuff, fresh new material that will tie it all together. It didn't take me long to get it down, once I'd figured it out.

So I've created the missing pieces and written down my notes on where they might work. But we need your designs to put it all together. You always were the one who saw the big picture. Your spells, to bind my ingredients.

I wanted to finish the Greatest Game of All together, Elliot. I don't think that details such as who's living and who's not should stop us now. Nothing ever stopped us. This was our first game. I want it to be our last. So while it's a bit overdue, I'd like us to go Double Dragon one last time and wrap this up like the friends we once were.

I want you to know that I love you and I'm so sorry. I fear that even in death, I'll miss you more than I did in life. I know you deserve closure. I want to give it to you. You might think that you're alone, but you're not.

So let's make this one count, okay? Let's build the Greatest Game of All, you and I. Because if we don't, then who will? Certainly not Howard Scott Warshaw :)

//Your best, best friend like forever

//Calvin

TWO

SPELLBINDER
SOFTWARE

Chapter 26

DOUBLE DRAGON STYLE

You remember that I told you about Lars, and that everything changed when he came around?

Well, as the heat arrived, he finally came around.

It approached Fjellhamn like a thin veil, stirring slowly as the temperature rose.

People stayed inside to sleep away the warmest hours. Some went for a quiet swim, dripping with water from their bodies and sweat from their foreheads. Others just left, to the air-conditioned city or to Norway. The bustling ambience from a typical Fjellhamn summer, with boats cruising the bay and children playing by the ocean rocks, was gone. Instead, there was the eerie calm of a ghost town. The air was still and difficult to breathe.

Despite our ambitions to build more awesome into the folder while searching for a computer, the rising temperature made things hard. Ideas came slowly, if at all. Finding new ways around old problems felt like a chore. We'd agreed that the best conditions for video game development were when the rain hammered on the windows and washed away the heat with the wind howling along, the kind of storm the fishermen had taught us to predict by watching the thin streaks of clouds and understanding how deceptive clear blue skies could be. As you can imagine, we were in the nightmare opposite now.

"Let's go for a swim," Calvin would say.

"I wanna finish this map," I'd reply.

He'd sigh and shake his head, like an old wife looking away in contempt from her farting husband.

"Wanna get an ice cream?" I'd ask.

And he'd go, "I'm drawing a purple dragon."

I would look at it and say, "Hmm," and his eyes would flare up and I knew he wanted to ask me what I meant with that, like that husband who couldn't stand his wife belittling him because he couldn't hold his gas.

Every morning, the heat advanced towards our shores until one day, you couldn't see it over the waves because now it was here.

On that day, we walked aimlessly along the thick hedges in the old villa neighborhood, shadowed by the wild oaks that grew from the yards. We'd gone for a swim and we'd drunk a lot of water. Even so, things felt hopeless.

Calvin stopped and pointed. "Look."

An ambulance approached. It passed us and stopped by one of the oldest houses in town, the one with the overgrown rose garden and dirty windows.

A man and a woman in uniform stepped out and went inside. We sat down on a stone bench and watched. Whatever trace of a breeze that had been here before was gone now. There were no birds or butterflies, only the sound of a fountain from somewhere down the road.

Half an hour later, they returned with a body on a stretcher and a crying old woman by their side. The man spoke softly to her while the young woman hoisted the body into the ambulance. After some hesitation, the old woman climbed inside. Then, they left.

Calvin squeezed his hands around the folder's edges.

"You ever seen a dead person before?" I said.

"Yes."

We got up and turned around, and that's when he appeared.

He seemed to come from nowhere, summoned from the boiling point, walking towards us like a ghost or a goblin emerging from its grave. He had one hand in his pocket, the free arm waving casually. He was blonde with a back slick, tall and dressed in a sailor's outfit. His legs and shoulders implied strength and even from a distance, his blue eyes glowed in the shadows from the oaks, like slices of ice in a winter night.

"Hey," he called and waved to us.

We waved back.

He came closer.

"I'm new here. Just moved in. Checking out the neighborhood. You're Elliot and Calvin, right?"

We said nothing.

"Sorry, I meant C-c-calvin." He stopped in front of us. He must've been two meters tall, maybe two or three years older than us. He smelled good.

"I'm Lars," he said. "My parents got a house here. The new one, by the cliffs. I'm sure you've seen it. We had to blow up parts of the rock to build it."

"Okay," I said. "Nice to meet you. We gotta go."

"What's that?" Lars pointed to Calvin's folder.

"N-n-n...noth—noth—"

"You're gonna say nothing, right? It's okay, I got it. Give it here, little guy."

At first, we didn't get it and we were relieved when we heard bicycles approach from around the hedge.

"C'mon," Lars said. "Hand it over."

"N-n-no," Calvin said.

"You heard him," I said.

"Barely," Lars said as the bicycles appeared.

I should've known.

These were the bullies that used to chase us through town with less enthusiasm than a jellyfish on antidepressants. Now, they were quiet as they formed a circle around us, pedaling slowly with a rhythm that made them into one.

"Give it here," Lars said to Calvin. "Come, come."

I felt him tremble against me. I heard him breathing. He didn't seem afraid, just revved up, but I had no time to wonder why that was, because Lars punched him in the face.

There was blood on the ground, not a scream but a whimper, and that compressed sound from a fist striking bone.

When Calvin hit the asphalt, he held the folder tight to his chest. Lars grinned through a few red stains on his face. He leaned down.

I shouted and threw myself at Lars. He laughed as he lost his balance and scraped his face, and then he was up on his feet and kicked at my legs. I fell, sensing but not quite yet feeling the pain. The biking bullies had stopped and looked as us with dead expressions. They all had a few bruises, traces of a black eye or two.

Calvin threw himself at Lars like a monkey on his back, pulling his hair to twist his head. Lars roared but as two of his goons approached, he said, "Not just yet, boys. This is too much fun."

I looked for an opening as he spun and threw Calvin to the ground. I came at him again. He turned around, grabbed me, and gave me a head butt. I almost fainted and one of the bullies caught me before I fell.

"Just stay away," he whispered. "It'll be over soon." His voice was thin, he smelled of sweat.

Lars raised his foot and aimed for Calvin's wrist, but Calvin dodged him and got up. I broke free and rushed against Lars, but my head was spinning and I fell again. I couldn't see anything. I heard a crunching sound and a gasp from Calvin.

Then, things got quiet.

Lars was crouching over him, prying the folder from his arms. He stood up.

"N-n-o," Calvin said. "G-g-give it b...ba...back."

"Please," Lars said. "The word you're looking for is please."

He tilted his head, holding the folder in his left hand.

"Tell you what. Say it without a stutter, and I'll give it back to you."

Calvin sat up, rubbing his wrist.

"Just the one word," Lars said. "It's simple. Please. There, I just said it. Now, you go."

I moved towards Lars. Calvin turned to me and shook his head. I didn't care, I was ready to throw anything at this giant and take whatever came after that, but honestly, I didn't know what I'd do even if I got close enough. And I could tell from Calvin's eyes, he really didn't want me to try. This was the kind of fight he didn't want to take. The kind that might get his mother to think it was time to leave.

"No, no," Lars said. "On your knees. Say please. Like you're begging for it."

"Forget it," I said. "Calvin, we'll start over. We don't need that stuff. It's all in our heads. We'll make it better."

I don't think he heard me. He was shaking. Lars was bleeding, his elegant outfit torn and dirty. He was radiant, as if this was his favorite suit.

Calvin closed his eyes.

He made a noise from deep down his throat. He was working hard to get the words out. He'd humiliate himself and then Lars would leave with the folder and we'd never see it again. Didn't Calvin realize that? We'd never get it back. And Lars would find another angle and come after us again and again. There's no way I'd let this happen. I'd take the fight for Calvin, if that's what it took.

I got an idea.

I quickly looked around. Thugs, bicycles, big hedge, lots of shade, no one else around. Yep, it would work.

Lars smiled at Calvin, dangling the folder before him. "Come, come. Not p-p-please. But please."

I was ready to make my move.

Calvin spat Lars in the face.

So much for my move.

I gotta hand it to my friend, though—he fired off a good, solid green one, mixed with snot and slime, as big as they came. While it was just some goo from his mouth, it hit Lars like a fireball from a Level Ten spell book. It even made a little sound as it stroked his skin and made its mark.

Lars blinked. The bullies gasped, like hyenas choking on their cadaver.

Calvin slowly rose.

"I'll wipe it off if you say please," he said to Lars. There was the hint of a smile in the corner of his lips.

Lars squeezed his grip on the folder. He shifted his feet and rolled it into a stick. His puppies whimpered and spread out.

I couldn't help it. Whatever was rushing through me, it was as electrifying and deceptive as fear and it was equally destructive. But it felt like the best thing ever.

Lars snarled. I took a stand next to Calvin.

"Let's go *Double Dragon*," I said.

"Let's do it," Calvin said.

We positioned ourselves, back-to-back, with our broken noses and torn faces, ready to face these thugs and a hundred more.

"Oh," Lars said as he moved towards us. "That's cute."

We raised our fists. We knew we'd die today. But fuck it, we'd die together. And I couldn't think of a better way to go.

Chapter 27

THE PHOENIX AND THE WRIGHT

Maybe I remembered the Fjellhamn summers as a lot warmer than they were. Or maybe things really were easier back then. But it felt like you could count on the weather. Politicians did their best. If a stranger approached you on the street, he was just lonely with no intention of hurting you.

Or perhaps the world was what it always had been, about as violent and beautiful as anyone would make of it. It wasn't heading in any particular direction, and my idea of today was colored only by how I choose to remember things from yesterday.

Because the world of today, and Stockholm in particular, had anything but predictable summers. I don't recall them being so damn unreliable when I was a kid.

I had risen, like the phoenix, from the ashes of my own self-pity, about as stable in flight as a prototype from the Wright brothers. Or maybe Calvin had pulled me out from the pile, like he always used to do. I don't know. But I'd left the chaotic spring behind, with its warm showers and raging snow storms, and arrived to a summer with floods and thunderstorms. I was wearing my t-shirts again, with my patched jeans and favorite sandals. My hair was back to its short but curly mess and if I had a beard, it was just a few days old and it made me look good.

I'd left my apartment and gone for walks. I'd read magazines in the park and asked a few friends if they wanted to see a movie. When I called, they offered congratulations on my recovery mixed with excuses related to their kids, and that's about as much honesty as I could get from them. I'm not sure if they didn't care, or didn't have the energy to. I went to a few of the stores I'd been a regular at once, and those still working there who recognized me nodded and smiled, but that was it. I went to a bar and had a beer, tried talking to someone I didn't know, and got a few polite replies, but no real interest to engage. I felt like a kid who had a birthday party with only himself as a guest, confused as to why no one came. And that was okay, because that's the way I remembered the world, and it hadn't changed since I was last out and about.

At least there was Skye, and we fell into the once familiar routine of having dinner at Nonna's, a place where the *Spellbinder* team always had gone to when crunches were intense and we worked on fumes. Nonna wasn't just a concept, it really was owned by a true Italian grandmother, and once the *Spellbinders* became regulars, she didn't take orders but served us whatever she felt we needed. We were always tired and loud when we squeezed through her door and pushed up the stairs, and even though the idea of getting back to work after midnight almost killed us, it was so absurd that we had to laugh about it. There was only one table that could seat us all, a square oaken desk by the street windows that had a century-old olive tree in the center. We used to arrive when Nonna was about to close, but she motioned for us to come inside. While we fought over the best seats, she hung up the sign that kept the rest of the city away.

When Skye and I went there now, we sat by the same table but surrounded by bankers and lawyers, hipsters, and their children. Every now and then, we spotted a few of the old vets, mixed up with youngsters we assumed were colleagues or prospects or maybe indie developers. There was a Battlefield producer or two from the Dice offices, the always-fuming art director and his entourage from Avalanche, and a few souls adrift from what used to be the Grin studio. The King pack were as loud as ever, and the Starbreeze crew hung in the darkest corners, avoiding contact. It was all familiar and slightly sad, a context where I'd once been someone and yet, my absence made no difference. Had this been a few years ago, we would have shared tables, traded ideas, and swapped discs. Now, the industry was full of secret projects and guarded patents, exclusive publishing deals and potential mergers, walls that kept you out or trapped inside.

"They wanna know," Skye said as she filled up her third glass of wine. "What the fuck you're doing here. Why you're back. They think you're dead or something. Or was that the other guy? Somebody died. That's what they're saying, as they're checking us out."

"I'm having dinner," I said. "With my friend."

"Fuck your friends."

One of Nonna's sons appeared and served us our pasta. He'd told us his mother was sick and didn't work in the restaurant anymore. We could tell, from the food.

"They're not real," Skye said while finishing her glass. "Kids are just a fucking excuse for not wanting to care."

"It's a good one," I said.

"That's why they can go fuck themselves."

"The kids?"

Skye laughed. She leaned back and exhaled.

"You sure you ready for this?" she said.

"You keep asking."

"I care."

"I'm not a kid."

She tilted her head and looked at me with a curious smile.

"No?"

We turned down dessert when the waiter arrived with a menu. Skye ordered coffee and we looked out the window at the slow summer rain.

"Be careful tomorrow," she said.

"I will."

She sighed, frustrated.

"I was in that room too, Elliot. Sean did what he did to you on purpose. He put a dagger in your back and pushed you into that room with all those execs."

We'd had this conversation countless times now, and she always got upset when we reached this part, red in the face and voice growing louder.

"He even made a joke about it," she said. "We were waiting for the ambulance. And he made a joke."

"I'm done talking about it," I said.

"I know," she said. "Doesn't mean I am."

"This shit happens all the time, Skye. The one disease that's gonna wipe us out is already here. We just don't properly understand it. Stress and exhaustion will kill us and plants will take over."

She put her hand over mine and squeezed it. She tried to be gentle, but that third glass of wine made her grip hurt. She burped.

"I don't want to lose you again."

"You keep sayi—"

"Don't argue. Be grateful that someone cares."

She followed me home. We were soaking wet from the rain but got straight to work by the dimmed ceiling light over the kitchen table. It wasn't a storm precluded by streaks of thin clouds, but it would have to do. A slow thunder rolled in over Stockholm and murmured through the night as we knocked out a few more drafts on an idea we hadn't cracked yet. But we knew we didn't have to. After tomorrow, things would be different and our work wouldn't matter. Trying to control it would be pointless.

An hour or two after midnight, we thawed a few slices of pizza, launched *Skype*, and waited as it echoed over the world to the beat of the rain.

Joakim was the first to pop up. He was a bit pale, despite his years in the Californian sun, his short hair cut into something that made him look like a boy. In twenty years, he hadn't changed a bit.

"Hey," he said. "How's it going?"

"It's raining," Skye said. "That's how it's going."

Angela appeared, her black hair tied into a tight knot. "Good morning," she said. "Or is it night? Afternoon? It's morning here in Kyoto, if you wanna know."

"Hey, all. Are we ready for tomorrow?" I said.

Joakim turned away, looking at another screen now. "I'm uploading the package," he said. "I took care of the last parts this week. The code that could be refactored and compiled has been. I made the final assessments this morning."

"What did you leave out?"

"Check the logs. You'll see."

"And the art?" Skye said.

"It's on the server," Angela said. She laughed. "I feel like I've had it easy compared to you, Joakim. It was just a matter of converting it and cleaning it up, especially the older stuff. I like it. There's a crude charm to it."

She made a pause as she looked at something on her desk. "I guess Calvin would've called it style."

Skye smiled. "The J Dilla of video game art."

"I gotta say," Angela said as she turned to us again, "I didn't think this would work when you called, Elliot. I agreed to this because I liked the idea. But now...well..."

"It's not going to work," Joakim said. "I can't see how it could."

"But you're coming anyway, right?" I said.

"Of course."

"Travel safe," Skye said.

Joakim hung up. Angela sighed. "Well, I'm on my way, taxi's around the corner. So yeah..." She got quiet again. "This feels really strange."

"It'll be good to see you," I said. "I mean that."

She smiled. "I know."

We went through what we had on the table one last time, and then Skye crashed on the sofa to the pale light of a bad Netflix show (she'd made it a point to avoid all the good ones, though that point was lost on anyone but her), her pants and t-shirt thrown into a corner. I sat by the window, one of the few spaces not yet covered with a drawing, concept, or otherwise printable asset. The walk-in closet had turned into a forest and the living room was a desert that blended into high mountains with snow-covered peaks. The shelves were littered with beasts and creatures, characters and wildlife. The walls were a mess, hung with charts, diagrams, and schedules. In the center, there was a picture of the sad, old man with his unkempt beard and long hair. His eyes followed me as I moved through the room.

I felt closer to this place, like that time when I'd first seen the Atari. It still made sense to me, that a bunch of pixels, which hard-ly resembled anything but a deformed mess, was more real and honest than anything in the actual world.

Skye was right. I should be careful. I shouldn't argue with her. She didn't want to lose me again. I should be grateful for that.

I rose with the sun and got dressed. I picked up the keys on the desk in the hall. Not the ones that led to my apartment because I already had those in my pocket, but the keys that I'd had only for a week, the keys that were still new to me. I'd rather forget my pants today than those keys.

Next to them was the stick drawing Calvin had made for me, the one with the two boys down by the pier.

The boys were laughing. The sun was setting. It had been a beautiful day.

"I remember," I said quietly.

I turned around.

THE GREATEST GAME OF ALL

There was only Skye there, sleeping on the couch.
I put the stick drawing in my pocket and left.

Chapter 28

SEAN

Sean was already at the hotel, waiting for me at the best spot with something in his glass and a cigarette in his hand. He looked shamelessly comfortable on the terrace by the street, reading a New York Times in a plush, white armchair dressed with linen. The parasol waved in the wind. He smiled when he saw me, and when I crossed the lobby to reach the terrace, he got up and reached for a hug.

If you just looked at him, you wouldn't think that he was in his late sixties. He was as lean and agile as a man half his age, cut like a guy who took his exercise routines seriously. His hair was gray, but it had been for as long as I'd known him. Calvin and I had asked him once if he was born that way. He'd answered that he didn't remember. You had to give it to the man—his timing was flawless. He always wore those expensive shirts with a slight shine and suit pants to match, and maybe that was the only real tell-tale sign of his generation. He dressed like middle management from the sixties, like the man who did all right but never got invited to the barbecues. But most executives in the video game industry didn't know how to dress, so perhaps it was part of his chameleon tactics.

He got his hug, though.

"Elliot," he said as he wouldn't let go. "My dear, dear boy. It's so good to see you."

"Thanks," I said. We sat down. "I hope I didn't make you wait."

"No, no, I just got here. Let me say this right away, that I wasn't expecting this but I'm glad you're here. Look at you, back from the dead."

I smiled.

"When I spoke with Skye," he said, "you were locked up in your place with your beard and your hair." He chuckled and put out his cigarette. "I was concerned, to say the least."

I kept smiling.

A waiter appeared with a silver tray. It had scones and biscuits, cheese and marmalade, and a tea pot with two cups to complement. While he served and poured with impressive precision, Sean made a gesture.

"I took the liberty," he said. "You always loved the afternoon tea here."

"It's still morning."

As the waiter left, Sean took a scone and applied some butter.

"I'm truly sorry, Elliot. Calvin was a good man and an amazing artist. There's no replacing him." He took a bite.

I gave myself a few moments, a few breaths.

Sean wiped his lips with a handkerchief. "I've offered to help Lisa," he said. "Must be tough, alone with the kids. I can't imagine what that's like."

"You've got kids."

"They're grown up. They'll do just fine without their old man."

The waiter arrived with strawberries. Sean watched him as he served us. He almost dropped a spoon, made a modest apology, and left.

"Doesn't seem so long ago," Sean said. "When I met you in Fjellhamn."

"Not long at all."

"Twenty-five years. Or was it twenty-four?"

"Who's counting?"

"You still got the house?" he said.

"You still got that scar we gave you?"

"I wear it proudly. Best accident I've ever had." He reached for his tea. "You kids. You still seem so...young, to me. There's something bittersweet about it all, don't you think?"

"I wouldn't know. I'm still young."

"I love my Northern studios. You're ruthless and disciplined, ambitious and aware. You even fail with grace."

"*Spellbinder* was never yours."

Sean laughed. "I'll say. And speaking of ..." He lit a new cigarette. "Sign the damn papers, Elliot. You know I want to buy the property. I'll be honest. I'm not sure what I'm going to do with it. But even if your titles are long dead, I see a slumbering potential. It's like an old franchise. Play it right, and it could be something still. I did it with *Terminator*. I'm doing it with *Blade Runner*. Yours aren't far behind."

I hadn't touched the tea or scones, but now I reached for the tray and poured myself something warm.

"You're certainly paying us more than anyone else would," I said.

"I'm sentimental. Feels like I played a part, somehow. Maybe we'll just remaster the games and release them for whatever console is relevant when we're done. Or do mobile versions for a new generation. Whatever we'll do, I'm ordering champagne. We'll drink to Calvin and for all the good memories. I want to give you the opportunity to let your games live on, even if it's not as you intended."

"I'm not sure we intended it one way or the other. We made them and people liked them."

"A lot of people. Anyway. Champagne."

Sean called for the waiter again and asked all kinds of questions about the bubbles they kept and how they kept them. What

Sean didn't know about drink and food wasn't worth knowing unless you worked in a restaurant that aspired to gain, or fought to keep, its stars. We'd had many dinners at his home in San José and he was the best host I'd ever known, the scorching sunsets from his rooftop garden some of the most beautiful I'd ever seen.

"I'm sorry," Sean said to me. "If I understand our friend correctly here," and he made a gesture to the waiter, "they don't offer anything beyond the dull defaults."

"It's okay. Thanks, Sean. I appreciate it."

"Not at all."

Our champagne arrived. Sean raised his glass.

"To Calvin, Elliot. A brilliant artist, a good man, and a true friend. He deserved a better selection, but this will have to do."

I didn't raise my glass. In fact, I didn't touch it.

"I'm not selling, Sean."

"All right."

"I don't want to waste your time."

"It's not a waste. It's just good to see you. If nothing else, this is closure. With Calvin gone, it's the end of something. Perhaps not an era. That ended long ago. You made sure of that. But it's the end of something, surely."

He drank his bubbles.

"You were never part of the beginning," I said.

"Oh, I most certainly was. If we're splitting hairs. Or mountains. But I know what you mean."

"And I know what you want," I said.

He put the glass away and leaned back, crossing his legs. Skye's words of caution were on repeat in my head.

But she'd known me long enough to know how this would play out.

"Once a guy tried to take our folder from us. He had no idea what it contained, of course. He just wanted it because he thought he could have it."

Sean reached for his glass and had a sip.

"I remember," he said. "You told me. Some local thug. Whatever happened to him? You never told me that. That's a story that needed closure." He took a smoke and looked out at the people on the street.

"We don't work with bullies, Sean. I made that perfectly clear once."

"We?" He shook his head. "You were always in your own space, Elliot. Made you hard to find, sometimes." His eyes narrowed. "Makes it difficult to talk about any kind of we, in any kind of sense."

"Well...we are done, I think."

I got up. He didn't.

He looked at me with his gray gaze, leaning his chin in his palm, cigarette between his fingers.

"You're gonna build it yourself," he said.

The wind had picked up. The parasol rocked back and forth. The other guests had gone inside. We were alone on the terrace. A cluster of thick, dark clouds drifted in over the rooftops.

Sean sighed. "A man with your condition, Elliot. You almost died. You must still be fragile. You have to be careful. You might relapse. Shouldn't you be done with this now?"

"Why did you come to my door every morning? Wasn't it enough that you dropped the news about Calvin's death on me, before you sent me into the pitching room? You had to keep twisting it?"

"I was only offering my condolences. I assumed you knew." He inhaled and blew out some smoke. "Clearly, I was wrong. You didn't know. These things can happen so fast, of course. Very sudden, all of it. You think you have time. Then you realize, you don't. And you'll wonder what you did with it all."

He fell back in his chair and crossed his fingers. "What are you talking about, anyway?"

"Every day, Sean. You came to my door."

"You're being absurd. I live in California."

"You're here now."

"I have studios here. I wanted to see you."

"Avalanche didn't ever need a visit from you. Or Starbreeze. Or whatever else you think you own."

"I don't own Starbreeze. Or Avalanche. Which is why they keep fucking up."

"You keep trying to get them to think they do, to give an idea that you're useful. But the kind of shit you wielded back when you had some publishing power doesn't work anymore. We don't need your millions. We don't need your marketing. We can raise the first and you were never any good on the second. We certainly don't need your fucking manipulating and humiliating ways. The publisher reign ended a long time ago. The emperor died. No one replaced him. You're just an old vizier who doesn't get it."

Sean got up. He put a hand on my shoulder. "Very evocative, Elliot. Very much you."

He smiled. "You're a remarkable person, my boy. After all you've gone through, with your mother and father, losing your friend and Spellbinder's fall, not to mention your current condition. You're the only guy I know who'd face a hundred enemies and still take the fight."

There was a spark in his eye. He squeezed my shoulder. "But that time has also passed, Elliot. You, too, are a relic."

"I know."

"I don't get the impression that you do."

"I just love a good ending, Sean."

He smiled. "I've talked to Skye. You know she's with you out of pity. She understands you'll get nowhere with whatever you got. You're a pariah. You've wrecked so many people and opportunities. No one will work with you. No one will publish you. You are alone. You always have been."

"Obviously, you care," I said.

He pulled up his wallet and dug up a few dollars. "I always care," he said. "You have to, when you do what I do."

He threw the money on the silver tray. The wind picked them up, shifting them around, considering whether to snatch them now or later.

"Think about it," he said. "Maybe you don't need the money. But Lisa lost her husband, her children lost their father, and who knows how many years Skye has left. You can't be selfish in this, Elliot. That's what got you here, after all. You owe them. I think it's time you realize that. Calvin left the industry with dignity. You didn't. But you could still get something out of this."

His phone rang. He picked it up and smiled apologetically. "Nintendo," he said. "Gotta take this." He answered in Japanese and before I had time to do anything else, like punch him in the face or throw him into the river, he winked and said under his breath: "Lovely to see you, and give my best to Skye," and then he walked away, speaking like a submachine gun now to some developer in Kyoto.

The waiter appeared and collected Sean's bills.

"These are dollars," he said to me.

"Yeah," I said. "He always does that."

I paid the waiter and left.

On my way back, I got a message from Skye. I read it while walking slowly along the streets by the water, holding the keys in my pocket that didn't go to my apartment. The message didn't say much, her texts rarely did, but it was epic, as most of her messages were.

Where the fuck are you? Everyone's arrived and as usual, we're all just waiting for you. Tell Sean to go fuck himself and get your sweet ass over here already.

Chapter 29

EXPLODING FISTS

So yeah, Lars was pretty good at this whole beat 'em up game.

A lot better than us, that's for sure.

And while I'd never had a bully pound at me with such relentless energy, channeled with a passion you almost had to admire—dedication was a rare thing, after all—it really didn't matter.

Lars had wiped his face from blood and sweat, kicked us one last time in the gut and then left, oddly frustrated by the whole event. He didn't seem to care if his goons followed or not. In fact, I don't think he even considered them part of his pack. They followed him, all the same.

Calvin and I got up. Assessed the damage done, accounted for items missing from the inventory (just the one, the folder).

And then, we shambled.

Through Fjellhamn, with our faces bruised like the flesh-torn palette of the undead.

When we found the flock, we sat down and watched them from a distance. They had ice cream while whispering and pointing at us, like they always used to do. When we stood up, they withdrew.

We followed.

If one of them broke out and approached us, we didn't move.

Calvin grinned at them through blood-soaked teeth. They pulled back, got up on their bikes, and left.

It wasn't about the concepts in the folder. *The Greatest Game of All* was in our head. We'd just make new drafts, better ones, updated ones.

Nor was it about the fact that the folder was a gift from Calvin's mum, and all the love she'd poured into the bold act of acquiring it. Obviously, that meant something. But in the end, it was just stuff.

If anything, it was about the fact that Lars and the Brady bunch had tried to stop us from making our game. That wasn't gonna happen. He had to squeeze our brains out first. You think a couple of exploding fists would stop us? I didn't think so.

However.

This was the kind of fight Calvin had mentioned. The trigger that would make his mum decide that they had to move. We had to work out a strategy.

So we took the long way home and went to the man at the café. Maybe he'd been to war, maybe not, but it felt like he knew his way around wounds and we needed some patching to make our story more credible.

His place was empty. When he saw us, he gestured for us to sit down. He didn't say anything when he brought out his first aid kit. He washed our faces and applied really painful liquid stuff on the deeper cuts. Then he poured us some water.

"Thanks," I mumbled. Calvin only nodded.

He smiled slightly and looked out the window. You could see the piers and the fishermen from here, working their nets in a downtempo pattern. They drank from their bottles, they'd swapped their t-shirts for linen clothing and strapped on their bandanas. The heat wasn't letting anyone get away.

"Sometimes, water is not good for you," the man said.

Calvin frowned. "How's that?"

The man got up from his chair and disappeared into his office behind the counter. Calvin and I looked at each other. Our faces hurt. Our legs hurt. Our brains hurt. It was all very confusing.

"What happens now?" Calvin said in a low voice.

"We should thank him," I said.

"But we did."

We approached him again. He had his back to us, his hands holding something, perhaps a photograph or a page from a book. He was humming, his voice breaking from beat to beat. We left, but he came out and called for us, waving two bottles.

"You must drink," he said. "It is very warm. Every day, you come to me now. And I will give you water."

We went home and told our parents we'd fallen from our bikes. My dad said that if I wanted to talk about what really happened, he was always around. I said that this was what really happened and he didn't need to worry about it. He looked sad when I said that, but I wasn't going to pity him. He was supposed to be the adult here, after all. Anyway, it didn't really matter what he thought, me telling him was just part of making our story more credible. Cornelia was the big challenge. If she didn't buy it, our game would be finished before it was done.

She was quiet when we told her. She was never quiet. She didn't always speak, but there was always some "Mm-hmm" or "Aah" and even the occasional "Hoo-kay," coming from her. But now, nothing.

When we'd served up our story, she poured herself some coffee. She waved the pot in our direction, eyebrows raised. Calvin shook his head. I was about to say sure, if this is the end, I might as well have coffee, but I remembered that I didn't really like it. So I also just shook my head.

"You're gonna need new pads," she said. "And pens."

She looked around and had a sip. "We might have to ask Mr. Svensson for more space." She broke out her arms to embrace the room. "Hell, I can hardly see the walls anymore, with your paintings all over the place."

She leaned back in her chair. I looked at Calvin. This could go either way, he told me with his eyes (no really, he did). Your guess is as good as mine.

"I like'm, though. Your stuff on my walls. Our walls." She looked at us with a sad smile. "You knew that, didn't you, boys? I hope I've told you so, again and again."

I smiled back. Calvin laughed quietly.

Cornelia motioned for us to come sit with her. We got up and she hugged us and as usual, there were tears involved. Cornelia could cry over a decent plate of pasta or a fresh pair of underwear, offering a "God Bless!" as she held them tight to her chest. But I was starting to like her hugs. They were intrusive, but they were nice.

The deep sound from distant thunder rolled across the Fjellhamn hills and woods. The skies were gray and the first drops from a soft rain hit the porch outside. It would seem that the best conditions for video game development had arrived.

Chapter 30

A REAL SPELLBINDER

It rained constantly now, but it remained slow and warm, like the air that had drifted in from the sea. It didn't do much to cool us down, but at least the skies wore a thin gray cover, which did its best to hide the sun.

We went to the café every day. The man served us fresh water and sandwiches. "You should be inside," he said. "Despite the rain, it is very warm. People here, they don't know. But you should be outside in the morning and in the evening. Not now."

We built a post-it puzzle across the window tables. On the rare occasion that another customer showed up and wanted to sit where we worked, the owner ushered them to another seat or told them to leave. Around noon, the church tower offered shade and if the rain allowed it, we took our breaks then and went outside to eat our sandwiches. We watched the cluster of pools and little streams over the asphalt and dirt roads, a small universe of river deltas, like a tiny bayou on the Swedish west coast.

It was on one of those days that a shape approached, riding her bike as if she didn't have a care in the world.

Sara, with her yellow sweater and white skirt and pink sneakers, dark hair in a perfect braid.

We hadn't seen her for a while.

She wasn't alone but whoever the other guy was, he wasn't riding a bike. He had to walk fast to keep up with her. He was big, a giant behind her.

"It's him," Calvin said.

Sara, friends with Lars.

Of course.

Sara, always neat and ready for a summer party. Lars, his hair perfectly combed and wearing a navy-blue shirt with white shorts. They were the young alpha couple of the Fjellhamn turf, the prince and princess of the festival.

They were coming towards us, slowly gliding through the puddles, but there seemed to be a distance between them, hardly possible to measure in inches but still as wide as a chasm when you picked up the vibe for it.

"Hey, guys," she said when they stopped before us. "What's up?"

Lars avoided our gaze as we tried to make sense of this.

Calvin's eyebrows bounced up and down and I felt like laughing and hurting someone at the same time.

Sara turned to Lars.

"You had something to say to my friends, didn't you?" she said.

He mumbled something.

"What's that, now? I didn't hear. You heard anything, Calvin? Elliot?"

We shook our heads.

"Again, please."

Lars' eyes wandered.

"I'm...sorry I..."

"Ah, no, dear god no. Like we rehearsed."

He looked at her, confused and angry. She pointed to the ground.

"But it's wet," he said.

She kept pointing.

He got down on his knees, staining his legs with dirty water.

Sara leaned closer.

"Look at them," she said. "While you say it. Look at Elliot and Calvin."

So he did.

I don't know what I saw in his eyes, there was such a chaotic mixture of rage and fear, anger and sadness, and to some extent, it took me out of the situation. I didn't know if I should gloat or hit back or ignore him. Or maybe, no matter how strange it felt, feel sorry for him.

"I'm sorry I beat you up," Lars said. "And I'm sorry I took your stuff."

"Yeah," Sara said. "About that."

She pulled Calvin's folder from her bicycle basket and threw it on the table between us. Calvin's eyes almost popped out from his head. He opened it and thumbed through the papers.

"It won't happen again," Lars said.

"And also," Sara chimed in.

He looked at her with a vain attempt to say, Come on, isn't this enough?

Of course it wasn't. Not for Sara.

"And also," he said and turned to us again. "I will buy you ice cream for a year."

"Cool," I said.

Calvin browsed through the folder. "It's all here."

"Yeah," Lars said. "I wasn't really gonna..." He fell silent.

"You can go now," Sara said. "Don't try this shit ever again."

He got up and wiped away the moist from his knees.

"I got a ZX Spectrum," he said.

As if this could get any stranger.

First, that this Lars guy had any clue about anything other than football and sailing.

Then, that he was here to say he's sorry for what he'd done (though arguably, under the influence of Sara Eastwood).

But finally, dropping the bomb like so—that he had a computer. And the inferior Spectrum at that! Daring to expose this flaw in character to us.

"Isn't that monochrome?" Calvin said.

"It has eight colors," Lars said. "But you can only use two at a time."

Now I felt truly sorry for him. Calvin shuddered.

"Anyway," Sara said. "Scram."

Lars turned around, shoved his hands in his pockets, and left. When he was gone, Sara said: "He lives at the end of my street."

"H-he said his house was at the top of some hill," Calvin said.

"That's where her street ends," I mumbled.

"I don't think his parents are home much," she said.

"Anyway," I said. "Thanks. I mean, we could've handled this on our own..." Calvin was shaking his head now. "...We had a plan for getting it all back and showing Lars who's the boss, but it's a good thing you stepped in."

Sara smiled at me.

"Because now," I said and felt warm, "well, now, we can focus on...uh, the game...and stuff."

She laughed.

"You do that," she said. "I'll see you around."

She got ready to leave. Calvin chewed his lip and looked around. She was shifting into gear when I surprised everyone— including myself—by saying with a loud and not impressive voice (there might've been a falsetto involved), "You're a real spellbind-er, Sara."

Yeah, I know.

It didn't sound good even in my head.

She looked at me. "I'm a what now?"

Calvin was equally confused. "D-don't call her names, Elliot. She's trying to being nice."

"No no, I mean—"

"Yeah, what the fuck do you mean?" she said.

"That's what we'll call our studio." I shrugged. "Spellbinder Software."

"We got a studio?" Calvin said.

"We?" she said.

"Who?" he said.

"Well, I mean...you know ..."

"The mighty Elliot Lindh," Sara said softly. "Suddenly lost for words."

"Yeah," Calvin said. "You're all out, man. Spellbinder's pretty lame."

"You think of something better, then."

"Oh, we will," Sara said.

"Stupid easy," Calvin said. "T-that name won't last longer than my sandwich."

Seeing as he only had a bite left of the sandwich in question, I can safely say that he was wrong.

Chapter 31

CIGARS

And now, I was holding that set of keys in my hand that didn't go to my apartment. They were worn and pale, from years of use, and I squeezed them hard, as if they'd been mine since the day they were molded. My meeting with Sean already felt like a distant memory, a nostalgia happening under the parasols of a hotel by the river, where we'd cleared up a few disagreements and then laughed at fond memories.

I stood outside a big, white door, one of those Victorian gateways that usually led to the stairway of an old house or the entrance to a mansion. But this one led to a cigar factory. It was on the third floor in a building with five, and it occurred to me just then that we wouldn't be alone here. The fourth floor had a lawyer firm of sorts, the top level a random humanitarian organization, and the bottom floors...actually, I don't remember. A restaurant, I think, run by a Greek or something. I could be wrong about the others, too.

But Pete had given me the keys.

And he'd brought his dog.

He always did. A sizeable one, as kind as he was big, content with life as long as he had a bone to chew on. They had that in common, though calling Pete kind would be unfair to his dog. He was many things. Kind was not one of them.

He hadn't been on my radar for years, nor I on his, but I felt pretty confident he'd answer when I called. We skipped the formalities, he was never one for small talk anyway, and I cut right to it and asked what his plans were for the old Dice house on Maria Street next to the old school.

"No plans," Pete said. "We're just bleeding it out for a year. Landlord's not trying too hard to find a new tenant. It's a cost for us."

"Okay," I said. "You're gonna give us that year for free."

He laughed. "Who's we? Why would I?"

"You wouldn't be running Activision now if it wasn't for me."

"I run Electronic Arts."

"Didn't the one buy the other?"

He could've kept laughing and hung up, or shouted at me for always being the same arrogant dick, or saying, "Sure, you'll get the place but you come work for me then," or some other shit he used to throw around, back in the days. All that would be Pete.

"What're you up to?" he said.

"Wouldn't you like to know."

"I'm late for a meeting. I'll call you back."

Which he didn't. He never did. But he sent me a text message a few days later. It dropped into my phone as Skye and I had our first cup of coffee for the day, at my kitchen table.

Meet me at the old Dice office tomorrow at 0900. // P

I showed her the message. She put out her cigarette in her cereal bowl.

"What did you offer?" she said

"Nothin'."

"Good deal."

So I went there to the yellow stone house that once held a cigar factory, and while I waited for Pete who was always late, I watched the kids play in the school yard across the road. The bell rang and they went inside. The street was quiet. A few minutes later, the man of the hour arrived in his custom-built Audi. He stepped out with his dog.

"Hey, Lindh," Pete said as Mellow bounced around, excited by all the familiar smells. "So what are you up to?"

It felt like whatever you said to Pete, you had to pitch it. A concept, a merger, a cup of coffee. I wasn't ready to do that.

But he just gave me the keys.

"It's yours," he said. "For a year."

I took them. "Thanks."

He looked at Mellow, who'd managed to find the only spot of dirt on Maria Street and started digging.

"Sean's in town," Pete said.

"Yeah. He wants to buy Spellbinder."

"You met with him?"

"Not yet."

"But you're gonna?"

"I feel like he's earned it."

Pete shoved his hands in his pockets.

"He hasn't, Elliot. He's an asshole."

We looked at the house where, after the last piece of fine tobacco had been rolled and shipped, a bunch of people had set up shop years later and built a couple of warfare video games. The place had just swapped one addiction for another.

"I don't know," I said. "Calvin and I took a lot of his people with us when we started Spellbinder."

Mellow bounced up to us with a stick in his mouth. Pete leaned down and tugged at it.

"You think he did some good. Found you. Took you in. Taught you. Trained you. But you guys were a force of nature."

"Yeah, but the way we did it...the way I did it ..."

Pete threw the stick, Mellow already in the air to catch it.

"Sean made a living out of humiliating people, Elliot. The industry applauded when someone finally humiliated him." He turned to me. "That guy had it coming. He still has, if you ask me."

This was probably the most profound discussion I'd ever had with Pete. I was surprised how comfortable it felt, how easy these searching moments seemed to come for him. Not that we reached for unexplored psychological depths, exactly. But at least it wasn't just business.

When Mellow returned, now with a worn plush in his mouth that probably once belonged to a kid in a stroller, Pete leaned down and scratched his friend behind the ears. There was a faint smile on his lips.

"Well, good luck," he said. "I'm sorry about Calvin."

"Thanks."

He got into his car. Mellow followed, jaws empty now. I covered my eyes against the sun and looked at him as he fired up the engine and turned the car around. He rolled down the window, his eyes on the road.

"You're gonna build it, aren't you?" he said. "That game you and Calvin always carried around."

"Nah."

"That's why Sean's coming after you, isn't it?"

"For a pile of sketches? I think not."

"Any publisher would've picked it up."

"We could've pitched shit. They'd pick that up, too."

Pete smiled. "Where do you go from there, though?"

"What do you mean?"

"If you make the greatest game ever, Elliot. What's beyond?"

I turned away from the sun. "I'll let you know."

Pete stroke his dog, already half asleep in the passenger seat. "Let's go, Mellow. Elliot's gonna have a moment now."

He stepped on it and turned at the crossroads with a speed that would've put him in jail if caught on camera.

That was the last I ever saw of Pete.

I kept hearing about him for a long time after all of this was over, sometimes wondering what his fight was about. We'd had many meetings over the years that had ended with shouts, screams, and threats. But this last one, that could've been the beginning to something entirely new.

I unlocked the door to Spellbinder's new studio and stepped in.

Chapter 32

BOUND BY THE SPELLS

I heard voices.

Lots of them, from inside.

Not inside my head, mind you, though I did consider for a brief while if this wasn't just too unreal to be true.

If I'd guess, I'd count them to a small crowd, about thirty or forty people. Relaxed and conversational, like guests in an afternoon ceremony.

I didn't have to guess, though. I knew there were twenty-eight of them. We would've been thirty if Calvin had still been around, and if Pete hadn't left.

I had imagined this moment a thousand times, and it had taken about as many turns every time, but I'll admit—I never expected this casual mood. I'd pictured everything from right out verbal attacks to fistfights or the whole thing being a staged return, just to show me how it could've been if things had been different. If I had done things differently.

But never once in these thousands of times did I think I'd walk into a garden party of sorts. However, as I closed the door, a cool wind must've swept through the trees because the conversation faded as the supposed guests turned around and looked at me.

Our reception area had no furniture. But it was filled with bags and coats, shoes and gear, strollers and baby seats, with travel notes and custom stickers attached to the handles. I could almost see the trail of dust from the deserts and mountains these people had crossed to come here. The once-a-cigar factory was like a ballroom with a ceiling that matched a mansion's, or like an old house that had once been occupied by a family of decent aristocrats, and then sold for a penny as times had changed and the industrial revolution became a way of life. At the very far left, one of the walls was covered by a worn, filthy curtain, a kind of washed-out gray. It seemed like the curtain you'd hang to hide a hideous work in progress by painters who never got around to finishing the job.

And here we were, messing the place up like an army of teenagers that invaded a parent's home, obscuring the floor underneath a mountain of shoes and sandals, building hills like gods with our stuffed jackets. The place certainly smelled like a bunch of rowdy no-gooders after gym class, partly I'm sure because everyone was in their socks. They'd taken off their shoes. They'd remembered. Shoes off.

Now, they all looked at me. Like one entity, with twenty-eight pairs of cold eyes.

My stomach hurt. I'd had too much coffee. I'd not had breakfast. I shouldn't have quit the vodka. Or met with Sean. Or read Calvin's notes. I should've stayed at home, close to my Eucalyptus plant, become the tree like Calvin and I had once imagined. There were too many people here, too many of them watching me, all of them waiting for a reason to leave. But there was something else as well, a soft but clear comfort behind all this, a distinct feeling of home. Of purpose. They were here, after all, because I'd asked them to come.

I could leave and close the door behind me. Call Sean, say it was good to meet and now that I'd given it some thought, maybe selling wasn't such a bad idea. It wouldn't surprise anyone. Most of them expected that kind of exit anyway, if not now, then later and perhaps they were just here to see the show.

Some of them were smiling, though faintly. Others looked angry. A few were blank, still confused that they'd agreed to this. Joakim and Angela were in the background, pretending to know nothing, blending in with the others. Filip had lost the last of his hair. He looked better this way. He seemed alone. He always used to be with someone. But not now.

Simon was divorced again and had dyed whatever hair he had left (and he used to have so much!). It would've worked if he was still twenty. Which he hadn't been for, I don't know, twenty years? Honestly, I don't think it would've worked then either.

Caroline was thinner, to the point of concern. She had her son with her. He was playing an old Game Boy Micro with headphones on. Good to see that he was being schooled.

Benjamin was larger now, hugging his wife with his left arm and their twins with his right. Though it hardly fit anymore, he wore his green Mushroom Boy t-shirt. I remember when we bought those. I still had my One Up-shirt somewhere in the drawers.

My mind continued to browse them all and, despite my dry throat and shaking hands, I felt good about this, like that roller coaster you finally decided you had the guts to embark. I just needed to find a way into the situation now, a channel to get started, and I couldn't have prepared for this because predicting what I'd face was impossible. I would have to improvise. I was always at my best when I improvised.

I looked for an anchor and found her, sitting on a crate the size of a container, next to a bunch of other crates, leaning against the wall. She smiled and shook her head as she put out her cigarette against the wooden surface.

"You gonna say something?" Skye said and jumped down from the crate. "Or are we supposed to fucking clap our hands and be grateful you even showed up?" At that, she clapped her hands, slowly, and it echoed through the studio halls.

I wasn't gonna smile. It wasn't funny. Besides, as I looked

around, I didn't see anyone else laughing. They all folded their arms, shifted their feet, tilted their heads.

"It's good to see you all," I said. "I want to thank you for coming here. But I'm not going to say I'm sorry."

No one seemed surprised by this.

"I didn't do this, all of this, to make amends." I stroked my hands through my hair. "You wouldn't have come, if I had."

I took a step forward. They stirred, reacting to me like fireflies to the light.

"It ended the way it did. We are not here to sort that out. This isn't about the past."

The sun broke in through the huge windows. It filled the halls and rooms, setting the dust on fire as the cobwebs sparkled in the corners.

"Then say it," Filip said. "We've come all this way. So say it. Just once."

They were listening now.

"I have things to be sorry for," I said, looking at Filip. "But not when it comes to you. Not when it comes to Spellbinder. Because," I said as they parted to let me through, "I ran it to the ground. I was reckless. I thought that was our only chance. I still do."

I stopped, right in the center. If they were a mob, I was in the worst possible place.

My hands were still shaking. I was sweating. I think they could tell. I hoped for an arm to reach out and carry me, but that didn't happen.

I remembered the room, the one with the blood on the carpet, and how that final nudge from Sean had pushed me across the ledge, how the news of Calvin's death had unplugged my brain and caused a short circuit I'd carry with me for life.

We'd always pitched together. We'd always owned the room. When he left Spellbinder, the room had owned me. My improvisations had turned into incoherent rambles, my laser sharp concepts into something blurred with potential, at best.

I looked at the wall with the worn curtain.

But now, we were pitching together.

From the corner of my eye, I saw Skye smoking again, watching me with her head slightly leaned back. She wouldn't come to my rescue. Not this time.

I faced the Spellbinders.

"We were great, weren't we?"

I saw a few smiles now.

"No one was as great as Calvin."

Yes. A few sighs. Tina's daughter, five years old, asking her with a whisper, "Who's Calvin?" And Tina, hushing him and saying, "I'll tell you later. But he was a great guy."

"You know," I said. "I never thanked you. For all the years we had together, for all the great games we made. But when Calvin left, there were no options left but the risky ones. I'm sorry for that. If I was the reason he left, then actually, I am sorry."

I let that one sink in, an image of a place wild and beautiful. And when the prince died, it burned to the ground by its own ambition and its inhabitants scattered with the ashes.

"Oh, come on," Yasmine said.

They all looked at her now.

"We're not here for a sermon," she said. "Of course we fucking know you're sorry, you fucking should be, you ran this shit to the ground. You got us unemployed, you selfish fuck. I don't know about the rest of you idiots," and she waved to the lot with a grim look, "no disrespect, I love you all, but I haven't agreed to anything. I came to hear you say something, anything, and it was worth the flight ticket alone which you paid so no loss, but I'm also here to give some goddam respect to Calvin, if nothing else, to just tell you all how much I miss his sorry ass. But if you're expecting me to quit my gig at Ubi to make another game with you, if that's why we're here, to bring back the studio again, you're fucking insane, with this staged excuse for a non-apology. How hard can it be to just say you're sorry for being such a dick?"

"I'm sorry for being such a dick," I said.

"I knew you were gonna say that. And you know what? It doesn't mean fuck to us, Elliot. My flight's leaving for Montreal tonight, so you got the afternoon to talk us into doing this with you, whatever this is, or we're fucking leaving and if I never see you again, it won't hurt."

I caught Skye's eyes. She moved a few steps closer to the crates.

"Just give me a reason, Elliot, just tell me why the fuck should I care or trust you ever again, you got my attention and now you got about one minute left of it, so go."

"Turn around," I said and made a spinning gesture with my hand, and they all did as a loud bang echoed through the halls. Skye had kicked backwards on the crate's front lid. It swung open and hit the floor, revealing its contents with a whirl of dust. The shadows wouldn't quite show the details.

"You're gonna have to move closer," I said.

And the Spellbinders did, as Skye chimed in, "And take a good look. These are your workstations, tailored and optimized for every single one of you. Including your Tempur pillow for your hairy ass, Yasmine, and that damn glass table with a backlight you always went on about. Maybe it'll shut you up until lunch. As for the rest of you ..." Skye turned around and looked into the gloomy crate, at the computers, screens, and customized furniture and assets. "Yeah, we got you covered. Obviously, computers and screens are state of the art. But there's a set of pipes for you, Filip. A vintage groove box for you, Jennie. A triple double console tier for you, Joakim."

"Why the fuck did you always have to use three consoles, anyway?" Ellie shouted from the crowd, and laughter broke through as Joakim said, "Because my code's three times as good."

"This is your slice of home as you once knew it," Skye said. "The kind of shit your employer won't ever know you loved."

"That's cool," Yasmine said. "Points for timing. You got something still. But we're not gonna stay because you bought us pillows and snacks."

"Depends on what kind of snacks," Helene said and got a round of laughs.

While Skye had taken the stage, I'd moved to the wall with the big curtain. I held a thin rope in my hand now, one that was tied to the top of the cloth.

Skye turned to me.

"Should I?" I said.

"You should," she said.

I pulled the rope.

The curtain dropped and revealed a massive explosion of art, sketches, and drawings—maps and monsters, places and items and houses and forests, all the work we'd done on the game since the dawn of time. Calvin's art taped, pasted, and arranged like a mosaic built through decades to the size of a castle, with the occasional note or appendix done by me. But where there'd once been a collection of whimsical ideas that didn't make any sense, I mean, they didn't have to, there was now something else. If you moved back, you could see it. All the pieces, old and new, coherent. For the first time ever.

There were a few impressed curses, some ooohs and aaahs, and gasping and momentary pauses of breathing, when even the Spellbinder kids put their consoles and tablets away and looked at the damn thing as it filled the studio with a presence divine. It was a piece of art, a collection of visuals, a journey through time and a map to something great. It was something else.

I turned to face them all. I put my hands together, not entirely unlike the preacher I'd been accused of resembling.

"Get your Jolt Colas ready," I said. "We're about to kickstart the greatest hackathon of all."

Chapter 33

THERE SHE WAS

"What's a hackathon?" Calvin said, his mouth stuffed with popcorn. "Can you eat it?"

"It's like a marathon," Sara said. "Only you make a game instead."

"But w-what's a mar—" And as the popcorn kept flying from his mouth like rapid fire from a submachine gun, Sara cut him short with a sigh.

"It's like a really long run. You run for hours and hours, until you're done."

"How long's long?" I said. "Couple of miles?"

"Ten million miles?" Calvin said.

"That's long," I said and Calvin nodded slowly at the truth of this.

Sara reached for the candy bowl and found some chocolate. "My dad's ran a few marathons," she said, munching away. "He's exhausted when he's done. But he seems happy. Content, you know."

I looked at Calvin. He looked at me. Happy and content after running for hours? Made no sense. And what did this have to do with video games, anyway?

"But we're talking about a hackathon now," she said. "You're missing the point. You always do. That's your thing, isn't it? Point's right there. Whoa, you missed it."

We were in her cottage again, door and windows open to let the sun and the wind travel through the room. The curtains waved in the breeze as it gently played with the paper mosaic we'd created on the floor, Calvin's art and my notes spread out like a map.

"I read about it here," Sara said and showed us a magazine, none of them British or American ones where we hardly understood a word and that she kept in droves in boxes, but an actual local Swedish paper about computers and video games. But she pulled it away and waved her arms.

"It's a thing you do," she said. "You get together, a bunch of people, and you work on your game until it's done. You don't leave the house, you don't take breaks, you only sleep if you have to. You work and work. For days, not hours. So it's like a marathon, but you make games instead."

We were both eating popcorn now, sitting in the sofa and looking at her.

"But why the hack?" I said.

"Y-yeah," Calvin said. "Why isn't it called a g-gamethon or a videothon or I don't know?"

"Again with the point you're missing."

"It sounds awesome," I said and Calvin nodded with his trademark head bounce. "So we can finish our game in just a few days, then."

"Yeah, I mean," Calvin said and pointed at the art on the floor, "it's all there. We just put it together and we're done."

"You speak the truth, brother," I said and reached for the chocolate. "It's more or less a wrap."

"Mum makes wraps for lunch sometimes," Calvin said. "They're really good."

Sara sat down on the floor, crossed her legs, and rested her chin in her hand as Calvin and I kept trading remarks on our excellence while eating snacks and juggling candy. She let us be for a while and then she said, "You have no idea how to make a game, do you?"

Calvin stopped chewing, his hand in the popcorn bowl.

Sara turned to me. So did he, loudly swallowing his last batch of snacks.

I was smiling, my hand hovering between the sugar-coated raspberry jellies and the raw salt licorice. Man, all these choices. I had to take my sweet little time to make up my mind here. One simply couldn't mix raspberry jellies with the black salt. It would have to be one or the other. But not both, not at the same time.

"You don't know either, do you, Elliot?" Sara said.

"Pfftehe," I said. And went for the popcorn.

Not my finest moment, but a necessary one, because it was time to accept the bleeding truth that I had absolutely no idea what I was doing. Now, the rest of the world was on to me.

But that was fine. I was still a kid and we all still were, and the idea of doing something real for a purpose beyond the moment felt so strange, so unreal, that I froze in that split second and couldn't go any further. But it seemed Sara was already on her way and maybe had been for years and for Calvin, just sitting down and doing it, was enough of a reason to do it. The sitting down was all, so to speak. They always seemed so peaceful, even when they were on fire.

Sara laughed. "It's okay, guys. Don't worry, as I said, missing the point's kind of your thing, so I saw this coming and I've recruited...hey, spectacular timing!"

Those last words she spoke over our shoulders to someone behind us, and this someone said:

"Hey, Skye. Sorry I'm late. Chain broke on my bike, I had to walk the last mile."

"No worries. It's like I thought. Elliot and Calvin have no idea what they're doing but come on in and we'll get started."

Calvin and I turned around.

And there she was. Smiling at us, stretching out her hand to say hello, her hair cut short and, what little there was left, tied into a pony tail. Despite the warm day, she wore jeans and sneakers, a t-shirt, and a blue fleece to cover the arms. She was never one to embrace the summer, as I've mentioned before.

"Hey, guys'," she said. "I'm Lisa. Skye figured I could help. I've done a few games on my Spectrum. And Mum's Commodore."

"And some stuff on some other crap systems too, right?" Sara said.

"Yes," Lisa said and laughed. "Don't mention the Vic 20. I think Mum's collecting bad processors to test me. So Skye tells me you've got this cool idea for a game."

We gaped at Lisa. We looked like hamsters with popcorn stuffed in our cheeks, as red in our faces as the raspberry candies in the bowl.

A girl. Who knew code. As in machine language code. We were still coming to terms with Sara's double agent moves within the Fjellhamn teenage community, but this was just too much.

"Bloorhe," Calvin said.

And me, I went for the classic: "Pfftehe."

"Don't worry," Sara said to Lisa, who looked amused and confused at the same time. "Once they start talking again, you'll learn to like them."

Chapter 34

THE TIME

I'd like to think that this was Spellbinder Software's first real meeting as a studio.

Sure, we were still kids.

And yeah, we had no idea what we were doing, and certainly not a perception that we were actually doing real work. So I don't know, meeting and studio are perhaps two words that make more sense as an afterthought, rather than to describe what was actually going on.

But as Lisa sat down on the floor next to us, and Sara fired up a game on the toaster computer, the day slowly burned down to a fading twilight and the air got cooler. There was a vibe in the room, a blend of sights that scared me and made me feel amazing at the same time, because while they were all so alien, they felt like something I'd yearned for without daring to admit it.

We were immersed in pixels and chip tunes as the shadows from the trees reached over the lawn. I had moments when I lost my breath or felt my tongue go dry. It should've been painful, or at the very least uncomfortable, but it wasn't, or at least not compared to any pain or discomfort that I'd had before. Even after I'd met Calvin, the haunts from my home were always present in my mind somewhere, sometimes like a vague itch, like a mosquito bite you could ignore but not forget and sometimes with full force, as a gut-wrenching stab in the belly. But now, I realized that it was completely gone. Not for long, but still. When those notions of the whispers through the wall returned and the images of a ghost-like shape that drifted through our rooms came with the dark, it felt more like the aftermath of a wound that was hardly ever there. Whatever the haunt was, it couldn't reach me now.

"We gotta get an idea of what's good and bad," Sara said. "A reference to what our game's gonna be."

"B-but we already know that," Calvin said. "Look." And he pointed to the concepts on the floor. "It's all there."

"Have you played every game ever made?"

"Nah...well, I mean...who has?"

"I think I might've," Lisa said and laughed.

"Yeah, you should see her basement," Sara said. "You think this is cool? Wait till you see her lair."

"I think this is pretty cool," Lisa said and pointed to all the artwork.

Calvin turned to her and said something, though the words came out as a mixture of vowels and sea gull cries, but Lisa had already gone for the controller next to Sara, as a game with a green, furry ball unraveled on the screen, a spherical being that tried to bring color back to the world where there was none left. There was also a cat around to help, if that made sense. It did for us, at the time. It still does to me.

So we played that game, passing around the controllers to take turns, and then Sara said, "Enough with the wizballs, it's time for the ninjas," and pulled out the cassette player hooked up to the computer.

"I got this one on disc as well," she said. "But I love the slow loading of the tape version. For the music. Ben Daglish wrote it, with Anthony Lees."

"I prefer Whittaker," Lisa said.

"We gotta have music in our game, okay? It can't be great without great music."

We sat back as the screen turned light blue when she put in the tape and pressed play, and then a strobing square appeared in the middle as patterns flashed around it and an oriental theme played from the television speakers, a slow and haunting composition that had a story of its own. As it unraveled, we were with the ninja in a wasteland of sorts, a solitude landscape where a white bird flew across the screen, over a shallow river with black rocks. The ninja had to cross these waters, or he'd never find his way to the vengeance that had set him on his path.

"It's kind of stupid that he can't swim," Lisa said.

Sara moaned. "Here she goes again," she said.

I turned to Lisa. "He can't?"

"Why does he have to jump on rocks to get across? Why can't he dive in and swim?"

"Ninjas can run on water," Calvin said, matter of factly. "Just run, Sara, you'll be okay."

"It doesn't work like that," she said. "It's the rules of the game."

"A ninja who dies by falling off a rock?" I said. "This guy's killed samurais and dragons, but he trips on a rock and falls into a river and goes 'Aaaw, man.'"

Lisa laughed. "Not much of a ninja, is he?"

But the game was awesome anyway, and as Sara showed the way through wilderness and palace gardens, her dad appeared with provisions on our journey, refills on popcorn and drinks, cheese doodles and chocolate, congratulating us on taking our shoes off. That was the rule in the Skye estate.

"This is a no shoes area," he said. "Leave your smelly shoes outside. If you're gonna work on your game, you're doing it with your feet bare from the sole of a shoe. Make that a rule. Shoes off."

"No one's wearing shoes, Dad," Sara said. "Just put the snacks there and go."

"I'm just saying. Dig in, kids. Don't stay up too late. Shoes off."

Sara rolled her eyes, making a show about how embarrassed she was about her father. But he gave her a quick smile before she left and she returned it from the corner of her lips.

I looked at Calvin, who laughed so hard he was crying when Sara was spinning a red car out of control from that Californian road she was driving on, right smack into the water by the beach. She threw the control on the floor with a loud cry and said the game sucked anyway. I'd known her all my life, and then I'd not known her for years, and on this evening it seemed those years had never happened and we were still five years old, our mums and dads having coffee in the shade and laughing at bad jokes while we were playing in the pool. Now, she'd been seen with us. She'd never get away with that. The girls in school would rip her apart.

And Lisa, who I'd hardly said a word to yet, who I'd never met before. She couldn't be from here. Wherever her bike ride had started, it hadn't been in Fjellhamn. But she stirred up this odd blend of known and unknown things whenever we exchanged a glance, however brief it was. Even if one of those moments only lasted for less than a second, they felt shielded from whatever else was going on, as if no one saw us and could ever know what we'd been up to while we were away. Calvin's shouts and Sara's cries were a distant echo and then they brought me back, into the room that would become the Spellbinder studio and far away from my home.

Lisa had this way of moving about, like she'd always been around, and when she threw the controller to me and said we should blast some space action monsters together before the sun got up, I looked out and saw that it was dark now. The air was cooler, the heat had drifted. I took the controller, slid down from the couch, and sat next to her. There was a buzz in my stomach that made me think of the years when I could still sleep between Mum and Dad, on nights when the rain fell hard and the thunder boomed over the sea, or our long Sunday breakfasts on the porch when Mum made pancakes and Dad did his freshly squeezed orange juice. I used to sit there in the parasol shade and watch them as they exchanged kisses, unaware that life could be different, that being in a good place didn't mean so much until you'd been in a bad one.

And Mum's lullaby, the one she sang to me about the boy who wandered, when the world seemed so big and I couldn't sleep. She'd stroke my hair and her voice was soft.

Tonight, there was a remaining rim on the horizon, a shade of blue that hovered over the Fjellhamn sea and kept the pitch black away. I realized I hadn't called home and told Dad where I was.

I turned to Lisa. "What time is it?"

She leaned closer. "Does it matter, Elliot?"

She smelled good.

I guess it didn't.

Chapter 35

THE HACKATHON

We opened up the windows, the ones we could reach, and Filip went to look for a ladder to get to those that we couldn't.

"You won't find one," I said. "There's just us and our stuff here."

"There's always a ladder somewhere," Filip said and stroked his bald head.

The afternoon sun had shifted its light to a colder glow, away from the typically intense glare of the Swedish summer, as the Spellbinders pulled out their gear from the carts and began to assemble their workstations around the wall.

It's not like my sermon had talked them into it. They hadn't agreed to anything, really. But they all knew they didn't bring luggage and kids just to watch me pitch, preach, or beg. I'd been vague enough yet precise where it counted, to let them know that it'd be worth a few days, at least. And now, here they were, and as Oscar had put it before, they snapped out of their awe of the wall—it's not like they had better plans. It's not like they weren't expecting *something*.

A vibrant noise filled the studio, like those birds in the spring that had just come home. Skye moved around and took notes on things missing and requests added, dismissed a few, laughed at most, and handed out hugs and kisses as the idea of seeing them all overwhelmed her. As those who'd acquired little ones over the years unleashed their toddlers and babies, their boys and girls, and the place was as much a playground for kids among wires and discs as it was a lair where we'd build a game, it seemed to dawn on the Spellbinders that it'd been a long time since most of them had seen each other. There were a few silent hugs but a lot of loud laughs, and as the assembling of the workstations emerged into people talking, touching, and crying, the work blended into something so emotional that teenagers would've told us to grow up and get real (or maybe the other way around).

Skye looked at the crowd, her arms folded.

"You didn't really expect them to get anything done, did you?" she said.

"I'm surprised they even showed up," I said.

"No, you're not."

I shoved my hands into my pockets and shrugged.

"Why do you always do that?"

"What? This?" I shrugged my shoulders again.

"No, that other thing. That backing away thing."

"I don't...I am?"

"You're like literally moving away an inch or two. Why do you do that? You've got nothing to worry about. I wouldn't be here if I didn't believe you were on to something. It's not charity, you know."

"Where did that come from?"

"I don't know."

"I trust myself. It's the rest of the world I don't trust."

"Hah. Good point."

"I don't always miss the point, do I?"

There was a spark in her green eyes and she quickly leaned forward and kissed me on the cheek.

"That's what happens when you don't back away," she said.

It was just a friendly thing, but I felt dizzy all the same. I think she had more to say, but before she got the chance, I turned to the crowd and clapped my hands, partly because it was time but also because I'm not sure where that move had come from. Now wasn't the time to find out.

They stopped buzzing and looked at me, like they had throughout the years whenever a new week started at Spellbinder Software. It already felt familiar, like our groove was back after just a few hours.

"Here are the hackathon rules," I said.

I paused.

Then:

"You can work in any constellation you like. Alone, or with others. Though good luck finding someone that wants to team with you, Filip."

Everybody laughed at this, as Filip nodded. "In the end, you will all ask for my help," he said. "Like you always do."

"Right," I said. "You can break it up and mix it around, tear down and rebuild. Do your own thing today, join forces tomorrow, split up by Sunday. It's up to you. As long as it's clear who's submitting what game when we're done, we don't care how you got there. You'll find that all software you need is installed on your workstations, as well as a bunch of assets to get you started. Just plug them in, download the package, and you're good to go. Deadline's at Sunday lunch. However...however..."

"You and your however," Bjorn called out. "You always say however."

"He's gonna go for 'Anyway' soon," Cecilia said.

"Maybe he meant whoever," Yasmine said. Laughter again.

I turned to Skye. "Should we tell 'em?"

"I don't know." She scanned the room. "Hey, Joakim. Angela. What do you think?"

Joakim had his enigmatic smile now, but he didn't say anything. Just the fact that he was smiling was comforting, though.

"Nah," Angela said. "I wanna see their faces."

I looked at the Spellbinders again, amused at their confusion when we'd exposed two of their own as part of the plan. A few of them had already fired up their workstations. They stared at their screens as the download commenced. Those who'd engaged in hugfest instead of work gathered around the others' stations.

The studio went silent, the air charged with electricity and the processor vents singing their own hymn.

Eric was the first one to see it, the first one to say it. His eyes grew wider.

"Holy fuck," he said. "You didn't."

"Of course we did," Skye said. "We did, didn't we, guys?"

"Seems like we did," Joakim said quietly. Angela laughed.

It took a few seconds for the rest of them to catch up, hypnotized by a few names and tags on a bunch of files that poured over the screen and regrouped into their place.

"You're in on this?" Yasmine called out to Joakim and Angela. "You did this? With Skye and Elliot?"

Joakim was about to answer but no one really cared. They'd all shifted into gear and grabbed their tables, already merging into teams and hooking up the cables that were still unplugged. Many of them said over the screens that there's no way this is ever gonna work, it's a waste of time to even try, it's just for the week, you can't build a game in a few days (at least not one so great at this one!), but then Bjorn shouted loud enough for all to hear, "Who gives a fuck?," and it was almost a cheer, a call to arms for a waste of time that'd you'd never be able to repeat, an outcome so impossible to predict that taking a trip to the sun was more likely to end well.

Chapter 36

THE KIDS

Afternoon became evening. We hadn't installed proper lighting in the studio and the rooftop bulbs were long broken and out of reach. When the shadows grew longer, the teams positioned their desk lamps to make the place as cozy as possible. The workspace became a pool of light in a growing matter of darkness, the soft and yellow mixing with the electric pale from our screens.

And the kids. I was most impressed by them. Once they'd realized they all liked candy, they became best friends and built a fortress with everyone's jackets and bags. Skye played monster with them for a while, until the youngest ones got scared and cried. I wasn't sure whose child was whose, although some of them wore obvious tell-tale signs that made it easier to guess.

But it didn't seem to matter, because when the Spellbinders dug into the art and code resurrected from our studio's glory days, and now refined by Joakim and Angela to work with today's reality, they were equally comfortable taking breaks to handle the kids. It came so easy for them to comfort a girl who'd tripped on her laces or play peek-a-boo with a boy hiding behind the jackets. And yet, their focus was of a quality I'd never seen at the time when we had nothing but time but felt time was the only thing of which we didn't have enough, despite the fact that all we engaged in now was a silly hackathon. Arguably, the greatest hackathon of all, but still just a hackathon. But they went at it like the seasoned pros they were and it didn't take long until strange and wonderful things emerged on the screens.

I saw space ships on fire from *Clear Blue Skies*, our first space shooter, over at Yasmine's team. I remember Calvin's first sketch of those. He made them when everyone was sleeping but us. We'd been on a porch, as the late August sun rose over Fjellhamn.

I heard a string orchestra play the familiar tune of *Fisherman's Fiend*, our only attempt to make an adventure game and the only *Spellbinder* game that hadn't done so well. Sean had sent flowers to our studio after the reviews came in.

At Benjamin's desk, there was that roaring beast from *A Dragon's Egg*. He'd already blended that with those pink, fluffy furballs Calvin had molded and Skye smeared with wine while we were drunk in Tokyo after a meeting with Square Enix at their own café.

Angela's guys were panning a camera around the sad, old man on the grassy hill. I heard her say they wouldn't be using music at all, just pull the sound effects from that library with all the sea and forest effects she'd always liked, and that she wanted to use Calvin's pastel textures for the skies.

That man had never appeared in any of our games. He'd just been one of those favorite assets that never found a place. Now, he was here again and perhaps this time, he'd find a home.

"It's the kids," Skye said. She was standing beside me now, outside the pool of light, looking at the teams. "They make you focus."

"How's that possible?" I said.

"You're forced to get your priorities straight."

I looked down on the floor, the old boards, the cracks and crevasses of worn oak. I felt Skye's hand on my shoulder, a light touch.

"Hey, Elliot," someone called. I looked up. It was Benjamin. He waved at me. "We need your eye on something."

Skye smiled. I smiled back. As new as all of this was, it was also so familiar that I couldn't even make a big deal out of it. Like a thousand times before, someone called for help and advice, to point out the direction through some kind of storm they'd whipped up for no apparent reason, and all I did was look at something and drop a few lines, and things would clear up. When I walked over to Benjamin and his group, passing by the clusters of developers and artists, I picked up that stride that I'd always had when I was on my way to something, somewhere. As a few of the others tried to catch me on my way, asking if I could drop by their desks when I had the time, I was right in the middle of it again, the very shape of that eye in the storm. Someone had to know the map by heart, the hidden steps on the path through the dark, a way to bind those spells together.

They wouldn't forgive me just because Skye and I, with Joakim's and Angela's help, had put together and updated a bunch of files from Spellbinder's time of legendary awesome. Even if you'd claim this hackathon was twenty years in the making, an impossible and unique opportunity because of the decades long dry run that went before it, it wouldn't matter. Now, we were here to make a game again, not any game but the *Greatest Game of All*, and if there was something we'd always known how to do, it was to make fucking awesome games. We'd been practicing for this one since we were young.

Soon, I was moving between the teams like a tornado, killing features, providing direction, and tweaking mechanics. If any producer from any publisher had been here to see how fast things were growing from nothing to something, from something to playable, they'd believe the whole thing was staged. Not sure how, but some kind of smoke and mirrors would've been involved to fool them into signing the damn deal and commit to a market strategy. Maybe our kind of recycling was cheating, or it was just us reaping the benefits of having perfected our craft over a lifetime's worth.

Not that the kids cared. Benjamin's daughter tugged at his arm and brought our priorities down to earth.

"Hey, honey," he said. "You okay? Here, look what your dad's been working—"

"I'm hungry," she said. "And Julian, too. I think all my friends are hungry."

Benjamin looked at her, at the other kids, and then at his watch. Some of the others stopped working and did the same.

"Geez," he said. "We gotta feed the offspring."

"We gotta feed you all," Skye said.

"Let's go to Nonna's!" I cried, and everybody cheered and bounced up from their chairs so fast that a few things crashed onto the floor.

"Elliot's paying!" Bjorn shouted, and everybody cheered even more, though nothing went boom this time, and they all reached for their jackets, swung up their children on their shoulders and went through the door and down the stairs and out into the blue summer evening.

Chapter 37

NONNA

We were a caravan of untidy developers and their children as we crossed the Stockholm streets to the restaurant that had sustained our crunches through the years. We drenched any noise from the cluster of party animals that roamed our turf, with our laughs and jokes that you'd have to be a Spellbinder to appreciate. When we arrived, as unlikely as it seemed, the grand table that always used to be ours was free tonight, all the other guests were spread out in the corners and by the windows, and we entered the place with such a bang that they wondered if they'd ended up at a private party and should leave before things got awkward. I was about to ask Skye if she'd done this, if she'd called and said we were coming, but decided not to. But she didn't seem surprised, and she had that quirky smile on her lips.

As if this wasn't enough—and you're gonna think I'm making this up, that I'm spinning a yarn just because I can because that's what I do—Nonna was there. Older and a bit frail, as her son had said, but she was there and she welcomed us with open arms.

"Where have you been?" she said with her thick accent, smacking those consonants like meat on a bench. "I've had the table ready for you, for so long."

"Now c'mon," Skye said over all the Spellbinder ratcheting. "It's only been a few years. I'm sure you've not had the time to miss us."

"I'll make you your favorite. And you brought your children. Time has passed, I see."

For a moment, she seemed thoughtful as she scanned us all. When she met my eyes, she nodded slowly, with a faint smile.

"Yeah," I said. "We miss him, too."

Nonna took my hands and squeezed them. "Nevertheless," she said, "as long as you are still here, you must eat."

"That, we must," Skye said. "Bring it, mama."

Nonna turned her gentle smile to the kitchen and shouted at her boys to whip it up or find a new job. That pasta wasn't gonna cook itself, though given their sense of quality—or lack thereof, maybe it'd be better if it did. When the waiters brought the wine and the gathering picked up in volume and spirits, I still felt the warm pressure from Nonna's hands and that growing hole in my stomach, that pain that expanded and pulled to the beat of my heart.

I knew it'd be back, stronger than ever, on this night.

I sat there for a while, knowing that if I got up, things would get a lot more difficult from here on.

You'd think getting the Spellbinders here and talking them into making a game again, even if it was just for a few days, wasn't hard enough.

So I got up.

But I felt a hand on my arm.

Skye was standing next to me now.

"Not tonight, Elliot," she said. "She can wait."

"They all wanna see her."

Skye leaned closer. "They're not here for Calvin, Elliot. Don't you see that?" Her green eyes glowed in the dim restaurant light. "Sit down, honey. Enjoy the food and the wine, and the people around you. We'll go back to the studio after midnight and crunch on the game again, okay?"

"I won't be long."

"You always say that."

She pushed me gently back into my seat. Benjamin, sitting next to me, was engaged in a conversation with Erik and Filip about the merits of story versus gameplay, waving around his glass of wine like a gardener wielded his water hose. When he saw me drop back to my place, he put his right arm around me and gestured towards the two gents.

"I know you got an opinion here, Elliot, join in and give me some love, I'm being thrashed." His breath was sweet from the wine, his eyes already a bit glazed. He never could handle more than a glass or two.

I looked at Skye, who shrugged and laughed quietly. She let her hand linger and as Benjamin insisted, she moved back to her place in the couch between Yasmine and Oscar, who were already sitting too close to each other anyway, their thing always a thing, apparently still ongoing as well.

I looked around at our people by the grand table as they got louder and warmer, switching places, moving around, helping each other to bread and wine as we waited for the food. Even the branches of the old olive tree stirred as we took it up a notch when Angela spontaneously rose her glass to Calvin, and we all cheered and applauded. I forgot about that hole in my stomach and when I remembered it again and it came back, it felt easier to let it go, to accept that it was there but couldn't do me any harm, at least not now. I dived into the debate with Benjamin on the one side and Erik and Filip on the other, slamming my hand on the table and saying: "You know *Metroid Prime* told an entire story just through its menus. The opening sequence? The helmet visor? Don't argue with me, you know I'm right."

"Oh, man," Erik shouted. "He's going for his *Metroid* references."

"I'm out," Filip said. "I can't argue story with a guy who's never played the *Last of Us*."

We laughed and changed the subject as Nonna's sons arrived with the food, setting the table with cold cuts and pasta, and we talked about the point of owning an original NES or getting the Classic Mini edition, if you could find one, or maybe we talked about the merits of Sonic against Mario and what Mark Cerny was up to these days anyway. But I caught Skye's eyes over the table and there was that hesitant smile from her again, the one I'd seen from across the street when I was in a diner once. She'd bought a cartridge for her Atari. It was faint, cautious, with no promise attached. But a smile, all the same.

Chapter 38

THE FARTHEST SHORES

If the Stockholm summers were a hypnotic whirl of blinding lights and warm showers, where people danced and drank through the nights, then Fjellhamn's darkest hours were like the calm you'd only find at the farthest shores of the west, just before dawn, when the skies warmed up to a lighter blue. You didn't know silence until you'd been to such a place.

When midnight approached, Dan showed up and asked if anyone was staying over and if we wanted another snack. Stuffed with popcorn and chocolate, Calvin and I had agreed that we would never eat again, that it'd make Cornelia really mad but we'd just have to deal with it, back-to-back, *Double Dragon* style. And yet, we did consider Dan's offer of a bologna sandwich with cheese and tomato and a few slices of cheddar on the side, because if we'd never eat again, then perhaps we should make our last meal a worthy one.

"But nah," Calvin said. "Thanks, Sara's dad. I think we might get sick if we eat more."

Dan yawned. "You're probably right. It's getting late. Should I call your parents, like a responsible parent, or just keep feeding you candy?"

"No one's calling anyone," Sara said over her shoulder. "We're gonna stay up and beat the sun to it." She was preparing the Commodore's cassette player with some kind of two-dimensional space shooter that apparently did parallax scrolling. (Delta, if you're obsessed with details, and if you really wanna know, Sara had a poster of Stavros Fasoulas in her bedroom.) We had no idea what a parallax was but we loved it already and as we grew older, Calvin always referred to this evening as the night on where he was introduced to the most glorious and beautiful way to create motion and depth in games ever invented. The parallax movements he made throughout the years after that were the best ones ever seen in games.

While Lisa explained the mathematics behind this technique to us, drawing charts and jotting down algorithms, Dan withdrew into the summer night with a slight smile.

So we passed the ghostly hour and went into the quiet space where the world drifted through the silence of a sleeping town. The Spellbinder studio was the only bright light in a garden that stretched into the shadows. We worked our way through tape after tape, disc after disc, crossing oceans on a dragon's back and competing in international karate contests. But eventually, Sara faded out and kept the controllers to herself, mumbling that she wanted to finish that ninja game now.

"She does that," Lisa said, "when she's tired of people."

I looked for Calvin, who'd been quiet for a while. He was sleeping on the couch. Loudly, though. I'd mistaken his snoring for a troll's roar in the last game we played.

"I should go," Lisa said. "I need to get home. It's not even late. It's just really early."

"But your bike's broken," I said.

"I'll grab a morning bus." She smiled to me. "Wanna walk me to town?"

Chapter 39

THE LONG WALK HOME

We slipped out, leaving Sara with her quest for martial vengeance and Calvin on the couch. The cool air energized me, like I'd taken a level ten restoration potion. I guess that's what walking next to a girl and almost holding her hand did to a boy.

We passed the dense tree alleys that led to the old asphalt road. Lisa would grab the morning bus from Fjellhamn's center and her mum would pick up her broken bike later. This, and much else, she talked about as we came to the beaten road between the rocks to the old fisher town. I didn't say much, partly because there wasn't much room for my words between Lisa's breaths, but also because I had no idea how to talk to girls. After Sara, there'd been no females in my life, only mothers, which all seemed troubled one way or another, so whatever practice most boys had had up until the age of twelve, I was way behind. But that feeling from Sara's house remained, that discomfort that still felt so right, that I was being slowly pulled out of my skin but kind of liked the idea that I had no power to resist. Or perhaps no will to summon that power.

And anyway, Lisa was a talker, so she didn't seem to mind. In fact, many years later, when we came back to this morning and about the stuff that happened next, she always said she found my silence comforting, as if I knew what was coming and took the time to find some calm in her voice.

That much was true. I did find a calm in listening to her, almost feeling her hand against mine, a subtle and different scent that wrapped itself around me and made me feel like everything was good in the world. If there was danger here, it was of the kind I'd felt when Calvin and I had gone up against Lars. Maybe this would be the end of me. But it'd be one hell of a way to go.

She bubbled with ideas and thoughts, jokes and reflections; she cycled through laughter and outcries, bursts and slowdowns, faster than anyone I'd ever met. In fact, most of what she was were versions of people I'd never met, if you know what I mean. She was thirteen (practically a grown woman!) and lived in Skaresund, which explained why I'd never seen her before, though I had this fantasy now that I'd passed her many times on my bike excursions across the hills or bus journeys. She'd known Skye for years. Skye's dad and Lisa's mum worked together and they'd become close as Skye's mum had died. "But not that kind of close!" Lisa said and laughed, "I mean, sure, my mum's divorced and all, but it's not a thing, they're just friends," and I didn't quite get what she meant, though I figured it had something to do with stuff. To Lisa, Sara had always been Skye. As strange as it was for Calvin and me to hear someone call Sara by another name, as weird was it for Lisa to call her Sara.

"Her mum was sick when we started hanging out, and she always called her Skye. I love that name. It's so beautiful. Don't you think? I don't mean to probe, but how come you stopped being friends? It's cool that you're back together, but she told me you used to be the best."

"We're not back together," I said. "We're making a game. There's a difference."

Lisa laughed again. "There is?"

"It should be."

"You're a moody one, aren't you? You feel old. A lot older than me. And I'm older than you. How does that make sense? It's difficult to be different around here. It's easier in a big city. Stockholm, maybe. Let's just say where I live, and I know you've been to Skaresund so I know you know what I'm talking about, there aren't a lot of kids into wiring their own computers."

"Yeah, Fjellhamn's not exactly crowded with video game clubs."

"They used to make fun of me, hit me and stuff. They threw my clothes in the water after gym class, cut up my tires, that kind of thing. Called me shit, as well. Real ugly shit."

She said it so casually, as if she'd just commented on a flavor of ice cream or the color of a shirt, that it took me a few seconds to pick it up. The idea that Lisa was anything other than the queen of her domain seemed so unlikely that I had no idea what to say or feel about this. She'd appeared indestructible and even now, when she opened up this new door, I didn't believe it.

But she was quiet now.

We kept walking. If I didn't say something, we'd be listening to crickets all the way to the bus station.

"But...you're so...uh..."

"Oh, he speaks. I'm so what, Elliot?"

"I just didn't think...I don't know."

"I'll tell you what I know. What unites all idiots across the world, Elliot?"

I shrugged.

"They're all idiots," she said.

Now I smiled.

"Yeah," she said. "Reason don't apply. They don't pick their targets based on looks or status. They just pick one. And then they find a reason."

"Some are more obvious than others, though." I thought of all the things I'd been called through the years. I certainly offered a few of the classic strikes for the conservative bully.

Lisa stopped. She took my arm and forced me to turn around and look at her. All kinds of things rushed through my body as she did, I got vertigo and had to take a few quick breaths, but she didn't notice. She was all fired up now.

"There's this world of ideals," she said. "In this world, we want things to be a certain way. We should be nice to each other, not give other people shit just because we're in a bad place, don't steal or lie or hurt others. Right? That's what we're being taught. That's what it says in our books and that's what our parents say. Right?"

I remembered all the talks I'd had with the school and my dad. About their ideas on how things should be, how my classmates shouldn't be, how clear it was that their behavior wasn't okay, how we'd decided on action plans and steps moving forward, and how once these meetings were over, they'd find me on the next break, drag me behind the building, and beat me up.

I nodded. She leaned her head to the side and smiled slightly.

"Then there's this other world, the real world, the one we live in. In that world, people lie and steal, bully and fight. They don't care about the ideal world. That's just an idea. They live in the real world. That's where the rules that actually have an impact apply. Unfortunately, you and I live there, too. Unless we decide to go insane, we're stuck with the idiots. So we can either call on the ideals and say that this isn't okay as they beat the crap out of us, or we can take the fight where it's at. Not where we'd like it to be. But where it's actually at. If you wanna make something better, you gotta see the truth of it first. You gotta start the change where it's bad. You can't do that, if you can't accept that things are as they are. Besides, the kind of people that spend their time talking about ideals, they're usually not around when the real world shifts into gear. So they're just words, anyway."

She sounded like a grown-up. Her words were like something my father could've said to a client on the phone, or Sara's Dad to a jury in court.

"Where did you learn this?" I said.

"I'm gonna ask you again, Elliot. I'm so what?"

"What do you mean?"

"You said before, or tried to say, that I'm so something or other, and I said, I'm so what, Elliot? Finish that thought, if you will, please."

It just slipped out of me, then.

"You're so pretty."

She touched her hair, pulling it to the side. The sun was coming up and we were in the middle of the road, the Fjellhamn rocks surrounding us and the turn that led to the last slope around the corner.

"See?" she said. "That's the real world. You just think I'm pretty. And hearing you say so, makes me feel good."

I was nervous now and noticed that she was still holding on to my arm.

In fact, pulling me slightly closer.

Gently, not forced in any way. But still, all kinds of alarm systems went off, brain approaching meltdown.

"Sometimes," I said with a strength that surprised me, "the real world's not so bad. Despite all the shit going on." I kept looking at her as I said so.

Lisa's eyes twinkled. "See?" she said.

"What?"

"You're smiling."

"I am?"

"You are."

She pulled me close and kissed me.

Chapter 40

NOT GOOD ENOUGH

But it wasn't like before, was it?

Because when the lights faded at Nonna's and she eventually told us we had to leave—I mean, even Nonna had to close at some point—we didn't go back to the studio. The kids were sleeping and their parents were yawning like lions after a day in the sun. A few of them had dozed off in the corners and some had left early, blaming jet lag. The remaining conversations transitioned into the kind of scattered talk that was left after you'd run out of the charming nonsense that only could sustain an evening with friends.

Those with children took them in their arms, said their good nights, and carried their little ones back to the hotels. Skye and I saw them drop off, one by one. No one said anything about going back to the studio and crunch until the sun was up.

"Why would they?" she said when we were the last to leave. "We're not young anymore. Most of them have traveled far. They got kids."

We walked through Stockholm. The night was warm and the streetlights showed us the way like a string of fireflies drawn over a map. We walked by the water, past the hotel where I'd met with Sean. It'd been just the two of us on a quiet morning, and now the terrace was crowded with people dancing, patterned by the moving lights from the rooftop's party beams. The base drum thumped through the city, and we all seemed to move to its rhythm as we walked, stopped, and picked it up again. We didn't speak for a while, Skye and I, and I loved the silence she could bring, the rare comfort of saying nothing. I didn't know where we were going. We just walked.

I took a few deep breaths. The night air was also young. It had been since I was a kid and spent the summer nights on our patio, in a sleeping bag with a pillow. Dad would come out with a lantern, put it next to me, and tell me that this would burn through the night to keep the ghosts away, and he'd keep the door open if I wanted to come in. And tomorrow, if that was a good morning, we'd go for cinnamon buns down at the bakery by the cinema. When the nights were warm like this, he never asked me to come inside and sleep in my room. If heavy clouds rolled in from the sea, he'd put up a sail cloth to protect from the rain. I listened to its quiet tap on the fabric as the lantern burned beside me. These nights could be quiet like that, or they could be cut in half by a scream that sliced through glass.

As if on cue, a warm rain fell over Stockholm now. It cooled the asphalt and sprinkled the crowd, to give us all that summer glow that made us look so young. I saw a few girls take off their shoes and run bare foot from one club to the next as they laughed through the shower. Then it ended and the low murmur from distant thunder told us that we got away easy this time.

"You're so fucking frustrating sometimes," Skye said.

We were at a crossroads now, and I realized we were on our way to my place. Or at least I was. She'd lit a cigarette and looked at the traffic, scanning the streets from left to right.

I frowned. "What do you mean?"

"You know what I mean."

We walked across the street as the lights turned green, surrounded by people drunk on summer's wine, moving in herds, talking out loud and laughing about anything. I felt lost in the crowd, but back on the pavement, I picked up my stride and followed Skye who was a few steps ahead of me. I was dizzy from all the neon lights around us.

"So tomorrow we'll continue," she said, "and you'll be looking for a reason to leave."

"I'm not going anywhere."

She spun around, her cheeks and curls wet from the rain. "What's your problem, anyway?"

She was drunk. As was I, I suppose. I tried to make sense of this. I stretched out a hand.

"Don't you fucking touch me," she said.

"I wasn't gonna...Skye, what the hell?"

"I'm not good enough for you?" she shouted. "Is that it? I don't tick your boxes, whatever the fuck they are?"

"What are you talking about?"

"How can I not know your boxes, Elliot? We fucking grew up together."

"You know me."

"It's just a fucking game. All of this, it's not real. They won't stay. When Sunday comes, they'll all go home to their houses and jobs and they'll get more kids, and you know what they're not gonna do?"

"Lash out?"

"They're not gonna stick around. This is just a big, fucking closure for all of them, and then they're gone. You get that, right? You know that? You know that shitty game of yours is never gonna happen? And who wants to work with the guy who doesn't go see his best friend when he's dying? Calvin never asked about you, Elliot. He fucking knew you wouldn't show. He knew your boxes."

I'd faced that argument so many times now. At least I could look at myself in the mirror and admit to that.

"I know they're here now," I said. "I know we're not selling to Sean. I'm okay with that. I thought you were, too. Isn't that why we're here?"

She was trembling now, her fists clenched. I wondered if she was going to punch me. She'd done that once or twice before and I knew she'd do it again if she felt she had to. As loud as our argument was, we blended in with the city's nightscape, where the quiet moments before dawn were still some hours away. No one noticed, everyone cranked up their own tune, singing from balconies or tripping out from clubs.

"I can't have this conversation," she said. "I'm too drunk. Good night, Elliot. See you tomorrow."

She turned around and walked away. I followed and reached out to grab her arm and pull her back, but she brushed me aside and slipped away with a snarl. I stopped and watched her disappear into the crowd, and while the world around me was as silent or loud as it had been a few minutes ago, and as confusing as ever, it did seem like a more lonely place now.

Chapter 41

CANDLE

I walked slowly through the city, oblivious to all the people and the noise around me. My clothes were wet, like someone had wrapped a warm towel around me and then left. I didn't mind, though. I had plans. My own thing going, my journey across the hills and rocks.

I looked up. This was a more quiet part of town, with villas scattered close to a park. The beats from the summer clubs weren't exactly distant, but a few blocks away now. Even so, they were like sounds from another world, an echo that bounced between the homes of people that wanted nothing to do with whatever was going on at the other side. Their windows were dark, just a night lamp or two burning on a ledge somewhere and the gardens slowly stirring in the shadows. Some of them had signs tied to their fences, saying they were for sale.

I sat down on a bench to watch an old stone house at the other side of the small street. It was one of those early twentieth century villas, carefully restored to preserve that which some called charm and yet maintained a decent platform for modern living. It was surrounded by a small and neatly cut lawn, a black and rustic fence with a gate that hung slightly ajar.

It had been like that for years. They never got around to fixing it.

The apple trees had bloomed, the ground and the garden toys littered with flower leaves were still fresh. Maybe the rain helped the last ones to let go. There was a tricycle there, a tire swing from one of the branches, and a sandbox with the usual set of shovels and buckets.

I watched this picture for a while, trying really hard not to travel with my mind's eye to the many shores of different outcomes. Resisting it was like holding a pack of cigarettes when you'd decided to quit.

The kitchen window lit up. I saw a shadow moving on the walls of the cabinets. Then she appeared and walked up to the bench to mess with the coffee machine. She wore her pajamas and a gray beanie, and I remembered that she'd put on one of those from time to time, before going to bed, to keep the hair in place.

"Yeah, I know," she'd say to me. "It's short. But my hair goes to all kinds of places if you give it a chance. I'm not gonna put you through that."

So she'd put a beanie on and slept with it. Not always. But sometimes.

The skies were a faded blue now, with a tone of purple in the horizon. The music had decreased to a slow beat and the guests that remained were saying their goodbyes.

Lisa sat down with her coffee by the table. The place wasn't as tidy as it used to be, with piles of cutlery on the table and a few big boxes close to the sink.

She looked out the window, at something which seemed to be far away. She held her cup with both hands. She looked weary and tired. But her eyes were clear, and I imagined that I could see their shine, despite the distance. Maybe she was as strong in her grief as I pictured her to be, and maybe her gaze was fixed because she saw good things beyond the present. But how would I know? There was a street, a fence, a garden, and a house between us and she was on the other side of a window, like she and Calvin always were when I'd been around. But he'd withdrawn from our world in more ways than one, fading into someone we could only observe from the other side, content as he was with his family and his art. He had no desire to return to crunches and hackathons.

A little girl entered the kitchen. She wore a blue night gown with white stripes and she carried a brown teddy plush. She climbed up in her mother's lap and buried her face in her chest. Lisa held her and leaned her head against her daughter's and stroked her hair gently.

Isabelle trembled from time to time, as if she had a cough. She said something. Lisa smiled and reached for a candle and a set of matches, close to the window. She put the candle on the table and gave the box to Isabelle. Carefully, the girl lit a match, but the flame died. She tried again and this time, the candle caught on.

Isabelle jumped down from her mother's lap, walked up to the kitchen light and turned it off. Then she returned to Lisa's embrace again. They sat there, watching the candle, holding each other.

I could never again picture what would happen if I'd opened that gate, walked through the garden, and knocked on Calvin's door to say hello. Nor could I sustain any images of meeting with Lisa after his death. Reality had seen to that.

But there were other things to say now, new circumstances that created new options.

I took out the stick drawing of the two boys by the piers. I stood up and I took a few steps towards Lisa's house. It felt so easy.

A little boy appeared in the kitchen, wearing just a blue shirt. He was short, even for his age, with blond bangs and blue eyes. He rubbed his eyes to get the sleepy sand out. Lisa stretched out her arm and Alexander climbed up in her lap, to join his older sister.

I stopped and put the stick drawing back in my pocket. After a few moments, I turned around and left.

Chapter 42

LISA

When she called our house the next day, my heart jumped and stopped. Dad answered from the kitchen, looking a bit puzzled as he handed me the phone, but he wore a slight smile as well.

Her kiss still lingered. I'd come home just before the sun got up with nothing on my mind but that, moved around in our house with that song in my head, that everything was gonna be all right, and it didn't feel like I was crossing a mine field where the traps changed every day. It's not like it was easier to disregard it. They just weren't there.

I took the phone from Dad, pretending I was all casual about it. It was the first time a girl had ever called me, and I'm just gonna lay it out to you and say that it felt awesome. Hence the heart jumping. But my fear that I'd lose whatever this was made my head hurt. That'd be the heart stopping.

"Hey, you," she said. "Wanna hang out today?"

"Uh, sure," I said. Was that what you said? What did you say, when you were something else than what you'd been before? But what were we, anyway? I hadn't known Lisa for more than a few days. There was hardly a yesterday to talk about. What the hell did I know about girls, anyway? Nothing. Honestly, I still don't.

"So my mum's gonna drive me to Skye's and we're gonna pick up my bike," she said. "If it's still there." She laughed. "Mum said she can take the bike home, and I can take the bus whenever I feel like it. You and I can go down to the water and have an ice cream, you can show me your favorite places in Fjellhamn, the ones you and Calvin keep talking about. Or whatever, you know."

"But...maybe we should meet at Sara's place. I'll bring Calvin."

"Why?"

"Because...the game. We gotta work on the game. We're doing that hackathon thing."

Lisa laughed again. "Hackathon schmakathon. Let's do the ice cream thing first, and then go see the others, okay?"

"Okay."

"And if we're feeling good about ice cream, then we don't have to see Calvin and Skye today. We can see them tomorrow."

"But I always see Calvin."

"Sigh. See you in an hour, Elliot. I'll be at the bus station."

We hung up.

Dad was gone now, nowhere around. I was alone in the kitchen. I'm sure he was listening from somewhere, smart enough to give me space.

I felt like I was being tested and if I failed, the world would laugh at me. But as scared as I was of being caught with my ignorance, as much did I realize that this rising rush had too much in it that I didn't want to lose. Of all the things Lisa could've done today, including working on a game, she wanted to be with me. I wasn't gonna lose that just because I didn't have the spine to have ice cream with a girl.

I found a clean t-shirt, my favorite sneakers in the hallway, and those patched jeans that made worn look good (or so Cornelia had told me once and that came back to me now). I left before Dad could ask me where I was going or before Mum woke up, got on my bike, and raced through Fjellhamn before I realized I was

THE GREATEST GAME OF ALL

going to Calvin's place and not to the bus station at all. I had this urge to tell him everything and yet not tell a thing, embarrassed or scared of what he'd say. Maybe he'd get upset that he wasn't my first call today (not likely), or maybe he'd be concerned that I'd be distracted when a girl was around (possibly) but probably, he'd just be cool with it and get on with whatever stuff he was doing.

I turned the bike around and headed towards the town center, feeling more anxious by the minute. What would I do, once we met? How did you say hello after something like yesterday?

There she was, sitting on a wall, dangling her legs, wearing denim shorts, a yellow t-shirt, and sandals. She saw me, smiled, and waved. I waved back, lost my balance, and almost crashed but recovered in a very inglorious way with a bang into the wall. She smiled and jumped down.

"You okay?" she said.

"Sure, no problem." I stood up and pulled my hands through my hair. I was suddenly aware that I hadn't washed for three days.

"Yeah?" she said. "You seem weird."

"Yeah, I'm..." I took a breath. "Yes. I was just..."

"Come on, we'll get some ice cream."

We walked down the road to the water. My heart raced and my tongue was dry, but strange as it was, Lisa being quiet helped. This was another side of her, not the tornado of words and ideas I'd met before but someone who appeared comfortable with saying nothing. After a while, I slowed down and felt something like a calm approach.

"I'm sorry if I was strange yesterday," she said. "Mum says I'm too much sometimes. It was such a special situation, you know. And...I like you. But I didn't wanna make you feel bad."

"You don't know me," I said. "How can you like me?"

"What a strange thing to say." She smiled. "Careful. I might change my mind."

"No, no, I'm sorry," I said, looking at her from the side now. "It's okay."

"You sure?"

I nodded.

"I liked it," I said with a low voice, as if I'd maybe get away with it if she didn't hear me.

Lisa was still smiling, looking at the road ahead of us now.

"We don't have to get ice cream if you don't want to. We can just walk, if you like. You can show me some cool places."

"I've got Fjellhamn branded as a map in my head. I'd be a solid bank robber if Fjellhamn ever had any banks."

"I'm sure," Lisa said and laughed. "But don't use your bike as a getaway vehicle." And since that was a pretty funny thing to say, I laughed too and again I had that feeling that maybe everything was gonna be all right.

Of course, I was wrong, Mum was now awake and waiting for me at home, but how could I know? So like I said, I was with a girl and actually, everything wasn't gonna be all right, because right now, it already was.

Chapter 43

JOHAN

I'd wandered the hills of Fjellhamn alone before I met Calvin, carrying my notebooks and water bottle in my backpack. My explorations along the coast had been a temporary escape, at best. When the sun set and the shadows grew longer, I had to go home. Sometimes, that felt okay. Sometimes, it did not.

But with Calvin around, I'd found a place where I didn't have to move all the time just to find some rest. I could have dinner with him and his mum, sleep over on a stormy night, or stay up for hours on a clear summer evening. We had places to go where it made sense to just hang out, and we had things to do that disarmed the sense of time, like riding our bikes or going for a swim or building a game. While I didn't completely forget, it helped me relax.

I could say things to myself, like "I'm at least not going home until I've had pancakes with Calvin and Cornelia," or "I won't be home until tomorrow, because I'm staying at Calvin's tonight," and things like that. Conditions that helped me take a break from Mum and Dad.

But with Lisa, it was different. I wasn't even aware that I felt so good. It was like a natural state, and I don't know how to describe that sense of not knowing something, when the entire idea is that you don't know and as a consequence, can't describe it. You don't know.

We walked down to the boat houses and the piers and she told me about her father, how he left them when she was very little but still came around to visit and that he and her mum seemed to get along. She didn't have many friends in Skaresund, she had always been a bit of an oddball (her own words) and loved machines and computers. Once, her father had stayed several days in their house and he and her mum built a computer with her and when it was done, they plugged it in and it caught an electrical fire and the entire place almost burned to the ground. Apparently, that was a good memory because she kept laughing when she told me about it, and I wasn't sure what my part in this was but I did my best, chiming in when it felt like I was supposed to, and I tried to appear interested and interesting at the same time. It was exhausting, to say the least.

She'd been bullied when she was younger but then she'd beat up a few of the girls and after that, she wasn't bullied anymore. She didn't get any friends from it, but at least they stopped bothering her. There'd been a few guys that tried to approach her, but soccer and sailing wasn't her thing. Like in Fjellhamn, growing up in a place like this and being just slightly out of the ordinary was boring at best and a fight for survival at worst.

"Skye was the only one I ever knew who was into computers and games," she said. "I've been told it's usually the other way around. Guys do this kind of thing. How am I supposed to know? My mum's an engineer. Dad's always shown me how to build stuff. You and Calvin are the only guys I know who know anything about video games. This is my reality. You're as rare as we are."

She kept going like this and I listened to her like I could listen to a good song, shifting the needle back to the record's beginning and enjoying the soft scratch from the vinyl with the singer's voice. We passed a few of the thugs who used to come after me and Calvin, and when they glared at us from the shadows of the trees, Lisa leaned across the bike and gave me a kiss on the cheek. Their mouths slowly opened to silent sighs, their dull expressions fired up for a few seconds when they tried to grasp the incomprehensible.

"Skye told me about that idiot that took your stuff," she said. "Did you know he used to live in our town? His parents are stupid rich. They're nice people. They're never home, though. Always out traveling. He and his sister are more or less on their own, all the time. He's really good to her. Takes care of her."

"Well, we showed him," I said. "He's not gonna mess with us anymore."

"You did, didn't you?" she said and laughed. "Apparently, he's got a ZX Spectrum. Only. Imagine that, you got all this money, but no Atari, no Nintendo, no Commodore. All your parents got you was a Spectrum."

"That's like abuse or something."

"For sure. You know what? Sara always said you were a talker. Stories and whatnot. But you don't say much. You think I'm boring? You can say so, it's okay. I mean, it's your problem if you think I'm boring, but I'd like to know."

"No. I like hearing you talk," I said.

And then, she said, "I know about your brother."

I kept walking, on automation, moving away from what she just said.

I knew this moment had to come.

I'd always thought it would be with Calvin. Maybe with Sara.

Lisa fell back into her own silence.

We had passed the piers now and came to the old docks, where abandoned boats were tied to concrete slabs eroded by the sea or marooned on shallow rocks. An old man sat by the end of the stony bridge, holding on to his hat as the wind tried to catch it and play with it over the waves.

I parked my bike against one of the anchor points. I sat down with my legs over the pier's edge and looked at the water, the world underneath.

Two crabs were circling a clam. A cluster of jellyfish hovered above, an audience waiting for the fight.

There was a slight chill in the wind. Even though we were still in July, I could feel that subtle drop that usually came with August. The heat was gone, for sure.

Lisa sat down next to me.

"We don't have to talk about it," she said. "I just wanted you to know that I know. It felt more honest. But it's not really a secret, is it?"

"No," I said. "Not a secret."

It made sense. She'd been friends with Sara for years and even if she hadn't, this was the kind of stuff that spread over bridges, across towns. Dad and I had never considered if people knew about Johan outside of Fjellhamn, because in the grand scheme of things, this wasn't such a big deal. It was to us, of course. The end of the world, in a way. Just not the end of the world everyone else lived in.

"I don't always think of him as my brother," I said. "I know he was. But...it's not like he was, either. You know what I mean?"

"I could say that I do," she said. "But I don't."

"Do you have any brothers or sisters?"

"No."

"Neither does Sara. Or Calvin. Strange."

"Why is that strange?"

"Everyone else has sisters or brothers. But we don't."

"I guess that is kind of strange."

I looked for the next thing to say. I'd never talked to anyone about Johan. Therapists and teachers didn't count. I'd dreaded the moment, but now I wondered why. It wasn't so hard, after all.

"Sara says your mum's not doing so good," Lisa said.

"That's one way to put it, I guess."

I was fine talking about Johan. But not about my mother.

"How old were you?" she said.

"Five."

I thought about when Calvin and I had stood, back-to-back, *Double Dragon* style, against Lars and the thugs. How we'd known he'd beat us into a bloody mess, take our work and burn it into ashes.

We didn't care. If we'd died on that day, that would've been okay.

"I only saw him in an incubator," I said. "The doctors said Mum should hold him. They thought that might help. She was in the room and Dad and I were standing on the other side, looking in. She sat in a chair, with Johan in her arms, rocking him slowly. She kept saying how much she wanted him to stay. How wonderful things would be, if he did. She promised him, if he decided to stick around, she'd love him like no other."

"I'm sorry," Lisa said and wiped her eyes. "Oh, look at me. I can't even...oh, I'm shutting up now."

"It's okay," I said. "I like your voice."

"Yeah," she said with a sob. "You mentioned."

I had to take a pause. While there was a strange calm over the situation, it was intense enough to get my heart racing. I was dragging something out from the shadows and whatever shape it had retained, it was different when the light fell on it. My story hypnotized me as I told it to someone else. It was entirely new and not at all what I'd imagined it to be.

"He was so quiet. Sleeping, in Mum's arms. He didn't seem sick. He looked peaceful. Like he had it all figured out. But he died after just one day. We don't know why. Doctors don't, either. But babies die, sometimes."

Lisa squeezed my hand.

"She sang him that lullaby that she used to sing to me."

"Which one?"

"Don't remember. But it's a haunting song. Maybe that's why it stuck."

Lisa sighed.

"Some of us just don't wanna be here," I said. "But some of us do, even if it's not always easy. I think we deserve some credit for that."

Lisa smiled. "You sound like me." Then she frowned. "What do you mean, though?"

But I was out of words now. I couldn't help it, but I was crying. Not much. Just a tear.

"We can just sit here," she said. "We don't have to talk."

So we didn't talk, but we held hands, and I kept thinking that as long as we did, I could stay here and never go home again.

Chapter 44

ANOTHER WORLD

But like all moments, this one ended too. There wasn't much left to say. We walked to the bus station and waited for almost an hour before the bus arrived. Not only was it a slow day for local traffic, this particular ride was late as well.

We sat on the edge of the same wall that I'd crashed into just hours before. That seemed far away now, so distant an experience that I slipped into my usual doubt if it had ever happened. I hadn't told Lisa about Johan, we were going for ice cream, and she was going to kiss me on the cheek half an hour later when we passed the bullies.

But there was one thing that was happening on this side of reality, that I wouldn't trade for any ignorance in the world. We were still holding hands.

I didn't realize, but I'd stopped thinking about the wonder of it, the fact that she didn't let go, that when we walked away from the piers and back to the town center, she still held my hand. It felt natural, like swimming. Difficult at first, possibly something you'd never really learn, because it seemed so damn hard, gasping for air and flailing with your arms. Then, some part of your body remembered, it had always known how to do this, and you flowed through the water.

"It doesn't have to be like this," she said to me.

I looked at her.

"I don't know what you're fighting at home. I don't need to know. I know enough. And I'm not saying we're gonna take the fight for you. If there even is a fight. But I am saying that your idea of being on your own, that's just not true."

"I've never said that."

"Yeah, you have."

She let go and stood up. The bus was approaching from down the hill. She shielded her eyes against the sun when she looked at me.

"Calvin's your best friend. Not just that. He's an amazing person. And Skye, and their parents, and that guy at the café, and the librarian and the fishermen." She tilted her head. "And now, me."

I wanted to say, "Yeah, but you don't get it. You have no idea." Not even Calvin knows all of it, what it's like at night when Mum haunted the house, when she looked at me from the porch not with cold eyes but just an indifferent stare, and the few mornings when she wasn't up and Dad and I could walk down to the bakery and get cinnamon buns. That was the one moment I still had left, where I still mattered. A slow walk, through rain or sunshine, snow or mist, to get pastry and talk about dragons and pitfalls. That was the one moment Dad hadn't traded away. I was lucky if it happened once a week.

The bus stopped and the doors opened.

"Whatever world you live in," Lisa said, "there's another one here, where people appreciate you. If you imagine anything else, you're wrong."

The bus driver glared at us. Lisa looked at him over the shoulder.

"Well, you're the one who's late," she said. "You owe us a moment here."

He was so surprised by this, he gave up a short laugh.

Lisa turned to me again and put her arms around me. She hugged me hard. I hugged her back and this now felt so easy, so amazingly great, like holding hands.

But even the patience of a bus driver in Fjellhamn reaches its limit, and he honked the horn now to show that he'd found his. We let go. She smiled at me.

"So I'll see you tomorrow, yeah?" she said. "Maybe you wanna come to my place?"

"Sure," I said. "I mean, I'd love to. That sounds amazing."

"It does, doesn't it? Like the greatest thing ever, you know? Like that game of ours?"

I laughed quietly. "Doesn't get any greater than that."

She got on the bus, waving at me as she did. The driver closed the door and I watched the bus as it went back up the hill.

Then, I got on my bike and I did go home after all, but this time for the last time in my life.

Chapter 45

PIECE

We worked hard on whatever ideas we'd come up with from the pieces we'd salvaged from our legacy. A low murmur of voices buzzing and machines humming filled the halls. The windows were open and a cool draft swept through the rooms. Someone had found a ladder, after all.

I had missed this thick, ambient wall where otherworldly sounds from strange places mixed with the slow beat from processor vents. But like a reminder that we were still here, there were also calm conversations on the merits of a specific design mixed with debates around a problem no one could've seen coming. The Spellbinders' kids were quiet today, hanging out in clusters where they drew with crayons or watched a movie.

Back in the days, every morning I'd arrive at the studio and someone would come up to me and say something like, "We got an unexpected crash in the rendering engine after submissions," or, "The AI went bonkers in the public beta and now the servers are down," (at which point someone always cried "Skynet!"–that joke never got old), or, "The levels won't render correctly when we've applied the new shaders." Stuff like that. Calvin called them "Oh, no" moments, because someone always went "Oh, no," when these things happened. So you'd be facing the impossible before your first cup of coffee, Skye would shout and throw things around and draw Gantt charts on the whiteboard, Calvin would sit down and try to rebuild whatever was broken, and I'd look for new ways to implement the design. We brought in anyone, developers and artists or animators and sound engineers though almost never publishers, since they panicked over everything and when they did, their marketing people arrived with their own ideas on game design and that was a real "Oh, no" moment. I'd take Sony's obscure PlayStation architecture any day, rather than the enthusiasm from a Marketing Director's chance to provide us with a design. Hell, we even preferred Jason's input, and every once in a while, he would sit down with us (always uninvited, though very comfortable, as it were), light a cigarette and say something like, "Just don't do it. Strike that idea. Move along."

But we always figured it out and if we didn't, we bought champagne, put it in the fridge, and said to everyone that once we'd cracked this, we were opening those bottles. If the season allowed for it, we'd have strawberries, too. If not, chocolate would do.

On this morning, those not already engaged in their work saw me and smiled, a few casual acknowledgements of yesterday's adventures. It was strange, how once we'd flushed this out of our system, how quickly we were back to the familiar. We were still drunk on our potential success before the launch of our first title, or high on the rush of a number of consecutive hits that eventually would rain across the world.

While I wasn't leading the Spellbinders like I used to, because the situation didn't really call for it, I remained in the center, the one thing that separated us from something finished and a damn mess. I moved across the workstations to bring perspectives and designs, to draw up wireframes, to tweak a camera or adjust an AI, or slap on a line of writing where an empty space called for it. Out of a hundred options by the hour, the teams called on me to point them to the one that would bring it home.

Skye pretended nothing had happened, that she hadn't been shouting in the rain and that there was nothing to talk about. I felt guilty for reasons that made no sense to me, so I was glad she dodged the subject.

"It was a few glasses of wine," she said, "and a strange day. Let's just get on with it."

"She should be here, Skye. I think she'd want to see this."

"You went to see her, didn't you?"

"I did not."

"Fucking liar." She put her hand on my arm. "I think you'd want her to want to see this. It's not like she doesn't know what's going on."

I felt like a fool and decided to drop it for now. Maybe Skye was right. She usually was. Besides, I didn't want to mess with perfection. As far as trailblazers go, there wasn't a producer to ever match her skills. And yet, even she was redefining herself now, raising a bar that most couldn't touch because they couldn't even see it. She directed the production with a clear but subtle harshness, mixed with clarity and the right amount of gentle. Too preoccupied with myself and my part in this, I didn't notice she was gluing the teams and their concepts together until coherence emerged. One by one, they realized their pieces would fit if they just made a few tweaks here and another implementation there. Once that thought got hold, there was no way we could stop it. However, as much as this is what you wanted in a proper production, that energy that would carry you across the finish line, it was treacherous today. It's not what I was after. And Skye could tell.

"There's no point in just making this into a hackathon," she said to me on Friday evening. "We'll merge all the code and assets into something coherent instead, and see what comes out of it."

"That wasn't the idea," I said. "I want them to leave with something finished. Their own version of what this could be. If they can take that, look at it, and say, 'I did this,' then they can imagine the greater game. They can see it."

"For what purpose?"

"You know why."

"Look at these people," she said. "You think a hackathon, as glorious as this one is, will make them sway? You're not Peter Jackson. You're not making *Lord of the Rings*. They're gonna return to their domestic lives and work on the annual FIFA, the next installation of *Final Fantasy*, or another reboot of the *Tomb Raider* franchise. It's not a bad thing. They don't need to be saved. They don't have to be inspired, to survive."

"No," I said. "They're here because they want a reason. Something strong enough to walk away from where they're at."

"Walk away from what? A home, a salary, a steady gig with an established publisher?"

"It's about what they'll get, not what they'll lose."

Skye smiled. She took a breath and looked out over the studio halls. Whenever she did that, she always reminded me of that guy that loved the smell of napalm in the morning.

"This is what I love about development," she said. "You have this idea, this map of something that'll take you to a place you think you wanna be at. Then, you see something from the side. You couldn't ever predict it. But once it's there, you can't let go. Now you know, this is where you really should be. Not here. But there. You wouldn't have found it without the map. But once you have, the map's useless."

She turned to me and put her hand on my shoulder. "You're hoping. As long as you do, you're wasting the moment. You're not getting what you need."

She looked me in the eyes. She seemed sad, all of a sudden.

"We're saying goodbye, Elliot. However strange it sounds, that's what Calvin's map was about. A way to get us to this point, where we could close this thing and put it behind us. He's around, as much as he can be. So that he can be a part of it, too. So that you can say goodbye to him."

This was making me angry.

"Why go through all of this, if it's just a few days' worth of time to you?"

"I need this too, Elliot." She pushed me gently back. "What do you see?"

I was going to snap back at her and then get out of the conversation, but I couldn't, because I was grabbed by the currents that flowed through the halls now, that growing sense of excitement that filled the studio as you realized you were on to something.

It was familiar and toxic, destructive and glorious, an emotion that crushed reason and laughed at all the user group tests and beta evaluations. There was no math here to prove you might have a hit on your hands, no tried-and-true formula applied to make sure the level of quality was right. It was only that sensation that spread to your hands and feet, electrifying your brain.

"You can't stop it," she said. "It's in the house now. No matter how this turns out, this is the way we gotta go."

I thought about this, feeling the fire on my skin.

Filip approached us, striking his hand over his bald head.

"Hey, guys," he said. "There's something going on with the LUA engine. It won't parse our scripts. Could be that I've forgotten the syntax, could be that it's just too old now."

"Oh, no," I said.

He smiled. "Yeah. Oh, no."

Skye looked at me from the side.

"All right," I said. "I'll be there in a second."

Filip nodded and left.

I turned to Skye.

"Okay," I said. "Let's do this your way. But only because I trust you, not because I think you're right."

"You're gonna have to explain the difference to me some time," Skye said and laughed.

Chapter 46

PRESS START

Despite the mess to merge all the branches together, it compiled. For those of you who don't know what I'm talking about, let's just say it worked. If my idea had been to let each team create their own flavor of what this game could be, it was clear that Skye's recommendation to bring it all together into one was better.

She'd mounted a big canvas on the wall next to Calvin's art and connected a PlayStation to a projector. She downloaded the final build an hour or so before Sunday lunch and didn't even test it before it was time to screen it.

"Maybe you should run it on your own devkit first," Joakim said. "To make sure."

"Nah," Skye said. "I mean, you and your guys don't write bugs into your code anyway, do you?"

"I don't know. Do we?" He looked over his shoulder at the team closest to us. They shook their heads in unison.

"I don't," Simon said, "and I'm pretty sure Yasmine doesn't."

"Please," she said.

Joakim turned to Skye again. He sighed. She smiled. "Why don't you go buy the beer and the snacks? Bring a few of the others. We're just about ready to go here. Oh, and make sure–"

"Helene handles the snacks," he said. "I know."

We'd always had this ritual before we shipped a game, that a few of us went out to buy beer and snacks by the truckload while someone prepared the final build on a big screen. Now, Joakim and Bjorn came back with cartloads of local brewery stuff and a few Carlsbergs as well, to make sure Filip had something to drink too, while Helene and Ellie had gone out for snacks. There was no one like Helene to find the perfect balance in what kind to get, the right amount of it, the perfect mix and the actual serving itself. She was like the snacks equivalent of a mix tape master. You'd think it was just a matter of getting some popcorn and chips, maybe cheezdoodles and chocolate, put it in bowls and then munch away. You'd be wrong. The ritual of sending out a patrol on beer hunt and asking Helene to take care of the snacks was as important as the playing of the game itself. If she wasn't around, if no one could get the beer, we'd cancel and wait until the next day.

I walked up to Joakim and the others to help unload the beer and put it in buckets of ice. Helene had taken a detour to buy some plates and bowls as well, and with a little help from Skye, they'd cleared a desk and used that as a serving table. Yasmine gathered up the artists to bring chairs and cushions, and we spread out over the floor like nomads in a tent when the canvas flared up with lightning and thunder and the opening theme played through the speakers. Everyone cheered and applauded, a brilliantly crafted start menu with an obscene amount of parallax layers unraveled on the screen and the camera panned over hills with green grass and a blue sky. It zoomed in on someone by a big oak and we saw that it was the sad, old man. The artists had made a few changes from the original model, closer to Calvin's sketch he'd shown me at the diner all those years ago. His hair was gray now, and it seemed longer as the wind touched it. He still wore his enigmatic smile, but there was a spark in his eyes, as if he'd seen something new.

"He looks a bit like you, Elliot," Skye said quietly. "If you'll ever be that old."

"He's handsome, for sure," I said.

"Right," Joakim called and held up a controller. "Who's first? Who wants to play?"

The game was still now. The music had faded, only the wind and the birds from the speakers echoed through our halls, chiming in with the draft from outside. The man looked at us. I couldn't call him sad anymore. It wouldn't do the image justice.

"Obviously, Elliot goes first," Benjamin said.

Everyone nodded to this. I felt some kind of relief as I walked through the crowd. It wouldn't have mattered if someone else had taken the first steps through whatever world we'd built this time, but there was a sense of peace in the halls as they let me through and gave up a spontaneous round of applause. Joakim handed me the controller. I took it and faced the Spellbinders.

"There's a funny story about the man on the screen right here," I said. "He's been around longer than any of us."

I paused.

They were all silent now, watching me. I looked at the wall, with sketches so old the paper was yellow and torn, with artwork so fresh, it looked like the paint was still drying.

There had been that time at the diner.

The first time I'd had coffee.

Where Calvin had said to this mother that I was his friend. We'd be making a game together. I had all these cool ideas. He was going to do all the drawing.

He'd opened his sketchbook.

The lines had poured out, they'd pulled me in.

That half-finished clearing with a small pond. I could still smell the morning dew. The beach that never ended, a sea with no horizon. The hush from the slow waves reaching higher with the tide.

And the man, standing on the hill, his eyes old and sad.

It remained as beautiful as ever, so painful I couldn't go there.

I had said to Calvin that our game's gonna be great. And he'd said back, The greatest game of all.

I turned around and looked at the canvas and the game on display. It waited for me to push start.

I faced the Spellbinders again.

I put the controller aside.

"You don't build a game in just a couple of days," I said. "But you can build something. A slice of an idea, a promise to something great. Even if it's just a piece, it can still be better than billion-dollar behemoths."

There were smiles and nods, a few murmurs, and cheers with raised bottles.

"Most of our demos," I said, "some of them made over just a week or two, were better than most of what's out there today."

They laughed quietly.

I felt a sting in my eye. I wasn't expecting this pain. But there it was and like an old acquaintance, I didn't fight it. We'd known each other for so long, there wasn't any point.

"I don't think you know how great a friend Calvin was. I'm saying that, well aware that you all thought he was one of the most generous and humblest people ever. Even you, Filip, liked him."

They laughed again, louder now. Some of them turned to look at Filip. He smiled.

"He saved me, in a way," I said slowly. "Not sure I deserved it. But he did."

I noticed Skye was the only one not looking at me now. She had her eyes on the floor, leaning her shoulder against a pillar.

"I think it's fair to say," I said, "that whatever this is, here on the big screen on our wall, we're dedicating this to Calvin. Don't you think?"

Yes! They cheered and there were more applauds but loud and rowdy, glass against glass and a call to arms that we should launch the game already, the beer was getting warm and the snacks weren't going to eat themselves. I made a gesture for them to calm

down, which of course they didn't, so I just picked up the controller and pressed Start.

Chapter 47

NATURE BOY

There was a slow thunder rolling in over Fjellhamn that night. The skies burned with lightning fire across the water. Through the dark stripes against the midnight blue, there was heavy rain by the sea.

I was home, in my room. I'd been there for hours, lying in my bed and staring at the ceiling. It was a barren place, hardly any signs that a kid lived here. I kept my notebooks and pencils in a chest of drawers by the bed. Dad and I had agreed to tell Mum that it was school work, that she couldn't touch those or my teacher would give me hell. She knew that I didn't really go to school anymore, in so much as that Dad had told her. Repeatedly. But I don't think it ever stuck. So we got away with it. But the rest of my stuff, she'd claimed, piece by piece, until the room became a place with nothing on the walls, nothing on the floor, a neatly made bed, a desk, and those drawers. I didn't mind. I never cared much about things, anyway.

I don't remember when I'd last spent so much time in my room. But it was a strange day, because I'd also never spent time with a girl in the way that I had, today. So I guess all bets were off now.

The rain came with the dusk and as the sun set into the sea, I opened my closet and took out my backpack. I shoved down most of my notebooks. Some weren't worth saving and the best ones were at Calvin's house, anyway. Then, I packed my t-shirts, jeans and shorts, my bathing pants and whatever clean underwear and socks that wasn't in the laundry basket.

I strapped it on. The rain was slower here and tapped gently on my window. I wondered if it was asking me for an invitation, to come inside for a casual talk about the weather.

But it was the other way around, of course. It was suggesting I come out, reassuring me that it was warm and soft, that I wouldn't be cold.

I opened my door and went out into the kitchen. Dad was there, editing something he'd typed during the day. The light from the ceiling was dim and bleak from a dusty bulb, and he had to squint whenever he marked something with his pen. The lamp cast a weak reflex against the windows and made the night seem darker. Only the lightning showed me there was still a world outside, followed by the thunder that echoed over the hills.

Mum was there too, of course.

She was always up at this hour.

She had a cup of tea in front of her. She hadn't touched it. It was probably cold by now. She wore a yellow gown and had her eyes closed, her face strained as if she endured a slow, burning pain.

"Don't worry, son," Dad said. "Thunder won't make it here. Not tonight."

"Okay, Dad," I said.

He looked up to give me a smile, but when he saw me with the bag, he was surprised.

"You going somewhere?"

I nodded slowly. "Yeah, I'm just...you know...I'm going out."

Mum didn't notice us. I don't know if she was pretending, or if she actually didn't hear.

"It's almost midnight, Elliot."

"I know."

"It's raining."

"I know."

He got up and walked around the table, towards me. He seemed tired.

"Hey," he said and reached out. "We'll get cinnamon buns tomorrow. We'll go down to the water, and we'll have them there. We don't have to go home."

I didn't move.

"You can tell me about that game of yours," he said. "All the places you can go to. All the beasts in the world."

He stroked my hair. I didn't want to answer, because I was afraid what would come out if I did. I was so mad at him now.

"Sure," I said.

I did manage that. But that was my limit.

I turned to Mum. "Hey, Mum," I said.

She flinched.

"Charlotte," Dad said. "Your son's talking to you."

Suddenly, she looked directly at me. I wanted to turn away, I was afraid that hands would emerge from the floor and pull me down if I didn't, but instead I faced her. Her eyes were gray, like the Fjellhamn rocks by the stone beaches.

"All right," she said. "What do you want, Elliot?"

"I was wondering..."

I lost my voice. It took me a few seconds to find it again. Something moved in her face, I wasn't sure if she was mocking me or if she was just curious, perhaps searching for her own emotional stake in this. But as I reclaimed my words, I spoke stronger now.

"You sang a song to me, when I was little. To help me fall asleep."

She smiled weakly. Maybe she remembered.

"About a boy," I said. "He learned something. The greatest thing of all."

Every time a sign from her had slipped through the cracks, I'd hoped. Maybe this was the day she'd come back. I think Dad gave up years ago. But a light touch or a gentle remark, that was all I'd needed to keep hoping.

"What was it called?" I said.

Mum looked to the side. Her face lit up with the clear blaze from a lightning strike.

"That was Johan's song," she said. "I never sang to you."

I nodded.

She turned to me.

"Why would I, Elliot?"

She moved her hand over the kitchen table, staring at the surface.

"Okay," I said. "Take care, Mum."

I walked out into the hall, but as I reached for the handle, Dad grabbed my arm. I looked at him, my eyes burning now.

"'Nature Boy,'" he said. "By Nat King Cole. She sang it to you every night."

We looked at each other for I don't know how long. Probably just seconds, though it could've been minutes or hours. But eventually, he let me go. I opened the door and walked out into the rain and towards my bike, parked under one of our apple trees. I was soaking wet when I got up on the saddle. Since the rain was nothing like the soft beat that had tapped on my window before, I didn't know if I was crying or if the weather was just beating me up real hard.

Chapter 48

WE HAVE TO FINISH IT

I don't know who you expect outside your door in the middle of the night, when you wake up to the sound of someone knocking relentlessly to get in. Especially when the rain's coming down and the thunder's banging away like Fjellhamn was its own base drum.

But apparently, Calvin was expecting me because the lights were already on when I arrived. He rushed to the door and I heard him shout to his mum that I was here now. He ushered me inside, as if my entering was part of something that went according to plan, a plan he knew all about and I nothing.

I was wet, through and through, and trembling like I'd walked through winter to get here. Cornelia came towards me, her hair wrapped in curlers and her face covered in a green and very weird (close to scary) looking beauty mask. She wielded a towel like she was fighting the wind, and pulled me close to wipe my face and hair dry.

"My dear, sweet Elliot," she mumbled in a voice I couldn't tell was angry or scared. "Your father called. He said you might be coming here. Thank the lord he was right."

She didn't seem surprised, and went about the task of drying me up as if she had been properly prepared for it for some time.

I was dripping on the floor, the rain coming off me like streams during early spring. I had no idea what to do or say. I was only half aware I'd managed to get here.

I felt so empty. So unwanted.

So Dad had called to announce my arrival. Picked up the phone, said a few lines, then gone back to work. Maybe talked Mum into going to bed, helped her get comfortable and take her medicine before she dozed off. Then went to sleep himself, on the couch or in the spare bed by the kitchen alcove.

I'd come here, with no one in pursuit, no one to follow me. I could've gone to the sea and kept going. No one would've known for sure.

"Hey," Calvin said. He was standing by me now, his hand on my shoulder. "You want some hot chocolate, Elliot? You can borrow my pajamas. And you can sleep here. Right, Mum? Elliot can sleep here, right? He doesn't have to go home again. He can have my bed. I can sleep on the floor." As if they had the space to spare, as if their shoebox of comfort had square meters to offer.

Cornelia kept looking at me, her dark eyes searching me through and through, her big hand touching my cheek.

Though the soft temperature in Calvin's and Cornelia's house was starting to warm my skin now, I still trembled. More than before.

"We have to finish it," I said.

They both looked at me. Calvin, slightly puzzled. Cornelia, waiting. I faced them both, my eyes darting between them.

"We have to finish it."

"Finish what, love?" Cornelia said.

"I think it's important...we try harder. To finish the game. Don't you think, Calvin?" I looked at him. "We gotta finish our game. Work on it, till it's done."

He nodded with enthusiasm. "Y-yes," he said. "For sure. We're just getting started. We can't stop now. Hey, I can show you some stuff I did today actually, I think you're gonna l-like it, it's pretty–"

Cornelia hushed him.

She'd dried my face and yet it was wet again. When she looked at me now, she had this serene expression, a gentle vibe that you wouldn't know such a grim face could wear if you hadn't seen it for real. Her fingers wiped away some of the moist under my eye.

"My dear, strange boy," she said. "You're much too beautiful for this world."

I felt a rush coming on. Something threatening to burst.

"You'll stay here now," she said. "Put on those dry pajamas. Go to sleep. We're watching over you. Tomorrow, I'll be making pancakes and bacon, and you'll be sitting there by our table with my sweet and wonderful son, and you'll be working on that game of yours."

"The g-g-greatest, Elliot," Calvin said. "Just like us, brother."

I cried now. Not a slow and dignified flow of lovely silver tears, but a gut-ripping, pain-wailing gush that poured over my face. My legs wouldn't carry me and I fell to the floor and wrapped my arms around myself like a baby warding off the ghosts. Cornelia sat down beside me and put my head in her lap and her hand on my head, stroking my wet hair away from my forehead. Calvin sat next to her and took my hand and held it until I didn't have anything left in me and my yells turned into empty sobs. But at the end of it, it didn't hurt so much anymore. Something had left me, perhaps not forever but certainly for a while, and as I got quiet, I listened to the rain on the rooftop and felt Cornelia's fingers in my hair and Calvin's hand holding mine. There was comfort but also strength, a pull to stand up and continue with a promise that I wasn't alone, after all. I had my best friend by my side, and we were going to finish the *Greatest Game of All* together or die trying.

Chapter 49

THE IMPOSSIBLE

So we took turns and the controller was passed around among us. We played the game on repeat, lining up to try again and to cheer loudly for whoever was engaging at the moment. It was just a few minutes of an experience and everywhere you looked, you saw something familiar. The trees from *Archipelago,* the rain from *Clear Blue Skies,* and *Dark Man Crying's* parallax scroll (Calvin's best ever). I felt like I'd brought my old friends to a place where they'd never been, and I saw them in a different light just because. I wondered if they saw something else in me today, or if I was just the same guy but with more gray hair.

There was a roundabout way to the design, an emergence that tugged at you to come back as soon as you'd put the controller down. The game had an ever-evolving beat, with small and constant changes, like an organism moving slowly through space. As soon as you were done, it served up this idea and you thought, I didn't think of that. I'll have another go.

Skye only played it once. She stayed in the background. There was a mood about her that made it difficult to approach her, and I wasn't sure if she wanted it this way or was waiting for someone to tear down the wall and bring her into the crowd. But I was in a moment that wouldn't come back, the kind of stuff you can base an entire story on, and I wasn't going to spend it on trying to figure her out. So I let her be, or ignored her if you will, and joined the Spellbinder fray as we played our slice of greatness on repeat.

But as the hours passed from afternoon to evening, the Spellbinders dropped off. They had different flights waiting for them to take them home, all across the world. Quietly, they left, one by one. I said goodbye at the door, as they wore their shoes and prepared to leave.

Ellie gave me a hug, told me not to be a stranger and that I should take care. Oscar said that he'd enjoyed this, he was glad to get a break from the FIFA games anyway, and that Calvin would've been proud. Of what, I'm not sure. Simon just said goodbye but then turned around and lunged forward and gave me a long, hard embrace. Filip was confused, wondering if this had been a waste of time or the best week in his life. He said he'd get back to me on that, once he'd figured it out.

But Yasmine lingered. She was the next to last one to leave, with only Benjamin still around.

"I don't have anyone waiting for me at home anyway," she said.

She was resting on the floor by the shoes, her back against the wall and her arm on her backpack. Her eyes were half closed and she looked at the canvas and the wall of art.

"This was special," she said. "Thank you, Elliot."

"Thank you for coming."

"You knew we would." She smiled. "You're good at these things. Calvin would've loved it."

I nodded. "Yeah."

"What're you gonna do now?"

Benjamin was putting on his shoes, checking all his bags and counting in the kids. We'd said goodbye already. I wondered why he was still around. I tried to pretend I didn't notice, but he was watching me now. Skye was nearby, sitting in a chair by an open window and smoking a cigarette. While she had her back against us, I knew she was listening.

"I'm gonna finish it," I said.

Yasmine laughed. "Okay, then."

"It's important that we finish it. So I will."

She sat up straight. "How?" she said.

"What do you mean?"

"I mean how?"

I looked at the game on the canvas. "We figured out the hard part," I said. "It's just the rest left."

Benjamin sighed. His daughter hugged her plush bunny. His son was deep into something on his Game Boy. His wife was already halfway down the stairs. Skye tipped her chair slightly backwards, rocking on its legs.

Yasmine laughed again, but it sounded more like a cough. "That's the kind of impossible that killed you the last time, Elliot."

Skye looked over her shoulder, not directly at us. She'd put out her cigarette, resting her hands on her stomach. Benjamin had left.

"This isn't impossible," I said.

"So what do you call all this, then?" She took in the studio with her arm.

"A goodbye, I guess."

"C'mon," Skye said. "I'll drive you to the airport."

"I'll get a taxi," Yasmine said.

"You'll miss your flight."

"I'll get the next one."

Yasmine stood up. She gave me a hug and a kiss on the cheek.

"For what it's worth, I'm sorry. I'm glad I came here to say so."

"I'm happy you did."

Skye lit another cigarette, observing her with a weary gaze.

"Okay. So I just wanna say..." Yasmine said and inhaled, "I just wanna say..."

"Here we go," Skye moaned.

"There's no way he'd make this work, this...this thing, right here."

I pretended I didn't get it. "Who, now?"

Yasmine smiled. "If he'd been the one still alive, we'd have shown up. For drinks and dinner at Nonna's, to celebrate your sorry ass. But when you called..."

She paused, shaking her head.

"When you called, Elliot...if there was just a slim chance you had your shit together, that fucking cauldron of yours that always made the potions work, it'd be worth at least the ticket to get here."

"Well, was it?"

Yasmine walked slowly towards Skye now.

"Sure. I mean, the good guys always show up."

She stopped at Skye and took her cigarette from her. She took a smoke. "You didn't, though. When Calvin was sick."

"So I'm a bad guy, then."

"I don't know. I really don't know you, Elliot. But I'm finding it hard to believe you'd bail on him at his final hour, just because you caught him with Lisa like...what, five years ago?" She turned to Skye with a thoughtful expression. "It was five years ago, wasn't it? Our last Midsummer party?"

Skye shrugged.

Yasmine blew out some smoke.

"I don't think so, Elliot. I want you to know that. I don't think so."

"He lied to me, Yasmine."

"You and Lisa weren't a couple. Hadn't been, for years."

I turned away.

"You don't know anything," I said. "These are just your fucking assumptions."

"As long as you're not talking, we're left assuming."

"I don't need to explain myself to you."

"But you'd want to, wouldn't you? If you had the guts to do it?"

I squeezed my fists, trying not to be angry. She noticed, though. She dropped the cigarette and stepped on it. "Anyway...shut this shit down. You've repented. I guess that's what I'm trying to say, in a very roundabout way."

"I appreciate the candor."

"You might be an asshole. As I said, I don't know. But even assholes have to move on."

Yasmine walked up to her bag and picked it up. Skye followed. They walked out the door, but then Yasmine turned around and looked at me. "You know, Elliot...for a guy who knows what he wants...you're really bad at saying what you want." She tilted her head. "Kind of ironic."

"People don't listen much anyway."

Yasmine laughed. "That's an answer, I guess."

"I'm fucking leaving without you," Skye said. "Getting on that damn flight myself."

Yasmine put a hand on her shoulder. "I think this moment was worth a missed flight."

Skye mumbled something about idiots and wasting her time as they walked down the stairs. Then, they were gone and the stair house gates slammed shut behind them. The place was quiet, except for the wind that howled from the game's speakers.

I sat down right where I'd stood, leaning my head in my hands. I breathed deeply.

The room was slowly picking up a spin.

I felt a pressure on my chest, a thumping in my head as the pulse increased.

I was in that office again, with the carpet that would soon have blood on it.

All I could think of was what Sean had just told me, that Calvin had died and here I was, trying to pitch something I didn't believe would ever work.

All exits were closed. There was no way out.

No one to catch me, when I fell.

Except for Skye.

She'd even been with me in the ambulance.

The room stopped spinning. I could breathe again.

I rose and walked up to the wall. I picked up the stick drawing from my pocket.

I found a pin and attached the note somewhere in the middle of it all.

Two boys, on a pier, as the sun was about to set. Laughing at something, their arms around their shoulders.

Calvin had written on that note: Remember?

I remembered.

But if this was redemption, I wasn't nearly done. In fact, I'd saved the most difficult parts for later. And now, later was here.

Chapter 50

BRINGING GIFTS

I wasn't expecting my father to come and pick a fight, just because I didn't come home. I'd been gone for just a night or two, after all. But I did wonder why he didn't call to ask me how I was doing, or maybe try to explain what was going on. I knew he talked to Cornelia, so he had the baseline covered. I had a place to sleep and someone who fed me. But why wouldn't he reach out to me?

In the meantime, Calvin did his best to pretend that this was a good thing.

"Now that we're 1-living together," he said, "we can work on the game all the time. And we can eat popcorn and watch horror movies when Mum's not home."

"I don't like horror movies." I frowned. "You know that."

"No problemo. I got Police Academy and Cannonball Run and...oooh, waaait for it...Ghostbusters."

"Okay. Cool."

But we didn't watch any movies and when we took our long walks through Fjellhamn down to the piers or the beaches, I didn't say much. I kept my eyes on the ground. Calvin talked, more than ever, but I wasn't biting. I think he went on because if he hadn't, the silence might've choked us.

We met Sara and Lisa by the dark man's café. Sara wanted to know where the hell we'd been. Calvin looked at me from the side and I shrugged my shoulders.

"We're here," I said. "Why?"

"I've called you," Lisa said. "Your dad says you're at Calvin's."

"He's right," I said.

"Well, you could've called me."

I looked at her. She wasn't upset or sad. She just wanted to know.

"It's only been a few days," I said.

"You don't wanna play with girls anymore?" Sara said. "You got plans or something? Hooked up with Lars?"

"He's got a S-s-pectrum. We'd never do that. Right, Elliot?"

It seemed there were a million good answers to that one. I found none. I was drawing a blank on anything that was fired at me now.

"You've been s...s...s-s-sick," Calvin said to me. "Fever and stu...uhff." He turned to Sara and Lisa. "B-broke out when we were helping Mr. Svensson clean up his b-b-b-back yard. What a mess that is. Mum said it's best Elliot stays with us until it's passed. Pretty exhausting, taking the bike home, when you're b-b-urning up."

Sara scanned us with her green gaze, applying her x-ray vision through our lies.

Lisa folded her arms. "A fever, huh?" she said.

"Yup."

"But you're fine now?" Sara said.

"Sure."

"Trouble with the words today, Calvin?" Sara said. "You nervous?"

Calvin shook his head, his cheeks turning red. "N-n-n-n...oooo. Uh-uh."

"C'mon, Lisa. Let's go build our own game." Sara pulled Lisa by the arm.

Lisa followed with some reluctance but she kept looking at me, puzzled. "What happened?" she said and stopped.

Sara moaned and rolled her eyes.

I shoved my hands down my pockets and raised my shoulders. "Nothin'."

"You can tell us. We're your friends. Aren't we? We're his friends."

Calvin nodded. Sara sighed. "Leave it alone, Lisa," she said. "Let him be."

She considered this for a moment. "Okay," she said. "For now."

She left with Sara. Calvin put his arm around my shoulder. "I'll buy you an ice cream, Elliot. And if you don't want to, you don't have to talk. I can t-talk for the b-b-both of us."

I looked at him.

"Is this the kind of fight," I said, "where you and your mum have to leave Fjellhamn?"

Calvin shook his head. "No," he almost shouted. "What fight? We're not fighting. W-we're not going anywhere. That's what Mum said. Remember? She told you, too. We're not g-g-going a-anywhere. We have to finish it. You said so yourself."

"I did say that, didn't I?"

"Yes, you did." He stretched his back and crossed his arms, like a superhero posing for a perfect picture. "I'm not going anywhere. You can count on me, Elliot."

"It's not really up to you, is it?"

"It's certainly not up to you. And I don't see anyone else calling the shots around here. Do you?"

I smiled faintly. "Nope," I said. "I guess it's just you and me."

Through those days, I imagined that I didn't have parents. I was slowly waking from a dream. I'd always been here with my friend and his mother, and was just coming around to the fact that I wasn't sleeping anymore. I recalled the idea of a mother and fa-ther, that it'd been nice when they'd been around, but it was so long ago and the memories were vague. Sometimes, I felt lonely. But I wasn't adrift. I had another family now, and they took care of me.

Dad showed up after a few days, on a Sunday morning at breakfast, right before coffee, and he'd brought cinnamon buns from the café by the cinema. He carried a cloth bag stuffed with pads and pens, some of the best I'd ever seen, and he'd bought me a new t-shirt. A really cool one, with a ninja printed on it.

When Cornelia opened, she gave my dad a glare that might've slayed the mightiest of giants. It only made him sway a little.

"Can I come in?" he said.

"And now you're a comedian as well," she said.

"Hey, Elliot," he said and waved to me from the doorstep.

"Hey," I said.

He turned to Cornelia. "I'm not leaving."

"Wasn't expecting you to."

"I wanna talk to my son."

"Go right ahead."

"So how's that gonna work if–"

"You can take him for a walk."

"I don't appreciate your tone."

"I don't appreciate you."

He sighed and rubbed his nose. "Look...thanks. For this. For everything. But you've got no right to judge me."

"The way you treat your so–"

"You don't know everything. Okay? So shut up. Please. I'm here to see my son. Nothing else."

"About time," Cornelia said.

I tied my shoes. Calvin stood beside me and when I was done, he said: "Let's go see Sara and Lisa when you're back."

"Why?"

"Or not. We'll see. Okay?"

"Okay."

Cornelia stepped aside and when I walked up to Dad, he

kneeled and hugged me. It was a big one, his bear arms burying me in sweat and body heat. I don't remember when he did that last. I closed my eyes, feeling the rough touch from his beard on my skin.

"Elliot," he said. "You know I love you, don't you?"

I didn't answer. I wasn't the kind of child raised to say I loved someone. I wasn't about to start now. Especially not for the sake of someone else.

I pushed him away and was about to walk out the door, but Cornelia stopped me.

"Let him do the talking," she said. "You don't owe him a word, Elliot."

Chapter 51

SWING

I don't remember where we went. It was a random stroll down some Fjellhamn road, past gray rocks with yellow grass and through a field of purple heather. Dad stopped by a stone bench and sat down.

"Come here," he said.

I joined him. He put his arm around my shoulders and tried to pull me close, but it was an awkward move. I shrugged him off.

"Are you mad?" he said.

"Don't know."

He put his hands on his knees. Didn't speak for a while. I heard the ocean strike against the cliffs. The sea gulls called their war cry as they dived for fish.

"I'm doing my best," he said. "I'm really trying. There's nothing more important than you. You're the son I got to keep."

I kept quiet, feeling a mix of confusion added to the anger. This could come out as anything if I put it into words. Better not try.

"We can be in this together," he said. "Like a family, not lonely people sharing a kitchen table."

"Mum never eats with us."

"You know what I mean."

"No, Dad. I have no idea. But I get it."

"You do?"

"Mum's sick," I said. "She can't help it. She is what she is."

Dad smiled sadly. "You really are the boy in the song, aren't you?" he said.

I turned to face him. "What's your reason?"

His smile remained, but now like a frozen frame. "What do you mean?"

"She's ill, Dad. It's no excuse. But it's a reason. What's yours?"

Dad put his hands together. He reminded me of Mr. Parkvik, who'd almost knelt in prayer when he'd sold our computer to someone else. "I don't understand."

"Maybe she can't choose," I said. "Maybe she really is lost. But you can choose, Dad. You're not where she is."

The wind caught hold and played in his uncombed hair. He was listening in a new way now, perhaps struggling to find a way through this when whatever map he'd had just became useless.

"When Mum's angry, you tiptoe around her every whim. When she's sleeping, you work or rest. Whenever she calls, you take her abuses and then you fix her dinner and coffee. You let her tear down my room, talk to me like I'm dead, or wishing I was dead instead of Johan. I can't bring home friends. I don't feel safe."

My father looked genuinely shocked now.

"She's like a ghost, Dad. When she's not sleeping, she roams our halls and slams the doors, wails and moans, and scares us to death. And you know why?"

He didn't move. Didn't speak.

"Because you let her."

"She's trying her best too, Elliot."

"Whatever you're doing, it doesn't make her better. Maybe you're making her worse. But I'm here and I have nowhere to go. There's no shelter for me, anywhere."

"But your friends...Calvin, and I heard you're seeing Sara again. And this new girl...you got this game you working on. I'd love to see it."

"You think that being okay now makes it all go away? Calvin's gonna move. He and his mum always do. When school starts, Sara will go back to her friends. And Lisa...well, Lisa...how's she ever gonna like me?"

He reached for me but I pulled away and fell. When he tried to help, I bounced up and lashed out at him. I wanted to hurt him, to hit him in the face and kick him in the gut.

"How can this be so fucking hard? To just take care of someone. To just do what you said you'd do."

"Hey." He withdrew. "This is what I mean. We can figure this out. You're smarter than the rest. You'll be fine. Maybe it doesn't feel like that now, but trust me. You'll do okay. More than okay. But this is exactly what I'm getting at. You're old enough to understand. This is a struggle and we're all doing our part, and your part is to accept things as they are, so that we can be together in this. You gotta receive, or I can't give."

Quiet rage fueled me now. I clenched my fists.

"How is it possible," I said, "that you think I can accept that you don't care? That would be my part? To give you permission to not give a fuck?"

"I do give a fuck," Dad says. "More than ever. Which is why we're moving to Gothenburg."

My mouth kept moving but nothing came out. An instant short circuit went through my body and shut down the brain before the shock caused too much damage. The air left my lungs when I sat down in the heather.

Dad leaned forward. "We're leaving, Elliot."

The world was spinning. My stomach hurt.

"After the Fjellhamn festival," he said. "By summer's end."

Just breathing was a struggle now.

"We'll get a lot of money for our house," he said. "When you got a home close to the sea, city folks go crazy for bids. And we'll be closer. To the clinic. I've found a place for Mum, where she can stay every other weekend. You and I will have more time together. I don't need to travel anymore. You don't have to start a new school right away, if you don't want to. We can explore the city. Find the place with the best cinnamon buns, and talk about dragon eggs and sea creatures. Oh, and there's this store where I buy all your note-books and pencils. I'll take you there. You can have anything you like. They have a big place where they only sell video games. We can go there, too. I'll get you a console of your own. You can have it in your new room. And a TV, as well."

He ruffled my hair.

I took a swing and hit him in the face. It hurt. A lot. To this day, I still don't regret it for a second.

Chapter 52

JUST LUNCH

It took me a few days before I returned to our studio at Maria Skolgata. The place was empty. Of course it was empty. Dark, despite the summer glow outside, and lights turned off. A bit cold from the drafts. Midsummer was coming and the notorious June wouldn't fail to disappoint, with a freezing wind to kill the strawberry fields and a cool rain to make sure the tomatoes stayed green. May was over. The real summer was about to kick in.

The screens were still on, the consoles humming along. Even the game remained on the canvas wall, next to Calvin's art. The place looked a bit like one of the scenes where everyone had picked up their things and left, as disaster was sudden and imminent. But it would've taken awhile for someone like me to pick up on the signs, because you didn't really turn off the equipment in the middle of development. The machines were just in different states of activity. In our first Spellbinder office, a century old apartment house in the center of Gothenburg, we'd pushed the circuits so hard that the entire building had blackouts once or twice a day. Once that was resolved by an electrician, who wielded some kind of voodoo with his flashlight and voltmeter to get our power station working, it still took a while before people in that building started to like us.

Anyway.

Maybe I was a fool. But I wasn't an idiot.

I never expected my reputation to wash away in a few days. I wouldn't have the currency to seriously suggest the Spellbinders should stick around to finish the work.

Still.

No one had stayed.

Despite the fact that we could build the greatest game ever. In the making for decades.

I heard steps in the stair house. My heart raced. I looked at the old Victorian door.

It would open. They'd come in. Take off their shoes and say, "Hey, Elliot, don't worry. We were just gone for a while. But we're back now."

As they poured in through the door and made a mess with all their jackets and bags, their children tearing up the place, Skye would be there to throw off her sandals, light a cigarette, and pull her hands through her hair while she shouted at the developers to get the fucking build in order or she'd shut down the Jolt Cola vending machine.

But whoever it was, this person passed the Spellbinder door and continued to one of the floors above.

I called Skye. It took her some time before she answered and when she did, she sounded tired.

"Hey," I said. "Did I wake you?"

"Kind of," she said. "What time is it?"

"About lunch. Wanna come over? We can get some burgers and talk about our next move."

She was silent for a while.

"What do you mean?" she said.

"You know what I mean."

"Well, I guess, but...hang on, okay?" She left the phone and said something to someone. A man answered, confused. Skye spoke louder, saying, "No, we're not gonna have coffee. You're gonna get the fuck out of here and you're not getting my fucking number."

"Okay," the man said. "I just thought it would be nice–"

"Oh my god, you're still talking!"

Then, she was back on the phone.

"Sorry," she said. "So, yeah. Elliot, I'm not coming over. We're done now, okay? It was fun. It was necessary. You did a good thing here, like Calvin knew you would. But it's over now. No one hates you. They never did. You did your best. I'm telling you, Lindh, as apologies go, this one's gotta count among the legendary ones. But drop this now. You got your life back. Go live it."

I leaned back in my chair and looked out the windows, as the world passed by. "No."

"No?" She laughed.

"Or I mean, yes. I'm living it. This is it."

"Oh, you sorry fuck."

"You're one to talk."

"Yeah, I know." I heard her light a cigarette. "We make quite the pair, don't we?" There was a loud bang in the background.

"What was that?"

"Hmm? Oh, this guy...he slammed the door when he left. Puppy eyes and all."

"Puppy eyes never did work on you, did they?"

"Hah. Dogs and men. Babies who never grow up."

I stood up. "You're not coming over, are you?"

She sighed as she blew out some smoke. "Of course not, Elliot."

"I can do this alone now. I'm not asking for your help."

She spoke slowly next. "Then what are you asking for, Elliot?"

"I'm...I...lunch, I guess."

She laughed again. "No. We really are done. For now, at least. I need the distance. I feel a bit used, you know. But it's okay, I went into this with eyes open. But now, Skye's gotta look out for Skye. And you're not helping."

"I can help. I wanna help. You've been there for me."

"And yet, you're such an ungrateful son of a bitch."

"You can just say no. You don't have to be a dick about it."

"I'm not equipped to know how. And no, you're not just asking for lunch. You're asking me to keep carrying you. I'm not doing that anymore. If you're going to do what I think you're going to do, you're a fool who learned nothing from Sean's stab. You won't get away with a bleeding head and exhaustion this time. Oh, fuck me, Lisa was right. She was always right."

"About what?"

"This game was always just a place for escape and recovery. That was the beauty of it. That was what made it great. And this time around, it was greater than ever. Everyone got to be a part and we said goodbye to Calvin and Spellbinder, and you got your closure. That's what he gave you, Elliot. A beautiful, lovely way to allow you to move on. Don't kill yourself with a release date now."

"I'm gonna finish it."

Skye screamed. I heard her kicking something. Maybe a chair.

"You're just not quite there, are you? The lights are on, but no one's home."

"You're making a burger and fries into an existential debate."

"Isn't that about fucking time? Aren't we finally getting somewhere? Don't you think you're ready for some goddamn real and honest truth?"

"I don't think anyone ever is. But you know what? I hear someone coming, I gotta check the door. Steps in the stairs. Could be the team coming back. See you around, okay?"

"Don't you fucking hang up on me, not now when we're finally getting somewhere–"

Chapter 53

A WOLVERINE

Now I was pacing, like a wolverine in captivity. I had my hands tightly clasped behind my back when I didn't wave them before me or squeezed them into fists. The next step was right there before me, literally shining as my phone's screen flared up. But whenever I reached for it, my fingers were made of lead.

Fuck you, Skye.

Fuck you for messing with my head like this.

I was just about to shift into next gear, and you had to ruin it all.

I only wanted to have lunch.

A festering thought took hold.

They'd laugh at me when I called. They'd wonder if this was a joke, or worse, they wouldn't even answer. Ignore me, until my dignity forced me to beg them to give me a sign that they got my messages.

You really were at the bottom of desperation's pool when you settled for acknowledgment that you'd at least been heard.

Maybe I was the last one to see this for what it was, a vain fantasy necessary for the fool to finish his errand. No one would want this game. No one would want to work with me again. I was the guy who wrecked one of the world's most famous studios. When the other guy left, the one with the real talent, I remained to burn down the house.

I screamed. I pounded my fists on the walls, tearing up the skin until I started to bleed. I wanted to cry but I couldn't, there was only rage. I turned around and shouted to the wall.

"If I died," I screamed, "and you brought them back, they would've stayed. You could've been great again. With me gone, there would've been nothing in your way."

After that, I sank to the floor and leaned against the wall of art. I cried, but I couldn't make sense of it, didn't know if I was going to explode in fury or drown in grief. I'd sworn to not become that creature of self-pity again, the one that wandered his apartment in filthy robes just a few months ago, but I still loathed myself. I didn't want to. I didn't think I deserved to feel this way. But I did, anyway.

The clouds parted.

A few rays of light shone in through the windows, to fire up the dust that floated through the space.

I looked at the slice of sun outside. The gray skies were already doing their best to cover it up. It'd be gone soon.

I heard steps in the stairs and again, my heart raced. This time, it'd be Skye. Or perhaps just a few of the Spellbinders, not all of them but the most devoted ones. Joakim, Yasmine, maybe Angela. They'd come and say that of course they want to finish this, you only get a chance like this once, and that's if you're lucky. You didn't think we'd pass on this, did you? Hah, you really did. Well, think again, because we're back.

The steps passed and continued to the next floor.

There would be no one to open that door again, no steps that would stop outside, scratch off the dust from their soles, and enter to take off their shoes. I was the only one still stuck in this, despite the chance I'd created to release myself from these chains. That had been Calvin's parting gift to me, like he said in his letter. He wanted to give me closure. And I'd made it into something I possibly couldn't finish, ever.

Despite the clouds' best effort to hide the sun, they failed.

They scattered, as the light pierced through the gray mist. Behind them, the skies emerged.

The clear, blue skies, as it were.

No.

I was not the last one to not see this for what it was.

I was the only one seeing this for what it really was.

Me, and that other guy. The one with the talent.

We saw it.

We had seen it since we were kids.

He'd known I'd still see it, once he was gone.

I stood up and looked at the stick drawing he'd made me. I touched it.

The dread was still there. But really, I'd settled my score with these demons some time ago. I needed to remind myself that they were guests at my table, not the other way around. Sometimes, guests don't behave.

"We always owned the room," I said. "Didn't we, Calvin? It was difficult without you. But you're still here, aren't you? You'll be with me when I'm going to Los Angeles, won't you?"

I removed the needle from the stick drawing and took it down. Folded it carefully into a small roll, and put it in my pocket.

Chapter 54

FEROCIOUS

Dad had been strangely cool about the punch. We walked back in silence to Cornelia and Calvin's house. He dropped me off and said he'd check in on me every day, and whenever I wanted to come home, he'd be there.

Then he left and it felt like Cornelia put a snare around me and slowly pulled me closer. She reached out in an almost casual manner, taking her affection for granted. I brushed her away with such force that she almost lost her balance. She pulled back.

"Well, now," she said. "Aren't you the angry little gentleman."

I backed into the corner of their kitchen. It didn't make much of a difference, considering the small space of their home, but it felt like a necessary distance. Calvin looked at me under his bangs, confused but his mind furiously at work as he opened and closed his eyes, shifted his feet, and spun a pencil between his fingers. I threw him a glance.

Cornelia took a step towards me but Calvin slid in between.

"No, Mum," he said. "Leave him alone."

"I'm not gonna hurt him." She looked over her son's head. "Elliot, c'mere. Tell us what's going on."

But Dad had told me not to. Not until the papers were sorted, whatever that meant. Not that he'd earned my loyalty. But it was an excuse for me to keep quiet, because if I said anything, I was afraid I would dissolve into a quivering pile and melt into the ground. And what would I say? That none of this mattered anymore. Because it didn't. Me and Calvin, our game, Sara and Lisa, staying here. It made no difference. Like that space in time before Johan was born only to die, I had lived in a bliss that was temporary at best. The future was nothing but a menace.

"Back off, Mum," Calvin said.

Cornelia looked at me, then back at her son. Her expression softened. She sat down by the kitchen table.

"What did you and your father talk about, Elliot?"

"Doesn't matter," I snapped. "If I tell, you'll tell. And he said I couldn't."

"Your father can't tell you what to do. Not anymore."

"Sure he can. He just did. It's not like I'm a grown-up. Just because you don't care about rules, doesn't mean they don't apply. He'll come back and get me. You know that. I'm not your son. You can't say these things. If you do, you're a liar."

Calvin turned to his mum as her face turned red, panic all over him now. "M-m-mum...he d-d-didn't mmm...mmm...mean that. He's just s-s-sorry. Aren't you, Elliot?"

I sank down to the floor. I leaned my head in my hands. "Leave me alone."

Cornelia got up. Suddenly, she seemed furious, in a quietly alarming way. I turned away and stared into the wall, but gave her a quick look from the corner of my eye.

"I don't care about rules," she said slowly. "No one ever asked me about 'em. That gives me the benefit of deciding m'self."

"Mum," Calvin said. "I don't wanna m-move again. Please. Elliot's my b-b-best friend. I don't wanna leave. Mum, please. Don't make this into a fight."

She turned to Calvin. "A fight?" she said. "Who said anything about a fight?"

"You know what I mean."

She took a deep breath. "Why don't you stay with Elliot, Calvin, honey? Call the girls, watch a movie, have some popcorn. I'll be home in a few hours."

"No," he shouted. "What're you gonna do? Don't leave. Stay here. Have coffee. Bake something."

Cornelia walked up to her apron, perched on a hook, and almost ripped it from the wall. Then, she folded it carefully over her arm.

"Calvin, honey. I gotta go to work."

"M-mum. Please."

She closed her eyes. She was gone for a few moments, trembling. "I'm running late. I gotta go."

She put on her apron. There was a tender silence in the house now, as she slowly moved her hands to tie the knots around her waist. "I'm gonna serve coffee and pancakes today, boys. To people I don't know. I'll be nice, Calvin, dear. It'll be hard. The hardest thing I've ever done. But I'll be nice. Do you know why, honey?"

He shook his head furiously.

She looked at me with a sad smile. "We're home."

She picked up her purse, holding it firmly with both hands. "I'm glad I've finally learned what a fight worth taking looks like."

"B-but you're not g-gonna fight, Mum. Are you?"

She looked at us. "No. I'm going to work."

She adjusted her apron and left.

Calvin walked up to the doorway. He looked at her as she strolled down the road to Fjellhamn's town square.

I got up. Wiped my arm over my eyes, and stood beside him. "What's she gonna do?"

He thought about this for so long that I wondered if he'd heard me.

"G-go to work, I guess. Like she said." He frowned. "She never puts on her apron at home. She wears it when she gets there."

She was almost over the hill now. Despite the distance, she

remained large, like the shape of gravity that kept the horizon in check.

I shuffled my feet. "You sure she won't go kill my dad or something?"

Calvin smiled. Then, he rolled his eyes and spoke with a creepy voice: "Do you waaant her too? Ooo-ooh?"

"Nah."

But I thought about it for a second.

"I mean, maybe just have a go at him with the frying pan or something. But kill? Nah."

"You know what?" Calvin said. "Let's go find Sara and Lisa. We haven't worked on the game for ages."

"Or at all, really. We just got your sketches and my notes."

Calvin grinned. "All the more reason to find them."

But as he moved to leave, scurrying about to collect his pads and pencils, my feet felt heavy, my shoes filled with rocks.

"I need to tell you something."

He stopped and looked at me.

"I'm not supposed to," I said. "But I'm doing it anyway."

He put his tools away, suddenly serious.

"W-we're gonna need lemonade for this one, aren't we?"

I sighed. "Yeah, Calvin. Lots and lots of lemonade."

Chapter 55

SIR CALVIN, LORD ELLIOT

We didn't really drink any of it, though. It was there, on the table, in a pitcher with two glasses next to it. He mixed it up, poured us one each but when we sat down and I told him I was moving, he didn't touch it. Nor did I.

The sun was out and there wasn't a cloud in the sky. The door and windows were open and a warm breeze drifted through the house like a friendly ghost. In the distance, we heard children laughing and some old jazz tune playing from a dusty vinyl recorder. Mr. Svensson was home, and his kids were there with their kids. It was a good day for him.

Calvin looked at his glass, filled to the brim with lemonade.

"I'm t-thirsty," he said.

I didn't say anything. It felt like I'd said enough.

But since that seemed to be about it from him, I eventually had to break the silence or it would've choked us.

"My mum's sick," I said. "This is better for her."

"You s-sound like your d-dad."

"You've hardly met him."

He stared into the table.

"I d-d-don't get it," he said. "Why are you moving?"

"I told you."

"How's moving making your mum better?" There was a slight tremble in his voice.

"Closer to hospitals. And stuff."

"My mum always says hospitals make you worse."

"Yeah, well, your mum also thinks you shouldn't go to school."

Calvin bounced up from his chair and lunged at me, one fist raised and another one waving. He punched me from my seat and before I'd hit the floor, he was screaming and came at me again. I hit him on the face and after that, we were just a tangled mess, rolling around on the floor, trading grunts and hits. We banged into the wall and something fell off from a shelf and broke into many pieces. I got out from his grip but he jumped at me again, but unlike the time when we'd fought Lars and his goons, we froze whenever we got an opening for a knock-out strike or a well-directed punch. After a few minutes, we stopped, sliding away from each other, breathing heavily. I had my back on the floor, he was leaning against the wall.

"I'm thirsty," he said. He got up and drank his glass in one sweep. He offered me mine. I stood up, took it, and emptied it.

This day. The worst. Ever. And that's saying something.

Calvin looked sad now. "I'm the one who's always moving," he said.

I nodded.

"You've lived here all your life," he said. "You can't move now. Not now, when I'm h...h...here."

"I know," I said.

"I'm home," he said. "You're here. I'm home."

He looked at me now. I saw sparks in his eyes, wet patches that gleamed in the sun.

"You know, Elliot, I never said...but I'm really sorry about your brother."

"You did say. Many times."

"I did?"

"Yeah."

He pointed to his nose and nodded at me. "Sorry about t...t-that, too."

"Huh?" But then I felt it, a small stream of blood over my mouth. It was warm and thick.

"It's okay. Besides, I think I got your eye. You're gonna get a bruise there."

"Got plenty before," he said. Then, he exhaled and sat down, like an old man with his hands resting on his knees. "So...h-how do we get your d-d-dad to change his mind?"

I had to laugh at this. "You don't want to get it, do you?"

"You haven't moved yet, have you?"

"He's given this a lot of thought. It's not like Mum's gonna get bett–"

Suddenly, Calvin bounced up from his chair but this time, I was prepared and rose with my fists ready for another go. Sure, he was waving his arms like before and he was red in the face again, but he was also stuttering so wildly that I thought he'd choked on a fly or something.

I lowered my fists.

"Hi...hi...hi got an i-d-d-dea," he croaked. "I g-g-got a g-g-great idea. The b-best ever."

I smiled wearily. It's not like I thought he'd find a way out of this. This was happening. I was already accepting it. But even if Calvin would someday end up in hell, wired to all the machinery and contraptions the devil could think of, he'd still think about ways to escape, confident that in time, he'd pull it off.

"B-because you know what this means, right?" he said.

"It means I'm moving."

"We already know that." He was almost annoyed by my answer. "No. It means, we got a deadline."

"For what?"

He rolled his eyes. "For the game, stupid." He kept dancing around, almost chanting. "We got a release date now. It's like you said. We gotta finish it. And now, we gotta finish it before you leave."

"How's that even gonna happen? I have no idea how to make a game. Neither do you."

"And neither do Sara or Lisa. But we're the smartest people on the planet." He spread out his arms. "We're gonna figure it out."

He was contagious, that's for sure. I did my best not to get pulled in by his strange enthusiasm. There was still blood on my lips. I wondered if he'd snap again, just in a different way this time.

"And we'll build the game," he said, "and sell it at the Fjellhamn Festival and make lots of money and then you don't have to move, then we'll have tons and tons of money and you can figure shit out when you have lots of money, like buy a bigger house or maybe hire a doctor to help your mum or I don't know...but people with money always figure shit out."

I laughed and shook my head. "Of all the crazy crap ideas you've had..."

"This one's by far the best! I know." He bowed with grace, grabbing his pen to wield it like a scepter.

I got up. He'd stopped bouncing now, looking at me with wide eyes, a wider grin, laughing with tears rolling down his face.

"I was gonna say," I said. "Of all the insane ideas you've had... of all the impossible shit coming out of your head...this one's happening. This one's going down."

"I know, right?" He was turning his right arm now, as if firing up an engine with a beat.

"This plan, sir Calvin of Shoebox Castle. This plan is about as goddamn foolproof as a plan can be."

"Why thank you, Lord Elliot of the Fjellhamn Hut. You are too good to me. Hey! It's gonna be so awesome. The *Greatest Game of All*, released on the Fjellhamn Festival. We'll be rich and you don't have to move and we can be best friends forever."

We were already on our way out the door and rushing to our bikes when we fired off those final lines, forgetting our stuff, forgetting to close the door, forgetting about reality in general, with a mission to find Sara and Lisa to reboot the production.

Yeah, well.

You already know how this is gonna end, don't you?

At least back then, I still had a team.

Chapter 56

CLEAR BLUE SKIES

If you wanted to know the right time to go fish, you just had to look up. Know your skies and you'd know if things would get rough. As the fishermen had told me and Calvin over grilled cod and slices of lemon when we were just getting started, before Sara and Lisa were a part of it, there was nothing as deceiving as the occasional streak of a white cloud.

"And nothing more enjoyable," one of the older men said, so worn by the sun and the salt that he'd made a dried plum look young, "than watching city folks set sail on their forty feeters, thinking they'll get a quiet night in a natural harbor."

They all guffawed at this, but Calvin looked puzzled. His mouth was full of fish. He chewed slowly.

"B-but whath's the differenthe bethween a thick fluffy cloud and a r-r-really...," and he had to take a pause to swallow now, "t-thin one?"

"The big ones," one of the men said, "they're obvious. They could've been storm clouds, but decided not to. But the thin ones... they're sneaky."

"Tricky little bastards," another one of the fishermen said. "Like puffs of smoke from a fire that's out of control. You just can't see it yet."

"You gotta respect the fury there."

"Like my wife," one of the younger men said. "She's expecting. Twins." They all nodded at this and gave him a camaraderie pat on the shoulder.

"We're gonna have clouds in our game," I said. "All kinds. Right, Calvin?"

He nodded, his eyes half closed now as a scholar acknowledging the obvious. Of course there would be clouds in our game. To think anything else would be daft.

As we'd once agreed, the prime circumstances for video game development were when the wind came and brought the rain with it, the kind of weather we'd been taught by the fishermen to spot by recognizing the sneaky streaks of thin, white clouds. Not the intense heat of a brutal July, but the cool, soothing shower from a soft May.

Now, every day when I woke up in my apartment, I made myself a coffee, sat in the window that faced the park, and looked to the skies. The damn summer wasn't about to throw me a bone, though, with either a thick, gray mist doing nothing or a constant blue with the sun glaring back at me.

A week went by like this.

I took walks. Went to see a movie. Had dinner in a place by the river. Bought a magazine, read it slowly. Tried a novel, but got tired. Had a drink in a place where a lot of cool people went.

I had moments where my hands shook, if only slightly, and brief episodes where my heart raced for no apparent reason. Like a fighter crawling out from the lair of an epic boss fight, barely alive but still breathing, I needed a power station to save and recharge before I went into battle again. I was ready. I just needed something to jumpstart me.

Sometimes, my walks led me close to Lisa's house. I saw it in the corner of my eye but kept going straight ahead instead of turning left, or I noticed its body between two other buildings if I was in the neighboring block.

Once or twice, I'd been at their gates with a bunch of notebooks in my backpack, my hand resting on the handle. Wondering if I had something with me now that was worth the mending, something that could bridge our worlds.

I'd played out in my head how I knocked on their door and maybe Lisa opened, or Calvin, and I'd say, "Hey, I got something I wanna show you now. I've finally got an idea that's worth our time."

Calvin would laugh and say, "It's about time you showed up, Elliot. You haven't even met my kids. But now you're here, finally. Come in. Hey, you can stay for dinner, maybe read a bedtime story to Isabelle. You were always good at telling stories."

But while I'd waited, doubted, with my hand on the gate's handle, time beat me to it. It's like Calvin had said to me in his note–it had gone so very fast, in the end.

After a few days, I took the left turn anyway and passed the house as if circumstance happened to put me here. I pictured that the day when I'd open the gates to enter the garden would be an ordinary one, comfortably familiar as if time hadn't passed. I'd feel it and know it and just go there.

The windows were dark. The toys were gone from the garden. While neat, the place looked abandoned. Slumbering, waiting.

They'd moved.

I sat down on the bench that faced the house.

Lisa had always traveled.

That had been our beat, as we'd grown out of our teens and into something that resembled the life of a responsible adult.

I'd gone somewhere with Calvin and Skye to make a game and Lisa had stuffed a backpack with socks, underwear, and a toothbrush and gone in the other direction. Then, a few months later, she would show up, tanned and dirty with unwashed hair and a big smile, directly from the airport with her bag still strapped on. She'd grab me, pull me close, and give me a long, warm kiss. She smelled of sweat and worn shoes. I loved it.

"This time, I'm not going anywhere," she'd say and lock me with her eyes. "What're you guys working on?"

"Some game," I'd say. "It's pretty cool. Wanna see it?"

"Do I ever."

She'd show up in the evenings with takeaway, sleep on a couch if it got late, try the game if there was a build you could play, offer feedback, or come up with an idea to crack a problem we'd been struggling with. But she never wrote a line of code, never opened the developer suite to check out the state of the architecture or chip in when the programmers were stuck.

"Just because you're good at it doesn't mean you should do it."

That was her answer, whenever we were stupid enough to ask her if she wanted to join the fray again. It bugged Calvin to some extent and Skye in particular, and they didn't always approve of her being there. But I loved the distraction, the affection she gave, and how easy it came for her to embrace and accept me. She lived with me in whatever place I had at the moment, and things sort of got brighter and had more color when she was around. The simpler things became something to appreciate, like sleeping close together or watching a bad movie on a rainy Sunday afternoon.

But whenever the game we were working on came close to release, there was an itch.

"What's gonna happen now, Elliot?" she would ask.

"I don't know," I'd say. "We're starting up a new production. Calvin's done some amazing art. I've got a few ideas on a new controller scheme."

"Okay. But what about us?"

"What about us?"

"You work ten to fourteen hours a day. Saturdays and Sundays included. Months before you let go of your current game, you're well into the next one. When are we gonna be your priority?"

"We got a chance to build our own studio. We don't wanna work for Sean forever."

"Why not?"

"You know what he's like. How he treats people."

"He's good at what he does."

"And what's that? Intimidating developers into sequels? Drafting up shit contracts in his favor? Shutting down studios, firing people, cancelling projects?"

"And yet, here you are. Pretty successful. He had something to do with that."

It always annoyed me, when she brought that up. It's not like Lisa justified Sean's infamous ways of working with his ability to acquire talent. It's just that I chose to see it that way. That annoyed her even more.

"There's a place for you in our studio," I said.

Lisa frowned. "Let's say that happened. You think you gonna put in less, when you got a studio of your own?"

"You can be a part of it. Like back in the days."

"We were just kids then. We were playing. Is that what you're still doing?"

"This is work. It's my career. You're an amazing developer. You'd be able to move mountains, if you joined us."

"I've been at the top of some of the greatest mountains. View's amazing. Can't see why I'd ever wanna move them."

Once these talks had begun, there was no stopping them.

Eventually, Lisa felt the wanderlust, and she left. We didn't really break up, because that would mean that there was a commitment to stay together in the first place.

"I'll see you around, Elliot," she said as we said goodbye.

"I'm gonna miss you."

"Sure."

And now, her house was empty. Cleaned out.

She'd probably picked up her bag one last time, helped her kids strap on theirs, and then gone on a plane with them, heading to a part of the world they'd never seen before.

The bench was getting cold.

People passed by. Continued to somewhere else, still laughing.

I pretended one of them was Lisa. She'd see me, break out from the crowd, and join me. Smile, maybe say nothing for a while, just sit there and watch me with her hazel eyes, holding my hand.

I looked up.

I saw sneaky streaks of thin, white clouds at the horizon. Tricky little bastards, drifting towards the city.

We wouldn't have clear, blue skies for much longer.

I smiled.

Chapter 57

THE JERRY MAGUIRE OF OUR WORLD

Like the fishermen predicted, the rain came the next day. It wasn't one of those brutal showers that we'd defined as ideal for development, but it seemed only fitting that this one was calm and slow, a curious and comforting chatter to accompany me as I went to the studio. On my way there, my heart beat to a groove it hadn't followed for a long time, the funk that slowly built over weeks until you entered the stage to serve your pitch. You were the actor preparing for the curtain to rise, a singer waiting for the opening chords. It'd be just that one time and then it would be gone. You'd live or die by the judgment that came with it.

I picked Christina at Microsoft first. I knew I didn't have to pretend with her. She'd always been one of the more gung-ho publishers I'd ever worked with, even before Spellbinder, when we were still with Sean. I knew she'd call my bullshit if I tried it on her, but that she'd go for it anyway. If you had the guts to pioneer the first launch titles on the original Xbox system, way back when the world was still scratching its head at Microsoft's attempt to build a video game console (and Skye and I were held in Seattle customs once, the guards had no idea what an Xbox was, and considered the possibility that our debug kits were weapons of mass destruction), you had the guts to hear me out.

And Christina did. And she laughed, all the way from Seattle to Stockholm. Thinking she'd never hear from me again, and it had been a few years, so she said she'd cancel any fucking thing she'd booked at the E3 show if I came, including that deal Microsoft had going with Zlatan Ibrahimovic, which she couldn't talk about anyway.

"But it's Zlatan," she said. "If I say it's a game about a demigod who comes to our world to teach us how to play soccer like titans and make love like the immortals, I haven't said too much. He describes it as the next *God of War*, but with him in the lead instead of Kratos. Obviously, he wants to do his own voice work."

"We can't all be Vin Diesel, can we?" I said.

"You tell Zlatan that."

We laughed so hard at this, we had to take a break.

Once we were back in the conversation, she said: "Kratos or not, Zlatan doesn't have a demo. And you do, Elliot. If Calvin was in on this, I wanna see it. If for no other reason than to pay my respects."

"I'm gonna be the Jerry Maguire of our world," I said.

"You gonna show me the money?"

"If you complete me."

"Who else you seeing?"

"Everyone but Nintendo," I said.

"They're not seeing anyone these days."

"Tell me about it."

"Just did. So you're meeting with Valve, then?"

"Well, okay, not Valve. Gabe's an–"

"I know what Gabe is. Spencer?"

"Sony, sure, but maybe not with Spencer. He's too vague. I'm too old for that–"

"–shit. Yeah, I know. Okay, so you're going multi-platform. PlayStation and the Xbox and not Nintendo, but maybe PC and mobile?"

"I don't know. I don't have a team, a plan, or a producer. How should I know?"

Christina laughed again. "Man, I'm looking forward to this. Your pitches, Lindh. Always were the best."

"Some even better than the games."

"Just when I thought I'd heard everything, here you are, raised from the dead, bringing another dead guy, saying that one of the most legendary studios of our time is about to rise again to make the best game ever. Makes Zlatan seem modest."

"You missed me, didn't you?"

"Did I ever. See you in LA, Elliot. And for once, not in June."

"Looking forward to it."

I left the studio with an umbrella, enjoying the rain's tap dance over my head, and walked to Maria Square, to a café where Skye and I had spent a lot of time in the early Spellbinder years. I had a coffee and a croissant, bought a paper, and read it from first to last page. Riding on my wave of inspiration, I called Kicki Hunt, now at Activision but once at Bioware. While she was her usual composed self, she did say that whatever grenade I'd bring, she was looking forward to being shellshocked, for once.

"Nothing's changed," she said matter-of-factly. "It's all sequels and franchises. Another *Call of Duty* for us, another *Battlefield for EA*. We're trading the same old punches. Except when we're not and someone tries to come up with something original. How's it even possible to invest in something that's statistically extremely likely to fail? How do you pitch that? Where are the studios like Rare of our age? The Looking Glasses or the Spellbinders, for that matter? You know how many failures it takes to come up with the Sims? The guts it takes to try again?"

"Not sure Wright ever did a bad game," I said.

"E3's moving from June to August and you show up. It's like it's making time for you."

I laughed. "After the Summit fail, I'm surprised they tweaked it again."

"Who cares? It's just a day in the calendar. Look, Elliot. Even failure can be beautiful. It has to be, or you won't succeed."

"So I'll see you there, then?"

"If this is your *Freddy* Mercury moment, I wanna be able to say that I was there. Don't bleed out on my carpet, though."

"Don't worry. Sean'll clean it up."

She laughed and we said goodbye. But I was left with a strange feeling. Was I just selling tickets to watch the freak dance one last time? More importantly—did it matter? It's not like my dignity was at stake. If it got me into the room, maybe that was enough.

I crossed a few bridges. The rain was passing now. I bought a ticket to a park and had an ice cream while I checked out some of the animals, considering who was next on my list. On a whim, I called Patrice Mechner at Ubisoft. He didn't answer. I left him a message and then I went for Martin Fitz at Capcom. He answered, but after a few polite exchanges on how things had been since last time and he was so sorry to hear about Calvin, he said that he's not making decisions anymore. None that counted, anyway. He was working in Europe now. I had to call Japan if I wanted traction, but he didn't have any names to offer.

I returned to the city and took the subway to nowhere in particular. The cool, dark underground calmed me down. I called Henrik Stahl at THQ Nordic. He didn't answer but sent me a text message that he'd get in touch next week, and Ninni Summers at Sony said that I should try and reach her after E3. Things were just too busy before then.

I felt a pain in my stomach, an unsettling sequence of stabs as something woke up and moved around in there.

"Glad to hear you're doing well," Ninni said. "Someone told me about your new ventures. I'm sure it'll be fine."

"Give me a meeting, then. Let me show you."

"No time, Elliot. My schedule's been locked for weeks."

"It's just a demo of the greatest game ever made, Ninni."

"Yeah, you told me. So did a lot of developers before you. Everybody thinks they got the next *Heavenly Sword*."

"Hoo-kay. Look, I always liked Tameem, but to call *Heavenly Sword* the greatest game ever…"

"My point exactly. We still remember *Ninja Theory's* pitch."

"They got a job, don't they?"

She sighed. "In a manner of speaking, sure."

"Anyway. Microsoft's on board. They want an exclusive."

"And I wish you the best with that. We'll talk after E3, okay? I promise I'll get you a meeting in August, or maybe September. It's not like we're not interested. But you know how these things work. What were you thinking anyway, calling when the show's just around the corner?"

"Might not be a game available after E3. You could be missing out."

"How's that my problem? Isn't that good for you, if that's the case?"

I didn't have an answer to that. She continued, "You got shit to prove, Elliot. Deal with it. Accept your rep. Meanwhile, I'll see you in the Los Angeles bars and you can come to our London office after the summer. That's not an empty promise. It's not like your name doesn't attract. But approach with caution, you know."

We said goodbye.

I had this brief memory, where Mum had once been up at dawn before I went to school. Dad had fixed me breakfast and he'd helped me with my homework. The kitchen smelled of fresh coffee. I was about nine years old.

Before I left, strapping on my backpack and tying my sneakers, she stroked my hair and said softly, "You'll never be great, Elliot."

I looked away. It stung, like the hit from a diseased bee. There was so much pain in that strike, a load that had to be moved or it'd consume whoever carried it, and she'd shifted it to me just before I left.

Dad had reached out to intervene, to pull her away or do whatever to stop her, but he'd been unable to, and all he could do was to send me off with a hug and a whisper. Mum stood by the window and had coffee, gazing absently at the rocks and the sea.

I got off the subway.

I had an impulse to send Skye a message, but I called her instead. I was somewhere further north now, not really in one of my favorite neighborhoods, so I stared into the ground when the phone kept ringing.

She didn't answer.

I called again.

No answer.

I sat down on a bench, looking into a building on the other side of the street. Don't remember what kind. Could've been a hospital. Or apartments for the wealthy. Maybe a set of office floors. Maybe not even a building, but a small park.

I did the journey back to the studio in a familiar but long absent haze. My hands were shaking again. I walked slowly to Maria Street and up the stairs to the Spellbinder lair. Halfway there, I stopped and looked at my phone to see if I'd missed Skye calling me back. She hadn't.

Apparently, I'd forgotten to lock the door. It was open. I entered.

Maybe it was the Spellbinders returning. Hah.

But why not?

Skye had told them that Elliot was going to be out almost all day.

"I know him," she'd say to them. "This is one of his walk and think days. We got time to stage a welcoming surprise before he gets back, to show him that we're here to finish the game. He'll have meetings booked, publishers excited, and we'll crunch to get it done and show the world what the greatest game ever, is like."

I looked into the void that was the studio hall.

The twilight shadows had grown long, stirring slowly around the glowing screens. The hum from the computers were a hypnotic drone, the darkness creeping closer to Calvin's art on the wall. The game was still looping, sighing with the wind from the speakers.

"How the fuck," I said to the ghosts in here, "how the fuck is it that I always end up in a goddam oversized room, surrounded by computers and a fucking game that I have no idea how to finish?"

Then, I noticed.

A pair of shoes, by the threshold.

Actually, not just a pair. But a couple. Three pairs.

One slick, black. Polished.

That'd be Oscar's.

A pair of sneakers. Very neat.

Only Filip wore sneakers that never looked worn.

And a brown, leathery pair, with thin, black laces. Expensive.

I wasn't sure about those. Could be Ellie's, though she'd have a higher cut. Probably–

"Hello, Elliot."

I looked up.

I hadn't seen him. He'd been there all the time, of course.

Sitting at one of the workstations, with two people I didn't recognize. Looked like lawyers, though. If people of the law had a look, this was it.

"I hope you don't mind," Sean said. "The door was open. We let ourselves in." He leaned forward. "Skye said you'd probably be here."

His grin widened. I even saw some teeth.

Chapter 58

BIG BABIES

What was that noise, a loud and frequent bang that fell like a hammer next to my ears? A nearby construction site, perhaps? A traffic jam outside?

Oh, right. My heart again. That constant, loud thump that seemed to shift between all kinds of familiar and unfamiliar grooves these days.

Sean looked around.

"Isn't this the old Dice offices?"

The other two were quiet. She wore a dress, he wore a G–Man suit. He had a tie, she had a Lara Croft braid. She had a thin port-folio in her lap, he had a thicker one.

"This is a little late for you," I said. "It's almost nine."

He smiled. "Sun won't set for an hour yet." He pointed to his feet. "See? We took off our shoes. I always liked that tradition. Skye's dad came up with that, didn't he? She says hello, by the way."

He kept smiling, hoping I'd take the bait but knowing I wouldn't. I could only assume that for whatever reason he was here, he was only getting started. Warming up. Trying out a few punches, seeing what worked today.

So he'd trimmed his offer. Made it into something I couldn't refuse, I'm sure. And he'd talked to Skye.

"Since you're here," I said, "coffee?"

"Thanks, but no. Maybe you youngsters want some?" He looked at the man on his right, the woman on his left. The man seemed bored, the way a parent could be when a child was past its bedtime. The woman was concerned. She stole a glance in my direction but dodged me when I returned it.

"We just moved here, you know," I said. "Not sure we got the appliances to make some."

"That's all right. I'll have some water, if you got it." He stood up but when the woman opened her folder and pulled out a pile of documents, he gave her a look and she put it back. Then, he turned to face the game on the wall.

I walked up to him. We stood next to each other, watching and listening.

"It's good, isn't it?" I said.

Sean nodded slowly.

"It's the kind of magic I always hoped I'd get from you kids. I still remember that day in Fjellhamn...what was it called?"

"The Fjellhamn Festival."

"Hmm." He smiled to himself, hands in his pockets. "Those were the days."

He sighed.

I noticed that the woman was standing now, her hands holding the folder. She looked straight at me.

"Can I just say that I love *Clear Blue Skies*?" she said. "I played it all the time when I was studying. I have so many fond memories from that game."

I smiled. "Thank you."

"And my son plays *Laser Fog* all the time."

This came as a surprise to me and for a brief moment, Sean and I exchanged looks. We laughed and while it lasted only for a second, it was real and warm.

"You tell her," Sean said. "It's your story."

"No," I said. "It doesn't matter." I looked at her. "I'm sorry. I'm Elliot. I guess you're here to cause some kind of damage, but that doesn't mean we can't say hello first."

She walked up to me and took my hand. "I'm Elin."

The man remained in his chair, browsing his phone, pretending he was busy.

"That's Henrik," she said. "It's okay. Nobody likes him."

Henrik looked up and gave us a faint smile. Then he returned to his phone.

Sean approached the wall. Elin fell back.

He was quiet for a while, watching the art and the game in an almost meditative state.

I wondered about his tactics, when he'd go for the kill, whatever it was. As far as I knew, no one had died, so he couldn't play that card again. And even if he'd offered me the world, I wouldn't sell. He was smart enough to know this.

That was the scary part about Sean. He'd imply by his very person that to know someone like him, you had to lack compassion yourself. Most people weren't built that way, so they lost the fight before it started. With a guy like Sean, you had to go *Double Dragon* or he'd take your folder.

But my hands weren't shaking anymore. My pulse had slowed down. The low hum from the machines were like a quiet battle hymn, their electric voices traveling straight through me, charging me up.

"My father was a musician," Sean said. "Quite accomplished."

"I know," I said. "You took us to one of his concerts once."

"I did? Maybe I did."

He kept looking at the game.

"You know what I was to him, Elliot?"

I shook my head.

"A man who nurtured artists. Someone who made concerts possible."

"Okay."

"According to him, that was just something that had to be done. Like driving a bus or working in a store. We had a duty. He had a calling."

He was silent for a while.

"He did put me in music school," he said slowly. "When I was a kid, I played the piano."

He faced me now. His eyes were cold.

"People like him wouldn't exist without people like me."

"They'd do okay, don't you think? The world would still want music."

"They'd have a hard time finding it."

"There's some truth in that, for sure."

Sean laughed. "Truth, he says. "You got a complicated relationship with truth. You know what I call it?"

"You're gonna tell me, I'm sure."

His jaw tightened.

"Ingratitude, Elliot. That's what I call it."

He reached out for the controller, positioned on a table close to him. He held them in a weak grip, as if he could drop them at any moment. I removed them from his hands and put them back on the table.

"What do you want, Sean?"

Sean was looking at the canvas again, shifting his gaze from the game to the art.

I felt a dry patch in my mouth now and a quick stab at my heart, muscles tightening with my breath. The electricity was still there, which made it all the more exhausting.

"He's suing you for all the property related to what we're calling the *Greatest Game of All*," Elin said.

I hadn't noticed, but suddenly she was standing next to me, papers in hand but not looking at them. She still seemed troubled, but she had a calm and composed manner now.

"You'll receive the formal paperwork in the mail tomorrow,"

she said. "It's been in process for a while."

"A while?" I looked at Sean, who pretended he didn't notice.

Elin cleared her throat.

"The assumption is that much of the assets, code, and intellectual property of this game were developed at Biosoft's offices during the time when you and the other owners of Spellbinder Software were still working there. Having employed Biosoft's equipment, as well as time and resources, to build something that would eventually be yours and not the property of Biosoft means they can claim that the game is theirs."

"I doubt you ever understood what *Clear Blue Skies* was about."

"Isn't it just a game?" she said.

But she withdrew, her eyes half closed. She adjusted her glasses and put the paper back in her folder.

I reached out and grabbed Sean by the arm. He woke up from his slightly hypnotic state, surprised and amused. He'd love to add abuse to this, I'm sure. A broken nose, a few bruises, and a black eye would've made his day. Not only was I a thief. I was violent, too.

"Why are you doing this?" I said. "What did I ever do to you?"

"Please," he said. "Let's keep this civilized."

"That's your answer?"

"On my time, Elliot. In my offices, with my equipment, you spent hours developing ideas and designs for this game that you're finally realizing. Then, you announced your departure and the rise of the Spellbinders at the E3 show, on stage, as you were presenting the last game you ever did for Biosoft. Everybody wrote about it. Talked about it. Laughed about it."

"So we're back to that, after all."

"I'm showing you the courtesy of informing you, before I make my move. If you'd done the same, I would've let you go. I'm not Pharaoh. You weren't slaves."

"You certainly made us feel like we were, sometimes."

"Oh, boo-hoo. Kid's got a job making games, earning lots of

money. But he feels like a slave. Come on, Elliot. Seriously."

I squeezed his arm, feeling the fuel pump through my veins. Throw a match in here and it'd all be over quickly, with no one left to tell the tale.

"You don't own Biosoft anymore," I said. "It was shut down years ago."

He looked at me with his stone gray eyes, and I let go. Took a few breaths, tried to calm down.

"Biosoft has no debts," he said. "It's still a shell for royalties. So that old place of mine, the one where I gave you kids a home and a career...that's still around."

"We haven't worked for you in twenty years. You don't have any hardware left with our material on it."

"We?" He laughed, as if he just realized something. "I'm suing you, Elliot. Not Spellbinder, or Skye or Lisa. I'm suing you."

Then, he waved it off, as if it was nothing.

"Anyway, I don't need the hardware." He nodded to the wall. "I know those assets. They're around, in property I used to publish."

"You can't point them out."

"Files leave marks, Elliot. There's a birth date to everything. Even a texture or a piece of code. I shouldn't have to tell you this, you're the artist. I'm just the one who nurtured you. Besides, I'll get a warrant. You got plenty of evidence right here. You might even go to jail. Don't worry, I'm not coming after the others. You've led them on. I sympathize with that. Sure, they're part of this. But you were always the architect. The one who held it together."

"This is fucking absurd. It could take you years to prove the point. You can't win this. It's vaporware."

Sean smiled.

He was starting to pace now, hands clasped behind his back.

"You looked healthy, when I saw you last. You were on your feet, doing well. Now, you're slipping again. You're more like the man I met before he entered that room and bled out on the carpet. The man that never made peace with his friend."

I didn't answer.

"You know what? You might be right. I might not win this. I think I will, but who knows? It'll be for the court to say. You're not gonna yield. Nor will I. So the battle begins, with your lawyers and my lawyers shifting papers back and forth. They'll claim your stuff and go deep, ask for your time and your thoughts, you'll be summoned to meetings and forced to remember things that happened a long time ago, and it'll be distracting." He nodded to himself. "Very distracting." He chuckled. "And expensive. Oh, my."

He turned to me and gestured to the wall. "You won't be able to focus on this. You'll want to be here. But you're always going to be there."

"I told you, Sean. We don't work with bullies."

"Again with the we. There's no one here, my dear boy. They all left. Yes, I heard about your party. It sounded nice. I'll be honest, I wish I'd been invited. But I can see why I wasn't." He chuckled again. Then, he got serious, pulled out a chair and sat down.

"But I can withdraw. Make you another offer. It'll be a fair one. You and Skye won't be lacking. And Lisa can provide for her children. I'll say it out loud, this is an absolutely lovely thing you got going here. The very magic I always knew you were capable of. And Calvin's art–"

"Which you're not getting."

"Of course I am. It's all part of it. I'll even go for the folder, that leathery thing Calvin always carried around, to complete the package."

"His mother gave him that."

"It's worth a shot. Anything I can connect to your reckless behavior, we'll throw in the mix. My lawyers are pretty good. But don't worry, once I have the stuff, I'll make sure to bag and archive everything with the care and caution it deserves."

"Bag it?"

"You don't think I'm going to publish this, are you? It'll never see the light of day. You were right. This game can't be done. Once

I've won the trial, I'll zip it, fold it, pack it and wrap it, put the folder on top and seal it in a box somewhere. Like the ark. Making sure no one will ever see it."

He stroked his mustache now.

"I've got publishers lined up," I said.

Sean leaned forward, waving his hand matter-of-factly. "You talking about the people you're seeing at E3? Oh, ha ha ha." He clapped his hands. "That's what I like about this industry. Despite all the money floating around, it's quite small. We know each other. We're friends. E3 is like our weekend trip. But then, Monday comes and you're back in reality." He fell back and crossed his legs. "You think anyone...anyone, Elliot...wants to buy property with a lawsuit hanging over it? No matter how great it is?"

Now, I felt like the guy in the ring who just took punch after punch, moving my head from one side to the other as each blow remodeled my face into oblivion. I didn't really know how to respond. But like Cornelia, as long as I didn't know the rules, I could always pretend I was winning.

So I pulled out a chair as well, and sat down in front of Sean. Close. We used to be friends, after all. He had his back against the main entrance, where his lawyers roamed now. Elin was restless. Henrik remained bored.

Sean smiled at me. He enjoyed the silence. The waiting game. He was looking forward to whatever I was going to throw at him now. The more curved the pitch, the more he'd enjoy his strike.

"Maybe we'd still be in Fjellhamn, if you hadn't found us."

He raised his eyebrows. Even laughed a little.

"Calvin working at a gas station. Me, part time in the old cinema. Sara would have kids and hate it. Lisa..." I paused for a second. "Actually, I think she'd do all right."

Sean nodded. "She always was the smartest of you."

"She got out, after all. But you...you'd be in publishing. Your catalog would be mediocre. Like now. You'd have a couple of sequels. A war game or two. Some movie franchise. And that'd be it. And those would be your good days. Now, you're hardly relevant. You're the music industry when Napster came around, television before Netflix."

He took out a cigarette. He lit it. Blew out some smoke. He looked at me from the side. There was a faint, red glow in his eyes from the cigarette's end.

"I can't imagine that you're suing me," I said, "because I left and took a few good people with me. Even if I did it with some... dramatic flair. But you had it coming. You've ruled publishing by humiliating, intimidating, and threatening developers."

"I treated you well."

"As long as we did what you told us to. But how's this relevant, anyway? This was a lifetime ago. I'm asking you again–what is this about, Sean?"

Sean leaned his chin in his hand.

He was quiet for a long time.

While whatever he said always came out as something he'd considered with care, to actually witness him preparing was rare.

There was a brief moment where a shadow moved over his face, where he looked away as if he'd felt a sting.

He faced me again, cigarette between his fingers.

"A man with your health, Elliot. You should take better care of yourself."

So that's the choice he'd made.

I would've offered the remains of my soul to find out the options he'd weighed. But the one he picked was very clear. His face was still, wrapped in thin lines of nicotine smoke.

"In the end," he said, "it's like Elin said. It's just a game. A good one, maybe. But just a game."

I got up.

"That's why you won't win this," I said. "To you, it really is just a game."

"How can it be anything else?"

"You should've asked your father."

Sean dropped his cigarette and stood up. It was still glowing, burning a black mark on the floor.

"It's like I said, Elliot. You're the only guy I know who'd face a hundred enemies alone and still take the fight."

I walked up to him and put a hand on his shoulder.

The sounds around us faded into a blur. My heart was so loud, my own voice echoed in my head like a man's cry from a sealed room. Sean looked nervous now, though he kept his grin. I could feel the strain in his shoulder. Just because a man was prepared to get his ass kicked, all according to plan, didn't mean he'd enjoy the hurt. But it would seal his case, for sure. It'd be worth it, for him. I already knew I'd regret it. But it would be an ending fitting for a song, at least. And most importantly, if Calvin had been here, he'd be the one to deliver the first strike, swinging his folder while we went down in flames together.

"Reckless," I said.

Sean shifted his feet.

"You called me reckless."

"Not in those words," he said slowly. "But sure."

I turned around.

Henrik was filming me with his phone. Elin was by the door, her hand on the handle.

I looked at Sean again.

"I guess I am," I said. "I guess I have been. From time to time."

I let go of his shoulder. He looked surprised. I backed away from him.

"You do what you do," I said. "I'll keep doing what I've always done. And we'll just have to take it from there, won't we, Sean?"

Sean put his hands in his pockets. He looked at the floor. He seemed old, his usually straight posture slightly bent in the weak light from the screens and the desk bulbs.

"I don't want to destroy something beautiful, Elliot."

"But you will if you have to. Because that's what you do."

Sean nodded slowly. "No," he said. "That's what you do."

He walked past me, to the door. Elin was already in the stair house. I didn't see Henrik anymore, I guess he'd already left. Sean crossed the threshold and closed the door quietly behind him.

For a moment, I pretended this meeting never happened, that I'd arrived to a studio where the Spellbinders had returned and were waiting for me to draw out the direction to finish the game. Then, I went further back, to the conversation we'd had on the hotel's terrace a few weeks ago, where we'd talked about how things can go wrong sometimes, but it's all good now, and he was only here to wish me good luck. He was retiring, in fact, and while he wasn't buying a house in France, he did plan to move to Europe. Buy a vineyard or something.

And then, I leaped. A couple of months back, where Lisa never showed up but instead Skye was outside my door and told me we were done with this shit now, and it was time to look forward and see what the future held. And then I was in Calvin's kitchen, we shared a coffee, the rest of the world was quiet, it hardly existed at all, and he told me in this peaceful void how happy he was that I was here. There was still time, he said. To not dwell in the past, to do that which mattered the most, with the days we had left.

As much as I realized that this was part of Sean's play, to make me feel bad and give up out of despair if nothing else, the past did seem to hold nothing else but opportunities for greatness. The future was a lonely place where I was on trial for most, if not all, of the things I'd done instead.

I sank down and leaned my back against the wall. Like so many times before, I wasn't lacking options. But to see them clearly, to know where to go now, that seemed more difficult than ever. I was afraid and confused. Maybe I deserved this kind of ending after all.

I went all the way back to my room in Fjellhamn, once littered with posters on the walls, piles of books, toys all over, plush animals and grand constructions. But piece by piece, mum took these things as her haunts led her to my room. These were Johan's, she said. Always had been. She pried them from my hands. Took them somewhere else. Told me tears made no difference. They certainly hadn't for her.

I heard a quiet noise. Metal against wood.

My phone, vibrating on the floor. A message, from someone, the screen shining like a lighthouse come to life in the night.

It was from one of the many publishers I'd talked to lately. I was in no hurry to read it. I couldn't handle a cancel right now and was unable to process a confirmed meeting. Or maybe it was Sean, hitting me with a final text before he went into the night. Perhaps his lawyers, forwarding the details already. Around the clock legal service.

Eventually, not knowing would kill me so I leaned forward, grabbed the phone, and looked at the screen.

It was from Skye.

I felt a rush.

I opened it.

All right, you big baby. You got me. One last time. But I'm telling you, whatever comes next better be good or you can go fuck yourself for the rest of your life.

THREE

THE
GREATEST

Chapter 59

THE BOMB

One morning in August, when we arrived at Sara's house to have breakfast before we got to work (that's what we called it now), we saw that she'd cut off her hair. She was in the kitchen, writing something on a piece of paper, and when she heard us crashing the hall and pouring into her home, she looked up.

Gone was the long, thick braid. Left were black curls that fell over her forehead like sprouts of evergreen reaching over an old wall. She wore jeans and a t-shirt, not a dress or tights. She was barefoot and had applied a light tint of lipstick and mascara, with a slightly odd color.

We looked at her. She stared back, defiantly.

I don't know about Calvin and Lisa, but there was a moment where I had to pause and process this, to consider the possibility that Sara was gone and replaced by this enigmatic creature. Or that I'd lost my mind and she'd always looked like this.

"Sweet," Lisa said. "Nice touch with the lipstick."

She walked up to Sara with her palm raised, high-fiving her as she continued to the kitchen table where Dan was making pancakes. I hadn't even noticed him. But I guess, if he was here, then it had to be Sara at the table.

"A-awesome," Calvin said. "You're the bomb. S-sorry, Sara's d-d-dad, can I say that?"

"You can today," Dan said from the stove.

"You're not so bad yourself," Sara said, trying to sound as if this wasn't a bigger deal than getting new sneakers.

"Looks good, right?" Lisa said to Dan as she helped herself to some pancakes. "Good morning, by the way."

"Oh, by all means, grab yourself some pancakes, Lisa."

"Thanks. They look delicious."

Dan turned around. He folded his arms over his apron and watched us all. Calvin sat by the kitchen table now. Lisa joined him with a plate and Sara put her pen and paper aside. I was still by the threshold, though.

"What're your friends gonna say?" I said.

She turned to me. "You're here, aren't you? You're saying it."

Dan picked up the plate of pancakes and put them on the table. Calvin and Lisa were already engaged in some kind of argument about the game, like they'd been every morning for the last few weeks. There was always something he wanted done, which Lisa said they couldn't do because a Commodore computer can't do that and even if it could, they wouldn't have time or they'd have to rip apart her code and miss the Fjellhamn Festival. He gunned for another layer in his parallax scroll or four monsters on the screen instead of three, or another frame of animation on the clouds or more pixels in the explosion effects. Lisa deflected his every suggestion until she didn't, paused, frowned and said, "That might actually work. We could try that."

This morning was no different and I sat down next to Sara, suddenly hungry for breakfast. She briefly touched my hand. I looked at her, surprised.

"It'll be good," she said. "Okay? Festival's not here yet."

I nodded. I felt a lump in my throat.

She smiled and pulled back her hand.

We attacked the breakfast like a pack of wolves. Dan made

more pancakes and handed out bowls of blueberries as we dug in, talking over the table about what was left to do. Lisa threw me the occasional kiss, laughing at my awkward attempts to return her casual affection. It came so easy for her. Calvin rolled his eyes and said it was gross and Sara said that there'd be no making out when we got to work, or this shit would never get done.

"Language, young lady," Dan said as he sat down, still wearing his apron and now wielding a cup of coffee. "Do I need to drive you somewhere or pick something up?"

"Nope," Sara said. "Today, we're just gonna play through the game and make a list of what's left to fix."

"Won't be much," Calvin said. "Just a bunch of scroll patterns and a few more enemies and—"

"Not happening," Lisa said. "We're fixing what's there. We're not adding stuff."

"Right, I forgot. You wanna make a crap game."

"But we'll fix my tweaks, right?" I said.

"Yeah," she said and fluttered her eyelashes. "You got priority."

"So unfair," Calvin said. "Elliot hooks up with the programmer and gets everything he wants." But he grinned. "Hey, you guys. We got gold. When we're selling this at the Festival, we'll make so much money, Elliot won't have to leave."

"Oh, for sure," Lisa said.

"That's the plan," Sara said.

I finished my last pancake. Dan was looking at me over the edge of his cup. He put it on the table.

"How much money can you make on a video game?" he said.

Sara glared at him from the side. Calvin swallowed. Lisa was suddenly deep into her notes. But I looked straight at him.

"You done some kind of estimation?" he said. "I mean, how much money do you need?"

"Richard Garriott is a millionaire," I said.

"And who's he?"

"Why do you care?" Sara said. "Festival's this weekend. We're busy. Shit's gonna have to wait. Including your bull."

He got up.

"Again with the language, Skye."

But he wasn't looking at me anymore. Somehow, that made it easier for me to breathe.

"Anyway," he said. "You got a plan. That's what matters. I'm home, if you need me. Now go forth, do your thing, and don't give a fuck about what others think."

We looked at Sara's dad with shock and surprise.

"Dad," she said. "Language."

Chapter 60

WORST GAME EVER

The game was a bloody mess. Pixels all over the screen. Controls as harsh as a whiplash over a naked back. Sound cutting through ears like fingernails on a blackboard. It was a stop motion disaster, an abomination that crashed every five minutes if it even started at all, a cruel joke from fate to show us how difficult, if not impossible, it was to make something that barely held it together.

We stood in the small house on the lawn. We were stuffed with pancakes and drunk on orange juice. We gazed at the unreal beings that moved across the screen, the crude and plain-colored creations that had once been fine ink drawings on Calvin's papers. We watched the incomprehensible patterns of those data-generated shapes that were my elegant and clever blueprint designs, now morphed into the senile version of a computer on crutches. The music followed no scale, the transitions were shock effects designed to provoke epilepsy among the dead.

"It's amazing," Calvin said.

"It's the greatest," I said.

"I love it," Lisa said.

"It's not done yet," Sara said.

The house had gradually transformed over the weeks from a

neat and organized space for ideas to grow into a cluttered mess with maps and drawings, Calvin's pictures from rough sketches to detailed portraits, my drawings of designs and mechanics, piles of matrix code with Lisa's notes and doodles (she'd drawn hearts around snippets she was particularly pleased with and skulls wherever she'd found a bug), books and magazines stacked in heaps and cassettes and discs spread out randomly over the shelves, and a big white canvas across one of the walls that held a timeline filled with things to do, ending with the Festival at the far right. In the very center, the TV shone with blue within blue light, the Commodore 64's signature gradient.

And the smell. Dear lord, the smell. When you were in the borderline of your early teens, but still struggled with basic principles on hygiene, spending time in a crammed space with your peers made it feel like you entered an old cabinet where someone had forgotten last year's Danish cheese and then rushed to call it an acquired taste. We didn't notice, of course. It was our scent, after all. Even the girls, who were years ahead of us when it came to these things, were deep into it. Whenever Sara's dad came by to bring us food or drinks, he put it outside and said: "I'm not coming in. It would be like facing Great Cthulhu. You can go to that place, but you can't leave with your sanity intact."

As we watched the game now, wrapped in our fumes, Calvin said: "We should send a copy to Nintendo. They might pick it up."

"I think they must," I said.

"We still need a name," Sara said. "Not many days left, and we still don't know what to write on the cover."

"Whaddayamean?" Calvin said. "We got a name."

"Yeah," I said. "It's the *Greatest Game of All*."

"Oh, c'mon. We need a real name."

"Whoa now, sister," Calvin said.

"Sister?" Sara raised her eyebrows.

"She's right," Lisa said. "The title sucks."

"It's the greatest title ever," I said and Calvin nodded quickly.

"Besides, if you don't agree, come up with a better one."

"I'm fucking busy," Sara said. "It's a full-time job to make sure you do what you're supposed to. I don't have time to come up with a better name."

"Maybe that's because it's already brilliant."

"It's a shitty name," Lisa said. "You know it."

"We'll just ask Nintendo, see what they think," Calvin said and pouted his lips.

"You know what?" Sara said loudly. "You call them. If they say it's a cool name, I'm gonna drop it. Okay?"

"Okay."

"Fine. And while we're waiting for that year to happen, let's see what's left to do before Saturday."

We played the game and called out things we wanted to fix, with Sara as our filter on what we'd actually do or not. She didn't write code, couldn't draw, had no design skills and was ignorant on sound and music. Still, whenever the debate got heated and Sara called the final shot, that was what settled it. There was even that part in the game where it just got real bad, real ugly–every game had one–but rewriting it was such a high risk that we might wreck the whole thing. Even then, Sara was the one who said no, to Lisa's relief and Calvin's and my dismay.

Today, when Sara handed out tasks, she'd put it on me to figure out a way to make the way you controlled the game's character flow more naturally, since it felt like your fingers were stuck in concrete whenever you played the game. Calvin had to reduce the complexity of his favorite monster since it was so big, it made the game crash. While Lisa was waiting for Calvin's new art before she could work on it, she hovered around me like a lost satellite until she was lost no more and sat down beside me. She rubbed her shoulder against mine.

"Whatcha doin'?" she said.

"Tweaking," I said, plotting numbers on a paper. I was getting nowhere so I didn't appreciate the distraction.

"Wanna take a break?"

I looked at her from the side. She stared at me with a sly smile.

"Sara's gonna kill us," I said. "I mean, if we...uh..."

Lisa gave me a quick kiss. "See? We didn't die."

I smiled. "Guess not."

Then, she sighed. Suddenly she was serious. "Hey, Elliot. When you move..."

"I'm not moving."

"Okay. But let's say your dad...uhm...moves anyway? Even if you buy a new house?"

"Not gonna happen."

"I'll still be here."

She held my hand now.

"And you can come see me, and I can come see you, and...well, you know...it might be nice, actually. Absence makes the heart grow fonder, my mum said to me a few days ago. I like that. It sounds nice."

"You already live in Skaresund. That's absence."

"Yes. But it takes a while to travel to Gothenburg. You take the bus or the train, so it's different. Like a small trip. So I guess...I suppose...wouldn't it just be easier if we slept over at each other's places then?"

Those last words came really quickly and she was blushing now.

"Like a slumber party?" I said.

"Yeah...something like that. Do you know what I'm saying, Elliot?"

I shook my head. But then I nodded. I guess I was doing some kind of confusing half circle.

"What I'm saying is," she said, "even if you move, I still wanna be with you."

"Thanks," I said and looked down into my papers. "But I'm not moving."

She sighed. "Okay, then."

I went back to my work. I stared at the paper. None of it made any sense now. I had no idea what my scribblings meant.

"I wanna be with you too," I said.

"Do you, though?" She stood up. "Sometimes, it feels like you don't."

"I just need to get my head straight. When this is over, when the game's done and we've sold it, then you and I can do more stuff together."

Lisa tilted her head and looked at me with a thoughtful expression.

"When the game's done?"

"Yeah."

She considered this for a few moments.

"I'm not sure it works that way," she said.

I shrugged my shoulders. "It's me being honest."

Lisa smiled. "Okay. I can appreciate that."

"Hey." We turned around. Sara was standing behind us, her hands on her hips. "How're the tweaks coming along?" she said.

"Uh...not so good."

"Yeah, you're messing around." Suddenly, she was upset. Real upset.

Lisa got up. "I'm gonna go now. You're right, Sara. Sorry."

Sara glared at Lisa as she passed her on the way back to the house. "Are you?"

"Not sure what you mean. Won't stick around to find out. Checking up on Calvin instead. Good byeeeh."

I looked at Sara. "Something wrong?"

She laughed out loud. "You played the game, Elliot?"

"Uh, sure."

"And still you ask?"

She growled, kicked up some grass, and left. I remained with a mess of failed tweaks, a pencil with a broken tip, and a growing insight that despite this summer's increased learning curve, whatever I knew about girls so far, I knew a lot more about making games. Seeing as our current one was in a state of emergency, that's saying something.

Chapter 61

IDIOT

The day after Sean served me his lawsuit, Skye came to see me at my place. It was a clear morning with no clouds. I'd made coffee and even picked up fresh croissants before she got here. When she knocked on the door, I was momentarily transported back to that window in time where there'd been a haunt outside that never showed itself. Mainly because I refused to open, but still. Now that memory was vague, as if it didn't really matter who'd ever been at my gates.

She entered quietly, a brief hello, smelling of sweat and liquor, her hair messier than usual. She'd grown an even deeper copper tan than usual and I was about to ask her if she'd been traveling, but she walked past me, poured herself a cup and didn't touch the pastry.

So that's the version of Skye I was gonna deal with now. Distant, not exactly aloof, but very much focused on the practicalities. The one that used to emerge when we approached launch, when marketing tried to cram ideas into production, when we'd miss our deadline by six months or...well, or when Calvin had left.

I was about to say that I was happy to see her and I'm sorry for a lot of things, but she turned around and looked at me, taking her first sip.

"Don't," she said.

I returned her stare.

"It's not like I don't have things to be sorry for as well," she said.

"But maybe we should–"

"Let's just get on with it. Okay? We'll save our sorrows for later."

"Why are you here?"

"Don't jinx it, honey. We'll have that talk. But not now."

I nodded.

We sat down by the kitchen desk.

"So here's how I see it," she said. "The Spellbinders left. They're done with your fairytale nostalgia shit. Unfortunately, they're still the team we need. Without them, this won't work. It'll be four times the time and budget and a team unfamiliar with our pipeline. Your meetings at E3 will be over in a split second. No publisher will bite."

"You don't know that."

"Oh, but I do. C'mon, you got like what, three or four meetings lined up? Seriously, Elliot. That's what Skype is for."

"But they're good ones. Microsoft. Activision. A few more on the fence."

"They're old friends, Elliot. They're returning a favor. The rest won't bite."

"Let's say you're right. What's the angle?"

"See, that's your problem right there. That you even have to ask, just...I don't know. It pisses me off. You know what? Sell it to me now. Tell me why I should care."

I thought about this for a moment.

As I'd been told through the years, I wasn't much for stating the obvious. But maybe the simple things didn't become clear, until at least someone had preached them at least once, at some point.

"If anything," I said, "this industry is about risk. We're doing something developers around the world dream of every day."

"It's a business. Even if you're only making textures for the next *Forza*, you're still living the dream."

"Where would you rather be? Animating mud particles for the next *Assassin's Creed*, or in the room when Shigeru Miyamoto says that the next *Metroid* should have a first-person camera?"

"Again with the *Metroid* franchise. Come on, Grandpa. Throw me a fresh reference here."

"But it would've been pretty awesome if you'd been in the room when he said that, wouldn't it?"

"A pitch that stands out gets all the love but none of the money."

"Once, we had both. And we didn't have the greatest game of all then."

Skye hummed, drumming her fingers against the table for a few seconds.

"It was so long ago I was in a proper pitch with you," she said, "I'd forgotten what it was like. But now I remember."

She looked at me with a wry smile. I smiled back.

"Okay...so here's the angle," she said. "You can't use pity. You can't play nostalgia anymore. Our people live in the real world. And you don't. Not entirely, anyway. You played your best card and they came, and that worked for that purpose. Now, you gotta do it the other way around."

I blinked. She made me feel like an idiot.

"You recruit them," she said slowly, "as you recruit for any project."

"Uhm..."

"I hear you. But let me finish. So you measure this as a real thing, against all other things they're working on. Make them believe this isn't the next *No Man's Sky*."

"Come on. That did quite well eventually."

"*Daikatana* then."

"Now you're just being nasty."

"But it's still better than *Laser Fog*."

I laughed. She smiled quickly.

"Look, position it like you've positioned any pitch. You'll find that what you got to offer is good on its own terms. A strong prototype. Publishers lined up. A credible track record. Granted, a bit tainted. But the magic's still there. And a trained team. Throw in a decent salary and a proper revenue share program, bring in a consultant to manage the relocations, and make them fucking understand that this could be their most rewarding and exciting production in their entire career...not because of what we once were, what Calvin wanted, whatever drives you to do this, not a startup fueled on ambition, not some shitty basement studio funded for three month and then we'll see...but because it's a fucking credible truth, no matter what. Do that. And they'll bite."

I shook my head. "I thought that's what I did."

That made her laugh so hard, she cried and gasped, "I can't breathe...I can't breathe...best part is, you're serious ..." until she could breathe, and calmed down.

"You're an amazing creative," she said and wiped her tears as I tried not to feel like an offended teenager. "But you're a terrible producer." She sighed. "The worst, you know."

"Yeah, but you–"

"No, no. Hush." She put a finger on my lips. "Moving on, Lindh. Moving on."

Chapter 62

HALF ALIVE

So yeah. It worked.

Kind of.

Joakim was done doing expansions for *Battlefield* anyway. Angela was between projects and she felt it was time to leave Japan. Oscar was looking for a reason to escape the *FIFA* sequels and Filip was writing lines for the *Toca Boca* games.

"Not my most challenging work, as far as drama goes," he said. "I created more plot that week in Stockholm than I've done in years."

"Not a waste of time, then?" I said.

"Not a waste, no."

And Yasmine. Well, she never left. She'd slept on couches and in guest rooms, in and around the city.

"I fucking knew you'd call," she said when we reached out to her. "I just wanted to hear it properly, you know? Making sure this wasn't all some crazy shit Elliot idea again."

"But it is a crazy shit Elliot idea," Skye said. "You were there, after all."

"Yeah, I know." She was quiet for a second or so. "So...Ubi sucks. Ancel's impossible to work with."

"You've been fired again, haven't you?"

"Fuck me. They're so frustrating. We're not the only ones who took a decade to get something done."

"Let's race them, see who finishes first. Besides, Oscar's on board, so if you wanna get so–"

"Shut up already. I said I'd do it."

So the ones to answer the second call were the same as those who'd been easily persuaded the first time around, the stray wolves, about as estranged from any kind of social defaults as Skye and I. They weren't exactly scraps from the talent pool, as I'm sure you know by now, but what they had in common was that they had nothing to lose. No family, no house, no marriage, no mortgage, no debt. Not even Sean's lawsuit made them flinch.

"He's a joke these days," Joakim said when I asked him about it, making sure he was aware that it existed, that it was real. "I almost feel sorry for him."

The rest of the Spellbinders couldn't, or wouldn't, join. Most of them made the verbal promise that they were on if we had a publisher lined up. They wanted to believe in this. But admittedly, given the history, they needed more than the best of intentions before they got on board. And a few said flat out that they wanted nothing more to do with this. Going back would render the closure pointless. Didn't we just do this? Were you for real, when you said you'd actually finish the game?

So there would be seven of us. That would have to be enough to iron out the bugs and wrap up the prototype in time for the E3 show.

They arrived over the next couple of days. It was awkward and familiar at the same time. The big things had been said. There wasn't much sense of a reunion. To talk about how long it had been, how good it was to see you again, that felt pointless. After the hugs and hellos, we more or less got to work at once, which was the only thing that felt equally comfortable and relevant.

There were no late dinners at Nonna's when the evening came. Those glorious treks through the night to find a place that was still open didn't happen. Crunching until midnight wasn't on the table. We stopped working at around five or six, said our See You Tomorrows, and went to our separate lairs to rest and sleep, wherever that was for the others. I couldn't even get Skye to go out and have dinner or a drink with me. She remained distant, often with some excuse as to why she couldn't hang out after work, and while we had our moments when it felt like things were like they'd always been, the space in between seemed wider by each day. Most of the time, I was the only one left in the studio after seven, playing and tweaking the game until I got so tired, I didn't go home but just slept on the couch.

Sometimes, I dreamed that Calvin was there, by his desk, working on something in the lone light from a desktop lamp.

He would look up at me and smile. And then go back to work.

I guess, in retrospect, there was a level of dignity to the situation. Because the Spellbinders, the ones we had been able to keep, they certainly took the job seriously. I'd never seen them deliver such quality, with such an edge, as they did now. If their last time around had been energized by memory's euphoria, this session found its glow from one very simple reason—they really believed this could work. So I was focusing on the pitch and the presentation around it. Skye got deep into the production plan to make this credible before publishers. The five developers we had made sure that Spellbinder's new game would shine more than any other when we went to Los Angeles.

Chapter 63

SLEEPWALKING

This was what I brought with me when I got into a taxi on an early August morning. It was three o'clock. Stockholm was still dark, with only a faded streak of blue moving across the sky's rim. This had been our only crunch, the day before Skye and I would leave. We'd compiled the latest build about an hour before the car arrived, wrapped it up, copied it to a few sticks and done a quick test run before I dashed down the stairs and out the door.

I'd brought a small set of clean clothes, a toothbrush, my notebooks and pencils, and a few copies of the game. And Calvin's folder, now stuffed with all its original material, carefully removed from the wall to do as little damage as possible to the sheets and drawings. Once again, I was leaving home with only the essentials stuffed into a bag I could strap over my shoulders.

I leaned back and exhaled, my arm resting on the backpack, as the car left Maria Street. The driver looked at me in the rearview mirror.

"Where you going?" he said, his accent mid-east heavy. He reminded me of someone. A man who once owned a café.

"Los Angeles," I said.

"Nice. I have cousins in San Diego. Is your first time?"

"Not really."

"You must like it."

"Sometimes, yes."

The first time I'd left Sweden was the first time we'd gone to California. Sean had invited the four of us to his home. He said he had an offer. It would be worth the trip, he assured us over a noisy landline. Since he was paying the tickets, whatever he had to say would have to be pretty bad not to be worth it.

Calvin and I were eighteen, Skye had just turned nineteen and Lisa would in a few weeks. We'd gone to the airport and when Calvin and Skye headed to the terminal that would take us west, Lisa and I had remained for a while. She'd put down her backpack and hugged me for a long time.

"No kissin'," she said. "That'd be too...I don't know. Too hard?"

"But we'll be back. You'll be back."

"Still. Too hard, Elliot. Say hello to Sean from me. Good luck with the game."

"It's your game, too."

She smiled and shrugged her shoulders. Then, she looked at me, her hands around my neck.

"Come with me, Elliot."

I laughed.

"I'm serious. Calvin and Skye can handle Sean. Come with me. We'll swim with the dolphins and drink coconut milk on the beach."

"You're going to India."

She laughed. "You know what I mean."

"You serious?"

"Yes."

I looked over my shoulder to Calvin and Skye, who had already checked in and were moving up the escalators. Skye threw a glance in our direction. She turned away when I caught her eyes.

"Hey," Lisa said. She put her hands on my cheeks and kissed

me. "Maybe next time, okay?" she said.

"I promise," I said. "This is our chance. A real publisher. We could actually get a game rele–"

"You've earned it," she said. "You really have. More than anyone. I'll write, okay? Whenever I'm at a place with a phone, I'll call."

She picked up her bag and smiled. Then she turned around and headed to her part of the airport.

Me, I stood there for a minute or so, unsure as to why I didn't go to the terminal immediately. But it wasn't until Lisa had disappeared and was truly out of sight that I got unstuck and walked towards the counters that would take me to California.

The taxi arrived to Arlanda. I paid the driver and got out. While the airport stores and terminals were busy enough despite the hour, there was a sedated quality to the mood, like we were all sleepwalking between perfume booths and liquor shelves. I had to go through special customs due to the large amount of memory sticks I'd brought with me, and you never knew how that could go down and what kind of abuse they'd show. But this time, it went smooth. The guards eyed the sticks briefly, scanned a few of them at random, and then let me through.

Our first trip had been a lot worse, when we'd have our only copies of the game stored on three point five inch Maxell discs and had to pass through the x-ray before we got to our gate. Skye had told the guards that they could look at the discs, sure. But if they touched them, or pulled them through the machine, she'd cry terrorist and promise that all planes to all parts of the world would be delayed with at least two days. That'd be a fortune for an airline, and maybe a few asses fired as well.

"What's it gonna be?" she said while holding the discs before the guards. "We're not sending these through your gates. We're not gonna leave until you let us pass."

And it worked. It was 1990, after all.

I took a cup of tea in one of the bars. Tried to think about nothing. To forget, for a moment. About Calvin. About Lisa. About the game. All our games. About Los Angeles and the show, my mum and dad and Fjellhamn.

To just sit there, and enjoy the idea that I might get a few hours of sleep on the plane. Strapped to a place where there was literally nothing I could do to influence the outcome of what would come next.

If I dared to go to that place, I'd feel how tired I was. I'd know the irregular strikes of my heart. Understand the unease that prevented my rest. Look at my hands, watch them tremble. Observe the world as it detached itself, while my head was hit with a throbbing pain.

Someone nudged me. I sat up, annoyed, and faced a guy with a mustache, wearing a blue jumpsuit and armed with a floor mop.

"Jason?"

He looked at me, slightly confused. "Sorry, sir," he said. "You were sleeping."

I shook my head and rubbed my eyes. "Thanks. I'm sorry. I appreciate it."

I walked slowly to the gate. The plane was only half full. It was a no transfer trip. You'd think it would be more popular. I was expecting to see some of our old competitors, maybe a few dicers and avalanchers, perhaps trade some banter over a gin and tonic with someone I used to know, but there were only suits and hipsters here.

When I walked through the alley between the seats, I saw her dark curls behind the back of a chair. She wore a tank top and patched jeans, loosely cut, already prepared for the Californian sun.

"That's my seat," I said as I leaned over Skye to put my bag in the compartment.

"About fucking time you showed up," she said. "I thought you were gonna miss the flight."

"You worry too much."

"You look like shit."

I sat down next to her. "This is gonna be a long flight, isn't it?"

"Don't worry. I brought entertainment. Bingo and stuff. And when we're done with that, I'll read my latest attempt at poetry aloud."

She winked at me. I smiled back.

"Nah," she said. "Let's get some sleep. Big days ahead."

I thought about the folder in my bag.

About the show, the pitch meetings, about Sean. And about her.

She had no idea how right she was.

"Good idea," I said. "Let's get some sleep. We're gonna need it, for sure."

Chapter 64

TEARS DOWN HER FACE

Of all the places I've been to, Los Angeles must be the hardest to describe.

It's not clean, like Tokyo. It's not continental, like Montreal. It's definitely not cold, like Reykjavik, but it's not as warm and moist as Singapore. It's certainly not safe, like I always felt that Seattle was.

I could go on. But if I'd use just one word to summarize what Los Angeles was for me, it would have to be this:

Colored.

The people. The places. The skies. They were all so bright, so radiant and shining, faded yet with style, like a photograph from an old album. It was a fitting image, because the sun never showed this place any mercy. It came down hard on the rocks and the streets, tearing up ever growing patches of dry land, spots of fire among the greenery that remained.

For an average white guy like me, coming from one of the safest places in the world, I couldn't claim to recognize your average Los Angeles dweller if my life depended on it. While all big cities were shapeshifters to some extent, with different characters emerging on different times of day, I'd experienced no metropole with cycles as defined as this one. The rules and its inhabitants literally changed at the strike of a certain hour. Sometimes, it felt to me like this city was the last frontier of modern civilization, because despite democracy and equality, it seemed like those who lived here fought against the realization that nothing really mattered. The edge of brilliance and beauty clashed with the disturbed and abusive, the very shape of no remorse seeking out the ones with a still innocent voice. You'd find both at the same table and understand that we'd never get any better than this, a constant circle of the sad seeking solace and finding it only at the feet of the hungry.

I was always told through the years that nothing was as fake as just about anything from Los Angeles, but I'd found it to be the most honest place. This is what the world was like, boiled down into one city, and we'd never get any better than this. It seemed appropriate that the most elusive yet widespread form of entertainment would thrive here, as primal as music, as striking as film, as capable as the novel, so hard to define for those who weren't in it, so easy to embrace once you'd swallowed its hook and line.

Our lure was different. We had the confidence of independence, stemming from the strength of subculture that we'd once been and still were. Sure, movies were made into games. Of course, it was great whenever someone like Beyoncé wanted to dip her toe into our world. But more frequently, the Spielbergs and the Gagas were our guests rather than the other way around. They were the ones who wanted in, to work with and understand an industry that remained an enigma, despite its size. But I guess if you could record a timeless classic on a four-track tape machine, you could build a million-dollar franchise on a toaster in your bedroom.

So yeah, Los Angeles wasn't–isn't–an easy place to describe. But on the day we landed at LAX, it was at least not sunny but cloudy, there had been a slow and cool rain to bring down the August heat a notch or two (or several, we were in Fahrenheit country now), but the air was warm and comfortable. As much as a day could be slow in this city, I'd say it was one of those when we got off the plane and walked towards the exits. I felt more a mess than ever and took a brief detour to the bathrooms to wash off my face. I sat down and closed my eyes. I fell asleep almost at once. But we'd soon be at the hotel. I could rest there. Thank god. I got up and went to find Skye.

Like me, she traveled light. She waited for me at the main gates, leaning against a pillar with her hands in her pockets, her soldier bag by her feet.

"Here we are again," she said when I approached her. "Twenty-five years later. Same city, same show."

"We go to the same retreat every year, dear."

"Maybe." She smiled. "But the magic's still there."

We left, got handed a taxi, and I slid into the backseat as Skye gave instructions to the driver. He nodded and waved but she shook her head and I heard her say, "Don't even try that trick on us, man. We know the roads and bridges better than most of you guys." He laughed and said that he'd marry her, if she wasn't taken.

She got in next to me and sighed. She looked out the window.

"You okay?" I said.

"Sure, sure. It's the jet lag. I'm not twenty anymore."

The driver took us away from the airport. I looked at the empty seat next to him.

"He'd be riding shotgun if he was here," I said.

"Calling to us in the back that this is gonna be the best E3 ever."

Then, we didn't say anything for a while.

I felt her fingers on my hand.

"That was some time ago," she said. She nodded to something in my lap.

I was holding Calvin's stick drawing in my hands. I wasn't even aware I'd brought it out. Or that I felt a lump in my throat, a sting in my eye. It caught the reflection of a million colors.

I looked at the drawing.

He'd told me to remember.

It felt like I had.

"It's not so long ago," I said slowly. "We're not kids in this picture."

"No? But it's Fjellhamn, right? Down by the piers? You look like kids."

"I think that's the way he always saw us."

She pulled back. "What's it about, then? When did he make this?"

I considered this for a few seconds of eternity, the many options that suddenly presented themselves now, so overwhelming that I got lost for a moment. I looked out the window, at neon lights and palm trees.

"Maybe you were right, Skye. Maybe I missed the point." I looked at her. "But if I did...I still need to be here to find out. Okay?"

"Hey," she said. "I came along, after all."

I put the stick drawing back in my pocket.

Suddenly, Skye squeezed my hand. "We're not going to the hotel."

"We're not?"

"We're gonna drum up the hype. And that's not gonna happen in a hotel room."

I was so tired now, I couldn't do anything but laugh at this. I wasn't sure I'd be able to stand up, much less embark on whatever odyssey Skye had in mind. But she wasn't wrong. It was the night before the show and everyone would be here, and no one would know what this year's Half-Life would be.

Skye laughed with me until tears ran down her face, holding my hand in a cramped grip until the car stopped. She opened the door and dragged me out into the sparkling Los Angeles night. I stumbled but my legs carried me, and I found myself stronger than ever as I inhaled the fumes from the gasoline desert.

"Come on, Lindh," Skye said. "Let's make this the greatest night the E3 show has ever seen."

Chapter 65

AN ENDLESS STREAM

The feeling I had sometimes, that maybe all of this was a dream and that each part of my life was a passing moment until I woke up, was always at its strongest when I was here. Los Angeles before the E3 show was a hypnotic whirl of light and music, where the strange mixed with the mesmerized in a vain search for the next profound experience. I guess all nights here were like that, only with different angles on the dream. What you were looking for seemed to be right there, you could see the colored arch dive behind the next hill, not the one you'd just climbed but the one after that, and tonight, that hill was some bar where the grapevine had told everyone to go.

This location changed from one year to the next, and there was never a formal thread or group where this event was organized. It could be on Sunset Strip. It could be somewhere in Downtown. Once, it was in the Venice District. If you had your ear to the ground, you'd know. I had always been deaf to these things, but Skye was quick to pick them up. Sometimes, I'm sure she was the one who started the rumor and got people to come to the place she'd chosen, but she always denied it.

We fell into a club with dim lighting and lounge music, rustic wooden furniture, and big booths. The rooftop was sky high and the bar covered the entire back, wrapped in vegetation, and walled with liquor shelves.

And everybody was there.

Publishers we'd worked with. Reviewers we'd partied with. Designers we'd befriended. Artists we'd admired. Community leaders we'd nurtured. Some still young, some pushing it now, clusters of familiar faces like a staged chronicle of our decades in the industry. Their heads turned, they waved from booths and desks, corners and pillars, calling out and saying hey, come here, we're just sitting down to eat or have drinks or grab a beer. Skye hugged, shook hands, kissed, high fived, bantered and joked her way through the crowds, throwing a glance to make sure I followed. People gave me friendly slaps on the back, reached out to say hello, put their arms around my shoulder, called out over the music and the chatter that it was out of this world to see me, so amazingly awesome, so unexpected but so cool. I was sweating, feeling the blood pump through my body at an alarming rate, but if I'd burst tonight, I'd do it with a grin on my face.

"Oh, we're here to pitch," I heard Skye say to someone as she passed him on the way to somewhere else. "We're seeing Microsoft and Activision tomorrow. Got most of the team back. Wasn't that hard, they were only on sequels and annuals now anyway. No, we're not talking to Pete. We didn't even call Nintendo this time. Who calls Nintendo these days? Do they even have a number?"

I was pulled down into a couch by a bunch of marketeers that used to do some solid work with us or whatnot, I don't remember, and they asked me if it was a sequel to *Clear Blue Skies* or maybe a spin-off to *Archipelago*? I shook my head and laughed.

"You have no idea," Skye said as she showed up again. "You're gonna be sorry you didn't bid on it when you could." She leaned forward. She was warm, sweat running down her neck and along her chest. "It's the greatest fucking thing ever."

"It's that game you and that other guy always worked on?" The man who said this smelled of chili nuts and beer. I didn't recognize him. "Where's he, by the way? Is he here, too? We'd love to meet you all."

Skye pulled me away, put her arm around me and then we were in another gathering and these people I knew from Ubisoft and Mechner was there. "Hey," he said. "You made it. How's it going?"

"Jet lagged. But that's okay. We've more or less sold the game. I'm just here to make an appearance."

Skye laughed and turned away. "Would you believe this guy?" she said to someone that happened to pass by.

"Who signed it?" Mechner said, clearly not believing me.

"Not you," I said. "But I'll send you a review copy once it's out."

The DJ threw out Avicii over the crowd, moving us from lounge to dance. The world was a time lapse and hours passed like minutes.

"Is it like *Super Mario* great, or just *Sonic* great?" someone said to me. There were arms in the air, waving to the beat. I think this someone was Mark, and I think he winked at me and gave me his trademark sarcastic smile.

"I dare you to leave Sony," I said. "If you do, I'll tell you."

He laughed and disappeared into the crowd. I was sucked into a mass of people, Skye tugged at me to join her on the dance floor, but I fell backwards into a couch and closed my eyes in an attempt to stop the world from spinning. I had a brief panic attack when I wondered if I'd been here for days and missed the entire show, but when an exec sat down next to me with drinks, I calmed down.

"I hear you're gunning for Valve's slot," she said and pushed one of the drinks over the table. I took it.

"But *Half-Life 3's* confirmed," I said.

She laughed. "It would be nice, though. If we had one of those titles, that levels the floor. One game that just did what it said it would do. I don't see why it can be so hard."

"What's hard?"

"To keep a promise. To just do what you'd said you'd do."

I looked at her. She had dark hair and a green suit, big red lips, and black eyes. I didn't know her. I'd never met her. But she seemed to know me. She smiled.

"It's not easy," I said. "To make a game. You mean it when you pitch it. But along the way...anything can happen."

The words felt strange as I said them. Each syllable was a struggle.

"I'm not coming after you," she said. "I know it's about as close to the impossible as we'll get, before we try to fix real problems. Global warming. Obesity and famine. Missions to Mars. That kind of stuff. Still...we never learn, do we?"

"I'm sorry," I said. "Who are you?"

Then, two or three friends of hers showed up as if they'd been dropped through a hatch, and everybody was laughing and drinking. She pointed at me and said to her friends that this guy's the Spellbinder founder and he's here to pitch a new game, they're like back with a new title and stuff. They all huddled together and looked at me with big, blurry eyes and shiny teeth, but an arm reached out and pulled me out of it.

"Come on," Skye said. She smelled of transatlantic travel, alcohol, and funk. "We're done. Now they know."

"I need to sleep," I said.

"Let's go."

We left the club and while the streets were rowdy now, they felt quiet compared to the infernal chaos that had pumped up the bar. We got into a taxi and I fell asleep. Skye nudged me when we arrived to the hotel and I could hardly walk as we entered the elevator. I leaned against the mirrored wall, breathing slowly.

"You okay?" Skye said.

"Yes. But tired. Long trip."

"Maybe this was a bad idea."

"No." I opened my eyes. "No, Skye. This was a brilliant idea."

We walked to my room. I went into the bathroom, threw up, and fell asleep with my head on the toilet seat. Skye forced me to wake up, made me drink a lot of water, then she dragged me to the bed. She put her hand on my forehead.

"You're burning up," she said.

"I just need to sleep."

She lay down beside me, her hands behind her head. I was drifting off again.

"Tomorrow," she said, "we're pitching. We're back in the room."

"Why are you doing this?" I said.

She turned around to the side, leaning her chin in her hand. "Haven't we had this conversation a million times?"

"I'm making it existential now."

She laughed. "You really don't know," she said.

Even though I kept talking, I think I was sleeping now.

And then, I was gone. Not sleeping, but hibernating, floating along an endless stream through darkness.

The air was cool. I was alone.

I only heard the water.

And Calvin.

Calling for me, saying that it was about time I got here. I couldn't see him, he sounded far away.

He'd waited for so long. Almost too long. But now that I was finally here, we could pick up just where we left off.

Chapter 66

BOOM

We met up at Sara's house on Friday morning, to a game that was finished. Well, as finished as it could be, given the circumstances.

We said a few good mornings to each other and sat down on the couch. Lisa and I cuddled up next to each other. Calvin looked at the screen, his eyes fixed on the blinking cursor. Sara put in the disc and typed the loading command on the computer. Outside, the colors of an early fall had splashed patches of red and yellow in the big garden. There was a chill in the air of the kind that made it clear that while it wasn't getting cold just yet, the warmer days were over. The night came sooner and the sun took longer to rise.

Sara pushed Enter. While the game loaded, she faced us.

"The Festival's tomorrow," she said. "Don't fuck this up now, and we'll make it. We just need to copy the game onto discs, wrap them up, and come up with a name to put on the label. Then we're done. Do we have a name yet, Elliot?"

I nodded. "Do we ever."

Calvin looked at me from the side. We do? he mouthed. I shook my head quickly, but also gave him my Don't Worry About It We've Got Hours Left To Figure It Out-look.

Sara grabbed the controller. "I'll play first."

And the game unraveled.

It didn't crash.

Sounds triggered on cue.

Things even flashed on the screen when they were supposed to.

Behind that pixel-generated mess, we'd managed to stitch something together during our last days that wasn't completely confusing. Honestly, it was like any other video game production. Not until everything was in place could you really see its potential. If the first draft of a game always was an abomination, the final draft was a thing of beauty.

If you got it right, that is.

Things were looking pretty good, until we came to that part. You remember the one, the one all games had, where things got real bad, real ugly.

But today, the game actually froze.

That had never happened before. It'd been slow and stuttering, but fine once you got past it and onto the next section.

But now.

Boom.

And not the good kind of boom.

"Strange," Sara said. "Let's try again. You play this time, Elliot."

She handed me the controller. We reloaded the game. There was an air of menace in the room now, a foreboding of dread. Errors of chance had a certain look to them. This wasn't it.

"I k-knew we should've fixed this," Calvin muttered. "Some kind of sneaky bug coming up to bite us now."

"Come on," Sara said. "Code don't just degenerate. Right, Lisa?"

Lisa, however, said nothing. She'd sunk lower into the couch and had folded her arms, her shoulders stiff. Sara kept looking at her as I played my way to the Part of Boom. The game froze again.

"Okay, so what the fuck is going on?" Sara said and stood up. "It didn't do this yesterday. Far as I know, we haven't touched the discs since." She was already raising her voice.

No one said anything. My gut hurt. Calvin rubbed his fingers on his forehead. Lisa stared into the floor.

"Anyone?"

"So I rewrote the code after all and copied the new version to the discs because I figured out a way to solve the problem," Lisa said.

She looked at us.

"That's what we wanted, right?" she said. "We wanted to fix it. We just decided not to, because we didn't know how."

"Oh," Sara said, scary calm now. "And now you do?" She pointed to the frozen frame on the TV set. "This is your fix?"

"It worked yesterday," she said. "When I tested it."

"I'm not gonna kill you today," Sara said. "Maybe some day. But not today. We'll just pull the version before yours from one of our backup discs and run that instead. I hate you, but we'll deal with that later."

She turned to the box on the floor where we kept all copies of the game from the day we started. It was stacked and each disc marked on its label with the date it was created. She pulled up the latest one.

It was dripping. From something gooey.

"Uh, yeah," Calvin said, nodding his head as if he suddenly remembered. "That'd be Coke, I believe. I...spilled some? Yesterday. Before...uh, before something. A pizza was involved. Your dad bought pizza? Remember? Those w-w-were the days."

Sara leaned down and picked up a few more discs.

They were all sticky with liquid sugar.

She turned to Calvin.

Red doesn't describe the color in her face. Crimson comes close. But really, she invented a new nuance all her own on this day, a deep and raging one that reminded me more of lava than anything.

"And then you thought, Calvin, that hey, now that I've spilled soda on our complete library of backup versions, I'll just tell no one and go home."

"I...uh...can't say I was thinking..."

"At all. Because that's not your thing, is it? Thinking?"

"I dunno. You're being unfa–"

"The fuck I am, Calvin. The fuck I am."

"Hey," I said. "Calm down. Let's talk about how to fix this instead."

She spun around.

"You serious, Elliot? You telling me to calm down? The festival's tomorrow and we have zero copies of the game and a broken piece of code, running on the only goddam disc we have left, because your idiot twin spilled drinks on our backup system. Why don't I just pull this out," and she did, from the drive, "and tear it apart, so we don't even have that? Why don't I? I'll just do that."

She held the disc in both her hands, bending it as if she actually meant it.

"Because it seems to me, it doesn't fucking matter what I do or say. You're not listening anyway, are you?"

"Look," Lisa said. "It's just a game, Sara. We all know...well, we all know..."

"What?" she shouted. "What do we all know, Lisa?"

"Elliot's moving," she said. "It's not gonna make a difference if we finish this game today or not."

Things got awfully quiet after that.

Calvin shuffled his feet, pulled them up into the couch and then swung them back on the floor. He mumbled something about no one's gonna move anywhere, but I don't think anyone but me heard him. Lisa and Sara stared at each other. Lisa looked sad. I felt a strange calm, as if no emotions were allowed to pass through me now and my only role in this could be to observe. Everyone was in orbit around me and if I acknowledged that, I'd be sucked dry.

Sara tore the disc in two.

She threw it on the floor.

"You didn't even come up with a fucking name," she screamed at me.

Then she ran out.

We were silent in the aftermath. Calvin made a few doodles on a block, retreating into himself. Lisa sighed and buried her face in her hands. The game was mocking us with its static image on an oval screen.

"I'm sorry," she said. "I really did think it would work."

Calvin looked up. "Yeah," he said. "I'm sorry, too."

Lisa leaned closer. "Are you mad at me, Elliot?"

I stood up, still empty. I looked at the broken disc on the floor.

I picked up the plastic shards and held them together. The magnetic tape was torn and scratched.

I turned to Lisa. "Can you interrupt the game?" I said. "Even if it crashed?"

She frowned. "We've got no lock on the code, so…sure."

"Then interrupt it."

I reached for the shelf and pulled a fresh disc from the box of unbroken ones.

"Copy it to this one. Then, make a few more. Don't let Calvin near them."

She smiled slightly. Calvin looked at me from under his bangs.

"Once done," I said, "fix the crash, Lisa."

"There's no time."

"We got hours. That's oceans of time."

"Okay, sure. I guess."

"We'll start making copies. Wrap them and label them."

"But…S-Sara's right," Calvin said. "I'm gonna need a name for the wrappers."

"I got one. And once I'm back, I'll let you know."

"Where you going?" Lisa said.

"To Sara. No way we're doing this without her."

Chapter 67

NOT ABOUT THE GAME

It's not like she'd run off to another village or anything. She was sitting on a bench in the garden, chin in her hands, staring into the pond where goldfish used to roam but then didn't. The sea gulls took them all.

I sat down next to her.

"Hey," I said.

"Fuck off."

"Language, young lady."

She glared at me. "Whaddayawant?"

"We can fix this."

"We can't."

"We still have the game on the computer. We'll save it to a few discs and then Lisa fixes the error, and we're good. Calvin's making wrappers. And I got a title now."

"Oh yeah? What is it?"

I was about to tell her, but she cut me off. "Doesn't matter. We won't make it."

"Festival's tomorrow. Plenty of time."

Sara took a deep breath. She closed her eyes and squeezed her hands around the seat. "I'm not talking about the game, Elliot."

"But I am, Sara. As long as we're still doing this, I'm not going anywhere. If we end that now, I might move the next hour. But as long as we're in this, I'm home."

"We're always talking about your stuff, aren't we?" She opened her eyes and looked at me. "Besides, that doesn't make any sense."

"I don't make much sense."

Then I saw something. An expression in her face, a sort of deep sadness that must've come from that place where she'd been when her mum left. It had probably been there for a long time, but right now, when the red autumn rays fell through the branches of the apple trees, I noticed her in that light and I felt so sorry for her.

"What are you talking about, Sara? If you're not talking about the game?"

She tilted her head and looked away. "I don't wanna say," she said. "Let's go back."

"No. Tell me."

She trembled. "I'm a girl too," she said. "You know…I like video games, too."

"Yeah, I know. I'm so glad we're friends again."

She made a noise. It sounded like she coughed, or lost her breath. Then, her features hardened.

While she seemed more herself again, and I was still wondering what moment we'd just had, she was colder somehow, like I'd never known before how warm she could be and now I'd lost it.

She stood up. "C'mon," she said. "You can tell me the name on the way back."

I followed and was a few steps behind before I caught up with her. I had the feeling I'd done something wrong, a kind of bad call that made Lisa's rebel hacking or Calvin's debauchery seem like kitty cat pranks in comparison. I stretched out my hand to grab Sara and ask her if everything was okay, but she gave me a quick glance over the shoulder and burned my fingers. I pulled back and slid up next to her and decided that the next thing I

would say would be the game's title. If that wouldn't cheer her up,
I didn't know what would.

Chapter 68

THE SECOND GREATEST TITLE OF ALL

It took Lisa the better part of the day to find and fix the error. She hadn't done many changes, so she didn't get why the game suddenly crashed. Once she found it, though–a comma she'd shifted one step too far–she moved it to the right spot, launched the game, and it worked. Just a stupid comma. That was it.

She was so angry with herself, she crawled under the sofa and wouldn't come out for another hour. Eventually, we had to ignore her and keep writing the game to the discs. We were aiming for a hundred copies and Calvin drew each wrapper by hand.

"Bleedin' awesome title, Elliot," he said and grinned to me as he wrote the name on the fifty-seventh copy.

"I know, right?" I said and stretched out my fingers. "It's not the greatest. But it's close."

Sara didn't say anything. She was moving in a drone-like state between the drives, rotating units and sorting them up.

The evening came. Dan showed up with drinks and snacks. The healthy stuff, to keep our energy levels right. Water, nuts, fruit, you know. He offered to help. Sara shouted at him to put the goddamn food on the table and leave already. As Calvin was on his last twenty, his hand slipped and he clipped with his eyes. By then, it was midnight. I told him I could make a few, and this made him and Lisa laugh so hard that he got his energy levels back. Even Sara smiled a little.

When she'd finished her last disc, she passed it on to Calvin and yawned. "Once you've wrapped it and typed the title, we're ready. You called your mum, right?"

"Now you ask," he said. "If I hadn't, it'd been way too late to do—"

"Well, did you?"

"Sure. She said she'd have the banner done by breakfast. And everyone who buys a game gets a slice of pie and a cup of coffee. Arshak makes the coffee."

"Who's Arshak?"

"The dark man? The café owner?"

"Oh, okay. Very cool."

Calvin rolled his neck, untying a few knots in his shoulders.

"Only ten more to go," he said.

Sara shambled to the sofa, sleeping before she hit the cushions. Lisa was snoring in the big chair by the Atari.

Outside, the garden was quiet. Summer's concert was over, the crickets and night birds were packing it up, preparing for the days that grew shorter, the nights that got colder.

I was standing in the doorway, looking out. There were a few beacons of decorative light that cut through the pitch black, a pearl band that faded into the shadows.

Tomorrow was the Festival. And however it would turn out, I knew it would be okay. Even a complete failure would still be some kind of accomplishment.

But then. After that.

Dad had showed up at Cornelia's and Calvin's house and showed me pictures of the new place. The sale of our home had gone really well. We were able to afford some stuff now.

My new room was big and had a wide and deep window with a view over a park. Dad had bought me a new bed and installed shelves where I could keep my video game consoles, once we'd bought them. He said I could pick whichever I wanted. He'd looked it up and said that these Nontendi people had something going on with some guy called Marius (or something), and then there was this other console you could get from...uh, Segal? He liked that one more, it had a game about a boy wonder, and he said that it reminded him of me.

He'd bought me a desk as well, one with drawers, where I could keep my notebooks, pens, and papers. The walls were white and soft. I'd be able to pin and sort stuff, use my room as a canvas for new ideas, and map the space to anything I wanted. And, he promised, no one would touch my stuff now. Not without my permission. New home, new room, new rules.

"And when you come to visit," Dad had said and turned to Calvin, "we can put your stuff up there, too. Like you've done here, in your house."

Calvin didn't say a word. Cornelia stayed away. She'd offered Dad some coffee and then gone out to the porch, where she'd rested in the shade under the parasol. I had been quiet, too, and after a while, Dad had taken his pictures and left.

I turned around now.

Calvin was huddling over one of his last wrappers, working with care to get the details right. We'd turned off most of the lights, to keep the night bugs away, and closed the windows. It would be too cold to keep them open.

Lisa was sleeping deeply now. She was smiling slightly, her spiky hair messier than ever.

And Sara. Resting in the couch, her dark curls dropping over the forehead to cover her eyes.

Calvin stood up.

"I'm d-done," he said.

He put the last disc, number one hundred, on the pile.

"We're not gonna wake them up, are we?" he said.

I shook my head. "Nah. They'll bite us if we do."

He smiled wearily.

We left the Spellbinder abode and closed the door. As we were about to leave, we saw Dan sitting in a rocking chair on the porch outside the house, blankets wrapped around him.

"Evenin', boys," he said. "You done yet?"

We looked at each other. Yes, Sara's Dad was insane, but now he was killing it.

"Uh...sure," Calvin said. "It's...like, two o'clock in the morning?"

"I know," Dan said. "Isn't it beautiful?"

"You been up all this time?" I said.

"Why wouldn't I be? Hey. See you tomorrow, okay?"

We nodded, turned around, and walked through the garden to our bikes.

We didn't say anything as we rode through the maple alley to the stone road. As we reached the downhill path, we let go of our handles and stretched out our arms. It was dark, no streetlights here, we only knew the twists and turns because we'd done this ride a hundred times before.

Silently, we rushed into the wind and closer to the sea, as our bikes picked it up to breakneck speed. Tomorrow, Spellbinder Software's first game would hit the market, our virgin attempt to pitch and sell a title that we'd made ourselves, with whatever we had at hand to make it work.

I didn't really care how it'd turn out. I had the greatest friends. We'd made the greatest game. I'd take that with me when I left this place. I'd keep it close, it would keep me warm until forever, or until the day I died, whichever came first.

Chapter 69

WALK THE FLOOR

We had breakfast. A slow one, despite its meager content. Skye didn't say much. She had coffee and a croissant. I ate nothing and drank only water. I could never eat before pitching anyway. I should be tired, but I wasn't. I was expecting a headache, but I had none. I was on fire, yet serene like a monk ready to face a dragon. If monks ever did that. I don't know.

"You good?" she said.

I nodded.

"You had a fever yesterday."

"I did not."

"Got your presentation in order?"

I patted my bag. "Yes."

Skye took a sip from her coffee. "It occurred to me, I haven't seen it. I have no idea how you're going to pitch this."

"And I haven't seen your production plan."

"You worried about it?"

"Not at all."

She fell back, hands clasped. She, too, was preparing for the storm, in the eye that was our hotel's lobby.

There weren't many people staying here. The porters and

clerks had to put an effort in, to look alert. So far, it was a slow day, with the morning sun already burning the asphalt and people gearing up with water bottles and sunscreen. We saw a few that looked vaguely familiar, but none of them said hello to us. Maybe they were just random people on vacation.

"We should talk about Sean," Skye said.

"I know."

"I've stayed away from it, you know...to keep it focused. Eyes on the target. But yeah...we're here now. And he's gonna make a move. A real one."

"Maybe."

"Maybe?"

"He's suing me, Skye. Not you or anyone else. They're still as-sembling the case."

"That's your answer? If a publisher asks you? That's what's gonna make them comfortable and go, 'Oh, it's okay, Elliot got this. Sean's just suing him. They're still just assembling their case.'"

I didn't answer.

"The property is tied to you, Elliot. He's coming for you. But it'll bring us all down."

"Yeah. He's shrewd that way."

"Even if you only used the napkins in his damn cafeteria to sketch your designs, they're still his fucking napkins."

"Calvin used napkins. I prefer notebooks."

"Don't be reckless. That's all I'm saying."

"Again with the reckless."

Skye frowned. "He's so relentless," she said. "Ever since we left, all those years ago...he couldn't let it go, could he?"

I sighed. Some of that monk's fire left me for a moment.

"I think I know where he's coming from," I said. "Took me awhile to figure it out, though."

Skye leaned forward. "You're a slow burner when it comes to these things, aren't you?"

"You're asking like you don't know me."

"It's taken me a lifetime, for sure."

"Then listen to this, Skye. Remember why we're here. Why we're doing this. Why we used to love this. Why we got into this in the first place. There's nothing like this world, and you know it. I'm asking you this now..."

She leaned closer.

"Are we gonna let Sean spoil the fun?"

She looked surprised. Then, she fell back and laughed. "Not in a million years, honey," she said and got up. "Not in a million years."

One thing we always loved to do when we visited E3 was to walk the floor. Not like sports agents or rockstars—we were neither, you know—but just because it was such a surreal experience, yet wonderful if you not only worked with games but were still into them, like a kid on Christmas morning.

Back in the days, Calvin, Skye, and I would arrive to Staples Center, get our passes, enter the gates, and hook up our arms to form a posse. Then we'd enter the circus, greeting *Resident Evil* zombies and high-fiving stone-faced *Metal Gear Solid* models. The entire center was an event constantly in motion, the exhibition halls a booth grid but the spectacle in between always changing. This was the only place where you'd find multiple Lara Crofts going after the treasure at the same time, while sport celebs and influencers had their time with a mike on a stage. *Princess Zelda* would be real but you could get lost in a land of toadstools trying to find her, and if you, like me, had a thing for Samus Aran, this would be the only place where you'd have a chance to meet her. Well, someone who looked a lot like her, at least.

The titan developers had their giant reveals here, shows before shows with invites only and, when well executed, a sense of drama that would put Steve Jobs to shame. Here, Microsoft unveiled their next Xbox. Sony unraveled the future PlayStation. But Nintendo was always the real thriller. You'd never know if they'd tank and completely miss the mark, or reshape the face of gaming.

Even when these shows weren't as live as they once used to be, now with videos and meticulously choreographed stage appearances as flavor, they were still a spectacle.

Of course, in Calvin's eyes, Nintendo never failed. Whatever they did, it was either plain awesome or bold progress, but usually both. If they had a bad year with confusing launches, and all the journalists said, "Okay, Nintendo's out and Sony and Microsoft will take it from here," Calvin would go, "Man, they're kings and queens." If they had a good year, with reveals that were on the mark and all the journalists said that they never doubted Nintendo would lead the way, he said: "God, they're brilliant." Or versions of the kind.

Now Skye and I wore our passes and faced the gates to what Calvin had always called the greatest show on earth.

We looked out over the sea of execs and devs, fantasy creatures and superhero characters, listening to the noise that was like a massive, amplified wall from an arcade hall.

Skye had her hands on her hips, scanning the crowds. I wore my bag over my shoulder, breathing slowly, trying my best to relax. People passed us. Someone bumped into me. Everyone seemed to be in a hurry.

We'd been here a few times after Calvin left Spellbinder. But without him, we'd never have anything worthwhile to show or tell. I'd made sure of that, by not listening to any kind of reason, running after all ideas at once and completely losing touch with... well, with most things. But it was through that lens I watched the theater before me now, and despite my fiery speech to Skye just before, I didn't feel like walking the floor.

I looked at her from the side. Her gaze was distant, as if whatever had her attention was far away.

Our first meeting was in an hour. With Christina, at Microsoft.

I looked at my hands. They were shaking. I held the bag's strap hard.

Just one more day. That was all I needed.

If I could hold it together just for today.

We walked.

Into the show, where we passed Max Payne taking a smoke in a filthy bar. We saw Donkey Kong relax with his kid on a barrel. They had a banana. There were three crow bars lined up in Valve's booth, and a big laboratory-like construction with shielded walls and tickets only allowance. Just like the reveal back in 2003. Electronic Arts was a country on its own and we stayed there and had popcorn while watching sports on a ridiculously large screen. There were also characters and studios I had no reference to, multiplayer behemoths and actors from the East, with titles I'd never heard of but who had apparently conquered continents. Even Rockstar's morally corrupt and savagely entertaining franchises were dwarfed compared to something from South Korea that was large enough to fund a third world country's debt sanitation. And an arcade hall with wooden cabinets for wealthy collectors, an entire section for merchandise, venture capitalist sections and...yeah.

I had to pause and sit down. Skye joined me, but she didn't say anything.

"There's so much I don't know anymore," I said.

"You think I can smoke here?"

"Why would you..." But then I looked at her. She was actually groping for her pack of cigarettes, pulling one out from the box while juggling the lighter.

"They'll throw us out," I said.

She put the pack on her left knee, the lighter on her right.

"We're seeing Christina in ten minutes, right?"

"Right," I said.

"Hey, Elliot."

"Yeah?"

I don't recall when I last saw Skye nervous. Angry, sure. Stressed out, frequently. Upset, yes. But nervous? Maybe never.

But now, she was. She didn't look at me and she actually lit the cigarette.

She took a smoke. Oddly, this made me cool down. It had never occurred to me that she might crack as well. She was invincible. Untouchable. She was Sara Johnson. They had nothing on her.

She turned to me, frustration all over her face. She put the cigarette away in a leftover coffee cup on a table, and pulled her hands over her face.

"You okay, Skye?"

"I will be. This is a special moment, you know. And I want you to know. You need to know."

I didn't like where this was going.

"Now who's reckless."

"I know, I know...it's not a...oh, fuck."

"Hey," someone called. "There you are."

That was Christina, cutting through the crowd and waving at us. Plain as I remembered her, jeans and a college sweater, pony-tail and no makeup, a big smile and shoes with plateau heels.

Skye sighed. "Never mind," she said. "I don't know what I was thinking. We'll talk later."

"You've hooked up with Sean. You're stabbing me in the back, just like he did, when I'm about to enter the room."

Skye stared at me. She gaped. Then she laughed and grabbed my shoulders hard. "Oh, you stupid, strange boy. Today, I got your back. I didn't last time. Today, I do."

There was something in this moment that made me forget that Christina was just seconds away from us. I should say something. I wanted to. But then, she was there and she pulled us up and gave us massive American-style hugs.

"It's so good to see you," she said. "I've been looking forward to this for weeks. C'mon, you can tell me on the way how you've been. How have you been?"

She was already walking as she said those words, and Skye took the lead and joined her. They fell into their banter at once, like the minute before hadn't happened, and I took my bag and followed to the area where you could have a coffee and a conversation without shouting your lungs out. I put my hands in my pocket to make sure that Calvin's stick drawing was still with me. Then, I picked up the pace to catch up with Christina and Skye.

Chapter 70

LASER FOG

The skies were gray on the morning of the Festival. Calvin and I got up early, despite only a few hours of sleep. We weren't tired. We should've been, but we weren't.

Cornelia helped us to breakfast and then picked up the banner she'd made. Before she left, she faced us from the doorway as we munched away on toast and eggs. "I'm mighty proud of you, boys. And I'm gonna let the girls know I feel the same about them. The four of you makes me think there's hope for the world."

Calvin grinned, mouth full of food. I smiled, but really, I just wanted her to leave. She nodded, made a humming noise to herself, and left with the banner under her arm.

There was a certain dignity to the morning, an air of serene silence. We were all done. Nothing left to fix or prepare except to get up on our bikes, ride down to the town center, and take it from there. We didn't speak on the way and we took it slow in the turns, feeling the wind against our faces, the breeze through our hair.

The clouds had parted when we arrived at Fjellhamn's town square. Rays of light pierced through the gray veil. Sara and Lisa were already there, setting up the booth. We were the only ones with a screen and a computer, in the company of tables with homemade jam and marmalade, hangers with sweaters and socks from the local farms, tents with coffee and pastry and a red wooden shack that served waffles with jam on fresh blueberries. These old ladies and worn men, their awkward sons and shy daughters, they all eyed us with an equal mix of confusion and curiosity.

Sara's dad had helped pack in the morning. They'd put all the equipment in the car and brought it here. He was doing some wiring now together with Arshak, pulling a long power cord from his café to our stand, which was a big oak desk with two poles on the side. Cornelia was fiddling with the cloth banner, tying it to one of the sticks. Lisa's mum, Elizabeth, was here. She had short flat hair, a hat, and a jeans dress. She was twiddling a few buttons on a large TV set, some kind of home brew screen with a wooden frame and radio-style buttons on the side. Our spot looked more like an electrician's messy work space than anything else. But Calvin and I stood and looked at it, our eyes big as saucers, mesmerized by the static from the big screen as Elizabeth calibrated it to match the game's colors, the pile of discs packaged in one hundred handmade wrappers and coffee and pie for everyone who bought a copy. To us, this was the greatest thing we'd ever seen.

While Cornelia tightened the last knot, Arshak came up to us. He didn't look so sad today. Not exactly happy, but at least content.

"Is this the story you told me about?" he said.

We nodded.

He smiled.

A slow, pixel-made fog rolled across the screen, layered in parallax to unravel the game's title in glowing red.

"It is beautiful," he said.

Cornelia gave up a small shout, as the banner unfolded between the two poles and framed the desk. It said:

Laser Fog

In smaller letters, underneath:

the Graetest Game of All

And then, even smaller:

by

Spelbinder Software

Calvin put his arm over my shoulder. I put my arm around his. "B-best title ever," he said.

People came from the neighboring islands on Festival day, parked their cars wherever they found a spot, and walked to the square to have something to eat and drink, maybe buy a local item or two, but mostly to enjoy a slice of time where our communities came together for waffles and wool. It wasn't sacred, but it was a bit like a pilgrimage, where parents carried their kids on their shoulders and grandparents wore their best weekend outfits. On a lucky day, even a tourist or two who traveled through Sweden showed up for some local west coast flavor.

As the first visitors appeared, at about ten in the morning, the four of us stood behind the desk and didn't really know what to do with ourselves. *Laser Fog* rolled on repeat, with two joysticks positioned in front of the computer for anyone to pick up and play. But no one seemed to get what we were, if in fact we weren't just part of the festival logistics, and they passed us with polite nods and excusing smiles. But as the first kids bounced off to our booth, pushing their mums and dads to explain what on earth this was that looked so cool, a small crowd gathered to see.

Sara nudged me from the side. "Go on," she said.

"What?"

Lisa nudged me from the other side. "What she said."

I turned to her. "But...uh..."

Calvin pointed to me and said out loud, for everyone to hear: "T-this is Elliot. This was all his idea."

For a moment, the crowd looked at me. Some were munching on a cookie. One guy had a coffee in a plastic mug. A mom with two sons studied the screen, as they moved inevitably closer, like it had a gravity of its own.

"Wanna try it?" I said to them.

Their heads bobbed in unison. I walked around to the other side, waved for them to follow, and grabbed one of the sticks.

"It's easy," I said. "Just watch me. So you play this guy here, and he's looking for his friends, and they're somewhere in this town. So this is how you move, and you can also climb stuff and jump over holes in the ground," at which point the kids went Whooaaa, "and then when you've found your first friend, you can combine your skills and…"

I kept talking, the kids kept gawking. I handed them the controller and they had a go, and I didn't notice that the crowd grew, how some waved for others to come watch, how Elizabeth subtly turned up the screen's volume and how Cornelia and Arshak got busy when a bunch of grown-ups handed over cash for a copy of our game with coffee and pie.

And this was the ebb and flow of the Fjellhamn Festival, that place where the video game community had never thrived, a town not known for its strong foundation to nurture a recently ignited passion for otherworldly digital experiences, if you recall. Perhaps the citizens of tomorrow would lead the way to organized grocery lists and other such emotionally involving interactive experiences, but not today.

But they were good people, and they didn't really believe that our Commodore computer was a toaster with a communist agenda wired into its circuits. Even Mr. Parkvik was here on this day, and when he showed up to present a bill on the table, he exclaimed that he was here to make a deal, and he was sure we'd both benefit from the transaction. But he smiled as Calvin gave him a copy, and he had his complementary coffee and pie with a gracious smile, telling anyone who was unfortunate enough to come too close that he always knew it had been a good idea to sell the computer to these kids. Cornelia shouted that we'd sold eleven games already, Arshak ran into his café to make more coffee, and Sara's dad paced around our booth to make sure no one tripped on our wires or cut the power.

Around lunch, the square was packed and loud as the street musicians arrived, and our mix of chiptune surrealism blended with violins and accordions. It became one of Fjellhamn's last summer days as the late August sun chased away the clouds and pushed the men to take off their jackets, the women to remove their shoulder sweaters. The fishermen set up a coal grill and a steel table, and served cod and lemon with fries and beer under the shade of a big sail canvas. One of them came over to us with plates and water in plastic glasses.

"It's on us, kids," he said and grinned, a few teeth missing. "Looks like you could need it."

He was right, and we thanked him for it, because while people circled the square for slippers or marmalade, they came back to us before they left. They tried to play the game, or they bought a copy without knowing exactly what it was, or maybe they admitted that "Actually, we have a computer at home. No idea what to do with it, but it'll be nice to say that we got something on it that's made around here."

For the first time in I don't know how long, I felt nothing but a calm yet intoxicating sense of joy. I'd forgotten that I was moving soon, that I'd never be with Calvin, Lisa, and Sara like this again. Fjellhamn wouldn't be my home for much longer. Even the sight of Lars did nothing to bring me down, as I saw him at the other end of the square with a waffle and a soda in his hands, his sister sitting next to him and eating an ice cream. He saw me too, and there was just this brief moment where he smiled a little. I smiled back. Arshak was doing an odd kind of dance as he served up coffee for everyone, a slow movement of the hips as if he was singing along to some old tune from his home. From time to time, he threw a glance at Cornelia and winked at her. She laughed out loud, scaring the youngest and alarming the elderly, and she waved at him to stop it this instance, but for every cup he served, she was there to slice up a piece of pie and put it on a paper plate to go with his black brew.

When we sold disc fifty-one, less than half remaining now, Lisa spun around and put her arms behind my neck and kissed me. For once, for the first time, I didn't resist in any way. I'd not been aware that I ever had, but now when it felt so obvious, so natural and easy to be with her, I felt bad about all the times I'd raised some kind of wall to guard myself from whatever fear I'd imagined might strike again. As if Lisa would ever do anything to hurt me.

And that's when my mum showed up.

Chapter 71

A FAVORITE

I saw her across the crowd, at the other end of the square.

She was standing outside, looking in.

Dad was there, she leaned against his arm. He had his best jacket on and his favorite jeans. She wore her blue summer dress with white dots, and she'd washed and combed her hair. Her lips were red, her face pale.

"You okay?" Calvin said.

I felt a pain in my throat as I swallowed. Things had been so easy. Now, I had no idea what to do.

"D-don't worry," Calvin said. "If you wanna sneak out, I'll cover for you. I'll tell them to leave."

Lisa looked at me, troubled. Sara was at the computer, showing the game to some of her dad's cousins.

"Thanks," I said to him. "I'll be fine."

My dad saw me and waved. I waved back, slowly. Mum raised her head and looked in my direction. A strain came over her and she tugged at his arm. He said something to her and they walked through the crowd, in my direction. She flinched and averted her eyes, as if the people around her lashed out, but most didn't even notice and those who did were just kind and offered her and Dad the space to help them pass.

It took them forever. But once they were here, it didn't feel so bad.

"Hello, Elliot," Mum said. She spoke slowly, in a low voice.

"Hello, Mum."

"Hey, son," Dad said. "It's a lovely thing you've done here. We're so proud of you."

Mum scanned our table. She didn't notice my friends or their parents, but kept her eyes on the computer, the screen, and the peripherals connected.

"This is the game he's made," Dad said. "You know, the one we've talked about at home. And these are his friends, Charlotte. This is Calvin and Sara. You remember Sara."

Mum looked around but didn't see her. She smiled quickly.

"And Lisa, of course," Dad said.

Lisa leaned forward and stretched out her hand. "So pleased to meet you, Mrs. Lindh. I'm Lisa."

Mum just held her hands in the air in front of her, not really responding to Lisa's grip. Then she took a breath and straightened up.

"So this is...is this...you made this, Elliot?"

"We did," I said. "Together."

"That's nice. I'd like to..." She turned to Dad. "We should buy a copy, dear. Don't you think?"

"We should buy two," Dad said.

"Mum...you don't have to buy it. I'll give you one." Sara pretended she didn't see or hear what was going on. Lisa and Calvin nodded, standing together now.

"No, no," Mum said. "I want to buy it. It'd be nice to have...to say that I bought something...my son made. How much is it?"

"Fifty kronor."

She laughed and made a dismissive gesture. "Quite the businessman, our Elliot," she said, sounding almost casual now. I had a glimpse of her as she used to be, maybe not a person without a streak of grief over her, but one that could still laugh and be generous as well as receive when others were the same to her. Or maybe that person never existed, and I'd just created her as the years passed.

Dad handed over a bill. I gave Mum a disc and nodded to Cornelia and Arshak. He was wiping away some stains from the table, but Cornelia watched us with a thoughtful expression.

"There's coffee and pie," I said.

Mum looked at me now. Her eyes on mine.

Behind those veiled pools, there was a flip book of emotions that turned the page every second. I wanted to understand it, I didn't need to like it but I had to comprehend and make sense of it or maybe I'd go insane one day. But it was impossible, of course.

"If you're not doing anything tonight," she said, "...how would you like...maybe you would like...do you want to come home?"

She held on to Dad now. He had his arm around her shoulder. I looked at him. He shrugged subtly.

"I'll cook something," she said. "Your favorite." She looked satisfied with this. "I'll make you your favorite."

I felt manipulated. But I don't think that was her intention. If it ever had been.

"Sure," I said. "I'll drop by."

"Oh. How nice." She looked at Dad and smiled. He smiled back and patted her on the arm. Somehow, that made me angry, because there was a condescending touch to his affection, dismissing her as you might with a relative confused by age, who really just tried to follow the conversation.

"Now, dear," Mum said. "Let's go home...let's try this thing... that our son made."

"Yes," Dad said. "We'll just get a computer first. And then we'll try it. See you tonight, Elliot."

"Mm-hmm."

They walked away from our booth, through the crowd, moving at their own pace among the festival guests. The band had taken a pause but now, they were firing away a cheerful solo on a violin as the singer dashed from left to right on the small stage, clapping his hands to work up the crowd.

Calvin came up to me.

"D-didn't go so bad," he said. "She was nice."

"I guess."

They were at the end of the square now, leaving the area, alone on the small road that led away from the piers, into the denser parts where the houses cast longer shadow over the streets.

"I d-didn't know you had a favorite," Calvin said.

They were gone now. I still had my eyes on the space where they'd just been.

"I don't," I said.

Chapter 72

STICK ON A TABLE

If you ever wondered what a video game pitch really looked like (I'm pretty sure you've never wondered), it's actually very straightforward. You'd be mistaken for thinking it's not, if you've seen what I've seen. But like we said before, stating the obvious only becomes a thing after it's been preached to a fault.

So I've witnessed everything from dry power point slides and confused scribblings on a wall, to light and music shows and naked people running around in ski helmets, complete staged productions, and downright rude visionaries who made it a point to sleep through the publisher's feedback.

But really, the only pitches that ever worked were the ones where you brought a good game into the room and let the people play. If you didn't have that, you'd fail at some point. No show staged by any agency on any planet could do anything about that.

So that's what I did. I brought out one of my memory sticks from my bag, slid it across the table to Christina and, while she installed the demo on her debug console, I took out Calvin's drawing, ironed out any wrinkles as best I could, and put it on the table. There were a couple of other Microsofters in the room, an assistant to Christina, some guy from marketing and a mid-level producer that already seemed to have her questions ready before she'd seen a single frame.

"I'm just gonna go ahead and play then," Christina said. "You wanna say something before we start?"

"Just play it. Then we'll talk."

"Really? Nothing?"

"Nope."

"No keynote? No slides? No show?"

"Not this time."

She looked at Calvin's stick drawing.

"No story?"

I shook my head.

"Confident, that guy," she said and turned to Skye, who smiled. "Almost rude, wouldn't you say, Sara?"

"I'd say so, yes."

"But we like that, don't we? No bullshit. Just the game. In fact, I think it's...oh, it's starting now. I'll be quiet."

The game faded in on the screen. Its bold title emerged, letter by letter, in glowing red across the black surface.

For a moment, the room was quiet. They all watched. Waiting.

The wind left the speakers and filled the room, as the camera panned over green hills. It stopped by a tree, and underneath that tree was the sad, old man.

He was looking at something on the horizon, breathing slowly, ready to wait for an eternity until someone woke him up.

Which Christina did.

I leaned back, hands behind my neck, and watched our game unfold.

This is how we pitched it throughout the day. After Christina, we saw Kicki at Activision and before that meeting ended, Skye had three messages in her phone. One from Francois at Ubisoft, one from Susie at Capcom, and one from Stephen at So Long Texas. She juggled their requests for appointments, made a call to another meeting we'd have in two hours and shifted that to a new slot to make it all fit. Before we entered our third session, she had another batch to handle. Suddenly, everyone wanted to see us.

Every time we entered a new room, I had Calvin's drawing with me. I touched it from time to time. Skye noticed, but didn't ask. Besides, she had her own part to play. Having a great something was essential, but you'd get nowhere without the credibility to execute on your grand ideas. I'd figured that Spellbinder's track record, my years in the industry, and my generally awesome ability to make anything seem like a good idea when I put my mind to it would be enough currency for now. But once the question came, from Christina first but also from Kicki, Susie, Francois and the rest, Skye gently put her hand on my arm, to make sure I shut up now.

"Of course we have a plan," she said and displayed a memory stick of her own. "Open the file and we'll take a look."

I was quiet, as she unraveled a yearlong production with tactics that would make the three hundred Spartans look like chess rookies in comparison.

"After all," she said, "most of the Spellbinders will be back on the team, so we'd have a velocity of more than seventy percent. How about that? Impressive, I know. So it's not just a game based on familiar assets and production pipelines, it's also made by the team who's developed these components over a decade. Normally, this kind of title would require three years, maybe more, and it would probably fail anyway. But you can prepare this for next year's Christmas launch. It'll be ready. Or I'll remove my tattoos."

"All of them?" Kicki had said.

"Yes," Skye said. "All of them. Including the one you're thinking about right now, you filthy lady producer, you."

While the game left everyone who played it sometimes speechless, sometimes touched, sometimes blabbering incomprehensibly, sometimes reaching for a phone to call in a negotiator and tell them to drop *Half-Life 3*, that one's never coming out anyway,

Skye was the one who took their blown minds and put them back together, saying that this was real. "Once your awe has settled, you will be confident to know that it's not just a mirage. This will happen. It's not only the greatest game ever. It's also backed by the greatest team with the greatest plan."

Some of them mentioned Sean's lawsuit, either in a passing comment or as part of a joke. It's not like the threat wasn't real. It's more that it came from a man who held more grudges than the ghost from a Japanese horror movie. As serious as it was, it was hard to take it seriously in the moment.

And they joked about the title. "So we're going for 100% on Metacritic then?" Sigur from CCP said. "That'd be all tens and hundreds through the reviews. But you're gonna make sure that happens, won't you, Wilfred?" he said and turned to a junior project manager who was still crying. "You'll help Elliot and Skye make sure Spellbinder pulls this off? We're counting on you, Willie. Oh, don't worry. Marketing will fuck it up somehow. I mean, you're from marketing, Jennie? You gonna come up with some stupid ideas and some silly prognosis numbers, won't you?"

"I sure will," Jennie said. "I got an entire team ready to wreck this thing with guesstimations. You can count on me."

They all laughed except Wilfred, who still cried. If it was because of the game's beauty, or because of the pressure applied, was unclear. But he did cry.

As six o'clock approached and the show was shutting down for the day, Skye had so many appointments booked for the next day that she had to cancel and decline a few. We'd already received offers as well as invitations to those exclusive dinner parties at the most expensive places, and one or two of the larger publishers had ideas for marketing and positioning.

"Can we use Calvin's death somehow?" they said. "Like, a game raised from the dead, by a voice from the grave? Or maybe work the lifetime in the making angle. You still got all the material from when you were kids? We can tap that. Build teasers, maybe.

You think his wife's gonna do interviews? The mourning widow? Maybe the kids, too. They never got to know their dad, but they'll know him through his games, like forever. Hey, you're Swedes, right? Is this like the video game equivalent of Stieg Larsson? Just when success would strike, he was taken from us, far too soon. There are only possibilities here."

Skye said we'd go to Christina's party first, to show that loyalty was important. But to not make an appearance at Sony's dinner afterwards would be downright stupid, and if we could round it up with late night drinks at Ubisoft's lounge, then this would be a very good day, indeed.

I was struggling to pay attention as she spoke.

My feet were like lead now. I could hardly focus on the next minute, let alone make a decision on where and with whom we'd eat. It felt insurmountable. I had fired my smart bomb to get through the day. Now, I was all out.

I tripped, but Skye caught me and pulled me up.

"Hey," she said. "Let's sit down. It's been a crazy day."

We were in the hotel lounge now. How did we get here? Maybe we'd taken a taxi. Maybe we'd walked.

We went to the bar. I dropped my bag, let out a sigh, and closed my eyes. I tried to shut out all sounds, all impressions.

She touched my hand.

"You did it, Elliot," she said.

I opened my eyes.

"Not me," I said. "We. You."

"You want a drink?"

"No."

She called for the bartender. We were the only ones here. The hotel was quite depressing, interiors and furniture reminding me of something that might've been a good idea in the seventies.

"You should get some rest," she said. "Before we go."

I nodded.

Then I remembered.

"You were gonna tell me something," I said. "Before."

Skye got her drink. Some kind of bourbon. She took a sip. "Is this your greatest moment ever, Elliot?"

What a draining question to answer. I was almost annoyed with her now.

"It's certainly not the worst," I said.

She took another sip. "What's the problem, then? Isn't this what you wanted?"

"If I could just get some rest..."

"What is the worst moment ever, though?"

I was surprised by her question, and by how quickly the answer came to me.

I took out the stick drawing and put it on the bar desk. It was getting worn now, from all its pocket travels in and out.

"This one, maybe."

Skye looked at it.

"There it is again. When was this?" she said.

I sighed. "About a month after our last Midsummer party."

"The one where Calvin and Lisa..."

"That'd be the one."

"I see."

I laughed. "No, Skye. You don't. You really don't."

She leaned closer. I felt her breath on my face. Her green eyes sparkled in the faded bar light. Everything in here was so cheap, which made her presence all the more unreal.

"Fuck the dinner parties," she said. "I owe you a burger. Let's do that. And talk. Really talk. I know a shitty place a few blocks from here."

"I love shitty places."

"Great. I'll just clean myself up. I wanna look good if we're going to a real dump. See you in the lobby in an hour."

"Make that two. I need that rest."

Chapter 73

BLOOD AGAIN

I went to my room. I fell forward into the bed and sunk into the mattress, like a slow dive from the Fjellhamn cliffs, into the ocean.

My head was hurting. I tried to get up, but everything was spinning. I had to let go and drop into the bed again.

There was moisture on my lips. I touched them and felt blood, slowly trickling from my nose, along the corner of my mouth. There were tears but I didn't cry, I needed water but to get up, to find myself a glass and something to pour into it, seemed beyond impossible. Gravity forced me to stay, and who was I to defy a law of the universe?

Then fear hit me, as someone pounded on my door—the ghoul was back!—and the walls flashed and rotated before me, on the one side being those that belonged to this hotel and the other side, my apartment where I'd roamed my halls like a busy little ghost, wearing nothing but filthy robes.

So this is where the dream will end, I thought.

In a hotel room in Los Angeles, where maybe I'd taken something now and was dying. Or maybe I was just seventeen and the meeting with Sean had gone really bad, or maybe this was my first stay here after Calvin had left and I had realized that this would never work, it was all over now, or perhaps I was in my apartment, time hadn't passed and I'd just had a really long and sweet wish of how things could've been, or I was still a kid and Calvin had never existed and I had created this world where I ruled the monsters and decided when they could hurt me and when I was invincible.

But even a wish came to an end, and now here I was.

I sat up.

I held Calvin's stick drawing in my hands, squeezing the edges hard, preventing myself from pulling the paper apart, staring at the letters under the picture.

Remember?

My hands shook. I felt warm, perhaps from that fever Skye talked about. I gnawed at my lips, closed my eyes and now I cried.

And the damn ghoul wouldn't stop rattling its bones at the gates, would it? It had the same groove as always, this fiend.

I heard a voice calling to me, shouting from the other side. The time was eleven or something. I was hours late.

"Elliot," Skye shouted. "Are you there? Are you okay? Why aren't you answering your phone?"

I wanted to, but a short circuit rushed through my brain. I fell again, backwards now. I had time to think that I'd hit my head and there would be blood on the carpet, but this time, no one would see me and pick me up.

"Nintendo called, Elliot. They want—a fucking—meeting."

She kicked on the door.

"They're here. It's happening. But you have to come out."

Now, I was smiling.

The headache was gone.

I was cold, but it soothed me.

Maybe I was back in that stream again, following its flow to the end, where my best friend was waiting for me. I still held the drawing, but gently now.

"Now," I said, "you get to work with Nintendo."

The lights around me faded.

An endless night fell.

"I—am—calling—security, Elliot. Open the fucking door, you motherfucker selfish piece of shit. Please, just open the door. Oh god, please, Elliot. Don't do this. Not now. Please, Elliot."

She, too, was crying now.

And I remembered.

Chapter 74

THE WORST MOMENT EVER

Sometime after Spellbinder's final Midsummer party, I got off the bus at Fjellhamn's Town Square.

It looked the same and yet it didn't. Like all the places you only remembered from your childhood, things were smaller and more worn when you came back. In my mind, this town was a place where summer was the only season. But now, I wore jeans and a jacket, with a thick wool sweater underneath. The trees were yellow and red, and underneath the gray skies, a cold wind swept in from the sea.

I walked down the road to the piers. Arshak's cafe was replaced by a vegan restaurant owned by a young couple. Cornelia's diner was a McDonald's now but the toy store on the other side was still there, owned by a passionate collector, as odd as it was curious. The library had become a museum for aquarelle art, with an added exterior that hosted a fine dining restaurant.

There weren't any fishermen by the piers these days. Their sheds and nets were long gone. There were a lot of sailing boats and even a yacht or two, but the old skiffs had been stranded or moved up north. Some of the bridges were torn and rebuilt with swim ladders, but they were empty today.

Calvin was waiting for me at the booth where we'd always had ice cream. It was just an empty box with an unhinged door now, and patches of red paint on the wooden walls.

He seemed sad, but he smiled at me. I didn't smile back.

"Y-you want one?" he said and pointed with his thumb to the ice cream booth.

But I wasn't biting. He looked at me from under his bangs, pushed them to the side, and shrugged.

We walked.

Despite all, the silence between us remained comfortable. From a distance, I saw the cliffs we dived from during the summers. Contrary to everything else, they seemed bigger, as if their death-defying heights could only be realized when you'd grown up. I almost called out that it was a wonder we never broke our necks, but then I remembered I was angry and kept quiet.

After some time, we sat down on a bench by one of the beaches.

"I'm l-leaving Spellbinder," Calvin said.

"Good. We don't need you."

It took him a minute before he said anything else. "It's not like you d-d-didn't have your chances."

"It's not like you told me you took one yourself."

"No one's cheating on you. You and Lisa weren't a couple."

"Shut up, Calvin. Shut—the—fuck—up."

"Okay."

So he did, and since it felt like the next move was on me, nothing much happened for about half an hour. We looked at the waves and the rocks. They moved slowly with the water across the beach, creating patterns of black and gray stone.

"Is she here?" I said.

"She's w...with her parents. In Skaresund."

"If you're gonna say that she says hi..."

"She does, though."

"You're really asking for it, aren't you?"

"M-maybe you should just hit me, and get it o-over with."

"I'm thinking about it."

He looked at me as if a punch in the face wasn't out of the question. But if that was the case, he seemed prepared for it, almost wanting it. Like he'd take a beating and then we were done.

"We were going to tell you, Elliot."

"Oh, you were, were you? That's nice of you. When? At the Christmas party?"

"We didn't plan for this. It just happened. But it's not just a thing. I feel...it's really...she's...it's real."

"Don't, Calvin. Just don't."

"You would be the first to k-know. I swear."

As angry as I was, I had to believe that. There was no denying the honesty or despair in his voice.

"I'm gonna go *Double Dragon* on you," I muttered.

Calvin looked at me, unsure how to react. He tried to hide a smile. Then, he couldn't help but laugh. Maybe it wasn't appropriate, maybe it was just the right thing to do. I didn't join, but it did something to thaw me up.

"Whatever happened to Lars anyway?" I said.

"He had a S-spectrum. So nothing good, I assume."

"Eight colors."

"And only two at the same time."

Then I sighed. I looked at Calvin. "I'm not mad," I said. "I'm trying to be. But I'm not."

Calvin nodded. He eyed me warily. "You're s...s-something, though."

"How about that ice cream?"

Chapter 75

BOYS ON A PIER

We walked slowly through town. We met a few people but no one we knew, no one who recognized us. There were a lot of younger couples here, some with babies in carts, some expecting their first. Over the last years, the government had built apartments and small houses in the Fjellhamn center, with a promise to expand the railway from Gothenburg. It was marketed as a place close to the ocean, but just a short trip away from the big city pulse, with shopping and entertainment.

"How's your mum?" I said.

Calvin shook his head. "Not better. Not worse."

He looked at me from the side. I knew what was coming next but I didn't want to talk about my parents, so I cut him short.

"She doesn't remember you at all now?"

"Sometimes, sure. She mixes us up, though. One day, I'm Elliot. Tomorrow, I'm Calvin again. Sometimes, I'm even Sara."

I laughed quietly.

"But she's always happy," Calvin said. "They take good care of her. I d-don't know. In a way, I think she always recognizes me. We talk and laugh, she tells me stories and she wants to cook me dinner and sure, she'd burn down the place if she did...but she's glad to see me. Try as I might, I can't be t-too sad about it. But sometimes, I can't help it anyway, and then she gets angry. That temper of hers, man."

"Banging away on pots and pans, throwing plates around."

"Like a ninja."

"One who can swim."

"The true last ninja."

I sighed. "I should visit her someday," I said.

"If you want to."

We came to the street where the hardware store once was. Now, it was a barber shop, one of those where the staff wore white uniforms, where the men had complicated mustaches and the women warrior braids.

"I'll get over it," I said. "About you and Lisa. Just give me some time, okay? I need to get used to it."

"Yeah...she says the same thing. Maybe you should talk to her."

"I'm gonna have to, I guess. But not right now."

Calvin nodded. "Okay." He didn't dare say more, afraid he'd jinx it now, when we were heading out of the woods and maybe into friendship territory again.

"Did you ever realize how big Fjellhamn is?" I said. "If you count the forests and the hills."

"We went pretty far," Calvin said. "I always wondered what would happen if we'd get a flat tire in the middle of nowhere."

"It'd be a long walk home. But that's about it."

He laughed quietly.

"It was a lot bigger when I was alone," I said. "It felt like it stretched on forever."

"I know what you mean."

"It's gone now, though. Isn't it?"

Calvin looked at me. "What's gone?"

"Us. We."

"Stupid. Look, I know I fucked up. It's on me, but I'll fix it."

"By leaving Spellbinder?"

Calvin pointed to a small kiosk. It looked new, a franchise for a big brand that didn't even exist when we lived here. We went up there, he bought me a cone with vanilla and chocolate and one with blueberry and whipped cream for himself. We went to the cliffs that faced west, and sat down on two rocks among white heather.

"I am a bit t-tired, Elliot. I'll admit to that."

I couldn't question this. Years of travel and crunches, marathon release schedules, no real concept of vacation—it all came with a price. One that was insignificant at twenty, but grew more relevant by each year.

"I wanna d-do other stuff," he said. "Maybe work on my exhibition...write a comic book. Have kids, even. Walk them to school. Pull back, rest, turn off the noise."

"Give it a year. You'd go crazy."

"I don't know. Those oceans of time...they're not ours anymore, you know."

"We're not exactly old."

He grabbed my arm. "That's my point. We're not gone. It's not over. You're the best man at my wedding, Elliot. You're the godfather of my child. You're the one I call when I need a sofa to sleep on. You're the one who's always been there, who will always be there. That won't change. Ever."

"But you owe it to Lisa to put her first."

"What's that got to d-do with anything? It's not a c-competition."

"But if it had been, I would've lost. And I'm fine with that. You need to be, too."

"Fucking nonsense. I don't know where you're going with this. You're pissing me off."

"You're doing your own thing now. You said so yourself."

"But you're a part of that."

I was about to answer, but he got up from his rock and dropped his ice cream.

"This is what you always do, Elliot. Stringing people along, calling on them when you need them and not giving a fuck when you don't. Even the toughest give in to your charms, and how do you repay them? Oh, you don't. You talked to Sara lately?"

"Every day. We work together."

"I mean, really talked, Elliot." Calvin bit his lip and turned away. "Never mind," he said. "I'm sorry. Fuck it...I do know where this is going, don't I?" He spun around and glared at me. "We're your friends. And you're using us. You're putting us in all kinds of positions and that makes us feel bad. That we can't reach you. Can't help you."

He was red in the face, his eyes on fire.

"I know," I said calmly.

"Oh," he shouted. "Okay, then. Well, that's just fine."

But clearly, he was expecting some kind of comeback, me raising the volume to eleven by shouting even louder and us resorting to name calling and a final go to hell and fuck off before we parted. That was the kind of fight you could come back from. Like misunderstandings, punches and insults could be mended.

I watched him with slow patience as he calmed down, and returned to his rock next to mine.

"I'm still that boy," I said. "And I'm tired of him. He exhausts me. That kid...he's a good kid. But he needs to deal with his shit now."

"Can't argue with t-that," Calvin mumbled.

"So you see how you can't be a part of that, don't you?"

"Fuck, no. You're an idiot. What's a k-kid without a friend? I'll come with you. Where we going? To some shrink? Sign me u...up. Shock therapy? I'll hold the cords. A yoga retreat to India? Mind the food. Not a p-p-problem."

"But how am I ever gonna be able to face this, if you're along for the ride?"

"Because that's how you do it. You get help from your friends."

"Yeah, maybe. If things would be different. But you're leaving the studio. And you're going with the only woman who could ever stand me." Calvin was about to protest but I raised my arms.

"You're not doing anything wrong. But can't you see that you're just adding to the pain right now?"

He looked at me with a desperate expression, dashing around in his head to find the words that would lead us right again.

"You're all grown up," I said. "Maybe you'll get a family. I don't know, even a real job. If you want to, I think you should do that."

"Sounds pretty stupid to me," he said. Then, after a few seconds: "Getting a real job, I mean."

I smiled.

"You want my ice cream?" I said. "I see you dropped yours."

"N-no. I'm hungry. But I know just the place."

We walked back to town, down to the piers where a small restaurant served grilled cod wrapped in foil, with slices of lemon to boost. We had one each and a beer, and went down to the bridges and looked at the water and the boats. It was getting cold now, but we didn't care.

"I'm not gonna call you," Calvin said when we'd finished our meal and enjoyed our beer. "I know you, Elliot. You won't answer. You won't call me back. This is on you, brother. I'm not gonna come after you. You'll just run away."

"You're being very literal about it now."

"You're a very 1-literal person. Words are practically your thing."

"True, that."

"However...one thing that's most definitely not your thing...as we know by now, not everyone can draw, after all..."

He pulled out a small sketch book from his back pocket and detached a blank ink pen from its cover. He opened the book to a blank page and quickly made a small stick drawing.

It had two boys on it. They were sitting on a pier.

"This is us," Calvin said. "Right now, actually. This place, right here. Look how handsome we are."

"Dashing, even. What're we laughing about?"

"I don't know. Some random joke."

It was just a few lines of ink, but so beautiful.

I felt that familiar pain again, an overwhelming despair that there was so much beauty in Calvin's strokes that the world would never see, so much of his work that got lost in concept. But then again, there was all that output that they did get to see, all those fantastic games and all the color and motion he'd applied to them through the years.

He tore out the stick drawing and gave it to me.

"Take this," he said. "And r-remember."

"Remember what?"

"That we're friends."

I held it and looked at it.

The sun was setting now, coloring the waves with the fall's crimson rays. We'd been in Fjellhamn all day. It didn't feel that long, more like one of those summer days when the adventure never ended and we forgot about time, until the skies were so dark we could barely see the road in front of us.

"No," I said. "You kidding me? I'm not gonna forget. I think you're making this into a bigger thing than it has to be."

"You can disappear sometimes, man. And I just have a feeling... hmm...I have a feeling..."

"What?"

"You'll be going far and away for this one. Doesn't hurt to have an anchor. To remember a reason to get back. Take the drawing now. I made it for you."

"Oh, c'mon."

"All right, all right. I'll k-keep it. But I'll send it your way, if I think you're dragging. Don't be gone too long. We got plans. Shit to handle. Time to kill."

"We're still young," I said. "Oceans of time ahead of us."

"I mean, we haven't even worked with Nintendo yet. So if nothing else, there's still that, right?"

"Right."

He raised his bottle. I raised mine, and we toasted to this as the sun sank into the ocean.

Chapter 76

BEST, BEST FRIEND

I don't remember what we talked about after that, but I think it was some nonsense about *The Last of Us* or how Peter Jackson should've stayed away from *The Hobbit*. It was dark when we walked to the station and as fortune favored us, the bus to Gothenburg was there and waiting. The skies were cloudy, a rain was looming, and this was the last ride back to the city.

When we got there, I shoved my hands in my pockets and looked around.

"So...this is your bus, then?" I said.

"Yeah, I'm going back to Gothenburg. You coming?"

I shook my head. "Nah. I'm going north. To Lysekil."

Calvin was silent for a moment.

"What's g-going on there?"

"Oh, nothing much. Skye has tickets to a concert in the park."

"Skye? Has tickets? To a concert? In Lysekil?"

"Uh, yep."

"She's tone deaf."

"She's not."

"But it's close to midnight."

"Yes."

"In August."

"It is, isn't it?"

"Skye's in Stockholm."

"Ah, nope."

"Okay. I'm gonna get on this bus, then."

"Yes."

"You have a good concert. And say hello to Skye from me."

"I will."

Calvin walked up to me and hugged me hard. The bus fired up its engines and prepared to leave. I hugged him back, harder.

"Elliot," he said, his voice slightly frail. "Thank you for being my best, best friend. Like forever."

"The same," I said. "Thanks for walking these hills with me."

We parted. His eyes were red. He patted me on the shoulder, a weak attempt at some male camaraderie to brush off all the emotions, and then he got on the bus. The doors closed. I saw him move to the back and sit down by the window. He waved to me as they left the station, and I waved back and smiled.

I watched the bus as it rode up the hill and crossed the high point. Then it was gone.

I sat down on the wall where Lisa had been waiting for me on our first date. I felt like that boy again, wondering if time had ever passed, no idea where to go now.

Chapter 77

INSIGNIFICANT

There was no need for Skye to call hotel security. After she'd screamed and banged on my door for some time, I pulled myself together, got up from the bed and opened.

"So you're the ghoul after all," I said.

"What? Oh, you idiot. You fell asleep, didn't you? Now you've messed up my mascara. And we've missed the dinner parties. I didn't even get a burger."

"You look lovely, though."

It just came out of me. She really did. While she'd never returned to dresses or sweaters after she cut her hair and wore green makeup all those years ago, she had a way to wear a simple t-shirt and a pair of jeans that made her look fantastic.

"It's the same shit I always wear."

"Maybe it's because you've showered, then."

"That, I don't always do. So sure, yeah. Could be. Anyway..." She took a deep breath and gave me a big smile. "Nintendo, Elliot."

I grinned back. "Yeah."

"How did you do it?"

"I ignored them. Consequently."

"That'd be a trademark of yours, wouldn't it?"

"At least I'm not talking about myself in third person." She leaned her head to the side. "Seriously, though. You never approached them, did you?"

"I did not."

"They always used to get our call. But not this time."

"Not this time."

She watched me in silence for a few seconds. It made me uncomfortable and warm.

"I'm not gonna say that you're on to something," she said. "But they do want to see us. In Kyoto, no less."

"This all sounds fantastic. But I need to rest, Skye. Let's have lunch tomorrow at that dump you talked about. And we'll go through the details."

"Sure. Okay. What do we do about the others?"

"Cancel everything. We got Nintendo now."

Despite the jetlag, I slept through the night and woke up late in the morning. Like on many other days, the sun was shining in Los Angeles today. I took a shower, put on some clean clothes, and made sure that Calvin's folder was with me as I left the hotel room. When I passed the reception, I handed them the keys and said I was checking out.

"Leaving early, sir?" the woman behind the desk said. "I'm afraid we can't refund the remaining nights."

"That's okay," I said. "Thanks, anyway."

I took a taxi to Staples Center. I had maybe two hours or so before I'd meet Skye and I walked around inside the trade center, watching all the games and characters on display, listening to symphonic sound tracks and electro-pumping beats. I said hello to those I knew, I stopped to briefly talk to those who wanted a moment, but I was looking for someone and I had a pretty good idea where I'd find him. In the section where most of the independent developers were housed, there he was in his purple shirt and gray suit pants, moving about like a confused king in a land where his subjects whispered behind his back.

"Hello, Sean," I said. He was talking to a developer from Finland now, a team of women that had a game rolling on their screen about exploration and combat in a gothic castle. I liked it already. Very Castlevania.

He turned around. He didn't seem surprised to see me, but looked at me calmly, the hint of a smile behind his mustache.

"Elliot," he said. "My dear boy. I didn't expect to see you here, actually, considering...well, you know. You got a lot of nerve. But I'll admit, you make it more interesting. Your game's the talk of the town." He chuckled. "Here, let me introduce you to these—"

"I'm sorry, Sean," I said.

He looked at the Finns, then at me.

"For what? Interrupting our meeting? Don't worry, we're on the trade floor. It's all part of—"

"No, Sean. I'm sorry if I ever made you insignificant."

His eyes narrowed. He took a short step back, as if I'd pushed him with a gentle touch.

"Spellbinder Software wouldn't exist without you," I said. "No *Clear Blue Skies*. No *Archipelago*. No *Dark Man Crying*."

"Considering that many in your team used to be my people, I have to agree."

"Your father was wrong, Sean."

He laughed. "He's also dead, son."

"Finding talent is a skill. Without it, we'd be nothing. And growing it, and training it. You were a good teacher. I never respected you enough for what you did for us."

The team had pulled back now. Even if Sean and I were right in the tempest that was the show, the immediate area around us was quiet and empty. I could hear him breathing.

He folded his arms. "I will use this, Elliot. In court."

"I'm not here for tactics."

He scanned me now. "Then why are you here?"

"I don't want to be ungrateful, Sean. I am not that person."

"If you're here to trade your dignity, save it."

"I was recently told I had none left." I put down my bag. "Is there someplace we can sit?"

He looked straight at me. "No." There were chairs all over the booth.

I was uncomfortable. But I wasn't raising any shields this time. I could feel him trying to overwhelm me, but I wasn't fighting it. That, in a way, made this scarier than most battles I'd been in. I was trembling again.

"I never understood where you came from," I said. "To me, you were a bully who took us in to learn your ways. I thought that was all you were."

"I gave you every opportunity. You were always too naive to see that."

"No. I just believed in myself more than you did."

"I don't even know what that means. Are we done here? I think we are."

I grabbed a chair and pulled it up. I offered it to Sean, and then pulled up another to sit down. With some reluctance, he sighed and sat, his legs crossed, his hands clasped over his knees. I caught him with my gaze and held him.

"You're not a nice person, Sean. But I've been told the same, from people who matter to me."

He was about to reply but I cut him short.

"Go ahead with your case. Maybe you can prove that assets and designs were developed on your watch. It's a stretch, but that's not the point. You just want to bleed me dry. You can afford to lose. Because the big win will be to see me fail, and go out like an even bigger tragedy than before."

"Nonsense. I only want what's fair."

I was dry in my mouth. I wet my lips.

"You know what's fair? I'm coming back to the fact that without you, there wouldn't be a greatest game."

Sean chuckled. "You're full of surprises today, son. I'll give you that."

"You were a part of it. Without your talent and your skills, we'd never learned how to build a proper production. We'd be firing shots in the dark while working at those gas stations and local cinemas. You gave us that, Sean. I never thanked you for it. But I'm thanking you now."

I put my hand on his knee. He flinched, ever so slightly.

"Thank you, Sean."

He moved his legs, and I withdrew.

"I think you would've done fine," he said. "One way or the other."

"Then why didn't you just ask?"

He seemed to lose interest now. Bored, even. "Ask you what, Elliot?"

"To be a part of it."

He looked at me for a few seconds. They felt like minutes.

"I did. From time to time."

And that was as true as anything I'd ever get from Sean. We'd said that the entire point was not to show it to anyone. That the beauty of it was that it was never meant for presentation or display, for an audience of any kind. It was ours. Our world. To which we could go, when we needed the peace.

But that wasn't quite right, was it? We had showed it to some. Just never to him. That he'd ever be able to contribute to such a thing of beauty was so unlikely, we didn't even think of it as dismissal when he asked and we said no.

"Your fight is with me," I said. "Not with Skye, the Spellbinders, or a video game production."

His eyes were cold now.

"But you got nothing to offer, Elliot, except for the property you own. A fight with you can't be about anything else than the collateral around it. You yourself...honestly...I don't know what's left to take. You as a person, you can't be reached."

"I can offer you to be a part of it."

He dismissed me with a laugh, almost choking on his breath. "I don't do sentimental, Elliot." Then, his gaze flared up and he leaned forward. "Your fake pity isn't working. This confession of yours...or is it an attempt at compassion? Not your strongest side, is it? You're selfish, Elliot. To a fault. That's why you used to be so good. Now, you're just a mess. Let's end this, before you've admitted to the whole thing and killed years of fun in court."

He was red in the face and he'd raised his voice as he reached his point.

"We got Nintendo," I said.

He laughed again and turned his head, as if we had an audience. But while the floor show was as crammed as ever, no one took any interest in us.

"You don't know when to stop, do you?"

I didn't answer, but watched him with a slight smile. After some time, he calmed down and returned my look.

"You did not get Nintendo," he said.

I shrugged.

"You've never worked with them," he said.

"Don't I know it."

"They don't compare. For better or worse. They might gut you at negotiations and you won't know until you're published. Electronic Arts are school yard thugs, compared to what Nintendo can be like."

"They seem like nice guys."

"Oh, for god's sake. A lifetime of video game development, and you're still in Fjellhamn."

I leaned my chin in my hand. "You're not, though."

"Dear god, no."

"You've worked with Nintendo."

"Many times."

"I'd like to see them try to gut you at the table."

And then, he got it.

I saw it in his face, how he tried to hide his surprise as he realized the full meaning of what I said. I didn't think it would take him so long. I'd been clear and upfront about what I wanted. But so had he, once. To get it, you needed to be aware enough to consider it.

Now, he was aware.

"Spellbinder needs your skills, Sean."

He smiled.

"I'm suing. And you're responding with a request for partnership."

"As equals."

He stood up.

"You're pathetic." He turned away. "And you're wasting my time."

I got up. "Think about it. I mean it."

I extended my hand. He looked at it, from over his shoulder. Then, he looked at me, as angry as I'd ever seen him.

"You patronizing fuck," he hissed.

I let my arm fall. "Okay. Take care, Sean."

I walked away. He remained, alone on the floor.

Chapter 78

CALIFORNIA SUN

I returned my pass in the reception desk before I left, despite protests from the clerk.

"If you hand it in, you got no access," he said. "You can't get a new pass this late."

"That's okay," I said. "I won't be needing it anymore."

I left Staples Center and walked down the broken pavement to Skye's burger joint. I decided to not think about my encounter with Sean right now. Unsure what to do with the outcome, I had something more important to bring up with Skye anyway. Whatever the fallout, I could handle it later.

It wasn't exactly close so it took me awhile, and I even had a little sunburn going on in my face as I got there. She saw me from her booth, pointed and laughed. "You never learn, do you?" she said. "You don't wear the wrong colors in Los Angeles and you don't go out without sunscreen."

"I think it looks good on me."

"Yeah, if you're into lobsters."

We ordered some kind of monster burger with more fries than anyone should ever eat, and brought in beers to go with that. Skye was hungry and it wasn't a pretty sight, to see her attack the food once it was served to us. I didn't have much of an appetite, but took a few polite bites from my burger.

"So anyway," she said and licked sauce from her fingers, "we'll go directly to Kyoto from LAX. I've talked to Joakim and Angela and apart from the fact that they're stupid excited that we got Nintendo," and she actually called out those last words so that everyone in the restaurant turned their heads, "they don't really need us back yet. They got enough to do for now."

"Nice," I said. "I've never been to Kyoto."

"It's lovely. Lots of temples and gardens. Very Japanese."

Skye kept talking about logistics and details, plans and releases, that it was time to bring back the rest of the Spellbinders now and fill in the gaps with fresh recruits from those who'd been clear before that they were done with this. I was there and yet I wasn't, I listened and offered replies that made sense, but when the waiter took our leftovers and we waited for coffee, Skye leaned back in her seat and pointed at me.

"What's wrong?"

"Nothing," I said.

But I reached down into my bag and pulled out Calvin's folder. I put it on the table.

"I'm not coming with you," I said.

Skye sighed. "Here we go again."

I slowly pushed the folder closer to her. "Look, Sara...this is yours. It always was."

"It's not...what are you talking about?"

"His ingredients, sure. And my spells, to bind them. But your magic, Sara. To make it real."

"You talk. You and words."

"I can't do this anymore. But more importantly, you don't need me to."

She moved forward, her arms resting on the table. I couldn't read her now, suddenly she wore no expression. But she didn't let me go with her eyes.

"I'm tired," I said. "In so many ways. I could keep this up, but it would kill me."

"They're quitting their jobs, Elliot. They're moving to Sweden for this. Because of you. It's real."

"Nothing's changed. You can do this without me. In fact, you'll be better off."

She fell back again, eyeing me with thought. "It would kill you, huh?"

She sighed.

"I should've known," she said.

"I think you did."

We got our coffees and a slice of apple pie. Skye didn't touch hers. I had a sip.

"Why didn't you ever call him, Elliot?"

She sounded angry. It would be hard to deny her an answer.

"What makes you think I didn't?" I said.

"You never wanted to talk about it. And he said, 'It's up to you now.'"

I had some water and looked at my hands. They were dry and red, sore from the sun. My throat hurt. Maybe I was getting a cold.

"Well, I did call him," I said. "To congratulate him when they got Isabelle. To send flowers when they got married. But things had changed. And time...well, time just passed."

Skye breathed slowly, her back against the seat now, her arms folded over her chest.

"Even when I learned he was sick," I said. "I figured...I gotta make this right. It's been so long. I couldn't just...show up, you know. There was still time, I thought. Time to make this right."

She gave me a hard look.

"You, of all people, Elliot, should've known how sudden these things can be. Life isn't a trade show in Los Angeles. You don't always have the option to stage your entrance."

"Clearly."

I kept my eyes on the table. It was difficult to face her.

"You wait too long," I said. "Something that seemed easy, becomes hard. You get these ideas, you think about ways to approach it, about the circumstances. You're thinking, I'll get around to it. I'll pick up the phone and say hi. Maybe drop by for coffee. But first, I gotta fix this. Take care of that. Get those things out of the way."

"Drop by for coffee? He was fucking dying, Elliot."

I was reaching, fumbling, stuttering like him. I had to pause, to breathe.

"I wanted to find a concept, Skye...or an idea or something, that would be worth it. So that when we met again, things would be...I don't know...familiar. The one thing we'd still have in common. And the excuses mount up, you know. They grow. Into something that was never intended. You're not even aware there's an end to everything. And then...well, one day...one day, he dies."

Skye looked away.

"Those oceans of time," I said. "One day, they're gone."

Her jaw tightened.

"I always knew it was something like this," she said. "Some stupid idea that things have to be a certain way."

It felt like she wanted those words to hurt. And they did.

"Why didn't you just tell us? Or me, at least. You needed some time to figure shit out. That's all it was. I mean, I get it. It's not like Calvin's innocent in this. I can see why you needed the distance. And he started a whole new life. He didn't make it easy for you. But that kind of nonsense doesn't matter when life happens. You fucking took it to the grave, Elliot."

"You think I planned to? I was getting there. I wasn't gonna wait for another five years."

"But you didn't get there in time, Elliot."

"Don't you think I know that? Don't you think I'm living with that, every day?"

She sighed.

"I don't know. You're making it very difficult for me to feel sorry for you."

"I'm not asking you to," I said.

"You could've told me, at least. What was the point of all this lonely brooding?"

"Oh, you'd be all over this. Trying to fix it. Thinking it's nothing, get over it, get a grip, pull yourself together. You'd have thrown it all right back at me."

"Damn right I would've." She pointed at me, her hand trembling. "You're a dweller, hiding behind time. Very convenient, when ignoring people is a trademark. How's that working out for you? You happy with the result?"

Those last words came out sharp. She was almost mocking me.

"Do you know what I think, Elliot?"

"I really don't."

"He was scared. That if he made a real effort to reach you... you'd withdraw even more. You'd be more busy feeling sorry for yourself than appreciate that someone's trying to connect. That shit hurts, you know. Better to save the pain and not even try. Especially when you're counting down the hours. Because that's what you do to people, Elliot."

I felt a stab when her eyes pierced me, but I didn't dodge her gaze. I hated this, but at least it was real now, in a way it hadn't been before.

"I don't think he even told Lisa," she said. "Whenever I talked to her, it felt like she didn't get it, either. Now, it makes even more sense. He respected you too much. You and your stupid integrity. You know what?" She leaned forward, her eyes moist now. "You never earned that respect."

"We'll never know, will we?"

"Oh, get real."

"I'm trying to be honest about it. I know this will haunt me for the rest of my life."

"You're pitching, is what you're doing."

I waited for a few seconds.

"We had this thing, Skye. Our lives revolved around these worlds we built. From the first day we met, we were making something, creating stuff, and that bound us ever since. When all that shattered...it was hard to see what we'd be. Him and Lisa... Spellbinder without him...that's not change. That's another world, to which he went. How do you get there? I hardly understand this one. I think, in the end, he was just happier in his new place."

"Like you said...we'll never know, will we?" She shook her head. "You know what? I don't wanna talk about this anymore."

She picked up the folder.

"So this world of yours, then. You're giving it to me now. Is that like a favor? Am I receiving the grace of the mighty creator? Am I finally being accepted into paradise? Or is it like a cup? You keep it until you're dying and then you pass it on."

"It's a little more than that. If you could just let me finish—"

"Why do you think I want it?"

"I don't. But I assumed—"

"Don't," she said and looked away. "Don't you assume anything." She bit her lip. "Things go bad, when you assume things. People die."

She was so angry with me now. It was all so fragile, I didn't dare speak. But I wasn't done. There were things left to say, and I had to consider the possibility that this would be the last time I ever saw her. I'd left things unsaid once. I wouldn't do that mistake again, despite the risk of high explosives before me.

Skye wiped her arm over her eyes. She pulled her hands through her hair. "Fuck you, Elliot. Fuck you for doing this to us. To me."

She looked at me now. She was shaking as she picked up the folder, like a fighter's club. "Dumping this shit on me, and then skipping town like you always do. After everything I've done, after all that's gone down...you'd think that you would've learned something. How the fuck can you do this to me?"

"It's like in *Gauntlet*. My life force is running out."

"No. You don't get to play that card. Calvin's life force ran out. You're exhausted. Maybe even on an existential level. I get that. But why do you have to throw this shit at me, telling me to go finish the fucking game while you sleep for a year? Is it my fucking problem that you can't deal? I'm sorry your little brother died. I'm sorry your mum was a psycho. I'm sorry your dad was a coward. But that's not on us, Elliot. You understand that, don't you? You get that, right?"

"If you could just open the goddam folder and…oh, give it here, I'll do it myself."

But she pulled back when I reached for her.

"You know what?" she said. "I don't care. We'll finish this without you. Won't be hard. I have the plan, we have the team. You'll just be in the way, mess things up, change stuff, come with bad ideas at the wrong time and be a fucking disaster all the way through. It's like you said. We won't miss you."

She got up, holding the folder close to her. "You are absolutely fucking right, Elliot. We don't need you. We don't want you. You've made sure of that. So get the fuck out of my life because I don't ever wanna see you again."

The restaurant was quiet now. Everyone was looking at us. Skye turned to the waiter and pointed at me.

"This man here," she says, "he's paying. For everything."

I raised my arms. "Fine. I'll pay."

She grabbed her jacket in one hand and held on to the folder in the other, managed to spill coffee over the table, and headed for the door. She kicked a few chairs along the way and shouted something when she threw the door open and ran into the California sun. I remained in the dim diner, with things unsaid spinning around me like taunts and teasing rhymes.

Chapter 79

SOUTH

History has a way of repeating itself. But some things you do in life stick, you know. And on that day, I'd spent what little currency I had left on the one person in my life that had endured with me through everything, and I'd failed.

I was sad for that, perhaps more so than having lost Calvin, because for what it was worth, I'd tried my sorry excuse for an effort here. It didn't work.

Skye would know, probably before the end of the day, that the folder was just a small thing. Within it, on top of the pile that was all our work on the *Greatest Game of All*, was the paper work where I'd signed over my assets and property to her. She could finish the game, give it to a museum, write a book about it or whatever. All the rights to my work through life were included as well. She could sell those, buy that house she always talked about and retire. If she wanted to.

Whatever else would come out of my showdown with Sean, his lawsuit would have no effect now. He could argue that the assets in the game belonged to him, but he'd fail. He always knew that. He only wanted to wipe me out, and he'd probably still pick the fight to do it, but with all my rights gone, the only thing left to destroy was myself. I'd like to see him try to find an angle on that one. My offer had been real and honest, after all. But so was his answer, I believe.

And really, at this point, all I wanted was to give Skye something that was as much me as I could imagine. To show her how much I cared.

For some, these things come so easy. Small gestures, such as a gentle touch or a kiss at the right time, is all it takes. A flower, or holding hands. Giving you the better part of the umbrella when it rains.

At the same time, something grand, charged with the best intentions, can wreck it all. I'll never learn these dynamics, will I?

It's like that therapist said to me when I was a boy, and had to face the fact that my mother wasn't capable of loving me even when she tried:

You have to accept this, before you can find a way to live with it.

Honestly, though, he wasn't a very good therapist.

I bought a ticket home to Stockholm. I got on the plane and looked around, scanning for dark curls in white tank tops. There were none. I sat down and closed my eyes. I fell asleep before we took off.

Arlanda airport was cold and gray when we arrived, and a thin mist wrapped the city. I got stuck in customs again and this time, they scanned me closely. But they were friendly and we talked about video games and consoles, as they went through what little stuff I had.

I took the train to Stockholm and walked from the central station to my apartment. I unlocked and entered.

The place was packed in boxes, the furniture wrapped in plastic. It was clean and neat, more so than ever, and it seemed smaller now, with its interiors ready to go somewhere else, the walls clean from any concept art that might've covered them once.

Jason was sitting by the kitchen desk, enjoying a cup of coffee.

The pot was on. As he saw me, he got up and poured me one. I dropped the bag on the floor and went up to the desk.

"Hey," I said.

"Mm-hm," he said. "You're early. How was your trip?"

"I love what you've done with the place."

"And it's not even Wednesday."

"No, seriously. You've actually cleaned it."

Jason looked around as he drank his coffee. "Could be my best work ever."

He took out a set of keys from his pocket and slid them across the desk, to me.

"So...where you going?" he said.

"South, I think."

"Good. South is good. Like Denmark south? Africa south? South pole south?"

I shrugged. "Just south."

"Okay. When you know, let me know. And I'll ship your stuff."

I looked at the boxes. Jason had marked them carefully with labels sorted after each console. One for the Nintendo Entertainment System and one for the Super Nintendo. Two boxes for the first PlayStation, three boxes for the second. Just one for the third. I never owned the ones that came after. Lots of boxes for legacy and collector items, designer's editions of certain games, mint copies of titles like *Radiant Silvergun* and the first *Sonic*, signed cards and old blueprints for games that never were released. I didn't have our original Commodore 64, though. I think, in the end, it broke down and Lisa used what parts were still working to build a small robot.

"You got kids, don't you, Jason?"

"Sure," he said. "Five or six of them. Just like you." He smiled.

"Why don't you take this, then?"

I swear to god, I've never seen Jason surprised. But now, he actually choked on his coffee.

"I mean," I said, "your kids, they like games, don't they?"

"Any healthy kid does."

"So take this. Bring it home, take a week off, and play some games with your children."

"But...this is a fortune. I can't...no, Elliot."

"Sure you can. You deserve it. You've done good work for me through the years."

"Have I, though?"

We both laughed at this.

We had some more coffee. The sun got out and cleared away the mist, and the oaken floor glowed once again from the light through the windows.

"How did the divorce go?" I said.

"We decided to try again."

"How's that working out?"

"Really bad."

"I'm sorry."

Jason put away his cup and looked at me.

"You don't know yourself until you've had kids, Elliot."

"Okay."

"Once you get some, you can't hide from yourself. They're the result of your best efforts. That's all you can do. Your best."

"And you're saying this, because?"

He fell into deep thought. Then he picked up his cup and took a sip. "It's just an honest thought."

I walked up to the window and looked out over the park. Streaks of red and yellow crossed the trees. There were a few people out there who already wore scarves and beanies. Summer was over.

I turned around, walked up to Jason, and put my hand on his shoulder. "Take care, Jason."

"You, too. I'll wrap things up, give my keys to the real estate agent and...well, I guess I'll send you a postcard?"

"I think it's the other way around. I think it's I who should send you one."

"After this," he said and swept his arm over the stuff I'd given him, "I think you deserve a post card."

I smiled.

Chapter 80

A DRAGON'S EGG

The Fjellhamn Festival had ended and we packed up our things. We'd sold all copies of *Laser Fog* and while Cornelia counted the money with Calvin, Sara helped her dad carry our stuff into the car. Lisa and I sat on a bench at the edge of the square and looked out over the water. We held hands. It felt nice.

"When are you moving?" she said.

"Pretty soon," I said. "I guess Dad will tell me now."

"You want me to come with you tonight?"

I pictured it before me. Lisa and me with Mum and Dad, having whatever meal they thought was my favorite, and talking about stuff and laughing sometimes, and Lisa helping clean the table while I did the dishes with Dad. Mum would've made an effort and decided to pull it together, to mend herself as best she could for our new life in a new city, and Lisa would be a part of that. This commuting thing maybe wouldn't be so bad. And it'd make going away from home even more exciting. Like traveling abroad, even.

But another part of me, much stronger than the one who tried to see the glass as half full, knew that this wouldn't happen. In fact, I had no idea what to expect tonight. I didn't want to put Lisa through that. And perhaps I didn't want her to fully see, at least not yet, what things were like at my home. I should deal with that first, before I exposed it to her.

"Next time," I said. "But tonight, Dad wants to talk to me about serious stuff."

"You could use the support."

"I know. But next time, okay?"

"Okay."

She kissed me, her hand around my neck.

"I don't know what it is about you," she said and smiled. "You're a very strange boy. But I like you anyway."

"I smell nice. And I make great games. So there's that, I suppose."

She laughed. "Yes, Elliot. I guess that must be it."

We got up and helped out with the last parts of the packing. Calvin was bursting with excitement as they'd counted the money and we had ended up with almost six thousand kronor. A few had been generous enough to not ask for change when they'd bought a copy. He danced around and clapped his hands. "If that won't get us a house," he said, "I don't know what will."

Lisa sighed. "He's right about the last part."

"Hey, Elliot. We'll get bunk beds. On even weeks, you sleep on top. On odd weeks, I sleep on top. And we'll rotate! Oh, oh, we'll get a place close to the sea so that we don't have to take our bikes every time we wanna go swimming. Man, this is gonna be sooo awesome."

No one said anything. We all knew he knew, too.

"Hey," I said to my friends. "I'm going home now. I'll come find you later, okay? And we'll do something."

"Come to our place," Cornelia said. "They'll be there."

"Okay. Cool."

I got up on my bike and looked at them over my shoulder. Calvin was still dancing around. Sara was shoving a box into the car. Lisa was helping out. I kicked up some dirt and left.

I rode through Fjellhamn, passing trees with early autumn leaves on the way and lawns with tints of yellow. The slow and steady rain from garden sprinklers hummed with the wind and the waves. I was cold and felt stupid for only wearing a t-shirt and jeans on an evening in late August, and I picked up the pace to get home as fast as I could. Once there, I threw my bike on our lawn and went into the house.

It actually smelled quite nice. I entered the kitchen. Dad was frying sausages in a pan and had French fries in the oven. He wore Mum's apron and it was almost painful to see how glad he was to see me when I showed up at the threshold.

Fries and sausages. That actually had been my favorite, when I was three or four. I remembered wishing to have it for my birthday.

"Hey, son," he said. "How'd it go?"

I looked around. The place was neat and clean. Brighter than usual.

"We sold all our copies," I said.

"I knew you would. Such an impressive thing you've done. Make yourself comfortable, dinner's ready in a minute."

So I did, feeling tired now. Dad paused by the stove and faced me.

"She's sleeping, Elliot."

"Okay."

"It's been a busy day. She took her medicine when we got home. She needs to rest now."

"Sure."

He sighed. Then he returned to his cooking and within minutes, he'd served up fries and sausages and produced a bottle of Coke to boost. For us, this was a feast.

We ate in silence. Dad didn't even try to make conversation. I wanted to get out of here, but I wasn't sure if it was because I couldn't stand him and the way he pitied himself, or if the walls were so tight now, the space so crammed, that I was choking.

"You don't have to move," Dad said.

I had stuffed a close to dangerous number of fries in my mouth, just to get this over with. I must've looked like a hamster staring into the lights of an approaching car, as I raised my head and met my father's sad eyes.

"I've talked to Cornelia. Or...she talked to us. She came here, a few weeks ago. In uniform and all. She said that you could stay with her and Calvin for as long as you like. I said no, of course. You're my son, Elliot. Why would I want you to live anywhere else than with us?"

I was chewing slowly now. Dad put his plate aside.

"But on our way home today," he said, "your mum talked me into it. She was holding that game of yours in her hands. And she told me...well..."

I wasn't sure if this was a good thing. I didn't know what to feel. I had a rising sensation of something, but it was conflicted and torn, like a comfortable warmth constantly cooled with buckets of ice.

"You need to live with someone that can care for you, Elliot. Today, when Charlotte saw...I think she realized..."

He couldn't continue. He leaned his head on his hand.

"But that's what you're supposed to do," I said. "Take care of me."

He didn't look at me when he spoke next.

"You can come and see us whenever you like, Elliot. There's a room waiting for you, if you wanna sleep over or...or come home. To stay. And you can move with us now, if you want to. We want you to. I want you to. But if we force you...it'd make you miserable. She saw that today. I've known this. But I didn't wanna see it. But she did. She's not being mean. She's trying to be as good as she can."

Were they giving me up? Or was this about as unselfish as a person could get?

"Say something, Elliot."

A warm and glowing sensation grew within me. Suddenly, this kitchen table here, Dad in front of me wearing a lady apron, a Coke by my plate with a mountain of French fries, did feel a bit like home.

I pierced my fork through one of the sausages and held it up.

"These are nice, Dad. Perfect, really."

He seemed confused at this. Then, he shrugged and made a gesture of acknowledgment. "Thanks."

"You really nailed it on the fries, too."

He tilted his head and looked at me. A curious smile spread across his face. "I did, didn't I? Fries in the oven. Takes a certain skill to pull that off."

I took a bite from one. "But you did it, Dad. And there's no one ever gonna take that away from you."

"I snatched them from that dragon, you know. The one we used to steal eggs from, to make an omelet."

"You did not."

"I did, too. And when we get to desert, delicious cinnamon buns from the bakery by the old cinema, I'll tell you how I did it."

Chapter 81

INTO THE SHADOWS

After dinner, he walked with me through the dusk. We spoke about the game, he asked me how we'd done it and how do you make a game, anyway? "It sounds so...I don't know, impossible?"

I told him it's not, it's just really hard, but so are a lot of things. "Clearly, Dad," I said. "Otherwise, we wouldn't have done it."

"I guess not," he said and laughed.

We approached Calvin's house. The door was open and light flooded over the porch from inside, like fading waves from a bright ocean. Inside, their shoebox castle was rowdy and over-crowded, where Calvin, Lisa, and Sara were having dinner by the small table, together with Arshak and Dan and Elizabeth. Cornelia was busy shuffling stuff around in the kitchen, throwing pancakes in the air with her left hand and juggling the bacon pan with her right. She was laughing. No idea about what. She was just laughing. We heard music from an old vinyl player, that familiar scratch from Mr. Svensson's records, some kind of jazz tune that sounded like the stuff Dad used to play when he was working.

He put a hand on my shoulder. I turned and looked at him.

"You go," he said.

"You're not gonna say hi?" I nodded to the people and the

party lights.

"No, I..." He coughed. Then, he pulled me close and held me.

I hugged him back.

Right then, I wished I didn't want to stay, that leaving with him and Mum would be the beginning of something new and exciting, and the good things about the present would still be there.

But like him, I'd finally reached the point where I realized that those shards of hope, they'd never be real.

He let me go.

Looked at me, and stroke my cheek.

He smiled and ruffled my hair.

"Good night. See you tomorrow, maybe?"

"Okay, Dad."

As he turned to leave, Cornelia looked out. She saw him, and waved at him to come in. He waved back, but took a few steps and then turned around to walk down the road. I watched him as he fell into the shadows. Soon, the growing twilight took him and he was gone.

Chapter 82

ANOTHER ONE

This was our first release party. Our game was out, we'd made some money and we celebrated our success with a selected crowd of guests. The music played on through the night and there were drinks until early in the morning, when we finally dozed off and fell asleep on blankets and in chairs. Cornelia hushed the adults to leave, telling Dan and Elizabeth that the kids could sleep here tonight and to Arshak that she'd drop by his place and see if she couldn't teach him a trick or two about how to make coffee and serve a good meal. Looks like he could use it. He smiled and said that he'd like that very much.

I couldn't sleep, though. While Lisa and Sara were snoring away and Calvin had his head in a position that would give him pain the next day, I got up and sneaked out.

I sat on the porch and watched the sun rise, my feet in the grass, cooled by the dew. I thought about nothing. I looked at the skies as they slowly warmed up to a lighter blue, pretending I was the only one in the world who saw this right now.

I heard steps behind me. Calvin sat down, blinking and yawning, a blanket around him.

"Hey," he said.

"Hey."

"What's going on?"

"Nothing much. Checking out the sun."

"It's very nice."

"It is."

He pulled the blanket closer, shuddering.

"M-mum says you're staying with us."

I smiled. "Yes."

"So...I don't know how you feel about that. With your parents and all. But I gotta tell you, Elliot, I think it's awesome."

"Yeah."

He sighed. "We're gonna f-fight, though," he said.

"No, we won't."

"Oh, c'mon. Friends fight."

"Okay, sure. But we'll figure it out."

"We will, won't we?"

"Always."

He wiggled his toes in the wet grass. "I've never had a best friend, Elliot. And now that I do...I don't wanna lose that."

"Me neither."

"I mean, if we get really mad, Elliot...we'll work it out, right?"

I looked at him. "Of course."

He smiled, shaking his head to get the bangs out of the way. Then, he turned serious. "I think you should be nicer to Lisa."

This surprised me. I faced the sunrise again, but looked at him from the side. "I am being super nice to her. She's the best. Why wouldn't I be? I really like her."

"Yeah, I guess..." He frowned, searching for philosophical depths now. "It's just...I don't know. I just think I'm better with girls than you are, Elliot."

I laughed quietly. "I have a girlfriend, Calvin. You don't."

He nodded. "Hmm. Yes. Good point."

But something still seemed to bother him. I knew what it was, it had bothered me too, but I also knew better than to push him.

We were quiet for a few minutes. Then, he said, "Okay, so now it's time for some real honesty."

I took a deep breath.

"You ready?" he said.

"Always."

"*Laser Fog*," he said. "It's not really...it's not the greatest game of all, is it?"

I exhaled. "I guess not."

But then, he grinned. "It's better than *E.T.*"

I grinned, too. "Lots better."

"And anyway, we'll make another one, won't we?"

"You got ideas?"

"I got a few sketches. What do you have?"

"I've jotted down some thoughts. Wanna see?"

"Do I ever."

We got up and sneaked into the house, picked up our sketch books and pencils and went out again. The sun was climbing the horizon now, and the first birds were awake.

Calvin opened his notebook, where he'd applied water colors on several layers of blue on blue. It looked like a sky, a clear, blue sky.

"So I was thinking," he said. "Lisa really nailed it on the parallax scroll. Let's say this is the sky, and you control a space ship or something..."

"Oh! Oh! And it's burning! It's already on fire! And you put the throttle on the button and the brake on the stick, like so," I said and made a quick drawing to map out the controller.

"Whoa. B-brilliant. Already close to being the greatest game ever."

And while he kept knocking out sketches to show his ideas, I made blueprints for the controller as well as features for the monsters we'd have. We were talking over each other, switching pencils and blocks, ripping out papers and building a puzzle on the porch, as the morning rays warmed the wooden floor. Calvin spread out his arms and flew like an airplane across the lawn, showing how our ship would dive deep to dodge the lightning and rise high above the clouds, while I ran in circles to whip up a storm.

Our cries echoed across the Fjellhamn hills and through the woods, as we imagined sounds and effects for our next creation. It was a call to arms that Calvin and Elliot were at it again, making a new game, the greatest one you'd ever see, together in life and death as best friends, now and forever, and nothing would ever keep us apart. Ever.

Chapter 83

THE MIGHTY ELLIOT LINDH

It's like I said in the beginning. I don't make much sense these days. Now that we've reached this point, maybe you'll agree. But a wise man once said, in the end, it's in the eye of the beholder.

I did buy that house in France. It's nice, a little stone building in a county somewhere in the middle of it all. You'll know the place, I'm sure, but I'd prefer not to tell. It has three rooms and a small kitchen, and a yard with olive trees that offer shade in the morning and afternoon.

One of the rooms, I've made into a small studio. Nothing will ever come out of it, but I like to sit there and write. I got Calvin's stick drawing framed and it's at the center of the table. I look at it almost every day. Sometimes, it makes me so sad, I feel like I can't take it. On other days, I remember all the good things about us and then, I feel better.

I'm learning French. I'm not very good at it. My tutor is an old man in his sixties, who shouts at me a lot. When class is done, we have some wine and I listen to his stories about women. He's got a lot of those, though I'm pretty sure most of them are made up. I hardly understand half of what he's saying anyway.

The people who live here are friendly. They nod and smile to me, they accept my novice French and help me out when I'm thinking I'm asking for bread in the grocery store and they wonder why I want to buy meds for the pain. I usually stay at home until lunch, and then I go out for errands, a stroll, or a slow coffee. I read a lot. Listen to music. Sleep. And think. The hills around here remind me of Fjellhamn in a way, endless and vast with no clear line between the land and the sky.

Sometimes, I pack a bag with a bottle of water, buy a picnic lunch at a small sandwich café, and head out. Usually, I'm not back until dusk. There are some wild animals around here and the townspeople worry about me. I don't think they should. I'm my own person and if something happens, it's on me.

I called Lisa a while ago. She didn't answer and I didn't leave a message. But she sent me a text after a day or so, saying that she wasn't ready to face me just yet. Perhaps she'd never be. "Despite all," she wrote, "you didn't show up for Calvin in the end." There's a simple truth to that, to which I'm not sure I'll ever be able to accept.

But she wasn't mad at me. Not anymore. She hoped I was well. She heard from Skye about our fight and she said it was too bad Skye and I never got around to talking about the stuff that really mattered.

Lisa is traveling the world with Isabelle and Alexander now, and if she would ever come to see me, it would be because of them. Her children are starting to hear about this Uncle Elliot they never met. To sit down with someone that knew their dad, that could tell them stories about him for years and years, that'd be better than any game or any movie. I've told Lisa that they can come and stay whenever they want. I've got spare beds in every room and they can have the master one, and be here for as long as they like. But I don't think that's ever going to happen. I don't think I'll ever see her again.

I hear from Sean's lawyers every now and then. His case is homing in to be about any financial damages I might've caused through my use of his resources, to develop a title that should've been rightfully his to publish. It complicates matters that there's little proof that this ever was so, that if it ever did happen then it was more than a decade ago, that at least one key witness is dead and that I offered Sean to join the production as Skye and I made our pitching rounds at E3. Suffice it to say, I've not yet been summoned to court. Last time one of the lawyers called, she seemed a bit tired, spending time on something that went nowhere but still received injections from a wealthy man.

A few days ago, I received a thick parcel. It came to the local post office and the old woman working there winked at me and said that someone's apparently popular. I almost managed to hold a conversation with her and she laughed at me and brushed me off, as it seemed I offered her a compliment bordering on the vulgar.

I walked slowly through town with the package under my arm. The sun was out and it was a busy day. I was invited for coffee with someone whose name I still hadn't learned to pronounce. He had five children, the youngest two years old, the oldest fourteen. They climbed over my shoulders and had me play hide and seek until afternoon turned to evening and I was asked to stay for dinner. We had lamb and roasted potatoes and after a few glasses, my French got a whole lot better.

When I came home, the house was dark. I put the parcel in my studio, on the desk next to Calvin's drawing. I already knew what it contained. I was in no hurry to open it. I was afraid of what it might do to me, or more specifically, I had no idea, and that scared me the most.

But I did open it, with next morning's first cup of coffee, and pulled out the folder. It was still in good shape. Skye had been kind to it.

I browsed it, not sure what I'd face. But it was the same old material, together with the work Calvin had done before he died.

On top of it, though, there was a bunch of print-outs, held together with a green paper clip. I picked them up and read them slowly.

They were reviews, of our game.

I had deliberately stayed away from this, from finding out. I knew Skye had decided to finish it after all, but that was about it.

But now, apparently, she felt that I needed to know. She'd circled what I assumed were the best parts from the top reviewers.

"It shouldn't really work," *IGN* said, "being the mess that it is. But maybe that's why it's holding together, because somehow, Spellbinder Software has managed to capture the idea of life in a game, without saying that they have the answers. It would've been ironic if we'd found them here, in a bleeding edge video game production. But not all that surprising."

And *Eurogamer* said: "Apparently, the game's been a lifetime in the making, the brainchild of not two but four creators back from the days when they were still kids. If I was a developer, I'd find only despair in that. Essentially, it means you need a lifetime to make something as great as this. But for the rest of us, we're thankful that someone was insane enough to try and pull this off and actually succeed."

And *Gamespot*: "The title makes a bold claim. The greatest game ever? Too early to say. There's still *Super Metroid* to beat, after all. But the greatest this year? For sure. Greatest of the decade? Quite possibly."

It continued like this.

I smiled.

It wasn't her words. But it might as well have been. And they hurt. Every single syllable hurt.

I have this fantasy. One day, Skye will show up in my doorway, backpack slung over her shoulder, dirty and tanned from the trip, here with a smile to lift me up and put the pieces back to together.

Like she always did, throughout our lives.

That's been the problem all along, hasn't it? These ideas on how things should be. How I'd want them to be.

I've been so lost in the world I made for myself, with those endless hills and wide oceans, that I've known no other comfort. I've been unable to see that Skye, too, has been in pieces. I've not been brave enough to leave my place and for once come to her.

"The mighty Elliot Lindh," she said once. "Suddenly lost for words."

She was right that time. I was lost for words. As I have been, whenever they've really mattered.

Calvin was right, too. I'm not good at these things. Lisa was the best, setting the bar for the rest of us on how to show that you cared. Calvin followed, though his obsession with his craft got in the way for a long time. Then there was Skye, and she tried to tell me things and I didn't listen, because I didn't have the courage and she wasn't all that good at getting the point across. What a match. But she was always ahead of me, even back in Fjellhamn when she got an Atari and aced *Pitfall* before I even knew what such a thing was.

But I get it now.

It's like that song my mum used to sing to me, about the boy who wandered near and far, and learned the greatest thing of all. Now, I understand the words.

That someone so magnificent, so beautiful, as Skye, would want to be with me, has seemed so unlikely. She was Sara Johnson, after all. And I was just Elliot. It's hard to find the words when you don't believe in them yourself.

However, I'm done with doubt.

I'm reaching out to Skye now. Not tomorrow. Not next week. But now.

I lost Calvin because I imagined there was time. I'm not gonna lose Skye.

I'm still that person who can come up with a hundred reasons why I shouldn't call her. But I've decided to listen to the one reason why I should.

I don't want to be alone anymore.

I don't think I deserve to be.

I want to be loved.

I think I deserve that.

But more than me, more than anyone else, so does she.

So I'm hoping, I'm daring to believe, that the greatest woman of all will answer when I call her again. That she's fine with my loss for words, that she'll hear me out anyway. That she agrees, and truly loves me back.